GRIM DISCOVERY

A squawk from a car radio. One of the uniformed men picked up the handset and answered the call, then waved and yelled, 'Mr. Frost. Control wants to speak to you urgently.'

'Right,' said Frost, leaving Commander Mullett with Webster, neither of whom could think of a thing to say to the other. Mullett dredged his mind for some innocuous small talk. 'Getting on all right?' he said at last.

'Yes, thank you, sir,' replied Webster tonelessly, his eyes fastened on Frost, who was leaning against the car, the handset to his ear, his expression revealing that something was terribly wrong.

Frost walked slowly back to the commander, his face grim. 'Mr. Mullett,' he said.

Mullett felt the cold of approaching bad news and shivered. 'Yes, Frost?'

'The constable, sir. They've found him — in a ditch about three miles from here, just off the new Lexington Road.'

'Is he all right?' whispered Mullett. A silly question because he already knew the answer. The expression on Frost's face simply screamed it out.

Frost looked down at the blood on the lane. 'No, sir. He's dead.'

Also by R. D. Wingfield

NIGHT FROST

and coming soon from Bantam Books

HARD FROST
FROST AT CHRISTMAS

A TOUCH
OF
FROST

R. D. Wingfield

BANTAM BOOKS
New York • Toronto • London • Sydney • Auckland

This edition contains the complete text
of the original hardcover edition.
NOT ONE WORD HAS BEEN OMITTED.

A Touch of Frost
A Bantam Crime Line Book / published by arrangement with the author

PUBLISHING HISTORY

Constable edition published 1990
Bantam edition / June 1995

CRIME LINE and the portrayal of a boxed "cl" are trademarks
of Bantam Books, a division of Bantam Doubleday Dell Publishing
Group, Inc.

ISBN 0-553-57169-9

PRINTED IN THE UNITED STATES OF AMERICA

OPM   0 9 8 7 6 5 4 3 2 1

A Touch of Frost

TUESDAY NIGHT SHIFT (1)

A cold, clear autumn night with a sharp wind shaking the trees. The man in the shadows was trembling. The palms of his rubber-gloved hands were moist, and warm sweat trickled down his face under the mask. Soon he would be able to see her. To touch her. She wouldn't see him, deep in the black of the moon shadow. She wouldn't know he was there until it was too late.

At first he thought it was a police trap. A girl, a young girl, in school uniform, walking all alone in Denton Woods at eleven o'clock at night. But how could the police know he'd be here? The other attacks had taken place miles away. And how could the police know it was the really young girls who turned him on. The police knew nothing. He was too smart for them. Far too smart. They had questioned him. They had cleared him. They had even thanked him for his co-operation.

Even so, he hadn't taken any chances. Only fools took chances. As always, he had carefully reconnoitred the area. Nothing. Nobody. For miles around there was no-one but him, and the girl. The girl! In that school uniform. Wearing those dark thick stockings. She couldn't be much more than fifteen . . . *a schoolgirl, young and innocent, unaware of her developing body* . . . just like the girl in the book, the book he had hidden away in his bedroom.

What was that?

He stood stock still, ears straining, his heartbeats booming in the screaming silence. He had heard something. Something moving. He tensed, ready to tear off the mask and run. It was only the mask that could give him away. Without it the police had nothing. No leads, no clues, nothing. Even if they brought him face to face with his victims, they couldn't identify him. The first they knew of his presence was the sudden suffocating blackness as the cloth went over their heads, and then the pressure of his fingers on their throats, squeezing, choking. One of the girls . . . the second, or was it the third? . . . had managed to tear the cloth from her face. But all she saw of him, before his fists pounded her into unconsciousness, was the mask. The black hood that completely covered his hair, his face, his neck. The newspapers had dubbed him the 'Hooded Terror'. Tomorrow's headlines would read *'Hooded Terror Strikes Again. Schoolgirl Latest Victim'*. He liked reading about himself in the papers. It made him feel important.

He slid deeper back into the shadows, his body tensed, his ears tuned. The sound again. A rustling, a snapping of twigs. His hand crept up to the mask as he listened, trying to make out what it was. Then a snuffling and grunting as something blundered through the undergrowth. Something small. An animal of some kind. A badger, perhaps, but definitely not human. He relaxed and eased forward. He could smell his own sweat, his excitement. Soon he would hear her.

Such a shame he would have to hurt this one. She was so young, so innocent. How wonderful if she submitted without protest, her eyes wide open and wondering. *At first terrified, but gradually, as she experienced the new delights, the unbelievable sensations he was offering, she moaned, as if in pain, gasping with pleasure, drawing him on* . . . the way the girl in his book reacted the very first time it happened to her. She was a schoolgirl, too.

His ear caught another sound. The dry whisper of fallen leaves on the narrow path scuffed by quick, nervous footsteps.

It was her. The girl. Again he held his breath. Stood stock still and tensed . . .

Ready to spring.

Police Constable David Shelby, twenty-five, married with two young children, shivered and stamped his feet as the wind, cutting down the deserted back street, found an empty lager can and rattled it across the cobbled road. He checked his watch. Twelve minutes past eleven. He wondered who the station would send, hoping it wouldn't be Detective Inspector Allen; but whoever it was, he wished he would come soon. He had far better things to do tonight than stand guard over a dead body.

Above his head an enamel sign, hanging from a wrought-iron frame like a gibbeted body, creaked as it swung to and fro in the wind. The wording on the sign read Gentlemen, with an arrow pointing downwards. Behind Shelby a broken metal grille sagged, no longer fit to perform its function of denying entry to the worn, brass-edged stone steps which descended to the dank darkness of the underground public convenience, built by the Works Department of Denton Borough Council in 1897 to commemorate the Diamond Jubilee of Queen Victoria.

The sound of a car approaching. Headlights flared as a mud-splattered, dark blue Ford Cortina rumbled over the cobbles, coming to an uncertain halt behind Shelby's patrol car. The door opened and a scruffy-looking individual wearing a dirty mac draped with an equally dirty maroon scarf, clambered out. In his late forties, he had a weather-beaten face flecked with freckles, his balding head fringed with light-brown fluffy hair. Shelby smiled, relieved that the station had sent the easygoing Detective Inspector Frost and not that sarcastic swine Allen, who treated the uniformed branch with contempt and who was bound to ask some probing questions. It would be a lot easier with Jack Frost.

The wind found the lager can again and dribbled it across to the inspector, who gave a mighty kick and sent it flying through the air, past Shelby's ear, to rattle and bounce down the toilet steps.

'Goal!' yelled Frost, ambling over.

Shelby grinned and swung his torch beam toward the depths. 'Shall we go down, sir?' He was anxious to get this over, but Frost was in no hurry.

'What's the rush, son? If he's dead, he'll wait for us. Besides, I've got my best suit on and I don't want to mess it up sooner than I have to.' He opened his mac to reveal a newish-looking, blue pinstriped suit with a fairly respectable crease to the trousers. It was the retirement party tonight. Police Inspector George Harrison was leaving the force after twenty-eight years in Denton, and the division was throwing a big farewell thrash for him in the station canteen. Although officially on duty, Frost had set his heart on attending and was going to take the first presented opportunity to sneak up there. Which was why his old blue-striped wedding suit had been parolled from its moth-balled prison. He could have done without Shelby's newfound efficiency in finding this lousy dead body.

Frost fished a battered packet from his mac pocket and worried out a cigarette. 'You'd better fill me in with some facts. How did you find him, and why the hell didn't you pretend you hadn't seen anything and leave him for the morning shift?'

'Well, sir, I was driving past on watch when I noticed the metal grille across the stairs had been forced back . . .'

'Hold on,' said Frost. 'You know what a slow old sod I am. What were you doing driving down this bloody back street at this time of night?'

'It's part of my beat, sir,' protested the constable, looking hurt. 'It has to be covered.'

'Highly commendable,' sniffed Frost, spitting out a shred of tobacco, 'but next time there's a party, stick to the main roads. And speed it up, son. The beer's going to run out before you reach the punchline.'

'Well, sir, I stopped the car, got out, and checked the grille.' He directed his torch toward the sagging grille and they both moved forward to examine it. 'As you can see, the padlock has been forced.' Frost gave the padlock the briefest of glances and stared pointedly at his wristwatch. Taking the hint, Shelby speeded up his narrative. 'As you know, sir, these toilets are locked up at eight o'clock.'

'I didn't know,' grunted Frost. 'I always pee in shop door-ways.'

'Anyway, sir,' continued Shelby doggedly, 'I thought I'd better investigate.'

Frost snorted. 'Investigate what? Illicit peeing after hours?'

'There's plenty of copper and lead piping down there, Inspector,' Shelby pointed out. 'They could have been after that.'

'Sorry, son,' Frost apologized, 'you're quite right. Carry on. I'll try and keep my big mouth shut.'

'Not much more to tell, sir. I went down and found this tramp sprawled on the floor. As far as I could tell, he was dead. Dr Cadman only lives round the corner, so I nipped round and brought him back.'

The inspector dragged on his cigarette. 'Pity you didn't just call an ambulance and let the hospital take over.'

'He might not have been dead, sir. The doctor would have been quicker.'

Frost nodded gloomily and said, 'You're right again, son. Pity you have to be so bloody right on the night of the big booze-up. What did the quack say?'

'Doctor Cadman found damage and bleeding at the base of the skull. He reckoned death was caused by a blow to the head.'

Frost stared moodily into the darkness. He knew Dr Cadman. Knew him well. Cadman had been his wife's doctor. It was Cadman who had diagnosed stomach pains as mere indigestion and kept prescribing the white peppermint mixture until the unbearable pains drove her to hospital. 'An old tramp, you say?'

'Yes, sir. I've seen him knocking around the district, but I don't know his name.'

'I suppose we can't put the evil moment off.' Frost pinched out his cigarette and stuffed the butt back into the packet. 'Let's get inside before people think you're trying to pick me up.'

One hand gripping the brass handrail, he followed Shelby's torch cautiously down stone steps worn concave in the middle from the traffic of thousands of hurrying feet. The echoing, monotonous plopping sound of dripping water grew louder.

'Do you know which police surgeon they're sending us?'

'Dr Slomon, sir. Mind that step . . . it's a bit dodgy.'

'Slomon!' exclaimed Frost. 'That snotty-nosed little bastard? He'll want everything done by the book. I reckon I can kiss the party goodbye.' He moved his foot down to the next step only to give a startled yell as something cold and wet leaped up and licked its way inside his shoe. 'Flaming hell, Shelby, it's awash down here. You might have bloody warned me.'

'It wasn't as bad as this before,' said Shelby. The reflections from his torch beam danced in the rippling water which lapped at the bottom step. 'One of the cisterns is overflowing and the body's blocking the drain.'

'This gets better and better,' the inspector observed bitterly. 'So where is he?'

Shelby swung his torch and illuminated a sodden shape huddled in one corner. 'I'm afraid we're going to have to get our feet wet, sir.'

They splashed over, the water finding holes in Frost's shoes he never knew existed and reminding him of the pair of Wellington boots lying idle on the back seat of his car. The heap in the corner looked like a mess of wet rags, but the light of the torch revealed it to be a man. A dead man. He lay on his back in the flooded guttering of the urinal stalls, his long, matted hair bobbing in the rising water, wide-open, sightless eyes staring unflinchingly into the burning glare of the torch. The mouth was agape and dribbling, the beard and ragged overcoat filthy with vomit that stank of stale, cheap wine. The body of a derelict, a tramp who had crawled into some dark corner to die.

Frost stared at the tired, worn-out face, a face long unwashed, grimed and greasy with dirt. 'Good God, it's Ben Cornish!'

'You know him, sir?' Shelby asked.

'I know him,' Frost replied grimly. 'And so would you bloody know him, Constable, if you spent more time on your job and less on looking for crumpet.'

In the dark, Shelby flushed. He believed his womanising was a well-kept secret, but nothing seemed to escape the seemingly unobservant Frost.

'He may look a bloody old man, Shelby, but he's not much older than you.' The inspector bent down, his hand slipping under the water to the back of the head, his fingers exploring and finding the sticky section where the skull moved under pressure. 'He's been living rough ever since his family chucked him out a couple of years back. He started out as a wino — cheap booze laced with meths or surgical spirit — then he progressed to heroin.'

'Heroin!' exclaimed Shelby, his torch beam slowly creeping over the emaciated figure at his feet. 'That's an expensive habit.'

'Well, by the look of him,' observed Frost, 'I doubt if he wasted money on nonessentials like soap and food. He used to be a lovely kid. A cheeky little sod. Look at him now!' He prodded the body with his foot, then turned away. A match flared as he relit the butt. 'I suppose you haven't been through his pockets?'

'Not yet,' the constable admitted. 'He's a bit messy.'

'Well, he's not going to get any bloody cleaner floating in pee, is he? Is there any way to stop this damn water rising? It's up to my ankles. I feel like a passenger on the *Titanic*.'

Shelby paddled over to the far end of the fetid room leaving Frost in the dark. 'I think it's this one over here sir.'

'Don't give me a running commentary, son. Just fix it.'

Shelby's torch beam bobbed, then pointed upward to spotlight a cast-iron cistern tank which was meant to flush the urinal stalls at regular, hygienic intervals. It was brim-full, and water was cascading over the sides and down the wall. Shelby reached up and plunged his hand inside the tank. He jiggled the ball cock up and down a couple of times, and suddenly the cistern gulped, emptied itself, then filled up and cut off. Satisfied, Shelby splashed back to Frost.

'That's done it, sir. If we can shift the body it should unblock the drain and let the water flow away.'

'Better not move him, son. You know what a fussy little creep this police surgeon is. And see if you can't find a light switch. Slomon's bound to moan about the dark.' He sneaked a look at his watch. How much longer before he could get to the party? Where was bloody Slomon?

His question was answered by a clatter of footsteps from the top of the stairs and a peevish voice that inquired, 'Anyone down there?'

Shelby's torch guided the newcomer down. Dr Slomon, a short, fat, self-important individual wearing an expensive-looking camel-haired overcoat, peered distastefully into the murk as Frost waded over. 'Inspector Frost! I might have guessed. Somehow one associates you with places like this.' His overcoat was unbuttoned, and beneath it Frost could see a bow tie, and a smart black evening dress suit.

'You needn't have got tarted up just to come down here Doc. Any old suit would have done.'

Slomon smiled sourly. 'If you must know, I was on my way to Inspector Harrison's retirement party when I got this call. I hope it's not going to take long.'

'So do I,' said Frost. 'Hold on a tick, we're trying to find the light switches.'

At first there didn't seem to be any way of turning on the lights, but eventually the beam of the torch followed the wiring down until it disappeared inside a small wooden cupboard on which was stencilled Switches — Keep Locked. In obedience to this request, the cupboard door had been secured with an enormous brass padlock that wouldn't have been out of place in the vaults of the Bank of England.

'It's locked,' announced Shelby.

'I don't think so,' said Frost, splashing over to take a look. There was a wrenching sound, a tearing of wood, and the padlock crashed to the floor. 'You see,' said Frost, 'it wasn't locked.'

The splintered door swung open to reveal its treasures . . . rolls of toilet paper stamped Property of Denton Borough Council, a huge bottle of disinfectant, and a pair of brass-domed light switches screwed to the wall. Two clicks and the fly-specked bulbs high in the ceiling fought a half-hearted battle against the darkness.

Frost surveyed his surroundings, the filthy, stained urinal

stalls with their cracked beige glazing turning an unpleasant shade of brown, the copper piping thickly crusted with verdigris, the brown composition floor awash with discoloured water and floating matter. Behind him a row of dark-green painted doors with brass coin locks guarded the lavatories. One of the doors was newly splintered, the coin lock hanging from loose screws; it yawned open to reveal a toilet with a broken seat stuffed with torn sheets of newspaper; over it dangled a length of discoloured string as replacement for the missing chain.

'Only my opinion,' commented Frost, 'but I think it was more romantic with the lights off.' He paddled over to the body. 'Here's your patient, Doc. I'd be obliged if you'd hurry it up. I want to get to that party, too.'

The police surgeon made no attempt to leave the bottom step. He looked first at the swirl of dirty water he would have to wade through, then at his highly polished patent-leather shoes. 'Do we know who he is?'

'His name is Ben Cornish,' replied the police constable. 'A dropout. Sleeps rough. He's on drugs and booze.'

Slomon nodded. 'I see. And what leads you to suspect that death is other than from natural causes?'

'I wasn't sure if he was dead, so I brought Dr Cadman in. He said he died from a blow to the back of the skull.'

Slomon's eyebrows shot up. 'Oh? And how did Dr Cadman reach that extraordinary diagnosis?'

'I think he did it by actually walking over and examining the body,' chimed in Frost, losing patience. 'He didn't do it by remote control from the bottom step.'

Slomon's cheeks ballooned with anger. 'I don't need lessons from you on how to conduct an examination, Frost. These tin-pot general practitioners don't know what the hell they are talking about. Even from here I can see that the most likely cause of death is the obvious one: he choked on his own vomit. I have no intention of soiling my clothes by wading through that filth just to confirm what is self-evident. Isn't there any way of getting rid of this dirty water?'

'Only by moving the body,' explained Frost. 'It's bunging up the drain.'

'Then move the damn thing! Surely you've enough gumption to do that without having to be told. And while you're moving it you might as well bring it over here to me.'

And this is the bastard who insists on everything being done by the book, thought Frost. Aloud, he said, 'You take his arms, Constable. I'll grab his legs.' As they raised the body, the water began gurgling and swirling down the cleared drain. 'Reminds me of the time,' said Frost, grunting as he took the weight, 'when I was a bobby on the beat and I had to pull this stiff out of the canal. He'd been dead a bloody long time but had only just popped up to the surface. I grabbed his arms to pull him out . . . and his bloody arms came off. I was left holding the damn things while he sank to the bottom again.' Both Shelby and Slomon winced at this choice tidbit of reminiscence.

'Will this do, Doc?' asked Frost, dumping the body at the foot of the stairs and shaking his sleeves where water had run up his arm.

Nodding curtly, Slomon bent forward, looked at the face with disgust, then moved the head forward so he could examine the base of the skull with probing fingers. It was a brief examination. 'As I thought,' he said, treating the inspector to a self-satisfied smirk, 'the head injury was not the cause of death and was not the result of a blow. The damage probably resulted from his head colliding with the stone flooring when he fell.' He looked around, then pointed to something glinting on the floor, by the wall. 'Something you missed, Inspector. Fortunately I keep my eyes open whenever I do an examination.'

Frost swore softly as Shelby retrieved a broken wine bottle from the gully. There was no way they could have seen it earlier, as the dirty water had completely covered it.

Stretching out a hand, Slomon received the bottle from the constable and cautiously raised it to his nose. A delicate sniff, followed by a smug nod of satisfaction at his own cleverness. 'Wine laced with industrial alcohol, a potent combination.' He handed the bottle to Frost for confirmation. Frost took his word for it and passed it to the constable. 'He drank himself senseless, then fell,' continued Slomon dogmatically. 'Then he choked on his own vomit. I'll arrange for the hospital to carry out a post-mortem first thing tomorrow, but they will only confirm my diagnosis.' He consulted his watch. 'The party calls. I'll leave the tidying up to you.' With a curt nod he was up the steps and out into the clean night air.

'I wish they were doing a post-mortem on you, you bastard,' Frost muttered. He again looked around his unsavoury surroundings. Why was something nagging away? Why was that little bell at the back of his head ringing insistently, warning him something was wrong? He looked around again, slowly this time. But it was no good — whatever it was, it wasn't going to show itself. And why was he worrying? Death was from natural causes, and he had the party to go to.

'Do we know his next of kin, sir?' asked Shelby, his notebook open.

'His mother and brother live in Denton,' Frost told him. 'The station will have their address.'

'Someone's going to have to break the news to them, sir.' Shelby paused and looked hopefully at the inspector. 'I'm not very good at it.'

Frost sighed. Why did he always fall for the nasty jobs? How do you tell a mother her eldest son had choked to death on his own vomit down a public convenience? He took one last look at the dripping heap of death sprawled at his feet and shook his head reproachfully. 'Ben Cornish, you stupid bastard!' The open eyes of the corpse looked right through him.

'All right, Shelby. I'll break the news to his old lady. You arrange for the meat wagon to take him to the morgue, and wait here until it arrives. I don't want any late-night revellers peeing all over the body.'

He trotted up the steps to the street, Shelby, who wasn't going to be left alone with the body, following hard on his heels. At ground level the wind was still prowling the streets. Frost took a deep breath. 'Doesn't fresh air have a funny smell?' He looked up and down the empty street. Or was it empty? He thought he saw something move down by the back entrance to one of the Market Square shops. As if someone had ducked into a doorway to avoid being seen. He caught a quick glimpse of the expression on Shelby's face. The constable had seen the movement, too, but he was making a determined effort to keep his face passive. Strange, thought Frost. Very strange. He wondered what Shelby was up to . . . but if he was going to get to the party before the beer ran out . . .

With a wave to the constable, he climbed back into his car. As he settled down in the driving seat, his sodden trouser legs flapped clammily around his ankles, and he felt the cold squelch of his wet socks as he pressed his feet on the pedals. On the back seat, unused and bone dry, his Wellington boots sat on top of a yellowing back number of the *Daily Mirror*.

He reversed, only hitting the kerb once. As he drove past the red-brick building with the creaking enamel sign, he realized he couldn't see the broken metal grille. It was halfway down the stairs and completely out of sight from the road. Yet Shelby said he had spotted it from his car. It vaguely worried him, but there was probably a logical explanation which could wait, whereas the party couldn't. The dull boom of the disco belting out full blast from the station canteen was waiting to meet him as he turned into Market Square.

She was nervous. The moon, a diamond-hard white disc in the starless sky, made the path as bright as day but buried the bushes in deep shadow. She had an uneasy, nagging feeling of danger. Of someone lurking. She felt in her pocket, and her hand closed reassuringly over the nail file. Not much of a weapon, but just let anyone try anything and she'd use it like a knife.

But she didn't have a chance to use it. He was too quick for her. A slight rustling noise from behind her, and, even as she was turning, the cloth blacked out the moon, the stars. She opened her mouth to scream, but choking hands squeezed and squeezed.

Inside her head she was screaming, loudly, deafeningly. But only she could hear.

TUESDAY NIGHT SHIFT (2)

Police Sergeant Bill Wells, sad-faced and balding, raised his head to the ceiling where all the noise was coming from and bared his teeth in anger. Upstairs, that was where he should be. Up there, enjoying himself, instead of being stuck down here as station sergeant, trying to cope with the running of the district with hopelessly inadequate numbers of staff.

He was one of the few members of the Denton Division forced to be on duty on this special night, the night of the big party. And what was unfair was that he *should* have been up there. Today should have been his day off. But at the very last minute, for his own peculiar reasons, the Divisional Commander had revised the duty roster, so now Wells was on duty, as was Jack Frost. This didn't worry Jack Frost, as he intended to sneak upstairs whatever the rosters said. You could get away with it in plainclothes but not if, like Sergeant Wells, you were wearing a uniform. There was no justice.

The skeleton duty force could only cope if the night was almost incident-free. Indeed, all duty men had been instructed not to look for trouble, to walk away from it if it crept up, and to turn a blind eye to all minor offences. But already things had started to heat up with the discovery of a dead body down a public convenience, and it was a well-known fact that shifts that started badly almost always ended badly.

And the damn phone, ringing almost nonstop, wasn't helping; the calls were usually from members of the public complaining about the noise. It was so unfair. The people upstairs were having all the fun and he was having to cope with all the complaints.

The phone rang again. He snatched it up and blocked his

free ear with his finger to try and drown out that monkey music from above.

'Would you mind repeating that, madam? I'm afraid I can't hear you.'

The woman caller was gabbling away excitedly, but even with the phone pressed so tightly against his ear it hurt, he couldn't make out what she was agitated about.

'Would you mind holding on for a moment, madam?' He covered the mouthpiece with his hand and relieved the steam pressure of his myriad grievances by yelling at young Police Constable Collier, who was painstakingly hacking out a report on the antique Underwood typewriter. 'Do something useful for a change, Collier. Get upstairs and tell those drunken layabouts to keep the row down. Some of us are trying to work.'

But before Collier could move, the lobby doors parted to admit the tall, straight-backed figure of Police Superintendent Mullett, Commander of Denton Division. The Superintendent, with his glossy black hair, clipped military moustache and horn-rimmed glasses, looked more like a successful businessman than a policeman. He was wearing his casual party wear: a tailored grey suit, a silver-flecked shirt, and a blue-and-silver tie. Wells and Collier immediately stiffened to attention but were waved at ease. The thump of the disco from above made Mullett wince, and he could feel his head starting to ache, but he put a brave face on it. After all, he was one of the lads tonight, like it or not.

'They seem to be enjoying themselves up there, Sergeant Wells,' he shouted over the din. 'Not too loud for you, is it?'

'No, sir,' lied Wells as he pushed the phone to Collier so the constable could take over the call. 'Nice to hear people enjoying themselves . . . for a change.'

Mullett nodded his approval, his gaze wandering around the dingy lobby with its stark wooden benches and the Colorado Beetle Identification poster flapping on the dark grey walls. 'I never realized just how dreary this lobby looked, Sergeant. It's bad for public relations. Do you think you could see about cheering it up . . . get in some house plants, or flowers, or something?'

'Yes, sir. Good idea, sir,' mumbled Wells, raising his eyes to the ceiling in mute appeal. Bloody flowers indeed! He was a policeman, not a bloody landscape gardener.

'Is Inspector Frost about?' asked Mullett anxiously. He was hoping the answer would be no. He preferred that Frost, with his unpressed clothes, his unpolished shoes, his rudeness, and his coarse jokes, should be well out of the way when the Chief Constable arrived.

'Out on an inquiry, sir. Body down a public convenience off the Market Square.'

A public convenience! Mullett flinched as if he had been hit. It sounded just the type of distasteful inquiry that Frost would get himself involved in, but at least it had the advantage of keeping him out of sight when the VIP arrived.

He leaned across the desk to the sergeant, taking him into his confidence with great news: 'The Chief Constable said he *might* look in, Sergeant, to say goodbye personally to George Harrison. You might ask one of your spare constables to keep an eye on the road outside . . .'

'I haven't got anyone spare, sir,' cut in Wells hastily. 'I've only got one constable with me to help run the entire station.' He indicated young Collier, who didn't seem to be making much progress with the caller on the phone.

'He'll do fine,' beamed Mullett, who had no intention of getting involved in these minor staffing problems. 'The instant the Chief Constable's car turns that corner, I want to be told. I'll be upstairs with the lads.' He paused. 'Sorry I had to put you on duty tonight, Wells, but there are so few men I could really trust to do a good job when we're short-handed.'

Wells gave a noncommittal grunt.

Mullett pushed open the door to the canteen and steeled himself. He was not a very good mixer as far as socialising with the lower ranks was concerned and would never have attended were it not for the promised visit of the Chief Constable. He squared his shoulders, then, like a front-line soldier going over the top, he bravely charged up the stairs.

Wells glowered after him, speeding him on his way with a blast of mental abuse. 'That's right . . . go and enjoy yourself. Never mind us poor buggers sweating our guts out down here.' He became aware of Collier's worried face looking helplessly at him, the phone still in his hand.

'What is it now, Collier? Surely you can handle a simple phone call on your own?'

'She won't talk to me, Sarge, and she's getting stroppy. She says she wants a high-ranking officer.'

A loud burst of sound and the crash of breaking glass from overhead. Wells hoped it was Mullett falling over the beer crates.

'She can't have a high-ranking officer, Collier. All the high-ranking officers are upstairs getting pissed.' He snatched the phone from the constable's hand. 'Go out and keep an eye open for the Chief Constable's Rolls . . . and get some bloody flowers.'

'Flowers?' queried Collier, but seeing the look on his sergeant's face, prudently decided not to wait for an answer.

Wells stuffed a finger in his ear and put on his polite voice. 'Yes, madam, can I help you?'

'What are you going to do about that bloody noise?' screeched the woman caller. 'I've got three children in bed and they can't get to sleep!'

'We'll look into it, madam,' promised Wells.

The sliding panel that connected the lobby to the control room slid back and PC Ridley, the controller, poked his head through.

'I've got Dave Shelby on the radio, Sarge. He's trying to get a body to the morgue. The ambulance men refuse to touch it. They reckon it's too mucky for the ambulance.'

'Mr Frost is handling that one,' said Wells.

'I can't contact Mr Frost, Sarge. He doesn't answer his radio.'

'Typical,' snorted the sergeant. 'Trust him to hide when there's trouble.' He consulted a typed list of funeral directors. 'Tell Shelby to try Mawkins in the High Street. They're cheap, they're not too fussy, and they keep begging us for work.'

'Right, Sarge.' The panel slid shut.

Wells was logging the last call in the phone register when he became aware of an irritating tap, tap, tap. He raised his eyes. Someone had the temerity to be rapping a pencil on the desk to attract his attention. He jerked up his head and there was the new man, that sulky swine, the bearded Detective Constable Webster, with the usual scowl on his face, tap, tap, tapping away. Furiously, Wells snatched the pencil from the man's hand and hurled it to the floor. Pushing his face to within an inch of the constable's, he said, 'Don't you ever do that again, Webster. If you want to attract my attention you address me by name, then wait until I am ready to respond. Understood?'

'Yes, Sergeant, I understand.' Webster almost spat the words out.

'So what do you want?'

'I want to know where the hell this Frost character has got to. I'm supposed to be working with him. Two hours ago he dumps six months' filing on me and says he won't be a tick. I'm still sitting in that pigsty of an office, waiting.'

A malicious smile slithered across the sergeant's face. 'You want something to do then, Constable?'

Webster gritted his teeth, trying to stop his irritation from showing. The way these yokels took a childish delight in emphasising the word 'constable'. But he wouldn't let them see they were getting through to him.

'Yes, Sergeant. I want something to do.'

'Right,' said Wells, smiling. 'You can make the tea.'

'Make it?'

'We won't get any tea from the canteen, Webster. It's out of bounds to the workers. So you'll have to make it manually, which I trust is not beneath the dignity of an ex-inspector? There's a kettle and other stuff in the washroom. Brew up enough for six.' He lowered his head and returned to his entry in the log book.

Webster didn't move.

Wells raised his head. 'Is there a problem, Constable, something in your orders that you don't understand?'

Webster's face was rigid with fury. 'You want *me* to make the tea?' He said it as if he had received an improper suggestion.

Wells chucked his pen down and bounced back Webster's glare with a scorcher of his own. 'Yes, Constable. Any objections?'

'Yes,' snapped Webster, jerking a thumb at young Collier, who was hovering by the lobby door, anxiously peering out into the road. 'What about him? Why can't he do it?'

'Because *he* is doing a very important job for Mr Mullett. And anyway, why should *he* be the tea boy instead of you? You're both the same rank . . . you're both constables . . . or have you forgotten?'

'No,' snarled Webster, 'I haven't forgotten.' As if the buggers would let him forget! He spun on his heel and barged out of the lobby, slamming the door behind him.

That's put the bastard in his place, thought Wells, feeling better now he had syphoned off some of his pent-up frustration.

Collier raced over excitedly. 'The Chief Constable's car, Sarge.'

'Well, don't wet your knickers about it, Constable. Go upstairs and tell Mr Mullett, quick.' Wells adjusted his uniform and made his back ramrod straight. He rapped on the panel and warned Control that the Chief Constable was on the way through.

The phone on his desk gave a little cough. Wells glowered at it, daring it to ring. It defied him. So did the other phone. Damn and blast! He'd planned a quick exchange of dialogue with the Chief Constable in which the Chief would look around the empty lobby and say, 'All on your own, Sergeant?' and he would reply smartly, with much diffidence, 'Yes, sir, but I can cope. I can run this place single-handed if need be . . .' And the Chief Constable would smile approvingly and make a mental note that there was some very promising promotion material here. Instead, the Chief Constable, in immaculate evening suit, breezed through, nodded curtly at Wells and said, 'Those phones need answering, Sergeant.'

The first phone call was from a man living in the senior citizens' flats off Arberry Road. Some idiot in a sports car was roaring round and round the block, cutting across the lawns and waking the oldies up. Wells scribbled details and promised action. No sooner had he replaced the phone than it rang again. He picked up the second phone. Another senior citizen complaining about the same thing. 'Yes, we've got it in hand,' he promised, reaching for the first phone — yet another old fool wanting the police to do something about this hooligan in the racing car.

As he was taking details, Wells was annoyed to see the Chief Constable pause to have a few morale-boosting words with young Collier, who ought to be answering bloody phones instead of fawning on the top brass. Behind Collier, the Divisional Commander, all atwitter, greeted the honoured guest and escorted him upstairs where the raucous noise had mysteriously abated.

And all the time this damn old man was droning away in his ear about the sports car and the inefficiency of the police who were never around when they were wanted. 'I don't suppose you managed to get its registration number, Mr Hickman?' he asked when the caller ran out of breath.

'No,' replied the old man, 'but you'll be able to trace him. His licence plate fell off when he hit the dustbins.'

'Right, Mr Hickman, thank you very much,' said Wells, scribbling out the details. 'We'll send a car over there right away.' He jotted down the time of the call . . . 10.53, and slid the note through to Control.

Ridley, the controller, checked his wall map. Arberry Road. Charlie Alpha would be the quickest. He depressed the microphone button. 'Control to Charlie Alpha. Come in please.'

The old man in the call box replaced the phone and dug his fingers hopefully into the coin-return receptacle in case there was any money there. There wasn't. He shivered as a gust of wind found the broken pane in the kiosk door. He was still in his pyjamas, with his overcoat as a dressing gown and his sockless feet uncomfortably cold in his hastily laced shoes.

That hooligan in the sports car. It was the second night running the residents had had to put up with it. Screaming tyres, the horn blasting away, speeding round and round the flats as if it were on the Silverstone racing track. Tonight was even worse. The car had left the road and had ripped up lawns and flower beds as it took a shortcut. Then there was that almighty crash as it hit the dustbins and sent them flying and clanging. But that was the driver's downfall. The impact had knocked off the licence plate. The police would get him now. Hickman hoped they'd take away his licence for life and fine him hundreds of pounds. Or, better still, send him to prison. What they ought to do is bring back the birch. That would make these lunatics think twice before they disturbed the sleep of innocent people.

He didn't hear the car coming back. He was halfway across the road when the blinding glare of its headlamps transfixed him. The horn shrieked at him to get out of the way. But the old man was going too slowly and the car far too fast.

As if in slow motion, he saw the car leap at him, saw every detail of the radiator as it grew larger, then a terrible, smashing blow as the headlamp shattered his face. The pain was awful. Screamingly awful. But mercifully it didn't last long before a massive cloud of red and black blotted everything out and he was sucked down, down . . .

Watching from her window, a neighbour saw the car slow down, hesitate, then rev up and roar away, leaving the crumpled heap lying in the road. She had no phone and had to rush out and hammer at the next-door flat, screaming for someone to call an ambulance. The commotion had woken many of the residents. It didn't wake Hickman's wife. Slightly deaf, she slept soundly through it all, thinking her husband was still at her side.

The woman who had seen it happen covered the old man's bleeding body with blankets as they waited for the ambulance. It was on the scene in exactly four minutes from the time the 999 phone call had been received. The same ambulance and the same two ambulance men who had refused to handle the vomit-sodden body from the toilets. Carefully, they lifted Hickman onto a stretcher and, in a little less than thirty seconds, were on their way to the hospital, speeding past the arriving Charlie Alpha as it turned the corner.

The area car slid to a halt in front of the call box, its tyres just managing to avoid the puddle of blood and the shards of broken headlamp glass. PC Jordan took statements from witnesses while his observer, PC Simms, was sent to find the fallen licence plate. Then someone remembered Hickman's wife. A woman neighbour went with Simms to wake her and break the news.

Max Dawson, managing director of Dawson Electronics, the big, modern factory complex on the new Denton Trading Estate, gave a gentle guiding touch to the wheel of his Silver Cloud and turned the car into the private approach road to the house. The car purred as it glided toward the garage. Dawson felt like purring, too. This year's annual dinner and dance for his staff had been the best ever. His wife, who usually acted like a spoiled brat on such occasions, had behaved herself and had stuck to her promised maximum of four drinks, and all the speeches and presentations had gone off without a hitch.

He stole a glance at Clare in the seat next to him. For some reason she had been edgy all evening, fiddling with her bag, lighting cigarette after cigarette. But at least she had behaved like a managing director's wife and not like some slut a lorry driver would pick up. She certainly looked stunning in that low-cut red-and-black evening dress. Too damn low-cut perhaps. He'd noticed the way two of his sales representatives had eyed her and sniggered suggestively to each other. He'd mentally noted their names. He wondered if they'd still be sniggering at the end of the month.

The outside lights were on to discourage intruders, but the interior of the house was in darkness. The quartz digital clock on the dash pulsated to show the time as 11.31. His young daughter, Karen, spending the night at her friend's house, would be in bed. Fifteen-year-old Karen, sweet and unsophisticated, who hadn't inherited any of her mother's less endearing habits, thank God.

A touch of the remote control, and the garage door glided upward to receive the Rolls. 'We're home,' he said to Clare, who had her eyes closed.

Originally an early nineteenth-century farm building, the house had been completely gutted and converted, an undertaking that had cost him nearly ninety thousand pounds, but it had been worth it. On the open market there would be no shortage of buyers at an asking price in excess of a quarter of a million.

They went into the huge, split-level lounge with its massive natural-stone fireplace, large enough to roast the traditional ox if the log fire had been real. He pressed the ignition button and the living-flame gas jets plopped into life and licked hungrily at the sculptured logs. The instant warmth and the friendly red glow from the flickering flames increased his good humour to the extent that he was only mildly irritated to see that Clare had gone straight to the bar and was pouring herself a drink. Well, at least she had rationed herself at the function, so he'd let this one go by without comment.

'I'll just give the Taylors a ring to make sure Karen's all right,' he told her.

'Why shouldn't she be?' his wife snapped.

A touch of jealousy there, he thought. He'd been noticing it more and more of late.

Loosening his bow tie, he walked over to the phone and jabbed at the push buttons.

Debbie's parents were in bed. It was her father who eventually answered the phone, yawning loudly and at first not taking in what Dawson was saying. 'No, Max, Karen's not here. Isn't she with you?'

Dawson stared at the phone in disbelief. Had the fool gone mad? 'What the hell are you talking about?' he shouted. 'She was going to the cinema with Debbie, then spending the night with you. It was all arranged.'

'I know,' yawned Taylor. 'Debbie waited outside the Odeon, but Karen never showed up. We assumed you'd taken her to the dance with you.'

'*You assumed?* Why the bloody hell didn't you phone to check?'

'Well . . . we assumed . . .'

'You stupid sod!' roared Dawson, his face red with anger. 'Hold on.' He put down the phone and charged up the staircase to Karen's room. Flinging open the door, he looked in. The curtains were drawn, and the room was quiet and still. No sound of breathing. He fumbled for the light switch and clicked it on. Karen's bed was empty, still neatly made up from the morning. He raced down the stairs, grabbed the phone, and shouted, 'She's not here! If anything has happened to my daughter, I'll kill you, you bastard!' He was shaking with rage.

'What is it?' asked Clare, clutching his arm. 'Where's Karen?'

'That's what I'm damn well going to find out.' He raised the phone. 'Is Debbie there?'

'Of course, Max . . . but she's asleep.'

'Then wake her, you fool. She might know where Karen's got to.'

As he held on for what seemed like hours, anger fighting with apprehension, Clare drifted over to the bar and refilled her glass. 'Your daughter is missing,' he snarled, 'and all you can do is get bloody drunk.'

Clare burst into tears. He turned his back on her and waited impatiently for Debbie.

He scuttled through the woods, eyes and ears alert. He thought he had heard something. A scream. A piercing sound that tore a jagged hole in the silence. But all was quiet now . . . as quiet as the woods ever were at night above the rustlings and the murmurings and the moanings. Sometimes, when he was lucky, the murmurings and the moanings came from lovers, hot, sweating, coupling lovers too busy to realize they were being observed. The things some of them got up to . . . you'd never believe it! And some of the girls were worse than the men . . . far worse.

He squeezed between two bushes, taking a shortcut. He knew all the shortcuts. There was something in the long grass. Something black. He picked it up. A brassiere. A black, lacy, deep-cupped brassiere, the fastener hanging by a thread as if someone couldn't wait to undo those fiddling little hooks. He pressed it to his cheek and slowly rubbed it up and down the side of his face then, folding it carefully, pushed it deep into his pocket.

On through more bushes. The moonlight gleamed on something silvery white. He stiffened and stood stock still. It was the white of bare flesh. Holding his breath and moving quietly, with the skill of long practice, he inched forward, parting branches so he could get a better view.

Dear sweet Mother of God!

On the ground, ahead of him, lay the naked body of a young girl, her face raw and battered, the mouth and chin hidden under a mask of blood. Her body was mottled with livid green bruises. Strewn around, on the grass, her clothes. He crouched, making himself smaller in case whoever had done this was still lurking about. He listened. Silence.

It seemed safe, so he inched forward until he could touch her. The flesh was cold. Ice cold. He lowered his ear to her bloodied mouth but could detect no sound of breathing. Slowly his eyes travelled down the bruised and bleeding body to her thighs, then her legs. She was wearing thick black stockings which made the flesh of her thighs appear even whiter by contrast. The pieces of clothing strewn around the body seemed to be a school uniform of some kind. The girl's black-stockinged legs fascinated him, the stockings' tops circled by wide red garters, garters that were meant to be seen, not hidden. He would have thought school wear was far less sexy. This one must have been a right little teaser, deserving everything she'd got.

How marvellous it must be, he thought, to have a partner of one's own as quiet and submissive as this one. He had never touched a naked girl before. He had sweated and groaned in vicarious excitement as he watched other men caress, fondle, and make love to them. But he had never touched one himself. Not properly. Kneeling beside her, he gently stroked the flat stomach.

A twig snapped. He whirled around. Nothing. But this wouldn't do. Suppose someone saw him touching the body. Saw him and told the police. The police would think he had done this. He stood up and backed away from her, then turned abruptly, crashing through the bushes to the path that would take him to home and safety.

As he neared the phone box he knew he would have to call the police. Tell them about her. He wouldn't say who he was, but if anything went wrong . . . if they suspected him, he'd say, 'But I was the one who phoned you. Would I have done that if I'd killed her?' Yes, that would be clever. That would be smart. His hand dug deep into his pocket to caress the lacy softness of the black bra.

Police Sergeant Wells nudged Collier and nodded toward the lobby doors, which were opening very slowly. Jack Frost tip-toed in, obviously hoping to sneak upstairs to the party without being noticed. Unaware he had an audience, he furtively crossed the lobby and pushed open the door leading to the canteen, letting a warm burst of happy sound roll down the stairs on an air current of alcohol.

With perfect timing, Wells lobbed his grenade. 'You can forget the party, Mr Frost. Mullett's up there.'

'Eh?' Frost paused in midstride and nearly stumbled before spinning around, looking as guilty as a choirboy caught with *Penthouse* inside his hymnbook. 'You frightened the bloody life out of me, Bill,' he began, then the import of the sergeant's words hit him with a clout. Mullett had made it clear to everyone that the party was for off-duty personnel only. 'Mullett? Upstairs?' He studied the sergeant's face in the hope that his leg was being pulled.

'I'm afraid so, Jack. He's up there boozing and licking the Chief Constable's boots while you and I have got to stay down here and work.'

'Flaming ear holes,' muttered Frost bitterly.

PC Ridley slid back the panel and called out from the control room, 'Mr Frost. Dave Shelby has radioed through. Your body's been taken to the mortuary. The post-mortem will be at ten o'clock sharp.'

'Great,' replied Frost. 'There's nothing like a bowlful of stomach contents to give you an appetite for dinner.' He then gave his attention to young PC Collier, who was waving two burglary report forms at him.

'Two more break-ins, Inspector.'

'Shove them on my desk, son. I'll stick them in the Unsolved Robberies file if I can find room, and in the wastepaper basket if I can't.' Denton was being plagued with an epidemic of minor break-ins and burglaries. They all seemed to be quick in-and-out, spur-of-the-moment jobs — no clues, no prints, no-one seeing anything. Only money was taken, small amounts usually, so, short of catching the villains in the act, there was little the police could do. With more than eighty reported incidents, and probably many more unreported, Mullett had decided there was little point in wasting time sending experienced police officers to the scene of the crime. There would be nothing to see but an irate householder and an empty drawer, vase, purse or tea caddy where the money had been. Instead, a form was provided so the householder could fill in details of the break-in. The forms were then cursorily examined, filed, and usually forgotten. Jack Frost was nominally in charge of the break-in investigations, and his file of burglary report forms was growing thicker each day. The accumulated figures made the division's unsolved crimes return look incurably sick.

Another roar of laughter from upstairs. The Chief Constable must have told his unfunny joke and Mullett's pants would be wet from uncontrolled giggling. Frost stared at the ceiling sadly, then brightened up. Surely Mullett and the Chief Constable wouldn't stick it out right to the bitter end. As soon as they'd left, he'd be up there, and would he make up for lost time! He ambled over to the desk and offered Wells a cigarette.

'Ta, Jack.' Wells flinched back as the flame from Frost's gas lighter seared his nose. 'You'll never guess what Mullett's latest is: He reckons the lobby wants brightening up. He only wants vases of bleeding flowers all over the place.'

Frost was only half listening. For some reason the face of Ben Cornish swam up in his mind, the dead eyes reproaching him for something he had overlooked. Then he realized he hadn't told Wells who the body in the toilet was.

'Ben Cornish? Oh no!' Wells slumped down in his chair. Cornish was one of his regulars, nothing too serious . . . public nuisance, drunk and disorderly . . . but lately he had been on drugs. Hard drugs. 'He was only in here a couple of days ago, stinking of meths and as thin as a bloody rake. I gave him a quid to get something to eat.'

'I doubt if he bought food with it, Bill. I don't think he's eaten properly for weeks. When I saw him tonight he looked like a Belsen camp victim on hunger strike. I reckon the jar of his stomach contents tomorrow will be absolutely empty. Whatever he bought with your quid was squirted straight into his arm with a rusty syringe.'

'I bet his mother took it badly.'

Frost smacked his forehead with his palm. 'Damn and bloody blast . . . I knew there was something I'd forgotten to do. I'll have to nip round there. Any chance of some tea first?'

'Shouldn't be long, Jack,' said Wells, adding with a note of smug triumph, 'Webster's making it.'

Frost stepped back in amazement. 'How did you get him to do that?'

'Simple. I gave him an order. Why shouldn't he make it? He's only a bloody constable.'

'He may be just a bloody constable now,' said Frost, 'but he used to be an inspector, and half the time he thinks he still is one.'

The subject of their conversation, Detective Constable Martin Webster, twenty-seven, bearded, was in the washroom filling the battered kettle from the hot tap for speed. He banged six fairly clean mugs onto a tin tray and slurped in the milk from a cardboard carton.

Is this what he had come to? A flaming tea boy? Six months ago he had been an inspector. Detective Inspector Martin Webster, wonder boy of Braybridge Division. Braybridge was a large town some forty-three miles from Denton.

Shipping him to this dump called Denton was part of his punishment, just in case being demoted wasn't enough, and the cherry on the cake was being saddled with that stupid, sloppy, bumbling oaf Jack Frost, who wouldn't have been tolerated as a constable in Braybridge, let alone an inspector. How did a clown like Frost make the rank? Someone had tried to tell him that the man had won a medal, but he wasn't swallowing that . . . not unless they handed out medals for sheer incompetence. Police Superintendent Mullett, the Divisional Commander, seemed to dislike Frost with the same intensity as he detested Webster. 'I'm not happy having you in my division,' Mullett had told him. 'I accepted you under protest. One further lapse and you're out . . .'

So how did Frost manage to get Mullett to recommend him for promotion? Webster smiled ruefully to himself. It probably helped that Frost didn't stagger into the station roaring drunk and punch his superior officer on the jaw. The memory made him shake his right hand. His knuckles still ached. So hard did he clout Detective Chief Inspector Hepton, that he believed, at the time, he had broken the bones of his hand.

He'd remember that night as long as he lived. The day before, he'd had that damn-awful row with his wife, Janet. The rows had been getting nasty, but this one was the worst ever. Janet didn't know how badly things had been going for him at the station. There had been complaints about his treatment of suspects. All right, perhaps he had been a mite overzealous, but he was getting results. But then there had been those two incidents, one after the other, where one prisoner had a black eye, and the other bruised ribs, and they'd screamed 'police brutality'. Both had been resisting arrest and were swinging punches, but Detective Chief Inspector Hepton had preferred to believe them rather than one of his own officers. Hepton had threatened to take him off CID work and put him back into uniform.

He hadn't told any of this to Janet. All she got was his bitterness, his resentment, and his temper. He couldn't remember how that last row started. It had built up until he swore at her and called her filthy names. Reacting angrily, she had whipped her hand across his face. He deserved it. That's what made it so hard to take: He bloody deserved it. He should have let it go, apologized, begged her forgiveness. But he had reacted without thought, the back of his hand cracking across her mouth, splitting her lip, making it bleed. She just looked at him with contempt, face white, blood trickling, then she slowly walked out, slamming the door behind her.

Later, the phone call from her mother's, saying she was leaving him. That's when he should have swallowed his pride and gone after her. Instead he preferred to wallow in self-pity and drink himself stupid on the contents of the cocktail cabinet.

And when he finally staggered into the station, unshaven, eyes red-rimmed, there was Hepton, Chief Inspector-bloody-Hepton, waiting for him, barring his way, that nagging, jarring voice scratching away at his raw nerve ends like a fingernail dragged down a blackboard.

And then things were very blurred. He recalled flinging a punch. An almighty punch which spun Hepton around, knocked him into a filing cabinet, and sent him crashing to the floor. Then the room was full of people, angry, shouting, holding him back. Someone must have taken him home because he next remembered waking in his own bed the following morning, his head split by wedges, hoping against hope that it had all been some ghastly drunken nightmare. But Janet wasn't in bed with him. The house was empty, her clothes gone, and his fist swollen and hurting like hell.

Suspension, Disciplinary Tribunal, demotion to constable, and transfer to Denton — and to Jack Frost, the cretin of the year.

'Webster. How much longer are you going to be making that bloody tea?' Wells's voice, calling from the lobby, dragged him back to the present. The room seemed to be in a thick mist, outlines blurred and indistinct as the kettle boiled its head off. A roar of delight from the party upstairs. God, how he could do with a drink. Just one. But they'd warned him. Be drunk on duty just one more time . . .

He turned off the gas ring and made the tea.

In the lobby, Frost and Wells were huddled together exchanging moans. Young Collier was at the Underwood, splashing correction fluid over a typed report as if he were painting a wall. Frost lowered his eyes guiltily as Webster handed him the mug of tea, knowing that he should have taken the detective constable with him on the Ben Cornish job. Indeed, it would have been better if he had — then Webster would have been the one floundering about in the wet and nasty instead of him. But he was finding the hair shirt of Webster's permanent scowl a mite too much to take without the odd break. He pulled the mug toward him. 'Thanks, son. Looks good.'

Wells accepted his tea without comment, but Collier, looking up from his remedial work, said, 'Thanks very much, Inspector . . . sorry, I mean Constable,' which provoked a muffled snort of suppressed laughter from the sergeant.

Webster's face went tight. Laugh, you bastards. My time will come. He rapped on the panel, pushing the mug through as Ridley slid it open. The controller nodded his thanks, then called across to Wells: 'That hit-and-run victim, Sergeant — they've taken him to Denton General Hospital. He's not expected to live. Oh, and they've found the licence plate from the car that hit him.'

'A licence plate from the car that hit him!' exclaimed Frost in mock excitement. 'Now that could be a clue!' He sipped his tea. 'It's never been my luck to have a bloody licence plate left behind. I'm lucky if I find two witnesses who can agree on the colour of the car.' Then he paused, the mug quivering an inch from his lips, and whispered, 'Listen!'

They listened — to comparative silence. No music. No stamping.

Putting his mug down, Frost hurried over to the door that led to the canteen and pushed it open. Various voices called 'Goodbye, sir . . . Thanks for coming, sir . . .' The Chief Constable and Mullett were leaving. Frost smiled to himself. The minute they left, he'd be up those stairs like a sailor with a complimentary ticket to a brothel.

Picking its moment, the phone rang. 'Answer that, Collier,' Wells ordered. He wasn't going to miss his chance with the Chief Constable again. But Collier was doing his doorman act, standing to attention, holding the main door open for the VIPs to pass through. Crawling little sod, thought Wells disgustedly.

Webster had skulked off to the office and Jack Frost had ducked out of sight as he always did when Mullett loomed into view. That left only Wells to answer the phone.

Mullett and the Chief Constable shimmered into the lobby in a haze of whisky fumes and expensive cigar smoke. The Chief was talking, Mullett was listening, nodding vigorously and murmuring, 'Couldn't agree with you more, sir,' whether he heard what the Chief was saying or not. At the door the Chief Constable paused, smiled approvingly at Collier, and said to Mullett, 'You've got a smart man there, Superintendent.'

'Couldn't agree with you more,' said Mullett, wondering why Sergeant Wells was looking daggers in his direction.

Wells shifted the phone to his other hand and took down the details. 'I see, sir. Well, try not to worry. I'll have a detective inspector over to you right away.'

He hung up.

Upstairs, whoops of delight. The record player started up again. Jack Frost scuttled out of his hiding place in Control and hurried across to the door. The sound billowed and beckoned as he opened it.

He never made it.

'You can forget the party, Jack,' said Wells. 'I've got a missing teenage girl for you.'

TUESDAY NIGHT SHIFT (3)

Out to the car park and the Cortina, Frost scuffling along behind Webster, the bright lights from the canteen windows looking down on them. Absent-mindedly, Webster slid into the passenger seat and stretched out as he used to in the days when a detective constable drove him around. Frost opened the passenger door and peered in. 'I think you might be sitting in my seat, son.' With a grunt of irritation, Webster shifted over to his rightful, lowly place behind the wheel, listening sullenly to the muddled directions Frost gave him as they drove off.

It was Frost who broke the uneasy silence.

'This might come as a surprise to you, son, but you're not exactly the flavour of the month around here.'

Webster, in no mood to accept any form of criticism, especially from a twit like Frost, stiffened. 'And what's that supposed to mean?'

'It means, son, that you've been behaving like a spoiled brat ever since you arrived. I know we're not God's gift to the demoted, but why don't you try and meet us halfway? The odd little smile twinkling through your face fungus wouldn't come amiss.'

'I treat people the way they treat me,' snapped Webster, slowing down to wait for the lights to change. 'I'm sick of having to put up with all this "Thank you, Inspector . . . sorry, I mean *Constable*" crap.'

'Young Collier's harmless,' said Frost.

'It's not only Collier,' said Webster, accelerating as the lights changed, 'it's everyone, especially Sergeant Wells. He delights in making me look small.'

'There's a reason,' Frost said. 'Bill Wells wants to be an inspector so badly it hurts. He's passed all the exams but the Promotion Board keeps turning him down. So when he comes across someone who was an inspector, something he's never going to be, and who chucked it all away, well, he's bound to feel resentful.'

'And there's Inspector Allen,' began Webster.

'Inspector Allen is a bastard,' Frost cut in. 'Lots of inspectors are bastards. I bet you were one yourself.' He peered through the dirty wind-screen. 'Turn right here.'

Webster spun the wheel, braking suddenly as the car headlights picked out a brick wall charging towards them. They had driven down a cul-de-sac.

'Sorry,' said Frost. 'I meant left.'

Stupid bastard, thought Webster, backing out with great difficulty. 'And another thing. Why was I deliberately excluded from that dead junkie investigation tonight?'

'Because I'm a stupid old sod who never does the right thing,' replied Frost disarmingly. 'I'm sorry about that, son, honest I am.'

The reminder about Ben Cornish made him feel guilty. He knew he hadn't been very thorough. All he had wanted to do was get out of that stinking hole and off to the party. And there was no mystery about it. Accidental death, like the doctor said. But something nagged, itched away at the back of his mind. He shut his eyes, trying to picture the scene . . . the filth, the body . . . the sodden clothes. Wait a minute, the clothes! He had the feeling that the pocket linings of the overcoat were pulled out slightly as if someone had gone through the pockets. Yet Shelby had said he hadn't searched the body. It wouldn't be the first time a copper had been through a dead man's pockets and kept what he found. Immediately he discounted this possibility. Shelby might be a lousy copper in many ways, but he wasn't a thief. Besides, what would Ben have had that was worth plunging your hands in vomit-sodden pockets to find?

He shook his head and erased the picture from his mind. Then he realized he still hadn't broken the news to Ben's mother. He sighed. There were so many things he had left undone. Which reminded him —

'Did you manage to finish the crime statistics?' he asked hopefully.

'No,' said Webster, 'your figures didn't make any sense.'

Frost nodded gloomily. They didn't make any sense to him either, which was why he had passed them on to the detective constable. The returns were a monthly headache. This month Mullett had received a rocket from County Headquarters because, yet again, in spite of firm assurances, the Denton figures hadn't been received on time. Fuming at his division's failure, Mullet, in turn, had castigated Frost, and County had reluctantly agreed to extend the deadline by thirty-six hours. This deadline expired tomorrow.

'First thing tomorrow, son . . . as soon as we get back from the post-mortem . . . we'll make a determined effort.'

Webster said nothing. Frost's intentions were always of the best, but when the morning came, and the question of doing the returns was raised, Frost would suddenly remember some pressing reason why he and Webster had to go out. Webster badly needed to make good, but his chances of clawing his way back to his old rank of inspector were being sabotaged by his involvement with this hopeless, incompetent idiot.

'Left here,' directed Frost. Webster spun the wheel and the Wellington boots on the back seat crashed to the floor.

Frost leaned back and picked them up. 'Must get the car cleaned up soon. We'll do it as soon as we finish the crime statistics.'

High up, ahead of them, a large house, its grounds flood-lit. 'That's the Dawson place, son. Dead ahead.'

Max Dawson was waiting for them at the open front door. He barely glanced at the warrant cards they waved at him, almost pushing them into the house and through the double doors which led to the lounge.

The split-level lounge, which ran almost the full length of the ground floor, was roomy enough to hangar a Zeppelin. It smelled strongly of expensive leather, rich cigar smoke, and money . . . lots of money. A welcome contrast to the gents' urinal back of the High Street, which smelled of none of these things, thought Frost.

The lower level, panelled in rich oak, gleamingly polished, boasted a bar as big as a pub counter but much better stocked, and an enormous natural-stone fireplace with an unnatural but realistic log fire roaring gas-powered flames up a wide-throated brick chimney. The room's trappings included a giant-screen projection TV posing as a Chippendale *secrétaire*, a concealed screen that emerged from the wall at the touch of a button, and at least five thousand pounds' worth of custom-built hi-fi equipment in flawlessly hand-crafted reproduction Regency cabinets. The carpeting was milk-chocolate Wilton over thick rubber underlay. It set off the deep-buttoned, soft-leather couches in cream and natural brown.

The second level, up a slight step, housed a full-sized snooker table with overhead lights, cue racks, and scoreboard. One wall was lined with what appeared to be banks of gilt-edged, leather-bound books that probably concealed a wall safe, the other with open-fronted cabinets displaying sporting guns, revolvers, and rifles.

Dawson came straight to the point. 'My daughter's been kidnapped,' he said, flicking his hand for them to sit. 'I'll co-operate with the police, but if there's a ransom demand, I intend to pay it. My only concern is my daughter's safety.' Then, as an afterthought, he indicated the woman seated by the fire, cradling a glass, 'My wife.'

Dawson, in evening clothes, the two ends of his bow tie hanging loose, was a short stocky man of about fifty with thinning hair, hard eyes, and tight, ruthless lips. Clare, his wife, was much younger and quite a looker, with dark hair, rich, creamy flesh, and the most sensuous mouth Frost had ever seen.

'Right,' said Frost, unbuttoning his mac. 'We'd better have the details.'

The door bell chimed. Dawson jerked his head to his wife. 'That'll be the Taylors. Let them in.' Obediently, she tottered out of the room. 'I want you to hear what this girl has to say,' he told the two policemen.

While they waited, Webster rose from his chair and wandered over to the second level, where he took a closer look at the guns. He removed a Lee Enfield Mark III from a rack and squinted down its sights. 'Are these genuine, sir?' he asked.

'Of course they're not bloody genuine,' snapped Dawson. 'They're replicas. I've got the genuine guns locked away.'

'I take it you have a gun licence, sir,' persisted the detective constable, forgetting he wasn't in charge of the case.

Annoyed at this digression from the main business, Dawson jerked open the drawer of a long sideboard and pulled out some papers. 'Yes, I bloody have. Do you want to waste time seeing it, or shall we talk about my daughter?'

Stubbornly, Webster held out his hand for the licence. Frost jumped in quickly before the constable got too entrenched in his detective inspector act. 'We can spare the gentleman that formality,' he said firmly.

Reluctantly, Webster's hand dropped. That's right, you bastard, make me look small, he smouldered, his expression mirroring his thoughts.

Clare Dawson returned with Mr Taylor, a nervous little man with a pencil moustache who entered the lounge hesitantly, as if not certain of his reception. He clasped the hand of his daughter, Debbie, whose face was hidden in the hood of a thick blue duffel coat.

'So sorry about the misunderstanding, Max,' he began, offering his hand.

'Misunderstanding?' snarled Dawson, knocking the hand away. 'You little creep. If anything's happened to my Karen, I'll break you . . .'

His wife tried to make peace. 'I'm sure nothing's happened to her, Max.'

Dawson spun round, his face furious. 'What are you, bloody clairvoyant all of a sudden? How do you know she's all right? You don't even bloody-well care!' He paused and waved his hand jerkily in what was intended as a gesture of apology. 'I'm sorry. I'm overwrought.' He squeezed out a smile for Taylor and the girl. 'Please sit down.'

Debbie unbuttoned the duffel coat and slipped it off. Beneath it she wore a green long-sleeved pullover. A serious-faced little girl wearing glasses, her hair twisted in pigtails, she looked half asleep, frightened, and a lot younger than her fifteen years.

'Right,' said Frost. 'Let's make a start so Debbie can get back to bed.' He checked to see what Webster was up to and was annoyed to locate him back with the guns. 'Do you think you might spare the time to take a few notes, Constable?' he called.

Webster's frown crackled across the room like a lightning flash as he dragged out his notebook.

'Karen's been kidnapped,' said Dawson. 'There was a man hiding in the house. You saw him, didn't you, Debbie?'

'Well, I *think* I did,' whispered the girl. She seemed too shy to look at anyone in the room and kept her head bowed down.

'You *think* you did?' shouted Dawson angrily. 'What do you mean "think"? You told me over the phone you definitely saw him.' He spun around to Mr Taylor. 'Have you been getting her to change her story?'

'Hold hard everyone,' pleaded Frost. 'This is getting confusing. I'm a bit on the dim side, I'm afraid, so everything has to be explained very slowly to me. How about starting right from the beginning with not too many long words?' He nodded for Dawson to begin.

'I'm managing director of Dawson Electronics. Tonight was the firm's annual dinner and dance, which my wife and I attended. As we wouldn't be back until late, our daughter, Karen, had arranged to go straight from school with Debbie to see a film at the Odeon — *Breakdance* or some such name — they're both mad on dancing. After the film they were going back to Debbie's house, where Karen was to stay the night. My wife and I got back home from the function a little after 11.30. I phoned Taylor to see if Karen was all right. He told me they hadn't seen her. Debbie had turned up outside the Odeon at the appointed time, but no Karen. Debbie waited and waited, but, as Karen hadn't arrived by the time the programme started, she went in and saw the film on her own.'

'Hold on a minute,' said Frost. 'You say Debbie waited for her outside the cinema? I thought the original idea was that they went straight there together — from school?'

'Tell the inspector, Debbie,' said Dawson.

'The school closed at lunch time,' said Debbie, her head bowed, talking to the floor. 'We were all sent home. The teachers went on strike.'

'Did you hear that?' demanded Dawson, quivering with barely suppressed anger. 'The teachers went on bloody strike! If they worked for me I'd sack the lot of them. And this isn't the state-run comprehensive school we're talking about. This is St Mary's.'

Frost nodded. St Mary's College for Girls was a very exclusive, extremely expensive private school for the daughters of the filthy rich.

'They kick the kids out, lock up the school, and don't bother to tell the parents,' ranted Dawson. 'If anything has happened to Karen as a result of this, I'll sue that bloody school for every penny it has.'

As the tirade continued, Frost's eyes wandered to Mrs Dawson, who was quietly topping up her glass. She certainly was a seductive piece of stuff. At a guess, she was at least fifteen years younger than her husband, but it was difficult to tell — those rich birds knew how to slow down the ageing process. Her low-cut red-and-black evening gown revealed acres of warm, creamy flesh just crying out for exploration. She was, if one were being hypercritical, just a trifle on the plump side, but warm and inviting nevertheless, just like an over-inflated sex doll. She's wasted on her husband, he thought. I bet he only has sex if it comes up on his agenda. *11.02-11.04, sex with wife, weather permitting.* As Frost tore his gaze away, his eyes met Webster's. He too was taking a sly surveillance. Frost leered and gave the constable a knowing wink. Webster looked away quickly, finding his notebook of consuming interest.

'So the pupils were sent home at lunch time, sir?' Frost prompted.

'Yes. Debbie walked back with Karen as far as the gates to the drive, and they arranged to meet outside the Odeon that evening.'

'What time would this be, Debbie?'

'About a quarter to two,' she told the carpet.

'You would be at work at that time, sir?' Frost suggested to Dawson.

'Of course I damn well was.'

'And where were you, Mrs Dawson?'

Clare began to reply, but her husband had no intention of yielding the floor and answered for her. 'My wife was out at the hairdresser's. That's the point. The house was empty, and yet Debbie saw . . .'

'Debbie can tell us herself,' cut in Frost. He beamed at the young girl. 'Tell us what happened, love, and the naughty man with the nasty beard will write it all down.' He had added this for Webster's benefit as the constable's notebook looked suspiciously devoid of shorthand.

Debbie spoke so quietly they had to lean forward to take in what she was saying. 'I left Karen at the gates at the bottom of the drive. My house is farther on. As I turned and waved to her, I saw . . . I thought I saw . . . someone at the window of Karen's bedroom. I didn't pay much attention. I didn't know the house was supposed to be empty.'

'Was it a man or a woman?' asked the inspector.

She stared hard at the floor. 'I can't be sure but I think it was a man. He was closing the curtains. I only saw him for a second.'

'Closing the curtains? You mean the bedroom curtains were open. The man you saw was pulling them together?'

'Yes. I thought nothing of it at the time. I didn't know it was supposed to be important.'

Frost rubbed his chin. 'Did you see Karen go into the house?'

'No, but I saw her walking up the path toward the house.'

'And she had arranged to meet you outside the Odeon at what time?'

'Half past five.'

'You arrived on time?'

'I was there five minutes early. I waited until six . . . that's when the programme started. She didn't turn up, so I went in on my own.'

'Were you surprised she didn't turn up?'

Her eyes blinked rapidly behind her glasses. 'Yes. She'd been excited about it for weeks — we both were — and she was looking forward to spending the night at my house.'

'Any idea where she might have gone?'

She shook her head. 'No. No idea at all.'

'We've phoned all her other friends,' said Dawson. 'It's bloody obvious. She's been kidnapped. The man was inside the house, waiting for her.'

'Thank you, Debbie,' said Frost, 'you've been a great help. Now, you go off home and back to bed. If you think of anything else, get your dad to phone me.' He dug around in his pocket until he found a dog-eared card, which he handed to Taylor. While Clare was showing father and daughter out, Frost asked for a photograph of Karen.

Max Dawson took a coloured photograph from a mosaic-topped coffee table and handed it to the inspector, who studied it, then passed it over to Webster. A photograph of a schoolgirl, dark, shiny, well-brushed hair, a scrubbed, glowing face with a hint of freckles, a snub nose, and a broad grin. If she was fifteen, then, like Debbie, she looked very young for her age.

'A pretty kid,' smiled Frost. 'When was this taken?'

Dawson snapped a finger for Clare to reply. 'About six or seven months ago,' she said obediently.

'And how old is she?' inquired Webster, writing the details on the reverse of the photograph.

'She was fifteen last Thursday,' Dawson answered.

'Thank you, sir,' said Frost. 'And now a couple of questions for you, Mrs Dawson.'

She started as he addressed her, catching her glass just in time to stop it from falling over. Then she tried to light a cigarette from a statuette of a visored knight in armour that doubled as a table lighter, but she had difficulty in steering the flame to the end of her cigarette. At last the cigarette was alight, but still she kept the statuette in her hand, fidgeting with it, clicking the flame on and off, on and off. 'Yes, Inspector?'

She was understandably nervous, and of course worried . . . but there was something else . . . something almost furtive about her. The same furtiveness Frost had seen in the face of Dave Shelby. Later, he would remember how he had linked her with Shelby — and all for the wrong reasons.

'What time did you leave the house to go out, Mrs Dawson?'

'This evening you mean?'

'Of course he doesn't bloody-well mean this evening,' snarled her husband, snatching the lighter from her hand and putting it on the oak mantelpiece above the fireplace, well out of her reach. 'He means when you went out to get your bloody hair shampooed and set.'

'Oh, I'm sorry. The appointment was at two. I left the house shortly after one.'

With a quick glance to make sure Webster was recording these details, Frost then asked, 'And what time did you get back home?'

'Five o'clock, perhaps a little later.'

'Three hours for a shampoo and set?' queried the inspector. 'I didn't think it took that long.'

'It only took an hour, but afterward I walked around the town, looking at the shops, then I went in Aster's Department Store and had afternoon tea.'

'When you returned home, was there anything that didn't seem quite right . . . any feeling that someone had been in the house while you were out?'

She considered this for a moment, then firmly shook her head. 'No, nothing.'

Frost smiled his thanks, then switched his attention to the

husband. 'You suggest your daughter has been kidnapped, sir. I take it there's been no contact from anyone claiming to be holding her, no phone calls or ransom demands?'

'There's been no approach . . . yet. But it will follow, I have no doubt about that. I'm a rich man, a bloody rich man. My daughter is missing, a man was hiding in here, waiting for her. You don't have to be a genius to see she's been kidnapped.'

Frost leaned back in the chair and stared up at the high ceiling with its indistinguishable-from-real oak beams and its crystal chandelier. He worried at his scar and chewed the facts over. He wasn't sold on Dawson's kidnap theory. If the kid had been kidnapped, surely her abductors would have immediately warned her parents not to contact the police. And here it was, some ten hours or more after the event, and they still hadn't made their approach. No, he couldn't buy the kidnap scenario.

Webster watched the old fool drifting off into his reverie, trying to find inspiration from the ceiling. Look at him, he thought. He hasn't a clue about what to do next. Well, if the inspector didn't know what to do, Webster certainly did. Abruptly he snapped his notebook shut and stood up.

'Right, Mr Dawson. Debbie saw a man in your daughter's room, so we'll start by taking a look up there.'

The inspector's face went tight, but after a couple of seconds he relaxed and forced a smile. Pushing himself from the armchair's cream-and-brown embrace, he said mildly, 'Upstairs is it, Mrs Dawson?'

Clare drained her glass and rose unsteadily to her feet. 'I'll show you.'

They followed her up a wide, deeply carpeted staircase to the first floor. Her tight-fitting evening dress did more than hug her figure. It intimately explored it, and they were treated to a glorious display of wriggling buttock cleft which Webster might have missed had not Frost nudged him and pointed.

A short wade through the knee-deep carpet of the landing to a dove-grey padded door, which she opened. She clicked on the light, then moved back slightly for them to squeeze past. It was a tight squeeze and she didn't seem to want to make it any easier. 'This is Karen's room.'

'Thanks very much, Mrs Dawson,' said Frost, taking her arm and steering her out of the room. 'We'll give you a shout if we want anything.' The door had barely closed behind her before he added coarsely, 'Though it's pretty obvious what you want, darling.'

Webster scowled but didn't respond. He was becoming inured to the inspector's tasteless comments on the people with whom they came into contact. But he would have thought even Frost would draw the line at a mother whose kid was missing.

Frost sprawled out on Karen's bed and bounced up and down to test the springs. He found a half-smoked cigarette hiding in his pocket and lit it gratefully. 'Well, you wanted to search the room, son, so search it. If you find any important clues, such as a severed hand, or a warm bra with the contents intact, let me know. Wake me up if I'm asleep.' He closed his eyes and relaxed.

'I was hoping for your co-operation.'

'Oh, it's *me* who's supposed to co-operate with *you*, is it?' he asked, as if understanding for the first time. 'I thought it was the other way around. I'll co-operate by keeping out of your way.' And he wriggled comfortably.

Who needs your bloody help? thought Webster.

It was a teenager's dream bedroom, straight out of the pages of an up-market pop magazine. The ceiling was finished in sky blue and dotted with a firmament of silver stars. Along one wall a custom-built unit held a music centre, a video recorder, and a small fourteen-inch colour TV to which was connected a computer keyboard.

Opposite, behind light-oak sliding doors, a built-in wardrobe travelled the entire length of the wall. Webster slid back the door to reveal rows of dresses and coats rippling on hangers. In a separate section a white ballet dress shimmered and rustled next to a cat suit and three pairs of leotards. Neat lines of tap and ballet shoes occupied the wardrobe floor.

Webster moved to the corner, where a small desk faced a

double row of bookshelves. On the desk were two blue-covered school exercise books with Karen Dawson, Form VB neatly written along the top. He opened one of them to read, in Karen's neat handwriting, *If I were Prime Minister, the first thing I would do on taking office would be to abolish poverty throughout the land* . . . He dropped the exercise book back on the desk.

Frost was still stretched out on the bed, eyes half closed, watching puffs of cigarette smoke drift like clouds across the star-spangled ceiling. 'OK, son, if you've got any theories, let's have them.'

'Well,' Webster began, 'if she has been kidnapped . . .'

'Kidnapped!' snorted Frost, reaching out for the exercise books. 'I wish she had been, son. A nice kidnapping case might make Mullett forget I hadn't done his lousy crime statistics.'

'The man Debbie Taylor saw . . .' said Webster.

Frost sighed deeply. 'Yes. I wish she hadn't seen him, son. That bloody man messes up all my theories. My theory is that Karen comes home, finds the house empty, and decides it would be a good opportunity to do a bunk.'

'Run away, you mean?'

'That's right. Teenagers run away from home all the time, especially when their parents are always rowing like those two charmers downstairs.'

'The father's a swine,' retorted Webster, 'but the mother's all right.'

'All right?' cried Frost. 'Her daughter's missing and she still finds the inclination to polish our buttons with her knockers as we have to squeeze past her into the bedroom? We could have had a quickie behind the door if we played our cards right. The pair of them aren't worth a toss, my son. Karen's run away, but give her a couple of cold nights and no clean knickers and she'll soon come crawling back to finish her essay about saving the world from poverty.'

'But the man . . .'

Frost ran his teeth along his lower lip. 'Yes, son, what about the man?' He crossed to the window, noticing that the curtains were open. Debbie had said she saw the man closing them. He opened the window and hurled out his cigarette, then leaned forward and peered along the drive, which sloped down to the main road, trying to locate the spot where Debbie would have been standing when Karen left her. Reluctantly, he was forced to agree that if there was a man, young Debbie would have been able to see him from the road. He withdrew back into the room and closed the window.

'If it was a kidnap,' said Webster, thoughtfully, 'then how would the man know Karen would be home from school early?' He thought for a second, then answered his own question. 'Suppose he was one of her schoolteachers?'

'The teachers are all women,' said Frost, poking another cigarette in his mouth, 'though a couple of them have got moustaches. The only man is the caretaker, but he's pushing seventy.' His fingers found a gap in his mac pocket. 'Sod it!'

'What's up?' asked Webster.

'There's a hole in this pocket. My lighter must have dropped out. Now when did I use it last?'

'About five minutes ago. It'll be near the bed.'

Frost went down on his knees and began patting the thick pile of the shag carpet. As his hand explored the area beneath the bed he touched something. He dragged out a small metal case covered in pale-blue leatherette. The legend on the lid read The Intimate Bikini Styler for That Sleek Bikini Line. Flicking open the lid, he looked inside. 'Here's a weird-looking electric razor, son.' He passed it over to Webster, who nodded curtly.

'They're called Bikini Stylers.'

'I know that,' said Frost, still searching for his lighter. 'It's printed on the lid, but I'm none the wiser.'

Webster looked embarrassed. 'Some of these modern bathing suits that girls wear . . . the bottom half is cut very low . . . they expose parts of the lower stomach . . . the very low lower stomach.'

Frost looked at him blankly, then his eyebrows rocketed up as the penny dropped. 'You don't mean . . . ? Are you trying to tell me that women actually shave themselves down there before they put their bathing drawers on?' He stared hard at Webster. 'You're having me on.'

'It's a fact,' Webster insisted. 'My wife uses one.' His eyes glazed reflectively. 'She looked a cracker in a bikini.'

Frost regarded the dainty shaver, shaking his head in awe. 'Now I've heard everything. I wish the hospital had one of these when I had my appendix out. Before the operation they sent in a short-sighted nurse with a Sweeney Todd cutthroat. That was the first time in my life I really prayed.'

He snapped the lid shut and poked the case back under the bed, wondering what a fifteen-year-old schoolgirl would be doing with a thing like this.

'By your left foot,' called Webster, pointing to the missing lighter.

Frost retrieved it, lit up, and flopped back on the bed. He yawned. 'I could stay here all night, son, especially if young Karen, all fresh, sweet, and clean-shaven, would slip under the sheets beside me.' He turned his head and saw the photographs. Two of them on the bedside cabinet, propped up against a tiny Snoopy digital alarm clock.

He sat up to examine them. One showed Karen in the white ballet dress from the wardrobe, standing *en pointe*, hands outstretched, looking demure and sweet. The other was a beach scene, brilliant sky, silver sand. Two girls — one, young Debbie minus her glasses, flat-chested in a one-piece dark-blue bathing costume, looking as embarrassed as if she were stark naked; next to her, smiling with the sensuous mouth she had inherited from her mother, Karen Dawson, long-legged, well-developed, posing in a white two-piece swimsuit that caressed and stroked every curve of her young body. An entirely different Karen from the scrubbed school-girl in the other photograph.

'No sign of five o'clock shadow,' muttered Frost, looking closely before handing the prize over to Webster.

The detective constable winced. Anything prurient and Frost flogged it to death. But the photograph certainly showed the girl in a different light. Unlike the inspector, Webster wasn't convinced the girl had left home of her own accord. There was one way to check, of course. He asked Frost to get off the bed, then he rummaged under the pillow and pulled back the bedclothes.

'I don't think you'll find her in the bed,' said Frost. He had pulled out the drawers of the bedside cabinet and was rummaging through the contents.

'I was checking to see if her pyjamas were there,' sniffed Webster. 'If she'd done a bunk I would have expected her to take them with her. They're not here.'

'But that doesn't mean she's taken them with her,' said Frost, pushing the drawers shut. 'She might be like Marilyn Monroe and wear nothing in bed but her after-shave.' He lifted the top sheet and brought it to his nose. 'Tell you what, though, my hairy son, she wears a pretty sexy perfume in bed . . . smells like that stuff farmers use to get pigs to mate. Mullett's wife smothers herself in it.'

Webster took a sample sniff. It certainly was pretty heady stuff for a fifteen-year-old. He was reassessing young Karen by the minute. 'Could we check the bathroom to see if her toothbrush and stuff have gone?' he asked. 'No girl would run away without her toothbrush.'

'Good idea,' said Frost, 'I'm dying for a pee.'

The first door they tried led to the Dawsons' bedroom, a vast room with a canopied bed, the walls covered in some kind of padded velvet. The next door opened on to the bathroom, fully tiled in red Italian marble. It contained a large circular sunken bath that could have doubled as a swimming pool. The bath had taps made of gold, as did the matching sink basin. A red carpet matched the tiles, and all the towels matched the carpet.

Frost surveyed the bath in awe. 'If I had a bath like that, son, I'd definitely have to get out if I wanted a pee.'

The bathroom cabinet was concealed behind a mirror over the sink. Webster opened it and was searching through its contents when the door burst open and Dawson charged in. He reacted angrily when he saw what Webster was doing.

'Who gave you permission to go through our private possessions?'

'We're checking to see if your daughter's toothbrush is still here, sir,' said Webster patiently. He had found two tooth-brushes in a beaker, one red, the other green. He showed them to Dawson. 'Do either of these belong to Karen? It is important, sir.'

'Karen's brush is orange.' He pushed Webster out of the way and rummaged impatiently through the cabinet. 'It should be here somewhere.' He yelled for his wife to come up. 'Karen's toothbrush —' he snapped as she entered the bathroom, 'where is it?' He moved so she could get to the cabinet.

Standing on tiptoe, she peered inside, moving things out of the way. 'It *should* be here,' she said.

'I didn't ask where it should be,' Dawson told her sarcasti-cally, 'I asked where it was. Apparently, it's important.'

'It isn't here,' Clare said eventually. 'None of Karen's stuff is here — her toilet bag, flannel, toothpaste . . .'

Webster leaned against the wall and folded his arms. An-noyingly, it looked as if Frost's theory was correct. The girl had run away.

'If Karen took her toilet things with her,' Frost told the parents, 'it does rather suggest she went of her own free will.'

Dawson's face reddened to match the Italian tiles. 'Are you suggesting Karen has run away from home? You're an idiot, man. A bloody idiot. You don't know my daughter. She loved her home. She wouldn't do such a thing.'

'Lots of teenagers do it, Mr Dawson,' said Webster. 'Not necessarily because of anything to do with home. There could be trouble at school . . . or an upset with a boy friend.'

Dawson regarded the detective constable as if he were an imbecile. 'A boy friend? My Karen? She's only fifteen, for God's sake, a mere child! And what about that man Debbie saw? What is he supposed to be, a mirage . . . a teenage sex fantasy?'

'I'm not convinced she saw anyone, sir,' Frost said. 'She had doubts herself.' He buttoned up his mac to show he was ready to leave.

'So you intend doing nothing?'

'Not a lot we can do,' said Frost. 'We'll issue her description, circulate her photograph, ask everyone to keep an eye open for her. I don't think she'll be away for long.'

They heard a phone ringing. Dawson snapped his fingers for his wife to answer, but when Frost suggested the caller might be Karen, he dashed out to answer it himself.

Frost sat down on the toilet seat and lit up his thirty-eighth cigarette of the day. He gave the woman a friendly smile. 'Anything you want to tell us while your husband isn't here, Mrs Dawson?'

Her face went white, then she pretended to be puzzled. 'I don't know what you mean.'

Frost shrugged. 'Then it's my mistake, Mrs Dawson.' He stood up as her husband returned. 'It's for you, Inspector — Denton Police Station. You can use the phone in Karen's room.'

The caller was Bill Wells. To Frost's delight, he could hear the noise of the party in the background. There was still a chance he would make it.

'Hello Jack,' Wells intoned in his usual gloomy voice, 'Can you talk freely?'

'Yes,' confirmed Frost.

'What's the score with Karen Dawson?'

'Zero. Her old man thinks she's been kidnapped, but my bet is she's done a bunk.'

'Don't be too sure she's all right, Jack. We might have found her.'

Frost caught his breath. Suddenly he felt cold and apprehensive. *'Might?'*

'We've had an anonymous phone call. A man. He says there's a girl's body in Denton Woods. I think you'd better take a look.'

Dawson poked his head round the door. 'Anything wrong, Inspector?'

'No,' said Frost. 'Just something we've got to look into. I might be back to you later on, sir. If there's any news, that is.'

TUESDAY NIGHT SHIFT (4)

Upstairs, the party was throbbing away louder than ever and showing no signs of breaking up. Wells heard stamping, shrieking, roars of laughter, and the sound of glass smashing. A load of bloody hooligans, he thought as he tried to hear what the caller was saying. 'I'm sorry, sir, bit of a disturbance outside. Would you mind repeating that?'

The man sounded out of breath and was barely whispering into the phone. 'I've found a body. In Denton Woods. A girl.'

Wells stiffened. Another body! Just when he was praying for a nice, quiet, peaceful night. With his free hand he knuckled the panel to Control and, when Ridley opened it, signalled for him to listen in on the extension.

'A girl's body, you say, sir?' He picked up his pen, ready to write down the details.

'That's right. A young girl . . . a kid.'

A kid! The sergeant's first thought was of the previous call he had logged. Karen Dawson, fifteen, missing from home since this afternoon.

'I see, sir. And where exactly is she?'

'I told you. In Denton Woods. Off the main path, behind some bushes.'

'Where in the woods, sir? We'll have to have the exact location.'

A pause, then a click and the line went dead. The caller had hung up. Wells replaced the receiver and cursed. 'Damn!'

'Sounded a nutter to me,' called Ridley, hanging up the extension.

Wells nodded. They were always receiving bogus calls from cranks with a grudge against the law, who took delight in wasting police time and money. But you couldn't take chances. It had to be assumed that all calls were genuine until proved otherwise. 'What cars have you got?' he asked the controller.

Ridley didn't need to consult his map. With half the strength drinking themselves stupid upstairs, only two cars were available, and one of them, PC Shelby's patrol car, was failing to respond. This was not untypical of Shelby! 'There's only Charlie Alpha, Sarge, and that's on the way to a domestic on the red-brick estate.' A 'domestic' meant a family row or disturbance.

'Forget the domestic,' he was told. 'I want Charlie Alpha to divert immediately to Denton Woods.' He vented his annoyance by kicking the leg of his desk. 'One bloody area car! How am I supposed to cover a division of this size with one lousy area car?'

Shutting his ears to the sergeant's moans, Ridley thumbed the transmit button and called Charlie Alpha. While he waited for the response, he asked, 'Exactly where in Denton Woods, Sarge?'

'How the hell do I know?' snarled Wells. 'I'm not a bloody mind reader! You heard what he said — off the main path, behind some bushes.'

A burst of static from the loudspeaker. 'Charlie Alpha to Control. On our way to domestic on the red-brick estate in response to your previous message, over.'

'Forget the domestic, Charlie Alpha. Proceed immediately to Denton Woods and initiate search. Anonymous report of young girl's body behind bushes, off main path. Over.' He waited, his thumb hovering over the transmit button, for Charlie Alpha to request the precise location.

'Would you give us a more precise location, Control? There are main paths running the length and breadth of Denton Woods.'

'That is all the information we have, Charlie Alpha,' replied Ridley in an aggravatingly reasonable voice. 'Over and out.' He heard the door open behind him as Wells came into the room.

'But there's four hundred acres of woods, miles of paths,

and thousands of bloody bushes . . .' Charlie Alpha pointed out.

Wells was getting fed up with this. He snatched the handset from Ridley. 'Then you'll be spoiled for bloody choice, won't you, Charlie Alpha? Just go and look for her and don't bloody argue!'

'Over and out,' said Charlie Alpha hurriedly.

Ridley stuck the marker for Charlie Alpha in the green-coloured expanse of Denton Woods on his wall map. 'They'll need some help, Sarge. Should we break up the party?'

Wells pinched his nose and gave it some serious thought. It was tempting, very tempting, and it would serve those noisy sods right to be turfed out into the dark and cold to search the woods. But if the call turned out to be a hoax and he had deployed half the force on a fruitless search, all on overtime, he'd never hear the last of it. Mullett would grind on and on about it for weeks. On the other hand, if it was genuine and he ignored it — He groaned. He was in a no-win situation.

To play it safe, he decided to phone Jack Frost. It might be his missing schoolgirl, and if the inspector wanted more men, it was up to *him* to ask for them. He picked up the phone and dialled the number of the Dawson house. 'Denton Police here, sir. Sorry to trouble you, but I wonder if I could have a word with Detective Inspector Frost?'

The traffic lights glowed an angry red in the darkness as Webster ignored them, speeding the car straight across the road junction. 'Slow down, son,' Frost murmured. 'There's four hundred acres of forest to search. The odd second isn't going to make much difference.'

Frost's request received the same sort of treatment as the traffic lights, and Webster's foot pressed down on the accelerator. Watching the street lights zip past at seventy-five miles an hour, Frost checked that his seat belt was fastened, then fumbled in his pocket for the photograph of the missing girl and studied it gloomily. I hope this body isn't Karen Dawson, he told himself. I'd hate to be the one who had to break the news to her father. Break the news! He sat up straight and banged his fist on the dashboard. 'Knickers! We were supposed to be breaking the news to Ben Cornish's old lady. What time is it?'

Webster twisted his hand on the steering wheel so he could see his wristwatch. 'Ten past one.'

Frost settled back in the seat, relieved it was too late to do it tonight. 'We'll do it tomorrow, first thing. It'll be our number-one treat before the post-mortem.' He paused for a second. 'Are you any good at breaking bad news, son?'

'No,' said Webster hurriedly. The inspector wasn't dumping that rotten job on him.

'Pity,' sighed Frost. 'I'm bloody hopeless. How do you tell someone their son was found dead, choked in his own vomit, floating in a pool of piddle. There's no way you can tart up that sort of news.'

They were approaching the dense blackness of the woods. Frost scrubbed the wind-screen with his cuff and squinted through, trying to locate Charlie Alpha. 'There it is, son,' he yelled, pointing to the white-and-black Ford Sierra tucked neatly into a lay-by. Webster coasted the Cortina snugly in behind it.

The wind slashed at them as they left the warmth of the car. Frost wound his scarf tighter and buried his hands deeply into his mac pocket as they trudged along a path in search of Jordan and Simms, the Charlie Alpha crew. Webster was the first to spot the dots of torch beams bobbing in the distance.

The path they followed twisted and turned, so it was nearly five minutes before they heard low voices. A sharp turn, and just ahead of them were the two uniformed men, Jordan and Simms, greatcoat collars turned up, huddled against the trunk of an enormous oak tree, dragging at cigarettes. At the approach of the detectives they spun around guiltily, pinched out their cigarettes, and snapped to attention.

'Hard at work, I see,' said Frost.

They grinned sheepishly. 'Have you come to give us a

hand, then, sir?' asked Jordan, who sported a drooping, Mexican-bandit moustache.

'You mean to say you haven't found her yet?'

'Found her, sir? Some nutter phones the station and says there's a body behind a bush, and me and Simms are supposed to search four hundred acres in the dark. It's bloody ludicrous.'

Frost showed them Karen Dawson's photograph. 'There's a chance it might be this kid. She's fifteen years old, missing from home since one o'clock this afternoon.'

They studied it under the light of Simms's torch. 'Why should it be her?' asked the moon-faced Simms. 'As many as twenty teenagers around here go missing every week.'

'A man was reported lurking inside her house as she came home from school. She hasn't been seen since,' said Webster.

Heads turned toward him. They hadn't seen the bearded bloke before.

'Are you the ex-inspector?' asked Simms. 'The one who got kicked out of Braybridge?'

Another sneering bastard, Webster thought, his hands balling into fists. 'What if I am?'

'Rotten luck,' commented Simms mildly.

The oak offered shelter from the wind, and Frost was in no hurry to move on. He offered his cigarettes around. Only Webster, with an impatient jerk of his head, declined to accept one. Jordan's lighter did the rounds.

Webster looked out on to the dark mass of trees which seemed to stretch on and on for miles. 'It's hopeless with only the four of us. We should ask the station for reinforcements.'

Frost forced out a stream of smoke which the wind snatched and tore into shreds. 'A full-scale search would have to be properly organized, so it couldn't even begin until the morning. Let's give it a whirl ourselves first — unless anyone else wants to chip in with a suggestion?' He looked hopefully at the two uniformed men, who shook their heads, engrossed in studying the branches of the oak tree. They were paid to do what they were told, not to work out campaign plans.

'Right,' said Frost, pulling himself up straight. 'Lacking

evidence to the contrary, we've got to assume that there is a body — a girl — alive or dead. While we're assuming, let's give ourselves a bit of incentive and make her alive . . . not only alive, but a rampant quivering nymphomaniac with enormous knockers, fully prepared to bestow her hot lusty favours on the man who finds her.'

Jordan and Simms grinned. At least Frost was making it interesting.

'Right,' he continued. 'Now keep that dirty picture in mind while we transfer our attention to the herbert who tripped over her and phoned the station.'

He dropped his cigarette end to the ground and crushed it under his heel. 'It's late at night. So what was he doing skulking behind bushes? Obvious answer: He wanted to do a pee and, either ashamed of or too modest to flaunt his equipment, decided to commune privately with nature behind a convenient bush, only to find this nympho's supine body. So he bottled it up and legged it to the nearest blower to call the cops. How does that sound?'

They paused to consider this. It sounded feasible.

'Sergeant Wells said the man was phoning from a public call box,' Frost continued.

'I noticed a phone box near where we parked the car,' offered Webster.

'There are phone boxes all over the bloody place,' said Jordan gloomily.

'We've got to start from somewhere,' said Frost, 'and that's as good a place as any. We'll go up the main paths, searching behind the bushes on either side. If we can't find anything, we'll go to another phone box. And if we have no joy in a couple of hours, we'll call in the heavy mob from the station.'

It was Simms who found her. And by pure chance, because Frost's reasoning was completely wrong. After getting himself entangled in a flesh-clawing clutch of blackberry thorns, he made a wide detour to take him clear of another thicket and bramble. He squeezed through a tight gap between two bushes.

And there she was, white and still, lying on her back. She

was naked, her cold, still flesh gleaming like silver in the harsh moonlight.

'Here!' yelled Simms. 'Over here.' He directed his torch beam into the sky like a beacon, then knelt beside her, shining his torch on her face. He shuddered. Her face was a swollen, bloody mess, the eyes puffy and blackened, the nose misshapen and broken. Blood from her nose had clotted, forming a sticky mask all over the lower part of her face and neck.

The body was blood-streaked, scarcely an inch free of livid bruises. Scattered on the grass around her were items of ripped-off clothing. She looked dead. He touched her. Her body was icy. He bent his ear to the wreckage of her mouth, holding his breath as he tried to detect the slightest whisper of life. Nothing at first, only the hammering of his own heart, but then the faint wheezing rasp of tortured lungs. Fumbling with the buttons, he dragged off his greatcoat and draped it over the girl.

There was a crash in the undergrowth as Frost lumbered through, Webster hard on his heels. 'She's still alive,' Simms told him. 'Some bastard's smashed her face in.'

Frost dropped to his knees and made his own check for signs of life, feeling for the pulse in her neck. Satisfied, he called over his shoulder to Webster. 'Radio the station. We want an ambulance bloody quick. And you can tell Sergeant Wells, with my compliments, that the party's over. We've got another rape victim.'

As Webster was radioing through, Frost studied the extent of the girl's injuries. It took some resolve to look at her face, which must have been kicked. He suspected the jaw was broken as well as the nose.

Jordan was the last to arrive. He stared down at the girl, and what he saw made him shudder.

'See what the bugger's done to her neck,' said Frost, indicating bruises cut deeply into the flesh where the rapist's fingers had gripped and squeezed her into unconsciousness.

'The same pattern as the other one,' observed Simms dispassionately. 'That nurse he raped over at the golf course. But she wasn't beaten up anything like this.'

Webster switched off the radio and dropped it into his pocket. 'Ambulance on its way,' he reported. Frost, still bent over the girl, acknowledged his message with a grunt, then ordered Simms out to the main road to home the ambulance crew in.

'Is it Karen?' Webster asked, only to wince and turn his head away as Frost moved back so Webster could see what the animal had done to the girl.

'If it is, then she's nothing like her photograph,' muttered the inspector. 'The poor cow's been kicked in the face. Give me just five minutes alone with the bastard.'

He pulled back the greatcoat so he could examine the rest of her. She was naked except for thick black stockings, the tops banded by sexy red garters. The stockings were short, coming not much higher than her knee, then there was an awful lot of white thigh. Somehow, it reminded Frost of dirty French postcards he had seen when he was a kid, all black underwear and white flesh. Her body, like her face, was mapped with huge green-and-yellow bruises. As gently as he could, Frost ran his hands along her sides. He thought he could detect at least two broken ribs. She moaned softly as he touched her.

Could this possibly be young Karen? There was no way he could tell from the face. The body looked too well developed for a kid of fifteen, but girls seemed to be maturing earlier and earlier these days. He frowned and bent forward. The nipples. There was something odd about them. The colour was wrong. He took out his handkerchief and rubbed. The red came off. It was lipstick. Lipstick? He stood up and stared at the red on the handkerchief, unable to believe it. It couldn't be Karen.

'It's Karen, all right,' called Webster, and he showed Frost the school blazer he had picked up from the grass. 'And there are pieces of school uniform all over the place.' His torch stabbed out at the straw boater, the gym slip, the navy-blue knickers.

'I've found this, sir,' called Jordan, pulling a white plastic carrier bag out of a clump of nettles. Frost delved through the contents . . . sweater, jeans, bra . . . a complete change of clothing. Also a purse which held about a pound's worth of silver, a worn, Yale-type key, and three packets of male contraceptives.

School uniform, red garters, painted nipples, and contraceptives. It wasn't making sense. And the Yale key, its chromium plating wearing away, looked far too old to be the key to the Dawsons' elegant front door. He put everything back into the bag. Where was the ambulance? It should be here by now. As if in answer, the piercing warble of a siren came floating over the trees.

Deep in thought, Frost followed the trail of flattened grass back to the bush where the rapist had stood hidden, waiting. He looked along the empty path, from where the girl would have come, trying to put himself into the mind of a man who would do such things to a kid.

Muffled sounds came from his jacket pocket. His radio was trying to talk to him.

'Sergeant Wells calling Inspector Frost.'

'Yes, Bill, what is it?'

'Message from Detective Inspector Allen. He's on his way with a full team. He said don't anyone touch anything until he gets there.'

'I won't even touch my dick,' said Frost.

'Is it Karen Dawson, Jack?' asked Wells. 'I'm getting phone calls every five minutes from her father asking if there's any news.'

'Hard to tell. The way the bastard's rearranged her face she could be anyone . . . Karen, Bo Derek, or Old Mother Riley. Keep stalling her old man. We might want him to identify her, but I'll be back to him as soon as there's anything positive. Over and out.'

He pushed the radio back into his pocket. No surprise that Allen was taking over. Allen was in charge of the 'Hooded Rapist' investigation and would want to get Frost as far away as possible the second he took command.

Car doors slammed, then Simms pushed his way through the bushes to report that the ambulance men were hot on his tail. 'Do you want me and Jordan to start looking around, sir . . . to see what we can find?'

He shook his head. 'We've been ordered not to touch anything. Mr Allen is on his way, so we can expect an arrest in seconds.'

Out of sight behind him, Webster grinned. It was common knowledge that Frost and Allen didn't get on, but then, coldly efficient Allen was a real detective, unlike the clown in the mac. Webster had successfully led many rape cases back in his old division. Tomorrow he would request a transfer to Allen's team.

'Where the hell are you?' came a cry for help from the ambulance men, floundering about in the dark. Simms waggled his torch like a cinema usherette and yelled, 'This way!' then, lowering his voice, said to the inspector, 'Something a bit odd about the girl, sir. Did you notice?'

'Painted nipples, you mean?'

'No, sir. Something else . . . lower down.'

'If it was something else, then I have missed it.' Frost pulled back the greatcoat again and Simms directed his torch. 'I keep feeling like a dirty old man every time I do this, Simms. What am I supposed to be looking for?' The torch beam moved down and pointed. 'Oh!' exclaimed Frost, very surprised.

He replaced the greatcoat and straightened up. 'You're probably too young to be told this, Simms, but that feature is known to us men of the world as "the sleek bikini line." You can buy special shavers for it. Webster's wife has one. That's why he grew a beard — he didn't want to share the same razor.' He called Webster over and showed him.

'It's got to be her,' said Webster. 'It's got to be Karen.'

Frost still couldn't convince himself. 'This is hardly bikini weather, son. Still, we'd better get her father to meet us at the hospital, just in case.'

The ambulance men forced their way through and lifted

the girl onto a stretcher, covering her with thick red blankets. 'Anyone travelling with her?' one asked.

'No,' Frost told him, 'but we'll be sending a woman police officer to the hospital as soon as we can.'

As the ambulance pulled away, a convoy of cars containing Detective Inspector Allen and his team roared up. There was a barrage of overexcited shouting and door-slamming as everyone piled out, immediately silenced when Allen bawled that they were all to get back inside their cars and wait. 'No-one to move until I give the say-so.' He didn't want people trampling all over the evidence before he had a chance to see it, especially as some of them were clearly the worse for drink.

Detective Inspector Allen, a wiry man with a thin sour face and a permanent sneer, looked sharp, alert and efficient despite being dragged away from the drinking party well after midnight. His assistant, Detective Sergeant Vic Ingram, slightly unsteady on his feet, his breath redolent of whisky fumes, was a thickset, charmless man of twenty-nine, cursed with a foul temper and a vindictive streak. He hated the newcomer, Webster, and delighted in giving him menial tasks to perform. If Webster hesitated to comply, he invariably taunted him with his stock response: 'Too lowly for a detective inspector, is it? Well, you're a detective constable now, Sunshine, and a bloody rotten one at that.' It was rumoured that Ingram was currently having domestic trouble, which everyone thought served him damn well right. He certainly had a cracker of a wife, much lusted after by all the red-blooded station personnel and, by general consensus, far too good for him.

'You've let the damn ambulance men take her away,' complained Allen. 'I wanted to see her.'

'Then you should have got here quicker,' said Frost.

'Fill me in,' said Allen curtly.

Don't tempt me, thought Frost. He told Allen how they had found her and the extent of her injuries.

Allen listened intently, his eyes flicking from side to side, missing nothing. When he saw that Webster, contrary to his instructions, was holding the girl's school hat in his hand, he raised an eyebrow to Ingram and jerked his head toward the detective constable. Used to his master's sign language, Ingram swaggered over to Webster and snatched the hat away.

'You bloody wally, don't you understand English? You were told not to touch anything.'

Webster snatched his hands from his pockets, ready to swing and to hell with the consequences. 'Who are you calling a wally, you drunken slob?'

Quickly, Frost, the peacemaker, thrust himself between the two men. 'Now cool it, lads. We've got more important things to attend to.'

'You heard him, Inspector,' appealed Ingram. 'He called me a drunken slob.'

'All he meant, Sergeant,' said Frost soothingly, 'is that you're a slob, and you're drunk. No disrespect was intended.' Over his shoulder he ordered Webster to wait for him in the car.

Ingram, swaying, spoiling for a fight, glowered as Webster stamped off. Allen decided to continue as though nothing had happened. Somehow, Frost always got the best of these unsavoury encounters.

'You reckon the victim is this teenager, Karen Dawson?'

Frost hunched his shoulders. 'It's possible. We're getting the father over to the hospital to identify her.'

'Let me know as soon as it's confirmed. I'll be there later.' Then, seeing Frost was making no attempt to move, he added, 'Thank you, Inspector, that will be all.'

Back in the car, Webster waited, seething. Frost slid into his customary position. 'Denton General Hospital . . . first on the left, then follow the main road.' As Webster jarred the car into gear, Frost radioed through to the station requesting them to contact Max Dawson and ask him to meet them at the hospital. That done, he slouched back in his seat, digging deep for a cigarette before he said, 'Ingram's a provocative bastard, son. He's out for trouble. Try not to rise to his bait.'

Webster growled a noncommittal reply, his eyes straight ahead, looking for the left turnoff.

'What you must remember,' Frost continued, 'is that one

punch and you're not only out of the division, you're off the force. You should also remember that Ingram is a great big bastard who could probably knock the living daylights out of you.'

'Spare me the sermon,' muttered the detective constable, spinning the wheel to turn into the main road.

'It's not a sermon,' said Frost, 'it's the gypsy's warning.'

Webster was well down the wrong road before Frost added, 'Sorry, did I say left? I meant right . . .'

Denton General Hospital had originally been a workhouse and was built, like the public toilets, in the reign of Queen Victoria, when things were meant to last. So it was as strong and solid as a prison, but not as pretty and nowhere near as comfortable. Over the years it had sprouted additional wings and outbuildings and was now a sprawling mélange of various styles of municipal architecture. It stood on the outskirts of Denton and was dominated by the huge, factory-type chimney poking from the boilerhouse, where, according to Frost, the incinerator was fuelled by amputated arms and legs.

They waited for Max Dawson in the porter's lodge, a small, partitioned cubbyhole just inside the main entrance. The night porter, a bright-eyed old man with a nicotine-stained walrus moustache, was pouring creosote-coloured liquid into three enamel mugs. Milk was added, then sugar was shovelled in from a tin marked Sterile Dressings. Frost always seemed to know where to get a free cup of tea at any hour of the day or night.

'Get that inside you, Mr Frost,' said the porter, sliding a mug over. 'And you, young fellow.'

Webster smiled his thanks.

They sipped, blinked, and shuddered.

'What's it like, Mr Frost?' asked the porter.

'Delicious, Fred. Do we have to sign the poison register?'

The old boy cackled, showing teeth browner than his tea. 'Your lot are keeping us busy tonight, Mr Frost,' he said, rolling a hand-made cigarette from a pouch of coarse, dark tobacco. 'First the old tramp in the morgue, then the poor kid who was raped, and last, that old man who was run over by a hit-and-run.'

'I hope we're getting our usual discount for bulk,' said Frost, steeling himself for another swig. 'Hello, you've got a customer.'

Someone was rapping on the frosted-glass panel over the counter. The porter slid it back to reveal a young woman in her early twenties, her bust in the high thirties, and her hair dark with a hint of auburn. She wore a light-blue raincoat over which was slung a white shoulder bag. Her eyes sparkled with pleasure when she saw the inspector.

'Hello, Mr Frost.'

Frost was up and out of his seat. 'Good Lord, it's sexy Sue with the navy-blue knickers. What are you doing here, Sue? They don't do pregnancy tests after midnight you know.'

She smiled, showing teeth as perfect as her figure. 'Inspector Allen sent me. I've got to stay with the rape victim and try and get a statement. He said you'd have the details.'

Frost trotted out the details, adding that the girl hadn't yet been identified but that a man who might be her father was on his way over. He caught sight of Webster staring at the girl in wide-eyed approval, his tongue almost hanging down to his stomach. It was the first time he had caught his assistant without a frown on his face. 'Sorry, Sue, I should have introduced you. The bearded gent at my side is Detective Constable Webster.'

'I've seen you about the station,' she told him, warming him with a loin-tingling smile. 'I'm Sue . . . Detective Constable Susan Harvey.'

'Take Sue up to Casualty,' Frost told Webster. 'Ward C3.'

And for the first time, Webster obeyed an order without a display of resentment.

Frost returned to his tea, sipping slowly as the porter puffed away at his evil-smelling homemade cigarette.

'We used to see a lot of you when your wife was here, Mr Frost.'

'That's right, Fred.'

'How is she? Did she get better?'

'No,' said Frost, 'she didn't get better.'

The main doors opened and footsteps rang out on the tiled passage. Frost went out to meet Max Dawson, who was shaking with rage. Beside him stood his wife, wearing a silver-fox fur. She was crying.

'Is it true?' hissed Dawson. 'Is it true?'

'That's what we want you to confirm,' Frost told him. He drew Dawson to one side and said quietly, 'It might be better if your wife stayed down here, sir.'

'No,' said Clare firmly. 'She's my daughter. I want to be with her.'

'How bad is she?' asked Dawson as they walked towards the lift.

'She's taken a very nasty beating. I think her nose, jaw, and ribs are broken,' Frost answered.

Dawson sucked in air angrily. 'When you find the swine who did it, let me have him,' he pleaded.

'I think there'd be quite a queue, sir,' said Frost, pausing to look around as a clatter of footsteps chased after them.

'Mr Frost!' called the porter. 'Telephone call for you. Ward C3 — they say it's urgent.'

An icy cold hand clutched at Frost's heart and squeezed hard. Karen Dawson was in ward C3. Had she died? *Please don't let her be dead.* The Dawsons had followed him and were watching him intently. He took the phone, then turned his back so the parents couldn't see his face. 'Frost,' he said quietly.

It was Susan Harvey's voice on the other end. 'Inspector, I'm with the rape victim. Did you say Karen Dawson was only fifteen?'

'That's right, Sue. Why?'

'Then this can't possibly be her. It's not a girl, it's a woman . . . she's thirty at least.'

Thirty! Flaming hell, thought Frost. 'Are you sure, Sue? I've got the parents with me.'

'There's no doubt at all, Inspector.'

He handed the phone back to Fred, took a few deep

breaths to compose himself, then slowly turned to face the Dawsons.

Max Dawson was pacing up and down, unable to keep still, anxious to be with his daughter. His wife, who had sat down on one of the wooden benches that lined the corridor, stood up anxiously as Frost approached, trying to read the message in his face.

He gave them both what he hoped was a reassuring smile. 'It's all right, Mrs Dawson, it's all right. . .'

Dawson pushed himself forward. 'All right? How can it be all right? My daughter's been beaten and raped, and you tell us it's all right.'

Frost took a deep breath and plunged up to his armpits into icy water. 'I'm afraid we've worried you unduly. The girl who has been raped isn't your daughter.'

Clare caught her breath, then began to laugh hysterically. Her husband grabbed her shoulders and shook her roughly. Still she laughed: He slapped her face . . . hard, the pistol-shot sound echoing on and on down the long corridor. She gasped, her hand touching the red mark on her face, then she shrivelled and burst into tears, dropping onto the bench.

Dawson stared into space for a while, then said, 'Not my daughter . . . ?'

'No, sir. It turns out she's a much older woman.'

The look of concern returned to Clare's face. 'But it could be Karen. She's very well developed for her age. We've got to check.' She stood up and frantically tried to push past Frost to get to the lift and the ward. He gently restrained her.

'It couldn't possibly be Karen, Mrs Dawson. The victim is at least thirty — maybe even older . . .'

Dawson froze, staring at the detective in open-mouthed incredulity. 'Am I hearing you correctly? You thought this woman, this thirty-year-old woman, was my daughter? My wife and I have been worried sick because you told us our daughter had been raped and beaten, and all the time . . . all the time it was a thirty-year-old woman!'

All Frost could do was shuffle his feet, mumble how sorry

he was, and wish that Dawson would push off home so he could face his own humiliation in private.

With a sudden lunge, Dawson grabbed Frost by the lapels of his coat. 'Sorry? Is that all you can say?' Then, with a look of contempt, he pushed him away and wiped his hands down the front of his coat. 'You stupid, bloody incompetent fool, I'm not going to soil my hands on you.' He took his wife's arm and led her out. At the main doors he paused. 'Find my daughter, you bastard,' he said, and then they stepped out into the dark.

Frost flopped down on the bench, which was still warm from Mrs Dawson, and fumbled for his cigarettes. Opposite, on the wall, a large red-and-white sign frowned its disapproval: No Smoking . . . Please! His hand returned from his pocket, empty. 'As you've said please,' he said aloud.

He heard someone clearing his throat. He looked up and there was Webster. 'Did you hear all that, son?'

Webster nodded.

'A stupid, incompetent fool!' Frost repeated. 'And he's right . . . that's just what I am.'

From his inside pocket he again took out the photograph and studied it. He would have to start thinking of Karen as a schoolgirl again, far too young for boys, too young to keep contraceptives in her handbag. So who was the anonymous victim, and why the fancy dress?

He pushed himself up from the bench. 'Come on, son, let's nip up to ward C3 and see what we can find out.'

'It isn't our case,' protested Webster.

'I know, son. My trouble is I'm such a nosey bastard.'

Sue Harvey was waiting for them by the door of C3, a small side ward with only four beds. 'The doctors are with her now,' she whispered, pointing to the end bed, which was screened off by curtains.

After a few minutes the curtains jerked open and a small Asian doctor in a white coat emerged, followed by the night nurse. Behind them, on the bed, a white huddle, absolutely motionless. The night sister whispered something to the doctor and pointed to the two detectives. He examined them with tired eyes, then walked over.

'How is she, Doc?' asked Frost.

'Still unconscious. She has been punched, kicked, and badly beaten. There are two fractured ribs, a broken nose, fracture of the jaw, and hairline skull damage. In addition, she has severe bruisings, and contusions all over her body. There are external marks on the throat, which is badly swollen, indicative of manual strangulation; also, of course, internal bruising. I imagine she was rendered unconscious, then repeatedly kicked and punched while she was lying on the ground.'

'Would the beating have been before or after she was sexually assaulted?'

The doctor frowned and looked puzzled. 'Sexually assaulted? Who said she was sexually assaulted?' He turned to the night sister and spread his hands in appeal. 'Did I say she was sexually assaulted?'

It was Frost's turn to frown and look puzzled. 'Are you saying she wasn't raped?'

'Raped? If my patient had been raped, do you think I am such a damn fool I would not have mentioned it?'

Frost shook his head, then wiped his face with his hands. He just couldn't believe this! 'You're quite sure, Doc? You wouldn't like to nip over and take another look?'

Indignantly, the little man pulled himself up to his full height. 'Are you questioning my competence, Inspector? I have examined her. There are definitely no signs of recent sexual congress, nor of any attempt of forced sexual congress. You obviously cannot take in what I am saying, so you will please excuse me. I have other patients to attend to.' He pushed past them, bustling out of the ward, his white coat flapping behind him.

Frost scratched his head and tried to make sense of this unexpected development. 'Not raped? He stripped her off but didn't rape her. It's like unwrapping your Mars bar then not eating it.'

'Perhaps he was disturbed before he could actually do it,' suggested Webster.

'Disturbed?'

'The bloke who made the anonymous phone call — perhaps he barged in on them at the crucial moment?'

Frost rubbed his chin. 'I can't buy that, son. I had a quick look at her clothes. There was no blood on them, which means he kicked and punched her after he'd stripped her. If he had time to kick her, he had bags of time for the old sexual congress.' He shrugged. 'Still, it's not our case anymore. Let Inspector Allen solve it.'

The ward door was barged open by a wheeled stretcher manoeuvred by a theatre orderly who had come to collect the patient for surgery. Through the open door Frost suddenly spotted Detective Inspector Allen, with Sergeant Ingram at his side, purposefully advancing toward the ward. He had no wish to be around when Allen learned of his foul-up with the victim's age, so he quickly looked for a way of escape. With a quick wave to Sue, he hustled Webster through a rear door, down some dimly lit stone stairs, then along another empty, winding corridor.

'You seem to know your way about,' commented Webster.

'My wife was in here,' explained Frost. 'I used to come every day.'

The detective constable remembered being told that Frost's wife had died recently and thought it best not to ask further questions. They turned right into the main causeway, which had wards leading off from either side.

Frost stopped and pointed. 'Look! The place is crawling with filth tonight.'

Webster saw a young police constable, dark curly hair, small moustache, leaning against the wall, engaged in animated conversation with a ridiculously young night nurse who had a wisp of stray hair escaping from her cap. Webster scratched his memory for the man's name; he had been introduced to so many people. Then he remembered. Dave Shelby, married with two young children but with the reputation of being woman-mad, or 'crumpet-happy,' as Frost had crudely termed it.

Catching sight of the inspector bearing down on him, Shelby quickly whispered something to the girl, making her blush, then in a loud voice, said, 'Thank you very much, Nurse.' She hurried off, giving an apologetic smile to Frost as she passed.

'Stay away from him, love,' Frost called after her. 'He meets men in toilets after dark.' To Shelby, he said, 'You want to try and stay off it for five minutes, son — it can make you go blind.'

Shelby grinned nervously. 'Just passing the time, sir. I'm a respectable married man.'

'So was Dr Crippen,' sniffed Frost. 'Anyway, what are you doing here?'

Shelby jerked his thumb at the glass-ported swing doors behind him. 'I'm with the hit-and-run victim. They're operating on him now.'

Frost squinted through one of the portholes. Not much to see. A huddle of green-robed figures, working silently. One of the robes was smeared with blood.

'Rather him than me. It looks like an abattoir in there.'

He looked over Shelby's shoulder. Farther down the corridor all alone, an old lady was sitting. She looked bewildered and frightened.

'That's the victim's wife,' whispered Shelby. 'She slept through it all. Didn't even know her husband had got out of bed until a neighbour knocked to tell her he'd been run over.'

'Poor old cow,' muttered Frost. 'What are his chances?'

Shelby gave a hopeless shrug. 'His skull is smashed, he's hemorrhaging internally, and he's seventy-eight years old.'

'The car that hit him was supposed to have shed its licence plate,' said Frost. 'Have we traced the driver yet?'

'I don't know, sir. I'm not really on this one. Mr Allen pulled the area car off to help with the search for the rapist.'

'That reminds me —' said Frost, staring closely at him '— have you been up to your larks tonight?'

Shelby started visibly. 'What do you mean, sir?'

'The woman who was attacked. You haven't been in Denton Woods tonight with your little truncheon at the ready?'

A wave of relief seemed to wash over the constable. 'No, sir,' he said, forcing a smile. 'It wasn't me.'

But you have been up to something, my lad, thought Frost, and for a minute you thought I was on to it. Well, I'm not on to it. I'm not that clever . . . I can't even tell the difference between a fifteen-year-old schoolgirl and a thirty-year-old woman.

They had to pass the old lady on their way out to the car. She reached up and clutched at Frost's arm. 'My husband —' she said '— they're operating on him. He is going to be all right, isn't he?'

'Of course he is,' beamed Frost. 'He's going to be fine.' He gave her a reassuring pat.

They walked on.

'Why raise her hopes?' asked Webster. 'He's going to die.'

'Then you bloody tell her,' said Frost.

TUESDAY NIGHT SHIFT (5)

'I can't give you any sort of description,' said the man. 'I never saw him.'

'You must have seen something,' said Wells. 'How are we supposed to arrest him if we don't know what he looks like?'

The phone rang.

'Answer that, would your Ridley,' yelled Sergeant Wells. 'I'm attending to someone.'

The man he was attending to had been robbed at knifepoint while drawing cash from the automatic cash dispenser at Bennington's Bank. 'He stuck a knife in my back,' said the complainant, 'then he grabbed the money and ran. By the time I'd plucked up courage to look around, he'd gone.'

'Was he short, tall, fat, thin, white, yellow, or what?' asked Wells.

'All I can tell you is he was a bloody fast runner,' said the man. 'He went off with my money like a dose of salts.'

The phone kept ringing.

'Excuse me a moment, sir,' said Wells. He pushed open the door to the corridor and shouted, 'Ridley!'

The toilet gurgled and roared, then Ridley appeared, doing up his belt.

'The bloody phone's ringing,' snapped Wells. 'You know I'm here on my own.'

'I'm entitled to go to the toilet, aren't I?' argued the constable.

'Not when we're short-staffed, you're not.' He turned back to the man. 'And how much did you say was taken, Mr Skinner?'

'Forty-five pounds. Nine five-pound notes.'

'Any idea where Mr Frost is?' called Ridley, holding the mouthpiece against his chest.

'You're on Control,' snapped Wells. 'You're supposed to know where everyone is.' It was really getting far too much. Every available man had been commandeered by Mr Allen after the rape attempt in Denton Woods. Even young Collier had been roped in, leaving only Wells and the controller, PC Ridley, to run the entire station. He wasn't good enough to go to their lousy party, but he was good enough to run a division almost single-handed.

'There's been a robbery and a coshing over at The Coconut Grove. They got away with more than five thousand quid.'

'Hard bloody luck,' said Wells. 'This gentleman's lost forty-five pounds, and he was here first.'

The lobby doors crashed back on their hinges, and in bounded Frost in his party suit with the sodden trouser legs and his everyday mac and scarf. With him was the new bloke, the bearded ex-inspector Webster.

Ridley waved the phone. 'Mr Frost!'

While Webster went on to the office to make a start on the crime statistics, Frost ambled over to Ridley. 'Yes, Constable?'

'Robbery at The Coconut Grove, Mr Frost.'

'Sorry, I'm only doing bodies down public lavatories to-night,' replied the inspector. At Ridley's look of reproach, he sighed and said, 'All right. Take the details.' He crossed to the corridor and yelled, 'Webster! We're going out again.' Then he caught sight of Wells struggling to get a report form into the typewriter. 'Everything all right, Sergeant?'

'No, it bloody well isn't,' snarled Wells, 'and I'm too busy for small talk.'

'I've seen a lady with rouged nipples,' said Frost.

'Are you going to take my details?' demanded the man who had been robbed.

'Just a moment, sir,' said Wells, waving him off as if he were intruding on a private conversation. 'You saw *what* Jack . . . ?'

Before it had time to blink at being brought out into the light, the crime statistics return was stuffed back into the filing cabinet and Webster was once again behind the wheel of the Ford Cortina, driving off into the night. As the car skirted the woods, they could see the firefly dots of torches dancing among the trees, where Allen's team continued its painstaking search.

The Coconut Grove was part of a large leisure complex development on the outskirts of Denton, just north of the woods. It consisted of clubs, bars, restaurants, bingo halls, a theatre, a sports pavillion, and myriad other amenities. The police suspected that it catered for the odd spot of prostitution on the side, but they hadn't been able to prove anything. It was run by a dubious character called Harry Baskin whose other enterprises included a chain of betting shops.

Baskin had bought the land cheap. No-one thought he'd get planning permission for his leisure complex because, under the new town development plan, the area was designated for agricultural purposes only. But, to everyone's astonishment, planning permission was granted. A couple of months later, the chairman of the planning committee resigned and retired to the Bahamas. Some cynics unkindly suggested that these two events were connected, but no-one said so to Baskin. People who got on the wrong side of Harry Baskin suddenly found they had become extremely accident-prone.

Harry Baskin! Webster wondered where he had heard that name before? 'He runs some betting shops, doesn't he?'

Frost nodded, 'He has thirty-seven all over the country. He also has subtle ways of making reluctant losers pay up. The punter wakes up one morning to find his dog's had its throat cut, or that his car has mysteriously self-combusted . . . little nudges like that. No-one owes Harry money for long.'

Leaving the main road, they followed large illuminated signs which beckoned THIS WAY TO DENTON'S FABULOUS LEISURE COMPLEX. A sharp turn, and there it was, a cluster of buildings in gleaming black-and-white mock marble, spangled with tasteful neon signs . . . Bingo . . . Fish and Chips . . . Striptease. Most of the satellite buildings were in darkness, but Frost steered Webster across a car park to the rear section, which a discreet blue neon sign proclaimed to be THE COCO-NUT GROVE.

They went through revolving doors into a dimly lit foyer where their way was barred by a wall of flesh, the bouncer, a hefty ex-wrestler in evening dress. He had been watching the approach of the mud-splattered Ford and had seen the two men get out. His orders from Mr Baskin were to exclude potential troublemakers, and these two were trouble if ever he'd seen it, especially the load of rough in the crumpled mac.

'Sorry, gentlemen. Members only . . .' he began, moving forward to urge them back through the exit doors.

'American Express,' said Frost, waving his warrant card under the man's nose. 'Tell Harry Baskin the filth are here.'

The bouncer muttered a few words into the house phone, then led them through a passage to a door marked Private . . . No Admittance. Above the door an illuminated sign in red announced Engaged . . . Do Not Enter. The bouncer rapped with his knuckles. The sign turned green and said Please Enter.

Baskin, dark and swarthy, in his late thirties, swivelled morosely from side to side behind a huge desk which con-

tained nothing but the remains of a smoked-salmon sandwich. He wore a midnight-blue evening suit, the sleeves of
the coat pulled back slightly to ensure an unrestricted view of
oversized solid-gold cuff links, which clanked on his wrists
like shackles. Everyone's in evening dress tonight but me,
thought Frost, his trousers still damp about his ankles, his
shoes squelching slightly as he walked.

On the walnut-veneered wall behind Baskin were framed
and signed photographs of the various celebrities who had
visited the leisure complex — boxers, film stars, pop stars —
their arms around, shaking hands with, or handing charity
cheques to a smiling Harry Baskin. But he wasn't smiling
now. His face was black with anger and furrowed in a frown
that could give one of Webster's a hundred-yard start and still
romp home. He didn't seem very pleased to see Frost.

'Oh, it's you, Inspector!'

'I'm afraid so, Harry,' acknowledged Frost, sitting unin-
vited in the visitor's armchair and rubbing his legs against the
upholstery to dry his trousers. 'All the good cops are busy on
a rape case. A woman attacked in the woods earlier tonight —
I hope you've got a cast-iron alibi?'

'Do me a favour!' pleaded Baskin, the cuff links rattling as
he flicked a hand to dismiss the bouncer. 'I can get all the
crumpet I want without moving from this desk. They come
knocking on my door begging for it.' He jettisoned the remains of the sandwich into a bin. 'I've had one hell of a
night. First the bloody stripper doesn't turn up, then the so-
called cordon bleu chef burns the bloody meat pies, and
lastly, this stinking robbery. So forgive me if I find it hard to
raise a smile.' He jabbed a finger in Webster's direction.
'What the hell is that?'

Frost introduced the detective constable.

Baskin found it possible to smile thinly as he recognized
the name. 'Webster! The cop they kicked out of Braybridge!
Blimey, we're getting all the rejects tonight, aren't we? You'd
better watch out for him, Mr Frost. He beats inspectors up.'

Webster fought hard to keep his face impassive, but behind the mask his anger was building up a rare old head of steam. It wouldn't take much . . .

Frost bounced a thin smile back to the club owner. 'He also beats up cheap crooks, Harry, so I wouldn't upset him if I were you. He could knee you in the groin so hard those ladies you mentioned would be beating on your door in vain. What do you say we get down to business?'

Baskin stood up and carefully adjusted the lines of his dinner jacket. 'This way.'

He took them through a maze of passages to an office near the rear entrance, its door newly scarred with deep gashes in the wood. Webster dropped to one knee to examine it. Baskin looked down with a sneer. 'You needn't get out your magnifying glass, sonny. My men did that. We had to axe our way in. A bloody good door ruined.' He opened the bloody good door and showed them into a small cell of a room . . . concrete floor, grey emulsioned walls, and a single high window fitted with iron bars. A cheap-looking light-oak desk and a nonmatching hard-backed chair comprised the furnishings. On the desk stood a phone and a wired switch.

Baskin checked that the corner of the desk was clean, made doubly sure by treating it to a flick of his silk monogrammed handkerchief, then sat on it.

'A lot of our trade is done by cheque and credit card, but we also get a fair amount of cash sloshing about. It jams up the tills, so twice a night we empty them, bring the cash here to be counted and checked, and then it's taken to the night safe at Bennington's Bank. There's a security man on guard in this room all the time the money's here. He locks himself in. Take a look at the door.'

They examined the inside of the door, which had two strong bolts top and bottom, a double security lock, and a thick iron bar which could be slotted into holders set tight into the concrete walls.

'Simple but effective,' continued Baskin, swinging his leg as he spoke. 'We bung the money in the bank's special bags, then a second security guard nips off to fetch the motor to take it to the night safe.'

'Do you use the same car each time?' asked Webster.

'Do I look that stupid, sonny?' scoffed Baskin. 'If anyone wants to rob me, I make it bloody hard for them. A different set of wheels, a different time, a different route each night.'

Webster said, 'And who decides on that?'

'I do, sonny, and I keep it to myself until the very last moment.'

'Don't call me sonny,' snarled Webster.

'Touchy little sod, isn't he?' grinned Baskin.

Frost had wandered across the room. Taped to the wall behind the desk was a collection of black-and-white glossy photographs, all of nudes, most of them strippers who had appeared at the club. As he scrutinised the various poses, he said, 'So, you've got one man locked inside, another fetching the car. Then what?'

'The motor's brought right up to the rear entrance, just outside here. The driver nips in, taps a prearranged signal on that door. The bloke inside gathers up the money bags, unlocks the door, and within five seconds he's inside the car on his way to the bank.'

'Is it a different signal each night?' persisted Webster.

'Of course it's a different bloody signal. I work it out myself and don't tell them until the very last minute. If the bloke inside gets the right signal, he opens the door; if it's wrong, he presses that switch, which raises the alarm. This was tonight's signal.' He rapped out a short pattern of taps on the desk top.

'I can name that tune in one,' muttered Frost, seemingly much more interested in the pinups than in the robbery. 'It sounds foolproof to me, Harry. Don't change it.'

Baskin raised his eyes to the ceiling and sighed theatrically. 'You'll have me in stitches, Mr Frost, with your droll humour. Well, it wasn't so bloody foolproof tonight, was it? Croll locks himself in with more than five thousand quid. His mate, Harris, waddles off to fetch the motor when, guess what? There's an urgent phone call for Mr Harris in the foyer. From the casualty ward of Denton Hospital . . . matter of life and death. The woodentops in the foyer call him over the

Tannoy. He legs it across the foyer, picks up the phone and this tart says, "Hold on a minute, please, and we'll get the heart specialist." As it happens, his old lady has a wonky ticker, so he swallows it and holds on.'

Frost said, 'Who spoke on the phone? A man or a woman?'

'A woman — supposed to be a nurse, wasn't she, the bloody slag. Anyway, this burke, this cretin, this lump of horse manure, just holds on for bloody ever listening to sod all. After about six minutes of deafening silence, it suddenly occurs to him that perhaps he's being taken for a mug. He hangs up and dials his old lady's house . . . and she answers the phone, bright and cheerful, fit as a bleeding fiddle. So then it's his turn to have a heart attack. He nips back here, wallops out the signal. No reply. He tries again. Nothing. Finally he plucks up the courage to come and tell me about it. Me and the boys come running. Takes us nearly ten minutes with a sledge hammer and an axe to smash our way in and . . . surprise, surprise! The money isn't there anymore, but Croll's out cold on the floor, blood trickling from his head, a surprised look on his stupid face, and a pain in the leg where I booted him.'

Frost poked a cigarette in his mouth and scratched a match on the desk top. 'So what happened? How come the foolproof scheme didn't work?'

Baskin stared at the desk top and tried to erase the mark of Frost's match with a spit-moistened finger. 'You tell me. The ambulance took him away before I could get any proper answers.' He took out his silk handkerchief and worried away at the mark on the desk. 'That won't bloody come off, you know.'

Frost puffed a smoke screen over the blemish. 'What did you say his name was?'

'Croll . . . Tom Croll.' Baskin didn't miss the quiver of recognition from the inspector. 'Don't tell me the little bastard's got form? Don't tell me I've employed an ex-con to guard my bloody money? I'll break both his bleeding legs.'

'Live and let live, Harry,' soothed Frost. 'If he doesn't mind working for a crook, why should you mind employing one? Tommy Croll's done the odd bit of time, but only for petty stuff. He hasn't got the bottle to pull off a stunt like this. Where's the other guard, Harris, the one who got the dodgy phone call?'

Baskin seemed preoccupied in watching his cuff links glitter in the light. 'He . . . er . . . had a bit of an accident — walked into a door — hurt his nose and blacked both his eyes. I sent him home to recover.'

'You're a nasty piece of work, Harry,' Frost told him. 'I hope he sues you.'

'What was the exact sum of money taken?' asked Webster, realizing that Frost had asked a lot of questions but hadn't touched on the basics.

'Five thousand, one hundred thirty-two pounds,' answered Baskin. 'One of our slack nights — the end of the week it could be nearer twenty grand.'

Webster jotted this down. 'And what time did the robbery take place?'

'Round about five past eleven,' said Baskin casually.

Frost, whose eyes had again been drawn to the magnetic north of the breasts and bottoms of the pinups, spun around. 'Five past eleven?' he said incredulously. 'That's more than four hours ago!'

Baskin spread his hands. 'So what? I had no intention of calling you in, but my expensive lawyer told me that as a crime's been committed I've got no choice. Your being here is just a formality to satisfy our insurers. What's a lousy five thousand quid to me? It's chicken feed! I can stand the loss, but what I can't stand is the humiliation. He who pinches my purse steals trash, but he who filches my good name gets both his bloody legs broken. So I'll find the bastard myself. Just take the details, go to the bar and have a free drink on the house, and then push off and forget all about it. Leave the hard work to me.'

Frost shook his head. 'Sorry, Harry, but we like to beat our own prisoners up. It's one of the few pleasures we've got left. What was the money packed in?'

There was a black fibreglass attaché case in the corner.

Baskin picked it up and showed it to the two men. 'It was in two cases like this.' He held it out for Frost to examine, but the inspector wasn't there. 'Where's the old git got to?'

'The old git's down here,' called a voice from behind the desk where Frost, on his knees, was almost rubbing his nose on one of the photographs. 'Just admiring your art collection, Harry.'

Making no attempt to hide his contempt, Baskin said, 'If dirty pictures turn you on, I'll find some. But in the meantime, could we just concentrate on the matter in hand?'

Still preoccupied with the nude, Frost asked if anyone had seen anything unusual at the time of the robbery.

With a snort, Baskin said, 'No-one saw a bleeding thing. Some slag legs it off with five thousand quid of my money and no-one sees anything!'

Frost seemed to lose interest in his questions. He ripped a photograph from the wall and held it nearer the light.

The old fool's going senile, thought Webster, deciding he had better take over. He opened the door and walked the short distance to the rear entrance. Down a couple of steps, and he was out in the car park where the night wind hurled a few handfuls of rain in his face. Despite the lateness of the hour, there were still quite a few cars dotted about. At 11.05, when the money was snatched, the area would have been crawling with motors and surges of arriving and departing customers. A man strolling to his car with a couple of small fibreglass suitcases, perhaps concealed under a mac, would attract no attention at all.

He stepped back into the building to escape the rain squall and bumped into Harry Baskin, a huge cigar wedged in his mouth.

'I left your inspector dribbling over that tart's photo. I suppose the poor old git hasn't had a woman since his wife died and it's making him go funny.' He pushed Webster aside to stare at a car turning off from the road and splashing over puddles as it crossed the car park. 'Who the hell is this?'

The new arrival was a Ford Escort, one of the pool cars from the station. Two men got out, heads down, and made their way to the front entrance. As they passed under an overhead light, Webster identified them. Detective Inspector Allen and his charming sidekick, Detective Sergeant Ingram. He nipped back to the office to warn Frost.

The inspector was now sitting on the corner of the desk, looking quite pleased with himself. He only grunted when told about Allen, but as soon as Baskin returned, he snatched up the photograph of the stripper and asked the club owner if it had been retouched.

Baskin frowned. 'What do you mean?'

'This lady seems to be devoid of hair in an area where I would expect to find some.'

Baskin took the photograph, holding it at arm's length. 'Don't you know nothing? Strippers have to make themselves look more artistic before they perform in front of an audience. The raw human body is quite repulsive if left to its own devices, you know.'

Frost dropped his cigarette on the floor and gave it the full weight of his foot. 'You said earlier that one of your strippers didn't turn up for work?'

'That's right. Paula Grey, the stripping schoolgirl.'

Frost turned to Webster like a stage artist awaiting an ovation, and Webster had the grace to reward him with a silent hand clap. The old fool wasn't always as stupid as he made out.

'She does a routine in schoolgirl uniform,' continued Baskin. 'It gives the dirty old men in the audience a cheap thrill to think they're watching a juicy young bit of under-aged crumpet peeling off. To be honest, we have to keep the lighting well down so they can't see how ancient the old cow really is — we don't want to put the punters off their meat pies.' A sudden thought hit him and he stopped in his tracks. 'Here, you're not suggesting she was involved in this robbery, are you?' He warmed to this theme. 'Hold on, though. It makes sense. I should have twigged the minute she didn't turn up to do her routine. She had inside knowledge . . . and she could have pretended to be the nurse on the phone.'

'No,' said Frost, 'it couldn't have been her. While you were being robbed, she was out in the woods getting herself booted in the kisser by the famous Denton "Hooded Terror".' Baskin listened, shaking his head in amazement, as the inspector told him what had occurred.

'Who in his right senses would try to rape Paula, Inspector? You could have her any time for the price of a packet of fags, and if you didn't have the price she'd lend it to you.' He grimaced with irritation as the door crashed open and Allen and Ingram barged in. 'What the hell? This is a private office. Get out!'

Allen ignored Baskin and stared past him to the scruffy figure by the desk. 'What are you doing here, Frost? I told you this was my case.'

Baskin looked from one inspector to the other. 'Blimey, you're not going to fight over it are you? Just find the joker who robbed me and you can split the money up between you.'

'Robbed you?' cried Allen, his lips quivering as he fought back a smile. 'Dear, dear, dear, what a tragedy! How much was taken? A not inconsiderable sum, I trust?' He shook with silent laughter. Ingram, leaning against the wall, obediently joined in.

'I've already had this patter from your number-two comic,' snorted Baskin, nodding his head in Frost's direction. 'If you're not here about the robbery, then what the hell do you want?'

Allen folded his arms and rocked with smug satisfaction on the balls of his feet, biting his lip to stop himself from laughing too soon. How he was going to love telling Frost that the girl he had identified as a fifteen-year-old school kid was an old scrubber. What sort of idiot could make a mistake like that? 'Do you know a girl called Paula Grey, Mr Baskin?'

But, annoyingly, before Baskin had a chance to reply, Frost chimed in with, 'Paula Grey? That name rings a bell!' He knuckled his forehead in mock concentration, then snapped his fingers triumphantly. 'Got her! Paula Grey, the stripping schoolgirl. She works for Harry. She's the girl who was attacked in Denton Woods tonight. Didn't you know that, Allen?'

Allen, completely put out, stopped rocking. 'Of course I damn well knew that. I've just taken a statement from her. But how did you know?'

Frost shrugged modestly. 'Intelligent deduction.'

'Is this a private conversation, or can anyone join in?' asked Baskin peevishly.

Allen transferred his attention to the club owner. 'Your employee Paula Grey was savagely attacked tonight. She claims you had threatened to sack her if she turned up late for a show.'

'That's right,' nodded Baskin.

'She overslept,' Allen continued grimly, 'so, to save time, she put on her stage clobber in her flat and took a shortcut through the woods, and that's where it all happened. The bastard jumped her, chucked something over her head, then squeezed her throat until she passed out.'

Baskin took his cigar from his mouth and shook the spit from the end. 'If he was after a nice young bit of the other, he must have been broken-hearted when he took the cloth from her face. I think the poor old cow draws her old-age pension next month.'

'You've got a heart as big and warm as Golders Green Crematorium,' observed Frost.

'He's right, though,' said Ingram, moving to the centre of the room. 'We think that's why he beat her up instead of raping her. He only likes young stuff, and Paula was a great big turnoff.'

The malicious glint in Allen's eye warned Ingram he would pay for having stolen his master's thunder.

Taking advantage of the situation, Webster thought he'd try a spot of ingratiation in the hope it would improve his chances of being transferred from Frost to Allen. 'How's the search in the woods going, sir?' he asked, politely.

'Search?' shrieked Allen. 'Don't talk to me about the search. It's a farce! I doubt if half of the search team are sober. I've called it off until tomorrow morning.' His head moved from Webster to Frost. 'I'm holding a briefing meeting to-morrow, at nine. You were there when the victim was found, so I want you to attend.

'Sure,' said Frost, wondering how he could fit in some sleep. 'I'll have to be away pretty sharp, though. I've got to go to a post-mortem.'

Telling Baskin he'd be back in the morning after he'd taken statements from the two security men, Frost signalled to Webster, busily engaged in a silent scowling match with Ingram, that it was time to leave. They were almost through the door when Allen fired his parting salvo.

'You will have the overtime returns done by the morning, won't you? You know it's the last day if we're to catch the computer.'

'Sure,' said Frost automatically while his brain shrieked at him in horror. The bloody overtime returns! Was it time for them already? In the worry of trying to get the crime statistics off, he'd completely forgotten the damn things. Quickly he closed the door behind them before Allen could think of any more horrors he should have done.

As they crossed the car park, heads down against the slant-ing rain, he told Webster to remind him about doing the overtime figures the minute they got back to the office.

'Sure,' said Webster. It seemed to be the 'in' word.

They didn't make it to the station. Control diverted them to Denton Hospital to follow up a complaint about a man prowling around the nurses' sleeping quarters.

Ridley was most apologetic. 'Sorry to dump this one on you, Inspector, but there's no-one else available.'

'I hope you realize, Constable,' replied Frost sternly, trying to keep the delight from his voice, 'that you're stopping me from doing the overtime returns.'

Tuesday night shift (6)

'It was horrible,' said the little nurse. 'He had these awful red, staring eyes . . . and his mouth was all dribbling.'

I'd be all dribbling if I caught a sight of you in the buff, thought Frost.

The little nurse in her shortie nightdress was all excited now she was the centre of attraction, and she was reliving her ordeal for the benefit of three other young nurses, none older than twenty and all in various stages of undress.

'I'd taken everything off . . . everything . . . when I realized I hadn't drawn the curtains. I went to the window to do it, and there he was.'

The lucky bastard! thought Frost.

A thrill of excitement ran through her audience. 'I screamed,' she went on. 'I thought he was trying to get in, and all the time I kept thinking about the nurse who was raped. I was terrified.'

Frost leaned forward and patted her warm, quivering young arm. 'Don't worry, love. We'll get him.'

A pointed cough of disapproval from Sister Plummer, the eunuch in charge of the harem, made Frost snatch his hand away hurriedly. Sister Plummer was the supervisor of the Nurses' Home, a gaunt, miserable-looking woman in her late fifties, with a hatchet face, and beady, suspicious eyes. 'She looks just like the nurse who shaved me for my appendix operation,' Frost later confided to Webster. 'She used to think a man's dick was just a handle to lift him up by.'

Webster returned from searching the grounds. 'No signs of anyone,' he announced, wishing it had been him who stayed with the half-dressed nurses and Frost who floundered about in the dark and the cold.

The nurse's shortie nightie was starting to slip down, and inch by inch, her beautiful, firm, young, creamy breasts were

emerging like mountains through clouds. Frost was ponder-
ing ways to make his questions last until the crucial moment,
when the eunuch said, 'Nurse! Cover yourself!' and the treat
was terminated.

'From the direction he was running,' said the little nurse,
'I think he went into the main hospital building.' Now she
tells me, thought Webster.

'Hadn't you better start searching the hospital, Inspector?'
rasped Sister Plummer. 'It's time the nurses were in bed.
They've all got busy days tomorrow.' The nurses all looked
too wide awake and excited for sleep, but Frost was forced to
take the hint.

'We'll go through the place with a fine-tooth comb,' he
assured them. 'If he's still there, we'll find him.'

Frost and Webster returned to the main building.

'How do you intend to carry out this search?' Webster
asked.

Frost grinned. 'You didn't think I was serious, did you,
son? That was just to keep that little nurse happy. This bloke
isn't going to hang about in the hospital. He'll be miles away
by now.'

'You can't be sure of that.'

'True, son,' agreed the inspector, 'but this place is a bloody
rabbit warren. Even if he were here, we'd never find him, so
we won't bother looking.'

'He could be the rapist,' insisted Webster, determined that
things should be done properly. 'He's already had one nurse.'

Frost laughed scoffingly. 'The rapist, son? Do you think a
man who strips off juicy young birds and has his wicked way
with them is going to be satisfied with peeping through a
window? This was just a Peeping Tom getting a cheap thrill
from a flash of snowy-white thigh, and don't I envy the
bastard. That little nurse was a goer if ever I saw one.'

At four o'clock in the morning the hospital was a desolate
and cheerless place. Frost told Webster that more patients
died at this hour than at any other time of day. 'If you hear a
trolley, odds are it's got a body on it . . .'

They trekked the labyrinth of corridors, past wards illumi-

nated only by the night sister's desk lamp, past a group of
anxious relatives talking to the little Asian doctor, who was
shaking his head sadly — 'Another body on its way,' said
Frost — past abandoned oxygen cylinders and trollies piled
high with red hospital blankets.

It was as they approached the turnoff that would lead
them to the exit that the nurse screamed.

They ran, Frost panting, out of breath, well behind the
constable.

'There!' yelled Webster.

Ahead, a nurse, white-faced, stumbled toward them in
blind panic. She looked up, mouth open, ready to scream
again when she saw the two strange men hurtling toward her.
Webster was the first to reach her. He waved his warrant card.
'It's all right, Nurse, we're police officers. What happened?'

Too terrified to speak, she looked from Webster to Frost,
her mouth working, then, still trembling she pointed back to
the open door of a storeroom. At last she was able to speak. 'A
man — in there. I went to get some clean sheets. He was
horrible . . .'

'Let's take a look,' said Webster, moving cautiously into
the dark of the storeroom and groping for the light switch.
The fluorescent tubes seemed to resent being woken up at
such an unearthly hour, but finally, with a half-hearted
crackle, they flashed and flooded out cold, blue light.

Inside the large room were racks of wooden shelving, all
neatly stacked with folded blankets, bed linen, rubber sheets,
and pillows. No sign of a lecherous intruder. Webster walked
around inside. 'Can't see anyone,' he said to the nurse, who
was hovering anxiously by the door.

Braver now that she had company, she joined him, her
head turning from side to side, looking, wanting to prove that
she hadn't imagined it. 'There *was* someone here,' she insisted.

Frost wandered in after them, his nose twitching. 'There's
a hell of a stink in here . . .' He sniffed again, his eyes slowly
scanning the racks, missing nothing. 'I spy with my little
eye . . . someone on the top rack . . . there!'

Webster followed his finger but couldn't see anything. He grasped the wooden supports and shook the racks as if he were shaking apples from a tree. 'Come on, you bugger. Down you get or I'll drag you down.'

A heap of blankets on the top shelf heaved, then slithered to the floor. A dirty brown overcoat struggled out, then two red-rimmed eyes peered down at them. Webster turned his head away in disgust as the smell wafted down to hit him in the face.

'I wasn't doing no harm,' whined the man.

'No harm?' cried Frost, 'You're stinking the place out.'

'What are you after — drugs?' demanded Webster as the old man, a tramp in his mid-sixties, climbed stiffly down.

Short and stooped, he had tiny, red-rimmed, deepset eyes; his face was greasy and black and grey with stubble. His nose, large and route-mapped with tiny red veins, cried out for the urgent attention of a handkerchief. Matted hair flopped over the dirt-stiffened collar of the brown overcoat, which had been made many years ago for someone much bigger. His hands, the nails chipped and black, reached up to the top shelf for a bulging brown carrier bag which he clutched protectively to his chest.

Frost identified him from the very first sniff. 'Blimey, Wally, hasn't the hospital got enough germs of its own without you bringing yours in as well?'

'I'm an old man, Mr Frost. Just looking for a place to rest my poor head for the night.' A dewdrop shimmered at the end of his nose. He gave a juicy sniff, which temporarily delayed its further descent.

'So you rested your poor head against the window of the nurses' bedroom?'

'I didn't know there was anyone in there . . . honest. I just happened to look in as she happened to look out — our eyes sort of met.'

'Sounds like something out of *True Romance*,' said Frost. 'So if you weren't after an eyeful of naked nurse, what were you after? And what have you got in that bag?'

He reached out for it, but Wally shrank back, clutching

the bag as tightly as he could. With difficulty, Frost managed to prise it from the tramp's greasy grasp and looked inside. Scraps of clothes, bits of food and a three-quarters-full wine bottle. 'I hope you haven't stolen someone's specimen,' said Frost, pulling out the cork and cautiously sniffing the contents. 'It's either meths or the stuff they pickle human organs in. Is this what you've sneaked in to pinch?'

'On my dead mother's grave, Mr Frost,' the tramp whined, 'I haven't come here to pinch anything.' A mighty sniff reprieved another dewdrop that was in danger of obeying Newton's law of gravity. 'I'm just a poor old man looking for shelter.'

'Well, you're not going to find it here,' said Frost, 'so push off before I kick you out.'

'I'm an old man, Inspector. Send me out in the cold and I'll die.'

'Promises, promises,' said Frost. 'Why don't you go and kip where you usually doss down?'

'I couldn't go to my usual place. There was a policeman standing outside.'

'A policeman?' queried Frost. 'Here . . . what usual place are you talking about?'

'The public convenience behind the Market Square. Me and Ben Cornish usually kip in one of the cubicles.'

'You won't kip with him anymore,' Frost said, and, as gently as he could, he broke the news.

The tramp, genuinely upset, clutched the wooden rack for support. 'We was good mates, me and him, Inspector. Ben wasn't eating properly. He was on drugs — used to inject himself with a needle. I told him it would kill him in the end, but he wouldn't listen.' He reflected sadly for a while, then said, 'Did he have any money on him? He said he was going to give me some for food. He promised me.'

'Sorry, Wally. He had no money. In fact he had sod all,' said Frost. 'Now beat it.'

The tramp's face fell. 'You've got to arrest me, Mr Frost. Put me in a cell for the night. I looked at that nurse . . .

saw all of her body. I lusted after her. I thought carnal thoughts. I deserve to be locked up.'

'You shouldn't have run away, Wally. She said she fancied you. Now hop it, or I'll tell my colleague to boot you out.'

'Please, Inspector. Look at the weather out there. You'll be signing my death warrant if you send me out in that!' He pointed dramatically to the windows, and, on cue, the wind lashed and hammered its fists at the glass.

Against his better judgement Frost relented. 'All right, Wally. Go to the station and tell Sergeant Wells I want you locked up for the night. Tell him I suspect that you're an international diamond smuggler.'

The dirt around the tramp's mouth cracked as he burbled his gratitude. They watched him shuffle painfully down the corridor, his arms folded around the carrier bag which contained everything he had in the world. Then the dead face of Ben Cornish swum filmily in front of Frost, the eyes insisting, 'You bloody fool . . . you've missed something.' As he later realized, Wally had shown him the answer, but he hadn't seen it.

Webster was saying something.

'What was that again, son?'

Webster's quartz digital was shoved under his nose. 'Four twelve. We'd better get back to the station.'

Frost winced. The station meant the crime statistics and the overtime returns and all the other mountains of paper work that had to be attended to. He thought hard. Surely there was something else they could do instead of going back. Then he remembered Tommy Croll, the security guard from The Coconut Grove. Why not interview him? That should waste a good hour.

'I'm looking for a bloke called Croll,' he told the nurse as she pulled sheets down from the rack. 'He came in tonight with concussion.'

'Then you're in luck, Inspector,' she said. 'He's in my ward.' She frowned at her tiny wristwatch. 'But it's very late.'

'I wouldn't ask if it weren't important, Nurse,' said Frost.

And what was more important than avoiding the crime statistics?

They followed her into a small ward where a ridiculously young student nurse was crouched over a desk with a shaded lamp, anxiously watching over the twin rows of sleeping, snuffling, and moaning patients, and hoping none of them died on her before the other nurse's return.

'All quiet,' she reported with relief. No sooner had she said this than one of her patients called out and started bringing up blood.

'Another one for the morgue,' Frost whispered to Webster.

'Mr Croll's in the end bed,' called the nurse as she and the student dashed off to attend to the crisis.

Their shoes squeaked as they tiptoed over the highly polished floor to the far bed where a weasel-faced man, his forehead decorated with a strip of sticking plaster, was sleeping noisily. Frost unclipped the charts from the end of the bed and studied them. 'Hmm. Both ends seem to be in working order. Give him a shake, son.'

Webster's gentle shake was about ten on the Richter scale. Croll snorted, choked in midsnore, then jerked his eyes open, flicking them from side to side as he tried to identify the shapes looming over him in the dark. He groped for the bedside lamp, blinking in surprise as he switched it on.

'Hello, Tommy,' said Frost, his voice generously laced with insincere concern. 'How are you?' He scraped a chair across to the bed and sat down.

'Mr Frost!' Croll fumbled under the pillow for his wristwatch. 'It's quarter past four in the morning!'

'I know,' agreed Frost. 'As soon as they told me you were in here, I dropped everything to come and see how you were. You're a hero, Tommy, a bloody hero.'

'Hero?' echoed Croll uneasily. He never knew how to take the inspector.

'The way you fought like a tiger to try and stop Mr Baskin's money being nicked. How's the poor head?'

Croll touched the sticking plaster and winced. 'Terrible, Mr Frost. Stabbing pains — like red-hot knives.'

Frost nodded sympathetically and stared down the ward. The two nurses had managed to calm the patient and were now straightening and smoothing the bedclothes. 'Tell us what happened, Tommy.'

'Not a lot to tell, Mr Frost. It was all over so quickly.'

'That's what my girl friends used to say, Tommy.'

Croll forced a grin. Frost always made him feel uneasy. And he wished the inspector would tell him who the bearded bloke hovering in the background was. He had such a miserable face, he looked like an undertaker. 'It was like this: Bert went to fetch the car, like always, and I locked myself in. After about five minutes I get the signal. Naturally I think it's Bert.'

'Naturally,' agreed Frost.

'I unbolts and flings open the door so he can come in when, wham, I'm welted a real right crack round the ear hole.'

'Did you see who hit you?' the bearded bloke asked.

'No, I didn't — but I sodding-well felt him,' replied Croll, his hand again tenderly touching the sticking plaster. 'It knocked me out cold. The next thing I know, I'm in here with this roaring headache. I can stand pain, Mr Frost, but this is just as though my skull was split open.'

'I saw a bloke with his skull split open once,' said Frost. 'A bus had gone right over his head — a double-decker, full of passengers — even eight standing on the lower deck. You could hear this scrunching and this squelching and then blood and brains squirted out all over the place. His eyes popped right out of their sockets. We found them in the gutter. I had a job eating my dinner that day.' He switched on a smile as he recalled the nostalgic moment, then abruptly switched it off. 'What did you do with the money, Tom?'

Croll, still shuddering from the description of the bus victim, was knocked off balance by Frost's sudden change of direction. 'Money? What money, Mr Frost?'

'The 5,132 quid you and Bert Harris pinched,' said the bearded one.

'May I drop dead if I'm not telling the truth, Mr Frost —'

Croll began, his hand on his heart, but Frost cut in before he tempted fate further.

'It had to be an inside job, Tommy. Whoever did it had to know the arrangements and the signal for tonight. Only three people knew: Mr Baskin, Bert, and you . . .'

Croll's head sunk back on the pillow, his eyes showing how hurt he was. 'That's a wicked thing to suggest, Mr Frost. Look at me — wounded in the line of duty. I nearly had my head smashed in.'

'But it wasn't smashed in enough,' explained Frost patiently. 'If your brains had been splattered all over Mr Baskin's floor and halfway up his wall, well, I might believe you, but as it is . . .'

And before Croll realized what he was up to, Frost's hand had snaked out and ripped the sticking plaster from his forehead. Croll yelled and clapped a hand over his wound, but Frost had already seen it.

'A waste of bloody sticking plaster, Tommy. I've seen love bites from toothless women cause deeper wounds than that.'

'I'm injured internally, Mr Frost,' said Croll, putting a finger to his forehead to see if he was bleeding. 'It don't show on the outside.'

More activity in the ward. The Asian doctor, who seemed to be the only doctor on duty in the entire hospital, flapped in and made for the patient who had called out. Frost now saw that the front of the student nurse's uniform was one dark, spreading stain of blood. The other nurse was rigging up an apparatus for a blood transfusion. She signalled to Frost that she wanted him to leave.

'We'll chat again tomorrow, Tommy,' said the inspector, moving away from the bed.

Croll pushed himself up. 'Mr Frost, I didn't do it. I swear . . .'

'I believe you,' beamed Frost. 'Just tell me where you've hidden the money and I'll believe you even more.'

When they reached the main corridor they had to press back against the wall so that an orderly, pushing a patient in a stretcher, could pass by. The patient, head swollen by a turban of bandages which were almost as white as his bloodless face, looked a hundred years old.

It was the hit-and-run victim.

At four forty-five in the morning Denton Police Station was a dreary mausoleum, and the flowers Mullett suggested would have made it look more funereal than ever. It echoed with cold emptiness. Only two men were on duty, Police Sergeant Wells and Police Constable Ridley, the controller. Wells, slumped at the front desk, stared at the ticking time bomb the computer had presented him with.

The licence plate found at the scene of the hit-and-run had been trotted through the massive memory banks of the master computer system at Swansea. The print-out read:

> Registration Mark: *ULU 63A*
> Taxation Class: *Private/Light Goods*
> Make/Model: *Jaguar 3.4*
> Colour: *Blue*
> Registered Keeper: *Roger Charles Miller*
> Address: *43 Halley House, Denton.*

What the computer didn't say was that Roger Miller was trouble. Big trouble. He was the son of Sir Charles Miller, member of Parliament for the Denton constituency. And Sir Charles was even bigger trouble. He had money and he had influence, owning businesses as diverse as security organisations, newspapers, and commercial radio stations. He constantly criticised the police in his newspapers, and he was a permanent thorn in the side of the Chief Constable. And it was his son, Roger, a twenty-year old spoiled brat, who had brought seventy-eight-year-old Albert Hickman to the brink of death.

Wells twisted his neck to see what luck Ridley was having in contacting Detective Inspector Frost. 'Control to Mr Frost, come in please.' Over and over, Ridley repeated the message, flicking the receive switch and getting only a mush of static in response. 'Still no answer, Sarge.'

'Damn!' said Wells, reaching for the phone. He dialled the first two digits of Mullett's home number, then changed his mind and banged the receiver down. 'Do you think I should phone Mullett?'

'That's for you to decide, Sarge,' was Ridley's unhelpful reply. 'You're in charge.'

'I'm not bloody in charge. Frost is in charge . . . or he should be. He's the senior officer.' Again his hand reached for the phone. Again he hesitated. Thanks to Frost, Wells was back in his familiar no-win situation. If he phoned Mullett he'd be castigated for disturbing him and for not using his initiative. And if he didn't phone, Mullett would say, 'Where's your common sense, Sergeant? If someone as important as Sir Charles Miller is involved surely it doesn't need a modicum of common sense to realize that I would want to know about it.' In either event, it would give the Superintendent a tailor-made excuse for turning down the sergeant's latest promotion application.

Wells felt like breaking down and weeping at the injustice of it all when suddenly he was dragged away from his self-pity by a most unpleasant smell, which elbowed its way across the lobby. The sergeant's head swivelled slowly until he located the source.

'Clear off,' he said, happy to have someone to snarl at. 'Get out of here before I turn the hose pipe on you.'

A brown overcoated figure clutching a carrier bag tottered toward him. 'I've come to be arrested,' said Wally Peters. 'Mr Frost sent me.'

As Wells searched for a suitable expletive, Ridley called out excitedly from Control. 'There's Mr Frost, Sarge.' Wells spun around in time to see Frost and Webster pushing through the main doors.

'I'm here, Mr Frost,' the tramp announced proudly.

'Yes,' agreed Frost, 'we smelled you from the top of Bath Hill. But I must dash,' and he went charging through the other door and up the corridor.

'Hold it a minute, Inspector,' yelled Wells, chasing after him.

The light was on in Frost's office. Relieved, Wells hurried forward and opened the door, but inside he saw only Webster, frowning at the car licence plate lying across Frost's desk.

'What's this, Sergeant?' he asked, picking it up.

Wells waved it aside. 'None of your business. Where's the inspector? We've got a bloody crisis on our hands.'

Webster put down the licence plate and sat at his own desk. 'He said something about going scavenging.'

'Scavenging?' Wells sank down in Frost's chair. 'What's he playing at? The man's supposed to be an inspector; why doesn't he start acting like one?'

'You sound just like our beloved Divisional Commander,' said Frost, staggering back into the office bearing a tray piled high with goodies: sausage rolls, sandwiches, crisps, pork scratchings, and salted peanuts. A clinking noise came from his bulging mac pockets. 'It's party time, folks,' he announced, pushing papers and the licence plate to one side to clear a space on his desk for the tray.

From pockets that seemed far too small to contain them came can after can of lager, a seemingly endless supply of miniature spirit bottles, and even a box of expensive cigars. 'You *shall* go to the ball, Sergeant,' he said.

Wells's eyes widened. 'Where did you get these?'

'From the canteen — the party.' He still hadn't finished off-loading, pulling more bottles from his inside jacket pockets. Proudly, he surveyed his haul. 'They didn't invite us to their stinking party, so we won't invite them to ours.'

In the top drawer of his filing cabinet he found three chipped enamel mugs and slopped in three generous helpings of seven-year-old malt whisky. One mug went to the sergeant, the other to Webster. 'Help yourself to tonic and salted peanuts. Sorry we haven't got any ice.'

Webster glared at his mug and pushed it away. 'Are you trying to be funny?'

Frost could only look puzzled. Then the light dawned. 'Sorry, I forgot. You've signed the pledge, haven't you, son? The beard that touches liquor will never touch mine.'

This had the effect of sending Wells into a fit of uncontrollable giggling, a fit that Webster's scowl only seemed to amplify.

Frost shared the contents of Webster's mug between the sergeant and himself. He pushed the tray toward the constable. 'Well, at least have a sandwich or some peanuts.' Webster flicked a hand in curt refusal.

'If you're not going to join the party, go and look after the lobby,' Wells ordered. When Webster stamped out, the sergeant slipped into his chair and washed down some cheese and onion crisps with a long swig from his mug. He felt warm and happy. It wasn't such a bad shift after all. He was trying to remember why he had been feeling so miserable before Frost came in.

Frost buzzed Control on the internal phone. 'Mr Ridley? If you wish to attend a booze-up, report immediately to Mr Frost's office.' He hung up and lit one of the cigars. 'This is great, isn't it, Bill? All we want now to make it complete are some pickled onions and a naked woman.'

'I wouldn't object if there were no pickled onions,' giggled Wells, unbuttoning the collar of his tunic. Frost's office seemed very warm. He felt the radiator, but it was stone cold. As he was trying to puzzle this out he remembered what he had wanted to talk to the inspector about.

'Jack, we're in a crisis situation. Do you know anything about this hit-and-run?'

'Yes,' said Frost, puffing out smoke rings almost as large as car tyres. 'We saw the poor sod spewing blood at the hospital.'

'Is he still alive?'

Frost removed the cigar and shot a palmful of salted peanuts into his mouth. 'Just about. I don't think they'll be cooking him any breakfast, though.'

'Damn,' said Wells, his worst fears realized. He emptied his mug in a single gulp. 'We've had the computer feed-back on the licence plate. The car belongs to Roger Miller.'

Frost stopped in midsip. He put the mug down slowly. 'Sir Charles Miller's son?'

'Yes,' agreed Wells dolefully, regarding the interior of his empty mug. 'It's tricky, Jack, flaming tricky. If we don't play this one right we could end up in the soft and squishy.' It took him several attempts to say 'soft and squishy.'

'Roger Miller,' repeated Frost, his eyes gleaming. 'Well, if we can chuck that little sod in the nick, the night won't be entirely wasted.'

Tapping at the door, Ridley looked in. 'You said something about a drink, Mr Frost?'

'More than a drink —' Frost told him, pouring out a quadruple shot of whisky '— a party, a celebration. We're going to arrest an MP's son tonight. Help yourself to a nosh.'

Ridley thanked him and took his drink and a ham sandwich back to the control room.

'Plenty more when you've finished that,' called Frost, biting into a sausage roll and coating both himself and the desk in a snowstorm of flaky pastry crumbs. The phone on his desk rang. 'Shut up,' he ordered. 'We're having a party.' It rang on and on until he shook it free of food crumbs and picked it up. 'Frost . . . OK, put them through.' He listened. 'Thanks for telling me. Good night.' He fumbled the phone back on the rest. 'That was the hospital, Bill. The hit-and-run victim just died.'

Wells stood up. 'You'd better phone Mullett, Jack. This could be dynamite.'

Frost waved him back into the chair, then refilled the sergeant's mug. 'Sod Mullett, Bill. I want to handle this my way.' He went to the door and yelled for Webster to come in. 'Put your coat on, son, we're going walkies. We've got to arrest a piece of puke called Miller.'

'Miller?' said Webster, as he unhooked his coat from the rack. 'You don't mean Roger Miller?'

'What do you know about Roger Miller?' asked Wells.

'I saw the name on a car-theft report on Collier's desk. When he went off he left a lot of his work unfinished, as I expect you know, Sergeant.'

Wells didn't know. He hadn't checked. 'I've only got one pair of hands. I can't do every bloody thing.'

Frost put his mug down very carefully and gave Webster

his full attention. 'Let me get this straight. Are you trying to tell me that there's an unprocessed car-theft report on Collier's desk, that Roger bloody Miller phoned us earlier this evening reporting his Jag had been nicked?'

Webster nodded.

'It's not my fault, Jack,' protested Wells, 'I didn't have time to look on his desk. Mr Allen had no right to take Collier away.'

'Never mind whose fault it was,' said Frost. 'What time did Miller phone in?'

Webster went out, returning with the report in his hand. 'Eleven twenty-four,' he said.

Frost sighed with relief. The old boy was run over at 10.58. 'He runs someone down, then he reports his car was stolen. Did he really think we'd fall for that?'

'Do you mind telling me what this is all about?' requested Webster.

Frost stood up and shrugged on his mac. 'It was Roger Miller's car that knocked that old boy down.'

'I see,' said Webster.

Slinging the scarf round his neck, Frost yelled for Ridley to contact PC Shelby on the radio.

'Dave Shelby has just come in,' Ridley shouted back. 'He's in the locker room.'

Frost dashed down the corridor and into the locker room. Shelby, busy ramming something into his locker, whirled around with a start. 'You frightened the life out of me, Mr Frost,' he said, quickly slamming his locker door and turning the key.

Hello, thought Frost, what are you up to now, my lad? When he had time, he'd check. 'Got a job for you, Shelby. See me in my office — now.'

Back in the office, Wells, fighting hard against the effects of the three brimming mugfuls of Scotch, was insisting that Mullett would have to be told about the MP's son. 'Let me arrest him first, then tell him,' replied Frost.

'Mr Mullett won't like that,' said Wells.

'I don't really believe I was put on this earth just to make

Mr Mullett happy,' replied Frost. Shelby walked in, and his eyes lit up when he saw the drinks and the food.

'Grab a sandwich and get this inside you,' said the inspector, draining his mug and filling it up for the constable. 'Don't sip it, swig it — you're going straight out again. The hit-and-run victim is dead. Do you know if any of the witnesses could identify the driver?'

Shelby bit into a sandwich. 'No, sir. All they saw was the car roaring off.'

'We've checked the registration,' Frost told him. 'The motor belongs to Roger Miller, the MP's son, and he's trying to kid us his motor was stolen and he wasn't driving.' He pused the car-theft report into Shelby's hand. 'I want all these details checked, double-checked and then checked again, right? We're dealing with a slippery sod, and I want to be one jump ahead of him.'

'Right, sir,' confirmed Shelby, raising his mug in salute.

'I want this bastard nailed, right?'

'You're not being objective, Jack,' said Wells, wondering why his headache was starting up again. 'He might be innocent.'

'Don't complicate matters, Bill. I haven't got time to be objective. Hickman is dead, and Miller is as guilty as hell.' He massaged some life into the scar on his face. 'The problem is going to be proving it.'

He twisted the scarf around his neck and was halfway across the lobby before he remembered to nip back into his office and stuff most of the remaining miniature spirit bottles into his mac pockets.

'There are a lot of thieving bastards in this station,' he explained. Then he took one of the miniatures and handed it to the sergeant. 'Send this down to Wally Peters with my compliments. Tell him to have a good-bye drink to Ben Cornish.'

Wells exploded. 'We don't give booze to prisoners, Jack. Besides, you know him. One drink and he'll piddle nonstop all over the cell floor.'

'Your trouble,' said Frost reprovingly, 'is that you expect everyone to be too bloody perfect.'

TUESDAY NIGHT SHIFT (7)

Roger Miller lived in Halley House, a newly built, multi-storeyed block of expensive service flats. Webster parked the Cortina alongside a public call box on the opposite side of the road and looked out at the towering hulk of Halley House, which loomed ever upward to the night sky. At that hour of the morning the only lights showing came from the entrance hall on the ground floor. 'What's your plan of campaign?' he asked the inspector.

Frost grunted and shifted in his seat. He didn't use plans of campaign. His method of working was to close his eyes, lower his head, and charge. 'Haven't given it a thought, son,' he admitted. 'We go in, chat him up, and see what happens.'

'If I were in charge,' said Webster pointedly, indicating that his way was the right way, 'I wouldn't mention the hit-and-run. I'd let him think we were here about his allegedly stolen car.'

'What's that supposed to achieve?'

'It could lull him into a sense of false security. When he's off his guard, we wham into him about the hit-and-run.'

'Then he cracks up, breaks down and confesses, like they did in those Perry Mason films?' Frost pursed his lips doubtfully. 'I'm afraid not, son. He'll know what we've called for the minute we poke our sticky fingers in his bell push.'

'How will he know?' demanded Webster.

'Because you don't get two CID men calling for a chat at this hour of the morning just because someone's taken your motor for a walk.' He drummed a little tune on the dashboard with his fingers. 'But I can't think of anything better, so we'll try it your way. You conduct the interview, I'll just chip in with the odd remarks as and when the muse grabs me by the privates.'

'If I'm going to question him, I want to know what sort of person he is,' said Webster, a firm believer in groundwork.

'His father is stinking rich, a Member of Parliament, and a pompous slimy bastard. Master Roger is exactly the sort of son a pompous slimy bastard deserves. He's arrogant, he's nasty, and he gets away with murder because of his old man. And if that didn't make you hate him enough, he also seems to be able to pull the most fantastic birds with throbbing tits and nipples sticking out like sore thumbs.'

'Sounds a right little charmer,' grunted Webster, 'but I reckon I can handle him.'

Frost unhitched his seat belt and opened the door. 'I'm sure you can, my son. But if you feel like giving him a welt, warn me so I can look the other way and swear blind I never saw anything. Come on, let's get over there.'

The wind tried to push them back as they raced, heads down, across the road. Some sort of down draught caused by the design of the twenty-three-storey block created a whirl-wind effect at the base, and they had to fight against it.

Three marble steps led up to bronze-and-glass doors which were security-locked and could only be opened with a key, or if one of the tenants pressed a release button from his apart-ment. Frost shook them until they rattled, but they refused to open. Through the plate glass they could see the red-carpeted lobby, the reception desk, and the lift. Beside the main doors was a bank of bell pushes marked with the flat numbers. Miller's number was 43. Frost gave the appropriate button a jab. Nothing happened. He tried again, then stepped back to stare up at the rows of windows. No lights were showing.

'Everyone's asleep,' muttered Webster.

'Not everyone, son,' said Frost, 'When you've knocked down and killed some poor old sod, you don't go to sleep. You stay awake and plan the lies you're going to tell the fuzz when they call.' He wedged his thumb in the bell push and leaned his weight on it for a good minute. 'That should wake the bugger up.'

It didn't wake the bugger up. No response. 'He's either not in or he's determined not to answer,' said Frost.

'Well, if he won't answer his door, there's not much more we can do,' said Webster.

Frost withdrew his thumb and looked at all the bell pushes. At the bottom was a button marked Caretaker. He thought for a moment, then smiled. 'You come with your Uncle Jack and I'll show you a way of getting inside someone's place that they never taught you at police college.'

Wondering what the old fool was up to now, Webster followed him back across the road to the phone box. Frost draped his handkerchief over the receiver and dialled the number of Denton Police Station.

'Denton Police,' answered a tired-sounding Sergeant Wells.

'I'm phoning from outside those new flats at Halley House,' said Frost in a low voice. 'There's a man on the balcony of the fourth floor trying to break into one of the apartments.'

'Can I have your name please, sir?' asked Wells as Frost whipped away the handkerchief and hung up.

'Back to the car, son, quick.'

In the car, Frost's hand hovered expectantly over the handset, snatching it up as Control called through.

'Control to Mr Frost, come in, please.'

'Frost.'

'Ridley here, sir. We've had a report of someone trying to break into the flats at Halley House. You're near there, aren't you?'

'Right outside,' answered Frost. 'We'll attend to it right away.'

The caretaker, an obsequious Uriah Heep in a thick grey dressing gown, kept yawning and jingling his bunch of keys like the jailer at the Bastille. 'This is most disturbing,' he said. 'The tenants won't like it one bit. But how could anyone climb up to the balconies from the outside?'

'These cat burglars can get up anywhere,' said Frost, wishing the man would just give him the keys and go. 'It was the third balcony along the fourth floor.'

'I'll come up with you,' said the caretaker. 'I don't want any of my tenants to be disturbed. It'll give the place a bad name.'

But Frost was quick to decline his kind offer. 'He could be armed. We don't want to expose you to any danger.' The keys were zipped into his hand. 'Thank you, sir. If you hear any gunfire, dial 999.'

The lift purred up to the fourth floor and deposited them onto a red-and-black-patterned carpet, which deadened their footsteps as they walked to a mat black door bearing the number 43. Frost pressed the bell push with one hand and hammered at the door with the other. He waited, then hammered again.

'Listen!' he exclaimed, like a bad actor. 'Is that a cry for help?' Before Webster could reply that he couldn't hear a damn thing, Frost unlocked the door with the pass key and stepped inside.

'Mr Miller?' Silence. Frost slid his hand down the door frame to locate the switch, and clicked on the light. The flat looked and felt empty. They were in a large lounge, its walls decorated with coloured prints of vintage racing cars; the centrepiece was a framed original poster advertising the 1936 Grand Prix at the old Brooklands racing circuit.

On the doormat were a couple of letters. Frost bent and picked them up. One was a circular, the other a letter from Bennington's Bank, Denton. 'Either he doesn't bother to pick up his post, or he hasn't been in tonight,' he said, dropping them back where he found them.

'Anyway, he's not here,' said Webster. 'Let's go.'

'Patience, son, patience,' said Frost and padded across to a half-open door which led to the bedroom. The bed was made up and didn't appear to have been slept in. Above the bed was a brushed-aluminum framed print of two naked lovers, facing each other, kneeling, mouths open, kissing, their bodies just achingly touching. Frost gave it his full attention, then starting poking into drawers, riffling through their contents.

Webster was getting fidgety and anxious. They had no right to be there, let alone search through private belongings.

If Miller came back and caught them, reported them to Mullet . . . 'We ought to leave,' he said edgily. 'We shouldn't be here.'

'*We* shouldn't, son,' agreed the inspector, 'but Master Roger should. According to his car-theft report, he was just off to bed when he remembered he'd left his briefcase in his motor. He went out to fetch it, and *presto,* the Jag had vanished. So why isn't he in bed, crying his eyes out?'

'I've no idea,' said Webster, inching toward the door. 'Let's talk about it back at the station — Now what are you doing?'

'Just being nosey, son.' He had opened the sliding doors of a huge built-in wardrobe to expose row upon row of expensive suits packed tight on the rails next to hangers sporting tailored silk shirts, all monogrammed RM. 'Don't you hate the bastard for having all these clothes?' he said. On the wardrobe floor, side by side in serried ranks of shoetrees, were dozens of pairs of hand-sewn leather shoes, intricately patterned in brown and cream. Frost measured one against his own foot. 'Do you reckon he'd miss a pair, son?'

Webster folded his arms and waited for the inspector to stop playing his silly games, his eyes constantly moving to the door, waiting for Roger Miller to burst in and demand to know what they were up to.

'All right,' said Frost at last, 'I've seen all I want to.' He looked at his watch. 'Sod the returns, son. Let's go home.'

I should bloody-well think so, thought Webster.

They gave the worried caretaker his keys back. He had been sitting by his phone, his ears straining for the fusilade of gunshots which, together with the two dead policeman, would give the flats some bad publicity. 'Seems clear up there,' announced Frost. He then asked where the tenants kept their cars.

'In our basement car park,' replied the caretaker. 'Why?'

'We'd better give it the once-over,' said Frost. 'He might be after nicking an expensive motor.'

The caretaker took them down to the basement in the service lift. Some forty cars were parked in areas marked off with the tenants' flat numbers.

'What do you expect to find?' Webster muttered sarcastically. 'The Jag dripping with blood? You don't think he'd be stupid enough to leave it here?'

'You never know your luck,' said Frost, turning to call to the caretaker. 'Where is Mr Miller's parking space?'

'Over there in the corner — that's his car.'

Frost looked at Webster in triumph. They squeezed through gaps between cars to reach the section marked Flat 43. But the car parked there wasn't blue and it wasn't a Jaguar. It was a black Porsche.

'Of course that's Mr Miller's car,' insisted the caretaker. 'He goes to his office every day in that.'

'What about his Jag?' queried Frost.

'There's only room for one car per tenant. He parks his Jaguar round the corner, down a side-turning.'

Webster didn't bother to hide his smirk at Frost's deflation. That was exactly where Miller said the Jag was stolen from. It looked as if his story about the theft might prove to be correct.

With slumped shoulders Frost shuffled back to the lift that would take them up to ground level. Then he remembered one last important question. 'Did Mr Miller drive the Porsche to the office today?'

'Yes,' replied the caretaker, 'I saw him.'

Webster couldn't understand why that answer made Frost look a lot more cheerful.

Back across the road to the Cortina. The car radio was buzzing away.

'Control to Mr Frost. Come in, please,' pleaded Bill Wells for the twentieth time.

'Frost!'

'Thank God I've caught you, Jack. I've just spoken to Mr Mullett about this hit-and-run business. He's going spare. He says on no account — repeat no account — are you to attempt to contact Roger Miller. He wants this handled with kid gloves and everything done strictly according to the book. So please, Jack, stay away.'

'But of course,' said Frost, sounding hurt. 'I wouldn't

dream of seeing Miller without Mr Mullett's express permission.'

He passed the handset back to Webster.

'I've had enough, son. Let's go home.'

WEDNESDAY DAY SHIFT (1)

The briefing room at Denton Police Station was looking very much less than its best. Like most of the assembled police officers, it was suffering from the effects of the previous night's party. Empty glasses and overflowing ashtrays were everywhere — on chairs, on window ledges, and dotted around the floor. In one corner a wastepaper bin had been knocked over, spilling its contents — screwed-up crisp packets, half-eaten sandwiches, and assorted rubbish — into a sticky, spreading puddle of lager.

There were a dozen or so police officers present, both uniform and plainclothed, some looking decidedly fragile. Most were sipping coffee from plastic cups, and the subdued burble of conversation was mainly about hangovers, upset stomachs, and the party.

Detective Inspector Allen stood outside in the corridor watching the second hand of his watch inching its way toward zero hour. Punctuality was his keyword, and he would not enter the briefing room until nine o'clock on the dot. Thirty seconds to go. He was annoyed to note that Frost hadn't shown up yet, although that bearded ex-inspector was there, sitting by himself in the corner and trying to look superior to everyone else.

Allen reached for the door handle. The minute hand of the wall clock quivered, then clunked up the hour. He flung open the door and swept in.

'All right, ladies and gentlemen, your attention, please.'

He climbed up onto the raised dais, where Detective Sergeant Ingram was in attendance with all the various files and photocopied orders laid out on the table. Behind the table was the wall map, and pinned on the blackboard next to it were photographs of the five previous rape victims, exactly as the inspector had requested.

The room went quiet. Allen paused, surveying the green-tinged faces, then his nose wrinkled. The room reeked of flat beer and stale cigar smoke. The inspector didn't smoke and wouldn't tolerate any of his subordinates indulging the habit in his presence. 'This room stinks,' he snapped. 'Someone open a window.'

Collier scrambled up from his chair and eased open one of the windows a fraction.

'I said open it!' bellowed Allen. 'Fresh air won't kill you.'

Collier flung the window open to its fullest extent, and the cold air came roaring in. The assembly shivered, which made Allen smirk with satisfaction. He had noticed a few barely stifled yawns as he entered. That should keep the bastards alert, he thought. A final scan of the room for the dirty mac and the maroon scarf. 'Mr Frost not graced us with his presence? Then we'll start without him.'

He rocked gently on the balls of his feet, his eyes travelling from face to face, making certain he had everyone's full attention. 'Those of you who were at Mr Harrison's farewell party will know that our old friend, the so-called "Hooded Terror", struck again last night. As we hadn't heard from him for six months, I'm sure we were all hoping that he'd retired or had some dreadful accident with a carving knife that would put an end to his raping career, but it seems he was just biding his time. Last night he attacked his sixth victim, a woman by the name of Paula Grey who works at The Coconut Grove where she does a striptease act under the billing of Paula the Naughty Schoolgirl.'

Someone sniggered. Allen's cold eyes searched the room for the offender. 'Have I said something funny?' He waited in case someone dared to answer, then went on. 'I said her name is Paula Grey, but she is also known as Nellie Drake, Sadie Kendal, and Molly Patrick, and under each of these has had the odd conviction for soliciting — for offering gentlemen the use of her body in exchange for a small fee. That, however, is by the way. She was not soliciting last night. She was proceeding in a lawful manner from her home to her place of employment.

'Like Mr Frost, it would seem that punctuality is not her strongest point. On several previous occasions she had been late for her spot, and her boss, nature's own gentleman, Harry Baskin, had warned her that if she was late one more time she would be for the chop. Last night she overslept, waking up at 10.35. She was due to go on at The Coconut Grove at 11.15. In order to save time, she slapped on her stage make-up, put on her stage clothes, which were those of a schoolgirl, and took the shortcut through Denton Woods. As I have so often pointed out to you, ladies and gentlemen, the shortest way is not always the quickest.'

He took a pointer from the table and turned to the wall map. 'She departed from her flat in Forest View at approximately 10.50. She went down this road, turned in to the woods, then took this path.' The pointer scraped the map as it traced her route.

'She left the main path here and cut down this little side route, which should have brought her back to the main road. But she never made it.'

From the back of the room the rasp of a match being struck. Allen froze. Without turning around, he said, 'I hope no-one intends smoking during my briefing.' The sound of a match hastily blown out. He relaxed and continued. 'She had reached this point here, where the path curves, and that was where the bastard was waiting for her. Exactly the same tactics as he employed with all the rest. The cloth chucked over her head, the hands around her throat to semi-strangle her into unconsciousness. Her attacker then dragged her from the path, behind some bushes, about here' — the pointer jabbed the map — 'where he stripped her down to her stockings. But at this point, to everyone's surprise, including his victim's, he deviated from his usual pattern. He didn't rape her. Instead, he viciously kicked and punched her, breaking her nose, her jaw, and some ribs.

'At five minutes to one this morning, Sergeant Wells received a telephone message from an anonymous male caller reporting the body of a girl in the woods. We don't know who this man was, but we want to trace him. This call was followed up by Constables Simms and Jordan in Charlie Alpha. They were later joined by Mr Frost and Inspector . . . I do beg his pardon . . . *Constable* Webster, our refugee from Braybridge District.' He smirked as Webster smouldered, and waited for the laughter to subside so he could continue.

As he turned back to the map he heard the door to the briefing room open and close. Obviously Frost trying to sneak in unseen. 'So kind of you to grace us with your presence,' he began sarcastically, but he was horrified to hear the scraping of chairs as everyone rose and sprang to attention. 'So sorry, Superintendent,' he said hastily. 'I thought it was Mr Frost.'

Mullett, in a mint-condition uniform straight from the tailor's, graciously nodded his acceptance of the apology, then smiled and waved a hand for everyone to sit. He then sat in one of the chairs in the back row, folded his arms, and assumed an expression of intense concentration. 'Please carry on, Inspector.'

'I spoke to the victim in the hospital,' Allen went on. 'As in the case of all the previous victims, she could tell me absolutely nothing about her attacker. I'm hoping to question her further today when the surgeons have patched her up, but the current position is that six women have been attacked and we do not have even the vaguest description of the rapist. All we know from semen samples is that his blood group is type O, a group shared by more than forty-four percent of the male population.'

The briefing room door was flung back on its hinges and a latecomer lurched in, managing to kick over an empty lager tin, which rolled down the aisle and bounced up onto the dais, only halting when it touched Allen's shoe. Delicately, the inspector pushed it to one side with his toe. He didn't look up. He didn't have to. There was no doubt this time who the newcomer was. 'Good morning, Mr Frost. I'm afraid we had to start without you.'

'That's all right,' said Frost grandly. 'I completely forgot about this bloody meeting. It won't take long, will it? I've got a post-mortem at ten.' He shivered. 'It's a bit nippy in here.' He slammed shut the open window, flopped into a chair in the back row, and lit up a cigarette.

Allen's eyes glinted. A chance to cut Frost down to size in front of the Superintendent. 'I don't like people smoking during my briefing sessions, Mr Frost.'

'That's all right,' beamed Frost, the cigarette waggling in his mouth. 'I don't like people jabbering away while I'm smoking, but I put up with it.' The burst of laughter that followed was withered to silence by the ice of Allen's expression. Grinning broadly, Frost puffed away at his cigarette, making as much smoke as possible. He turned to share the joke with the person sitting next to him, and to his horror it was Mullett, all immaculate uniform, gleaming buttons, and wintry disapproval. 'A word with you afterward, Inspector,' he hissed.

'Yes, Super, of course,' muttered Frost, wriggling uneasily in his chair and wishing he'd chosen somewhere else to sit.

Allen's smirk tightened. Now to rub salt into Frost's raw wound. 'By the time I arrived on the scene the ambulance was taking the victim to hospital. Mr Frost, who'd seen her, told me she was fifteen years old. During her short ambulance ride she must have aged twenty-three years, because when I saw her in hospital she was thirty-eight. I'm not sure how anyone could have made such a mistake, but perhaps the inspector would care to explain.' He moved back, extending an open hand, inviting Frost to take the stage.

Frost's fixed smile clearly said, 'You bastard!' but he kept his face impassive as he ambled up and leaned against the table, his eyes half closed against the smoke of his cigarette.

'As Mr Allen has told you, I made a real right burke of myself last night — not for the first time, and certainly not the last. We'd just come from a house where a fifteen-year-old kid called Karen Dawson was missing. She hadn't been seen since she left school yesterday lunch time. The woman in the woods was stark naked. Her face was smashed in and smothered with blood from where the bastard had booted her. Scattered around her were articles of school uniform, so I jumped to the wrong conclusion. I shouldn't have made such a stupid bloody mistake, but I did.'

He paused, took the butt end from his mouth and used it to light another cigarette. 'The scene when we got there? As I've said, the poor cow was naked, except for stockings. She was lying on her back, her clothes scattered on the grass around her where they'd been torn off. There was also a carrier bag which contained her non-working clothes and a purse. That's really all I can tell you.'

'Thank you, Inspector,' said Allen, moving back to the stage. Frost spotted an empty chair in the front row and sat down. It was the farthest from Mullett he could get.

'Any questions?' asked Allen.

A plainclothes man in the centre row raised his hand. 'Any idea why this one wasn't raped, sir?'

Allen nodded. 'I formed a theory about that.' He pointed to the five photographs pinned on the blackboard.

'These are the first five rape victims. Number one, Peggy Leyton, nineteen, a student nurse, raped on April 4th while taking a shortcut across the golf links. Number two, Sarah Finch, eighteen, an office worker, raped on April 5th, also on the golf links. Next we have victims three and four, Genette Scott, unemployed, aged twenty, but looks a lot younger, and Kate Brown, a student, also twenty. Both were attacked and raped in Meads Park, April 20th and 21st. Last, we have Linda Alwood, a shop assistant, aged nineteen, raped May 2nd on a piece of waste ground near the Denton Factory Estate. All these attacks took place some eight miles from Denton Woods, but they each have one thing in common. The victims were all very young and in some cases looked a lot younger than their age. My theory, ladies and gentlemen, is that the Denton "Hooded Terror" likes fresh, young meat. He can only make it with young birds. When he saw Paula Grey prancing through the trees in her schoolgirl clothes, he must have thought he'd hit the jackpot with a nice, tender young virgin, but when he found he'd got an old boiling fowl he did his nut. Old women are a turnoff to him.'

Webster, in his corner seat, nodded. Allen's theory made a lot of sense. You might hate him as a man, but he was a damn good police officer. He sneaked a look at Frost, lolling in his front row chair, looking as if he'd spent the night in the gutter. There was no comparison between the two men. One was a policeman, the other was rubbish.

Allen bent down and picked up a bundle of clothes which he dumped on the table. 'These are the clothes the girl was wearing prior to the attack.' He bent again and added a white plastic carrier bag to the pile. 'This is the bag she was carrying. We've had photographs taken of a model of similar appearance to Paula Grey, dressed in this clothing and carrying this bag. You'll each be given a copy. I want every house in the vicinity of Forest View and on the way to the woods to be called on. I want every single resident to be shown the photograph. Did they see a girl wearing these clothes last night? I'm sure a well-developed, thirty-eight-year-old woman wearing school clothes must have caught someone's eye. Did they see her? Did they see anyone following her or taking an interest in her? Did they see any strangers loitering? Has anyone going through the woods during the past week or so seen a man lurking, acting strangely? Has any woman been assaulted and not told us? A thorough investigation, ladies and gentlemen. I'm sure I don't need to spell out the questions you should ask. All witnesses, even those who only think they *might* have seen something, are to be brought to the station so I can question them personally. Understood?'

A few grunts of confirmation.

'I'm splitting you up into teams. Sergeant Ingram will give you details as you leave. Team A will be knocking at doors, asking questions, Team B will be doing an inch-by-inch search of the area of last night's attack, and Team C will be locating, and bringing in for questioning, all known sexual offenders in the area — even those who were completely eliminated from our previous inquiries. Any questions?'

He looked around expectantly, but no-one had anything to ask. 'Right. Off you go.'

They were shuffling through the door, passing Ingram, who handed them their duty allocation briefing sheets, when Allen suddenly barked, 'Hold it, everyone.' They all stopped and turned, except for Frost, who hared it off to his own office. Allen had completely forgotten Mr Mullett, seated in solitary state in the back row. 'Did you want to address the teams, sir?'

Mullett stood and showed his whiter-than-white teeth. 'Only to say "Good luck everyone",' he boomed, just like a vicar starting off the whist drive.

They all clattered out, clutching their briefing notes and duty schedules. Methodically, Allen replaced his notes back into the folder and waited as Ingram unpinned the photographs from the wall board. Mullett glided over. 'An excellent briefing, Inspector. A model for us all.'

'Thank you, sir,' said Allen, suspicious of the Superintendent's motives. He took the photographs from Ingram and dismissed the sergeant with a curt nod, then made great play of consulting his watch. 'Did you want to see me, sir? I've got rather a tight schedule. The press will be screaming blue murder when they hear about last night's little shindig in the woods — "Hooded Terror Strikes Again . . . Police have no clues".'

Mullett nodded sympathetically as if distancing himself from any criticism that might be levelled against the police. 'Don't talk to me about the press, Inspector. My phone's been ringing nonstop about this wretched hit-and-run business . . . the press, the Chief Constable . . . even Sir Charles Miller himself.' He looked at Allen, hoping that the recital of this all-star cast would impress him.

Allen again looked pointedly at his watch. 'What was it you wanted to see me about, sir?'

The Superintendent adjusted his gaze to a spot a few inches above the inspector's head. 'What cases are you working on at the moment?'

Allen's eyes narrowed. 'I hope you don't intend dumping

anything else on my plate, sir. I'll be working all the hours God sends on this rape investigation and there's going to be no time for anything else.'

'I fully appreciate that,' said Mullett, twisting his neck to look at the large-scale wall map, avoiding having to look the detective inspector in the eye. 'I want you to hand the rape case over to Frost.'

Allen stared at Mullett as if he were mad. 'Over my dead body!'

'Only for a few days, Inspector.'

'Not even for a few minutes — and that's just how long it would take Frost to sod everything up.' In his agitation he began to stride up and down, pounding his palm with his fist. 'Why, sir? Please tell me why!'

Mullett raised a placating hand. 'I've got another case for you — one that requires all your skill, tact, and expertise.'

'Oh yes?' said Allen warily, knowing that it would be a real stinker.

'Do you know anything about this hit-and-run?'

'Only that Roger Miller was involved.'

'That isn't certain. He claims he wasn't driving, that his car had been stolen.'

Allen straightened the papers inside the folder and tucked it under his arm. 'Balls!' he said bluntly.

Mullett, who could never stomach crudity, winced. 'His father, Sir Charles Miller, is convinced of his son's innocence.'

'I hardly think Sir Charles is that stupid, sir.'

Pulling a chair forward, Mullett sat down after hitching his trouser legs to preserve the lethal edge of their creases. 'This is all top-level stuff, Allen. Sir Charles phoned the Chief Constable this morning, and, as a result of that call, the Chief Constable phoned me at my home. If this case goes to court, Sir Charles intends to engage a top-flight QC.'

'Rich man's privilege,' sniffed Allen.

'Precisely, Inspector. But a good QC would tear a badly prepared case to ribbons, and that would reflect badly on this division. I do not intend for that to happen.'

'If we get a good prosecuting counsel, then it won't happen,' said Allen.

'All right,' said Mullett, 'I'll put my cards on the table. There's a slim chance that Roger Miller is telling the truth and that his car was stolen. If we can prove that he's innocent, it would buy us a lot of goodwill with Sir Charles. He's always been antipolice — what a feather in our caps if we could turn this man our way.'

'But supposing our investigation proved his son to be guilty?' asked Allen.

'Then at least we'd go to court with a watertight case. In either event the investigating officer would come out of the affair with credit.'

'Would he?' asked Allen shrewdly. 'With respect, sir, you're being naïve. This case is a political hot potato. Sir Charles Miller isn't short of enemies, also in very high places. Feelings are bound to be running high . . . a poor old boy knocked down and killed by a rich man's son. If we clear Roger, there'll be screams of "Police cover up," and if we prove him guilty, well, it's no secret that Sir Charles can be a vindictive swine when he likes. He'd use every dirty trick to get back at the man who nailed his beloved boy. Each way we lose, so I'm having no part of it.'

Mullett sucked in his cheeks. It was time to exert his authority. 'What you want, or don't want, doesn't come into it, I'm afraid. By arrangement with the Chief Constable, Sir Charles Miller is calling here this morning. He has been promised that a senior officer will carry out this investigation, and that means you. I can't give it to a rank lower than inspector.'

Sir Charles calling here this morning! thought Allen. So that's why the virgin uniform has come out of mothballs. 'You don't have to give it to a rank lower than inspector. Give it to Frost.'

A scornful laugh. 'Frost? On a case as delicate as this?'

Allen moved nearer to the Superintendent and lowered his voice. 'Consider this, sir. If there's got to be a loser, Frost is the ideal man.' He paused, then added significantly, 'He's the one we can spare the most.'

Mullett chewed this over and liked the taste. A chance of getting rid of the troublesome Frost. It was tempting. Very tempting. But how could he possibly introduce that scarecrow to Sir Charles and claim he was the best they had. 'No way, Inspector. No way at all. I'm sorry. I'm ordering you to do it.'

Allen quietly produced the trump card he had been holding back for such an emergency. 'You know, sir, if the story were leaked to the press that a senior officer was taken off a serious rape case in order to try and clear an MP's spoiled brat of a son, it could be very nasty. Very nasty indeed.'

Mullett looked at Allen. Allen looked at Mullett. Mullett's look said, 'You wouldn't dare', Allen's said, 'Just try me.'

The Superintendent was the first to lower his gaze. He stood up and started to stride around the room, scratching his chin thoughtfully with his forefinger. He stopped as if struck by a brilliant thought and turned slowly to the inspector. 'Come to think of it, Allen, Frost would be the ideal choice. He's got bags of local knowledge, he's got, er . . .' He paused because he had run out of things to say in Frost's favour.

'He's got the George Cross,' said Allen.

The George Cross! Incredible but true. The previous year Frost had blundered into a hostage situation at Bennington's Bank, where an armed robber, high on drugs, was holding a gun on a woman and her baby. Believing the man was bluffing, Frost had tried to take the gun away, getting himself shot in the face for his pains but managing to overpower the robber in the process. For this he was awarded the George Cross, the civilian equivalent of the Victoria Cross. Frost rarely spoke about it, and the medal was jumbled up with other debris in one of the drawers of his untidy desk. But it would very much impress Sir Charles, thought Mullett . . . ! 'Yes, Sir Charles, one of my best men — he's got the George Cross, you know.' He smiled at Allen. 'Yes, Frost is definitely the best man for this job.'

Allen took his leave hurriedly before Mullett changed his mind. Mullett dashed back to his office and told Miss Smith to get out the best coffee cups. Only the best was good enough for Sir Charles Miller.

Frost was at his desk, rummaging through mounds of paper like a housewife searching for bargains at a jumble sale. He didn't find any bargains, only the overtime returns and the crime statistics which should have gone off the previous night. He piled them on top of the other papers in his in tray. Somehow or other he would have to find time to do them. He picked up the latest burglary report, and skimmed through it, ready to lay it to rest with all the others in the filing cabinet.

> Householder's name: *Lil Carey (Mrs)*
> Address: *26 Sunford Road, Denton*
> Scene of crime (if different from address above): *As above.*
> List of goods (not money) taken (with approx. value): *Nil*
> Value of cash taken: £79

At first glance it appeared little different from all the others. A quick in-and-out job with seventy-nine pounds in cash being taken. The thieves always took cash — it was instantly negotiable, it couldn't be traced and it made the task of the police almost impossible. Frost sniffed. He knew Lil Carey. She was an unregistered money lender, lending out small sums of money, usually to housewives, at exorbitant interest rates. She'd never miss seventy-nine pounds. He wished the thieves had got away with more. But then he realized the '£' had been scratched through by the reporting officer and the word 'sovereigns' added. Seventy-nine sovereigns! Frost wasn't sure of the current rate for sovereigns, but that quantity must surely be worth much more than four thousand pounds for the gold content alone; even more if they were

Victorian and in mint condition. He stuffed the report in his pocket. They would call on old mother Carey this morning without fail.

The door was kicked open and Webster entered with the two cups of tea, his expression making it quite clear how much he relished being asked to perform these menial tasks.

'Thanks, son,' muttered Frost, who had learned that it was best to ignore the constable's repertoire of frowns, scowls, and grimaces. He disturbed the mud of sugar with his ballpoint pen and took a sip. 'Tastes like cat's pee.' He swivelled in his chair. 'Something important we had to do this morning. For the life of me I can't remember what it was.'

'The dead man in the toilets. You had to break the news.'

'That was it!' exclaimed Frost.

'Mr Dawson phoned,' Webster told him.

'Dawson?' Frost screwed up his face. 'Who's he?'

'The father of the missing schoolgirl. He wanted to know if there was any news. I told him we'd circulated her description.'

Frost nodded. 'Ah yes. Young, clean-cut, clean-shaven Karen. If she doesn't turn up soon, I'll have to try and sneak a chat with the mother without the father being present. There are one or two things about Karen that don't quite add up.' His attention was caught by a note in his own writing which he had circled in red as important. He studied it with a puzzled frown. 'PM 10.00? We're not expecting Mrs Thatcher are we?'

'The post-mortem,' explained Webster wearily.

Frost tipped the remainder of his tea into the waste bin and reached for his mac. 'Life is one round of constant pleasure. Come on, son, we mustn't be late.'

There was a brisk knock at the door. 'Not today, thank you,' called Frost.

The door opened and Mullett walked in. His expression didn't indicate that his life was one round of constant pleasure. Frost quickly pulled the crime statistics from his in-tray and put them in the centre of his desk as if he were working on them. 'Sorry, Super. Didn't know it was you.'

Mullett gazed stiffly around the room. What a shambles the place was. Piles of paper everywhere, even on the window ledge, where the piles were held down by unwashed teacups. There were even salted peanuts and bits of potato crisp dotted around the floor. 'This office is a mess, Inspector. An utter and disgusting mess!'

'We were just about to tidy it up as you knocked, sir,' lied Frost cheerfully. 'Shift the muck off that chair, son, so the Super can sit down.'

Webster removed the dog-eared stack of files, looked for somewhere to put them, then decided his own desk top was the only free space. He offered the chair to the Superintendent who declined it with a disdainful sniff. He wasn't going to risk his brand-new uniform on that. His eye caught sight of the overtime returns in Frost's in-tray. 'Some talk of the men not getting their overtime payments for last month, Frost.'

'Yes,' agreed Frost. 'It's that bloody computer. It's always going wrong.' He stared Mullett out, then remembered the busy morning he had planned. 'Have you just come in to give me a bollocking, sir, or is it something important? I've got a hell of a lot to do. They're filleting Ben Cornish down at the morgue in half an hour.'

'I've something more important for you than that,' snapped Mullett. 'Roger Miller . . . the hit-and-run. I'm putting you in charge of the investigation.'

'Right, Super,' said Frost. 'I'll have the little bastard put away for you, don't you worry.'

Mullett gritted his teeth and wished he hadn't let Allen talk him into this. 'You don't understand, Frost,' he said, and told him just what was expected of him.

Sergeant Johnson, the duty station sergeant for the day shift, had been down to the cells to check on the occupants. He was irritated to find that Frost had let Wally Peters stay the night, with the inevitable result. The cell was being hosed down now.

'Mr Frost!' he yelled sternly as Webster and the inspector cut across the lobby on their way to the car park.

'Yes, Johnny?' called Frost from the door.

'We've got a friend of yours downstairs. He's piddling all over the floor and stinking the place out.'

Frost's face creased in mock perplexity. 'What is Mr Mullett doing down there?' he asked.

WEDNESDAY DAY SHIFT (2)

He hovered in the hall, by the letter box, waiting, and as soon as the boy pushed the newspaper through he grabbed it, opening it up to the headlines. The big story was COACH CRASH HORROR — FIVE KILLED! Nothing about the attack. He turned from page to page, his eyes racing over the various headlines. Nothing. Back to the front page. And there he found it. Four blurred lines of stop-press squeezed as an afterthought down in the bottom right-hand corner. *Woman attacked in Denton Woods. A woman was assaulted and raped late last night in Denton Woods. Police are looking for a man believed to have carried out similar assaults in the area over the past few months.*

Four lines! He felt like crying. It was so unfair. Part of his pleasure was reading about it afterward. Sometimes the papers included an interview with the girl in which she described her terror at what had happened. He loved reading about it. It made him feel excited all over again.

Four lines. Four miserable little lines. And the paper was lying this time. It said he had raped her. He hadn't. He couldn't. He had picked her because he thought she was a young, untouched schoolgirl. But she was a tart. A dirty bitch with painted breasts who sold herself to men and was probably crawling with disease. She'd even tried to pick him up two nights before. The cow, the slag. Wearing those clothes to lure him on.

He screwed up the paper and hurled it to the floor, then

went into the bedroom and took the well-thumbed book from its hiding place. Time was running out. He would try again tonight. For a young one. He opened the book and started to read.

They had arranged the unpleasant jobs in this order: first, the call on Mrs Cornish to break the news about her son, Ben; second, the post-mortem. But for Frost, arrangements were made to be broken. There was another call he now wanted to make first. 'A quick diversion, son,' he said, pulling the burglary report from his pocket and filling Webster in on Lil Carey and her sovereigns. 'Could be the break we're looking for with these petty robberies. Shouldn't take us more than a couple of minutes.'

Webster looked at his wristwatch. There was no way they were going to make the post-mortem in time. They were late already, and here was Frost making yet another detour.

'Pull up there, son. By the lamppost.'

Sunford Street was a row of dreary-looking terraced houses. Out of the car, across the pavement, and they were in the porch of number 26, a house even drearier-looking than its neighbours. Frost hammered away at the knocker. They heard low, shuffling footsteps from within, then a harsh female voice demanding to know who they were.

'Jack the Ripper and Dr Crippen,' called Frost through the letter box. 'Come on, Lil, open up. You know bloody well who we are. You've been giving us the eyeball through the curtains ever since we pulled up.'

The clanking of chains being unhooked, keys turned and bolts drawn, then the door creaked open. Facing them was a small, wiry old dear wearing a moth-eaten fur coat over a too-long nightdress, the bottom of which was black with dirt where it constantly dragged over the floor. Her ensemble was topped by an ill-fitting, ill-suited brown nylon wig in a Shirley Temple bubble style; it wobbled and threatened to fall off each time she moved her head. Her face was knee-deep in make-up, the cheeks rouged like a clown's. She was at least seventy years old and possibly much nearer eighty.

'Tell your mummy the cops are here,' said Frost.

'Never mind the jokes,' she retorted. 'Where was you while I was being robbed?'

'Paddling in pee down a toilet,' answered Frost. 'Can we come in, Lil?'

She took them into the front downstairs room, a cold, damp little box packed tight with heavily carved, gloomy furniture treacled with dark-oak varnish. In the centre of the room a knock-kneed table sagged under the weight of bundles of ancient newspapers tied with string. A piano, complete with candle holders, cringed sulkily in a corner; it, too, carried more than its fair share of bundled newspapers. The one window was hidden by thick, dusty velvet curtains, tightly drawn so that passers-by couldn't get a glimpse of the treasures within.

Frost thumbed through one of the yellowing newspapers. 'Looks as if Mr Atlee's going to win the election,' he said. He pushed it away. 'Right, Lil, so what happened?'

'You know what happened, Inspector,' she said, the wig wobbling furiously. 'I put it all down in that form. It's all rotten forms these days. Soon you'll have to fill up a form to go to the lavatory.'

'I fill up a bucket myself,' murmured Frost. 'My hairy colleague can't read, Lil, so tell him what happened.'

She gave Webster a searching look and decided he just might be worthy of her confidence. 'You listen, young man, because I'm only saying this once.'

The day before, she had travelled to Felby, a town some fifteen miles away, to visit her sick sister. She left the house at three, catching the 3.32 train from Denton Station. A few minutes before leaving she had checked that the sovereigns were safe. She was indoors again by ten o'clock that night but, tired out after the journey, went straight to bed.

'If I'd known my life's savings had been stolen, I wouldn't have slept a wink,' she said. 'First thing after breakfast I went to the hiding place and I nearly had a seizure on the spot. The tin was empty — all the money I had scraped and saved for, my little nest egg, my burial money — all gone. They should bring back hanging.'

Poor old girl, thought Webster. 'Where did you keep the tin?'

'In the piano.' She waddled to the corner, removed two piles of newspapers and opened the piano top, then, standing on tiptoe, plunged her hand into the depths. With a twanging of strings, she pulled out a biscuit tin decorated with pictures of King George V and Queen Mary. This she opened, holding it out by the lid to demonstrate its complete emptiness.

'It's empty, all right,' agreed Frost. 'I've never seen a tin more empty. Who else knew where you kept it hidden?'

'No-one!' she said.

'The thief knew,' said Frost.

'Was anything else taken?' asked Webster.

She wobbled the wig from side to side. 'No, thank God. I've checked everywhere. Just my seventy-nine golden sovereigns.'

'What sort of sovereigns, Lil?' asked Frost.

'They were all Queen Victoria,' she answered. 'My old mother, God rest her soul, left them to me on her deathbed.'

'Would you know them if you saw them again?'

'I know every mark, every scratch on them. I'd know them as if they were my own children — and I miss them as much as if they were.' She dabbed her eyes and trumpeted loudly into a large handkerchief which looked as if it, too, dated from Queen Victoria's time — and hadn't been washed since. The wig slipped down over one eye.

'And the tin was put back again in the piano?'

She nodded.

Frost prodded his scar. The same old pattern, a quick in-and-out job, but this time the thief knew exactly what he was after and where to find it. So how did he get in? The window, perhaps?

He squeezed past the table and pulled back the curtain, then tried to open the sash window. It wouldn't budge. Early in its life it had been thickly painted with cream paint which had seeped over the catch to seal it tight. So the thief didn't get in that way. More than likely he came in through the front door.

The front door almost wilted under the weight of the hardware attached to it — bolts, bars, and various heavy-linked security chains. But none of these could be applied from the outside, and when Lil went to visit her sister, all that had secured the door was the door lock. It looked solid enough, but, as in many of these old houses, the pattern was such that the lock could easily be snapped back with a flexible piece of plastic.

'Odds are he got in through this door,' he told Webster, 'but you'd better take a look around the rest of the house in case there's any sign of forced entry.' He gave the old dear a grin. 'You'd better go with him, Lil, in case he pinches any-thing. You know what sticky fingers we cops have.'

Webster didn't think it at all funny, especially as Lil took the remark seriously and followed him suspiciously through every room of the house.

Left on his own, Frost quickly began opening drawers and peering inside. Then he lifted the bundles of newspaper off the piano lid so he could get to the keyboard. Lying on the yellowed keys were various bank-deposit books, post-office savings accounts, and building-society savings books. He quickly thumbed through them to see how much money the poor old dear had. That done, he shuffled through a wad of family-allowance books kept together by a thick rubber band. These were at the other end of the keyboard. He was pre-vented from studying these in detail as he heard footsteps descending the stairs. Quickly, he replaced everything where he found it, moved to the window, and put on his most innocent expression.

Webster had found no signs of forced entry, but he was shocked at the poverty-stricken conditions in which the old lady lived. The bedroom was a horror with no heating, bare boards on the floor, and old coats on the bed instead of blankets.

They knocked on a few doors, but none of the neighbours

would admit to seeing anyone suspicious lurking about the house the previous day. There was little else they could do, apart from Lil's suggestion that they should inform Interpol.

The biscuit tin was dropped into a plastic bag to be tested back at the station for alien prints, and then it was time to go. She saw them out, plucking at Frost's arm as he was about to leave. 'Please get my money back for me, Mr Frost.'

Frost shrugged. 'If we can, Lil, but we've got a lousy track record. We haven't recovered a penny of anyone's money up to now.'

With her lower lip quivering she looked pathetically at Frost, as if he had told her that her entire family had been wiped out in an air crash.

'It was my burial money,' she said, blinking hard to hold back the mascara-streaking tears.

Webster felt choked-up as he slid into the driving seat. 'Poor cow,' he said. 'I feel so sorry for her . . . and you should see the rest of the house. She probably hasn't got two half-pennies to rub together.'

'You should see her bank book,' said Frost. 'She's got at least twenty thousand quid in the building society, fifteen thousand in the bank, and God knows how much more in her other accounts.'

'You're joking!' exclaimed Webster.

'I'm not, son. I had a little nose around while you and she were up to no good in her bedroom. Years ago she used to carry out back-street abortions — fifty bob a time, including a cup of tea and a digestive biscuit afterward. She was known as the "Fifty Shilling Tailor." If it weren't for Lil and her crochet hook we'd be suffering from a population explosion. But as soon as the government made abortions legal she went over to money lending . . . short-period loans at exorbitant rates of interest to people desperate for ready cash — house-wives who've spent the housekeeping on Bingo and don't want their old man to know, loan club organizers with sticky fingers. She also makes loans to young people behind on their HP payments, usually taking their family-allowance books as security. There was a wad of them in her piano. You needn't get your beard wet with tears over her, my little hairy son.'

Time was hurtling on. The visit to Mrs Cornish would have to wait until after they had attended the post-mortem on her son. Webster broke all speed records driving to the mortuary, pulling up with a screech behind a Rolls-Royce hearse, all agleam with black and silver like Mullett's new uniform.

Out of the Cortina, up a slope and through double doors into a small lobby where the notice on the wall read *All undertakers to report to porter before removing bodies.* At the inquiry counter two undertaker's assistants in funeral black were arguing with a little bald-headed mortuary attendant who was firmly shaking his head as he thumbed through the papers they had presented to him.

'But I keep telling you,' the exasperated undertaker was saying, 'the bloody funeral is in an hour. We're burying him at twelve.'

'Don't you swear at me,' said the attendant, drawing himself up to his full height. 'Without the death certificate you're burying bugger all!'

'Excuse me,' said Frost, elbowing his way through like a referee parting two boxers. He showed his warrant card. 'I'm here for the Cornish post-mortem.'

The attendant craned his neck up at the clock. 'You're a bit late, Inspector.'

'Don't tell me it's started?' asked Frost.

'Nearly finished, I think. You know how punctual Dr Bond is. He don't sod about.'

They pushed through another set of double doors into the white chill of the green-tiled autopsy room, where a sharp antiseptic smell held a cloying aftertaste of something nasty.

A sheeted trolley stood against the wall to the left of the entrance doors. Frost twitched back the sheet and looked down on the blue, shrivelled, waxen face of an old lady. 'Sorry, love,' he murmured gently, covering her. 'I thought you were someone I knew.'

At the far end of the room a rubber-aproned mortuary

attendant in abattoir-style Wellington boots was hosing down
the guttered and perforated top of a post-mortem operating
table. Water suddenly overflowed as something blocked one
of the drains, but the assistant cleared the blockage with his
finger and carried on with his work. Webster shuddered to
think what the blockage was caused by. Frost tapped the
attendant on the shoulder. 'The Ben Cornish post-mortem?'

'All over,' said the attendant, too engrossed in his work to
stop. 'The pathologist has gone, but Dr Slomon's in the office
waiting to see you.'

In the office Slomon was pacing up and down, very agitated and worried. As soon as Frost entered, he dashed over
and grabbed him by the arm. 'Thank goodness you are here,
Inspector.' His worry increased when he saw Webster. 'Who
is this?'

Frost introduced his assistant. Slomon hesitated. 'It's a bit
delicate,' he said, making it clear he wanted Webster to leave.

'If it's police business,' answered Frost, 'then he's in on it.'

Slomon compressed his lips, checked the hall to make sure
no eavesdroppers were hovering, then closed the door firmly.
He lowered his voice. 'We're in trouble, Inspector.'

'I'm always in trouble,' said Frost, finding himself a chair.
He didn't like the way the doctor had said '*We're* in trouble.'
His tone seemed to imply that Slomon was in trouble but
wanted Frost to share a large part of the blame. He listened
warily to what the man had to say.

'No-one could examine a body properly in the conditions
we had to cope with last night, Inspector. They were intolerable and if we missed anything it was through no fault of our
own. It's important that we each stress that fact in our reports. People are always too ready to point the accusing finger.'

Now Frost was really worried. What the hell had they
missed last night? 'What did the post-mortem show, Doc?'

'Come with me.' Slomon took Frost's arm and steered him
into the adjoining storage area, with its neatly tagged refriger-
ated units set into the wall like filing-cabinet drawers. 'Where
are the frozen peas?' asked Frost. Slomon was in no mood for

jokes. He tugged at one of the drawers, and a body, smoking with curling wisps of frozen carbon dioxide, slid silently forward on rollers.

The haggard, strangely clean face of Ben Cornish stared up, horrified as if in protest at the indignities the post-mortem had subjected him to. 'Look at this!' Slomon indicated a nasty-looking green-tinged bruise in the area below the corpse's left eye.

Puzzled, Frost crouched over the body. 'How come we didn't spot this last night, Doc? It looks so bloody obvious now.'

'Last night,' explained Slomon, 'he was covered with filth and vomit. This only came to light when the body was stripped and washed clean. There was no way I could have spotted it.'

He pulled the sheet down to expose the torso and upper legs. The dead man's right arm was one angry mass of suppurating sores where he had been injecting himself. The chest and abdomen were vividly slashed with extensive autopsy wounds, which had been crudely restitched after flaps of flesh had been torn back to facilitate the removal of internal organs from the stomach cavity. The flesh of the stomach was one massive, sprawling, yellowy-green bruise.

Slomon traced the bruised area with his finger. 'As you can see he was beaten up pretty badly just before he died.'

Frost's heart dropped down to his own stomach cavity. He was beginning to realize what was coming. 'Did a fist do this?'

'Not a fist,' replied Slomon. 'A boot. He was punched, knocked down, then, when he was helpless on the floor, his assailant brought up his foot and stamped with all his weight on the abdomen.'

Frost gritted his teeth and winced. He could feel the pain shooting across his own stomach. But Slomon hadn't finished. From a stainless-steel cabinet in the corner he brought over two sealed specimen jars containing a mass of mangled human offal half immersed in a bloodied liquid. The sight of it made Webster flinch, and his stomach gave one or two protesting churns, but Slomon lectured dispassionately as if to students. 'As you can see, his liver has virtually exploded. In the whole of my professional career I have never seen such terrible internal injuries. Further, the blows actually split the pancreas, and the main blood vessel to the heart is torn. Really shocking injuries.'

'And that's what killed him, Doc?' Frost asked, fearful that the sheet might be pulled down to reveal further horrors.

'They would have killed him,' answered Slomon. 'In fact there is no way he could have recovered from such injuries. However, the initial blows to the abdomen caused the expulsion of the stomach contents. He choked on his own vomit, so, to my credit, in spite of the appalling conditions, my diagnosis was perfectly correct.'

To your credit? thought Frost. No-one comes out of this with any credit, Slomon. He stuck his hands deeply into his mac pockets and swore softly to himself. Why the hell wasn't any of this spotted last night? Damn bloody Slomon for not wanting to get his feet wet, and damn my own bloody incompetence. I was so keen to get away to that lousy party, I bungled the investigation. I should have insisted Slomon do a proper job.

'I don't want the body touched further,' he said. 'It'll have to be photographed. I'll send one of our blokes down . . . and I'll need his clothes for forensic examination.' He looked again at the dead face and then recalled the scene in the toilet the previous night. The cubicle with the splintered door. He could picture the scene. Ben cowering inside in terror while his assailant kicked the door down, then dragged him out and stamped him to death. He draped the sheet over the dead face and pushed the drawer firmly shut. 'Come on, son,' he said. 'Work to do.'

'Don't forget to emphasise in your report that we did everything possible last night,' called Slomon as they were leaving. Frost waved a vague hand. He would report exactly what happened, nothing more, nothing less. He had no doubt that Slomon's report would dump all the blame on the police, but he hadn't time to play such games.

They pushed through the swing doors and out into the

mortuary lobby, where a side door had been opened to allow the two undertakers to carry a coffined body straight through to the waiting Rolls-Royce hearse. Behind his desk the mortuary attendant was booking out the corpse and adjusting his stock records. He was whistling happily as if someone had tipped him a fiver. There was no sign of the death certificate on his clipboard.

Outside the air smelled marvellously fresh and untainted. As they waited for the hearse to move away, Frost said, 'Why would anyone want to do that to a poor old sod like Ben?'

'Robbery,' suggested Webster.

'He had bugger all to pinch,' said Frost.

'Drugs?' was Webster's next suggestion. 'Another drug addict wanted Ben's heroin so he killed him for it?'

For a few seconds Frost stared into space. Webster wondered if he had been listening, but then Frost turned and said, 'I've been bloody stupid, son. I knew I'd missed something.'

'What?' Webster asked.

'His carrier bag. That's where he kept all his worldly possessions — food, odds and ends, his hypodermic. He was never without it. But it wasn't with his body last night. Whoever killed him took it.'

He drummed his fingers on the dashboard, then leaned over for the handset and called Johnny Johnson at the station. He wanted to know if Wally Peters was still in the cells.

'No, thank God,' was the reply. 'We kicked him out half an hour ago. Now we've got all the windows open, and we're burning sulphur candles and scratching like mad.'

'I want him brought in,' ordered Frost. 'Get the word out to all units.'

'Brought in, Jack? Why?'

'We've just come from the post-mortem. Ben Cornish was murdered.'

'Murdered?' gasped Johnson. 'Why would anyone want to murder him?'

'Probably for the few bits and pieces in his carrier bag,'

replied Frost. 'It's missing . . . and Wally was seen lurking about outside those toilets last night. So I want him.'

'Right,' said Johnny. 'Consider it done. By the way, Jack, you won't be long, will you? Mr Mullett's got Sir Charles Miller, his son, and his solicitor sitting in his office, all craving an audience with you about the hit-and-run.'

'Flaming hell!' cried Frost, 'I forgot about them. We're on our way — shouldn't be more than ten minutes.'

He replaced the handset. 'Back to the station, son.' Webster reminded him they hadn't yet called on Ben Cornish's family. 'Hell,' said Frost wearily, 'we'll have to do that first.' As they were on their way to the house, he remembered that he had meant to ask Tom Croll some more questions about the Coconut Grove robbery while they were at the hospital. His finger gave his scar a bashing. There was so much to be done, and he didn't seem to be getting through any of it.

Then he saw her. 'Stop the car!'

Webster slammed on the brakes and the car squealed to a halt.

A young girl in school uniform was looking into the window of a dress shop. Frost's hand was moving toward the door handle when the girl turned and stared directly at him.

She was blonde, wore glasses, and looked nothing like Karen Dawson.

'Drive on, son,' said Frost.

WEDNESDAY DAY SHIFT (3)

Frost banged the knocker a couple of times. This started a chain reaction of noise from inside the house. A dog barked, setting off a baby's crying. Footsteps thudded down uncarpeted stairs; a sharp, angry shout followed by a yelp from the dog, then the front door opened.

'Police,' said Frost. He didn't have to show his warrant card. Danny Cornish knew him of old.

Danny didn't look at all like his brother. Four years

younger, stockily built, he had thick black hair and bright red cheeks which betrayed the family's gypsy origins. His meaty hand was hooked in the collar of a black-and-brown mongrel dog whose immediate ambition seemed to be to sink his teeth into the throats of the two policemen.

Webster stepped back a couple of paces as the dog's jaws snapped at air. Frost was looking warily at Danny, whose face reflected the savagery and hatred of the dog and who seemed all too ready to let his hand slip from the collar. The mongrel, almost foaming at the mouth, was getting more and more frantic as its efforts to rip the callers to pieces were frustrated.

One eye on the mongrel, his foot ready to kick, Frost said, 'You'd better let us in, Danny. It's about your brother.'

The man cuffed the dog. It stopped barking but, instead, began making menacing noises at the back of its throat, its lip quivering and curling back to expose yellow, pointed teeth.

'Ben? What's he done now?'

'Don't let the bleeders in.' Behind him, advancing out of the dark of the passage, they could see a young woman, not much more than nineteen. She carried a ten-month-old baby, its squalling almost drowning the snarls from the near-apoplectic dog. This was Jenny, Danny Cornish's common-law wife, once pretty, now hard-faced, her features twisted with hate.

His head snapped around to her. 'Shove it, for Christ's sake. And keep that bloody kid quiet!' His angry tone caused the infant to howl even louder, and this, in turn, spurred the mongrel on to greater efforts. Cornish yanked its collar and dragged the animal down the passage where he slung it out into the back yard. As he slammed the door shut, there was a resounding thud as the dog hurled itself against it, trying to get back in.

'In here.' He took them into more noise — a small kitchen where a whistling kettle on a gas ring was spitting steam and screaming for attention in competition with a transistor radio blasting pop music at top volume. Favouring neither, he pulled the kettle from the ring and snapped off the radio.

At the sink a gaunt, straight-backed woman of sixty, hair

and eyes jet black, a cigarette dangling from her lips, was methodically dicing vegetables with a lethal-looking knife. She didn't look up as they entered.

'It's the police, Ma,' said Danny. 'About Ben.'

She turned, hostile and belligerent, then she seemed to read something in Frost's face. Carefully, she set the knife down on the draining board, then wiped her hands on her skirt. 'Sit down if you want to,' she said.

They sat at the stained kitchen table with its cover of old newspapers. Frost fiddled for his cigarettes. He needed a smoke to bolster his courage.

Webster's foot was nudging something. A large cardboard box tucked out of sight under the table. He bent and lifted it up. An unpacked VHS video recorder. He looked at the man. 'I suppose you've got a receipt for this.'

Frost winced. 'For Christ's sake, son, there's a time and a place . . .'

But he was too late to stop Danny from snatching an old Oxo tin from the dresser and emptying the contents out on the table in front of the detective constable. 'Yes, I have got a receipt.' He scrabbled amongst odd pieces of paper, then, in triumph, stuck a printed form under Webster's nose. 'Here it is. You'd better check it in case it's a forgery.'

Webster took the receipt, read it briefly, then handed it back. 'I'm sorry.'

'Sorry you haven't caught us out, you mean?' The receipt was stuffed back in the Oxo tin. 'Now say what you've got to say and get the hell out of here.'

Stone-faced, Webster stared out through the uncurtained kitchen window into the back yard, which was strewn with parts of a dismantled motorbike. The dog had given up trying to break down the door and was nosing a mound of rusted tins. The nonstop wailing of the baby filtered through from the passage.

'It's about Ben, Ma,' Frost said softly.

'That shit,' Danny snarled. 'He's caused enough pain and misery in this house. If you've nicked him, you can lock the door and throw away the key as far as I'm concerned.'

Frost got up from his chair and offered it to the woman. 'You'd better sit down, love.'

She shook her head. 'Just say your piece, then go.'

Frost took a deep breath. 'He's dead, Mrs Cornish. I'm very sorry.'

She stood stock still, then felt for the chair and sat down. 'He died last night,' Frost added.

Danny put a hand on his mother's shoulder, but she shrugged it off. 'How did he die? Drugs?'

There was no way of tarting up the facts in fancy clothes. Frost told them about the beating, and how Ben had choked on his own stomach contents.

The woman's face showed no sign of emotion. 'In a public lavatory?' she repeated tonelessly. 'He couldn't even die decently.'

'Good bloody riddance,' said her son.

Frost lowered his eyes to the newspaper covering the table. 'We're trying to trace his movements up to the time he died. When did you see him last?' Out of the corner of his eye he thought he saw Danny and his mother start at the question and exchange a look of guilt. But it was over so quickly he could have been mistaken.

'We hadn't seen him for months, and we didn't want to,' said the man. His mother nodded her agreement.

Why don't I believe you? thought Frost. 'Did he have any enemies who might want to cause him harm?'

Danny laughed scoffingly. 'Enemies? Has a dog got fleas? He'd lie, cheat, or steal to get money for his drugs. He didn't give a damn who he hurt in the process. He had enemies in this house, Inspector, and I, for one, am glad he's dead.'

'So am I,' said the mother, but her eyes were fixed on a photograph pinned to the dresser shelf, a photograph of a much younger version of herself, smiling happily, holding the hand of a small, serious-faced boy of about four or five. The boy was clutching a wooden fire engine. Sensing she was being observed, she tore her eyes away and heaved herself up out of the chair. 'You'll have to excuse me. I've got work to do.' At the kitchen door she paused. 'We don't want him back here. The state can bury him. He's caused us enough pain and misery.' The door closed behind her.

Frost squashed out his cigarette in a saucer. 'We'll need someone to do a formal identification,' he told Danny.

'Sod that,' was the reply. 'You don't get me looking at dead bodies.'

Frost stood up wearily. 'It's got to be done, Danny. It'll only take a couple of minutes.' He signalled to Webster that it was time to leave.

'I'll think about it,' mumbled Danny as he ushered them to the front door.

From one of the upstairs rooms, Frost thought he could hear a woman crying, but, again, he couldn't be certain.

'Thank God that's over,' said Frost, grunting as they climbed back into the Cortina. Webster shifted about in the driving seat trying to make himself comfortable. All he seemed to be doing of late was climbing in and out of this battered car, listening to Frost droning his inanities.

'Where to?' he asked mechanically. God, he was tired. It had been days since he'd had any proper sleep.

'The lavatories where Ben was killed,' answered Frost. 'We should have gone there first — people have been peeing all over the evidence since eight o'clock this morning.'

Webster reminded him that the Divisional Commander was expecting him at the station to see the MP and his son.

Frost gave his forehead a wallop with his palm. 'Flaming rectums. Mullett will never forgive me for keeping dear old Sir Charlie-boy waiting. Right, son, this is what we'll do. I'll drop you off at the toilets. Turf everyone out whether they're finished or not, and seal the place off. Then search it from top to bottom for any sign of Ben's carrier bag, or blood or anything I should have spotted last night. And radio the station for a scene-of-crime officer to help. He can take photographs of the graffiti and dust the toilet seats for fingerprints. I'll drive on to the station for the hit-and-run interview. Remind me when we meet up that we've got that other security guard to interview about the robbery — the one Harry Baskin duffed up. Oh, and remind me about seeing Karen Dawson's mother.'

Webster nodded wearily. He would never get used to Frost's method of working. Webster liked order and forward planning. Frost seemed to thrive on chaos, lurching from one crisis to the next. He considered reminding the inspector that they still hadn't started on the overtime returns, let alone finished the crime statistics, but what was the point?

Frost shouldered through the swing doors of the lobby carrying, in a large polythene bag, the filthy, vomit-sodden clothes removed from Ben Cornish.

'Bought yourself a new suit, Jack?' called Johnny Johnson. 'I must say it's an improvement on the one you're wearing.'

'It's cleaner, anyway,' said Frost, holding the bag under Johnny's nose and watching him recoil. 'I might do a swap.' As he swung off to his office to make out the forensic examination request, the sergeant, reaching for the phone, called him back.

'Mr Mullett's been screaming for you for the past half hour. He wanted to know the minute you arrived.'

'I can't think what's keeping the inspector, Sir Charles,' said Mullett for the sixth time, his lips aching from the effort of maintaining the false smile. His phone rang. He snatched it up. 'What? No, don't send him in. I'll be right out.' He expanded the smile. 'Mr Frost has just arrived, Sir Charles. If you'll excuse me, I'll pop out and brief him.'

As he passed through his outer office he instructed Miss Smith to make some more coffee. Strong this time. He felt he would need it.

Even before he reached the lobby he could hear Frost's raucous laughter bellowing down the corridor. And there he was, slouched over the counter, exchanging coarse comments with the station sergeant, completely indifferent to keeping his Divisional Commander, and an important VIP, waiting.

'Your office, please, Inspector,' ordered Mullett brusquely, marching down the passage. When he reached Frost's office he was extremely annoyed to find that he was alone and that he had to stand there, fuming, until Frost had finished relating some anecdote to the sergeant.

'We've been waiting for you, Inspector. For over half an hour. Sir Charles Miller, his son, and his solicitor. I specifically told you they were coming. I specifically asked you to be present . . .'

Frost wriggled uncomfortably in his chair. He hated Mullett's bawlings out. He always had such difficulty keeping a straight face. As Mullett burbled on, Frost spotted a pencilled note on his desk telling him that Mrs Clare Dawson wanted to speak to him about her missing daughter. His hand was reaching out for the phone when he realized that Mullett was still in full flow, so he adjusted his face to a contrite expression and tried to form a mental picture of the luscious Clare Dawson, all warm, creamy, and bouncy in a topless bikini, her sensuous lips parted, her tongue flicking over them . . . A strange silence. He switched his ears back on. Mullett had stopped speaking and was leaning back, ready to receive Frost's grovelling apologies.

'Sorry, Super, but something more important turned up.'

Mullett's mouth opened, poised to demand what could possibly be more important than a summons from one's Divisional Commander, when Frost continued.

'That stiff I found last night . . .'

'The tramp?' asked Mullett. 'In the public convenience?' He wrinkled his nose in disgust, his expression indicating that he held Frost personally responsible for the fact that the body had been found in such unsavoury surroundings.

Frost nodded. 'It now looks as if he was murdered. The autopsy shows he was beaten up and his stomach jumped on while he was on the floor. You should have seen his internal organs. The doc reckons his liver had exploded.'

The mental picture of an exploded liver made Mullett shudder. This case was getting more and more unsavoury by the minute. He gritted his teeth and listened as Frost filled him in on the details, including a graphic, stomach-churning description of the human offal floating in the specimen jars.

When, thankfully, Frost had finished, he was forced to admit that, under police rules, a murder inquiry took priority over everything else.

Frost offered a little prayer of thanks to Ben Cornish for getting himself murdered and saving him from a grade-A bollocking. But Mullett wasn't going down without a fight.

'What I don't understand, Inspector, is why none of these facts emerged last night. It's now more than twelve hours since the body was found, and we have no photographs of the body, no forensic examination of the surroundings, and only now is a search being made for the missing carrier bag. The question I have to ask myself is whether you are competent to be trusted with a murder inquiry, even one as hopeless as this.'

'The body was blocking the urinal drain,' Frost explained patiently. 'The place was flooded. When you're up to your armpits in cold wee you're inclined not to be as thorough as you might be. To add to the fun, he'd spewed up all over himself.' As proof, he heaved the polythene bag of clothes under Mullett's nose.

'All right, all right,' pleaded Mullett, queasily waving the white flag. 'We'll talk about it later.'

The internal phone rang. Frost answered it, then handed it to the Commander. 'Your secretary.'

Miss Smith reminding him that Sir Charles was getting restless.

'Make some more coffee,' said Mullett. 'We're on our way.' Then he saw Frost's shoes. Scuffed, unpolished, and water-stained from the previous night's adventures. If there had been time he would have insisted that Frost repolish them and give his suit a thorough brushing. But there wasn't time. Sir Charles would have to take him, crumpled suit, unpolished shoes, warts, and all. But he made Frost put the polythene bag down.

The cleaners hadn't found time to clean up the briefing room because Mullett had commandeered them for his own office, which now sparkled and gleamed and reeked of polish. Added to this was the rich smell of cigar smoke.

Sir Charles Miller, MP, buffed and gleaming from good living, sat in one of the blue moquette armchairs, which were reserved exclusively for important visitors, and glowered at his watch. He seemed singularly unimpressed with the nondescript scruff that the grinning-like-an-idiot Mullett introduced as Detective Inspector Frost. If this piece of rubbish was the best they had to offer . . .

'Sorry I'm late, Sir Charles,' breezed Frost. 'I was held up on a murder inquiry.'

'A murder inquiry?' exclaimed the MP, leaning forward with interest. 'How fascinating!'

Mullett pushed forward a hard chair. 'You'd better sit here, Inspector,' he intervened hastily, determined to stop Frost from enlarging on the unpleasant details. Then he pointedly placed a large glass ashtray within easy reach on the corner of his desk. No use telling Frost not to smoke. He'd do it anyway, and if there was nowhere to put his cigarette ends he was quite likely to drop them on the blue Wilton and crush them under his heel.

'It might be better if I explained to the inspector what this is all about,' said the MP, determined that things be run his way. Mullett nodded weakly.

Miller sucked hard on his cigar. 'I'll be brief, Inspector. Through no fault of his own, my son, Roger, has been involved in this nasty hit-and-run business. Roger wasn't driving; he wasn't even in the car, but, as you can imagine, my political opponents are sharpening their knives. You can picture the headlines: "Son of Law-and-Order MP Butchers Old-Age Pensioner in Hit and Run." Now, I'm not asking for special treatment just because I happen to be an MP. All I want is a fair and unbiased investigation.'

'You'd have got that anyway,' said Frost.

'I don't doubt that for one minute,' went on Miller in his sincere voice. 'Your Chief Constable, who happens to be a personal and very good friend of mine, has already assured me of that. My son, of his own free will, has come here to assist you in any way he can. The important thing is to prove his innocence so conclusively that we can scotch rumours before they have a chance to spread.'

There was the rasp of a match as Frost lit his fourteenth cigarette of the day. Mullett edged the ashtray forward to receive the spent match, but was too late. Frost's foot ground the carpet, and the smell of burning wool joined the other aromas.

The cigarette waggled in Frost's mouth as he spoke. 'If your son's innocent, I'll prove it, Sir Charles, but if he's guilty I'll prove that as well.'

'That's all I ask,' said the MP. 'Do your duty, Inspector.' A pause, then, slowly and significantly, he added, 'Clear my son and you won't find me lacking in gratitude.' Frost's eyes narrowed as the implication registered, but Mullett was up, steering him by the arm, and pushing him through the door before he could snap back.

'Roger Miller is in the interview room with his solicitor, Inspector. I want you to see him right away and let me know the outcome.'

Police Sergeant Johnny Johnson stilled his rumbling stomach as the wall clock told him he had another forty-nine minutes to go before he could take his lunch break. A breeze from the lobby doors as Jack Frost clattered through on his way to the interview room. The very man! He flagged him down.

'Mr Frost!'

Frost ambled over. 'I'm very busy, Johnny.'

'Too busy to notice the smell?'

Frost tested the air, then smiled. 'You've got Wally Peters for me?'

'He's down in the cells awaiting your pleasure.'

'I'll see him now,' said Frost forgetting all about Roger Miller. He turned toward the cells.

'Hold it. I've got stacks of messages for you.' He scooped up some notes. 'First, from Mr Baskin of The Coconut Grove. Wants to know what's the latest on his robbery.'

Frost took the note and, without reading it, screwed it into a ball and tossed it in the rubbish bin. 'If he phones again, tell him we're vigorously pursuing our inquiries. Next.'

The second note was passed over. 'A Mr Max Dawson asking if we'd found his daughter. He wants to see you.'

This note Frost put in his pocket. 'I'll fit it in as soon as Webster gets back. Any more?'

'Yes. Message from the hospital. Tommy Croll discharged himself this morning.'

Frost whistled softly. 'Did he leave a forwarding address — Las Vegas or the Bahamas?'

Johnny lowered his voice. 'You reckon Tommy nicked that money, then?'

'I sincerely hope he did,' replied Frost, scratching the back of his head. 'He's the only suspect I've got. Send a car round to his house and bring him in. Is that the lot?' Hopefully, he turned to go, but the sergeant had one last bullet to fire.

'Mr Gordon of County buzzed through. It seems that the absence of Denton Division's crime statistics is holding up the computer return for the entire county.'

Hell, thought Frost. When am I ever going to get the chance to do them? He went down the stairs to the cells.

The cell area had its own peculiar smell. From the drunk cell the stink of stale beer, urine, and vomit; from others the heady aroma of unwashed bodies, too-long-worn socks, and carbolic. But all of these well-established odours were fighting a losing battle with the unwashed Wally Peters. Frost paused outside the cell door, lit a cigarette, took his last lungful of nontoxic air, then marched in.

'Blimey, Wally,' he spluttered, 'you stink to high heaven!'

'I don't make personal remarks about you, Mr Frost,' retorted Wally huffily. He was seated on the edge of his bunk bed, huddled over an enamel mug from which he noisily sucked tea with much working of his Adam's apple. 'What am I here for?'

Frost rested his back against the painted brick wall. 'It's about Ben Cornish, Wally,' he said gravely. 'About what you did to him.'

Wally didn't even blink. He took the mug from his mouth and belched. 'I enjoyed that, Mr Frost.'

'I thought so from the sound effects, but what about Ben, Wally? You'd better tell me.'

Wally sniffed hard and looked up at the detective. 'You told me he choked to death, Inspector.'

'I was wrong, Wally. He was murdered. Beaten up and jumped on until he died.'

The tramp's lower jaw sagged and tea dribbled down the dirty grey stubble of his chin. 'Murdered?'

'That's right, Wally, and all his belongings pinched. What have you done with them?'

'I wouldn't hurt a fly, Mr Frost, you know that. And I wouldn't hurt Ben — we was mates. Murdered? God, I'm never going to sleep down them lavatories again.'

Frost flicked cigarette ash on the stone floor. 'You were hanging about there last night. Did you see anything?'

'Only that copper sniffing around.'

'When did you last see Ben?'

'Yesterday afternoon, about four o'clock down by the railway embankment. He was twitching and sweating and he kept clawing and scratching himself. He said he was going to meet some blokes down the toilets that evening who were going to sell him some drugs.'

'What blokes?'

'A couple of new blokes. He said they hadn't been in Denton very long.'

'And how was he going to pay for the stuff?'

'He said he thought he knew where he could get some money. He wouldn't tell me where, though. That was the last time I saw him, Mr Frost, on my dead mother's eyesight, I swear it.'

Frost shook a couple of cigarettes from his packet and gave them to the tramp. 'Thanks, Wally. You can go now if you like.'

'They're getting me a dinner, Mr Frost,' explained Wally. 'I'll go when I've had it. Thanks for the fags.'

'All part of the service,' said Frost, banging on the cell door to be let out. 'Tell your friends.'

Webster was waiting for him in the office. A search of the convenience and the surrounding area revealed no trace of anything like a plastic bag, full of Ben Cornish's odds and ends, or empty. The scene-of-the-crime officer had crawled over the premises and had probably found the fingerprints of everybody who had used the toilets since Queen Victoria's Jubilee, but none likely to be of any help.

Frost filled Webster in on Wally Peters and the claim that Ben Cornish intended to buy drugs from two new pushers. 'Get on to Drug Squad, son. I want to know about two new suppliers who are supposed to have come into the district recently. And ask them to check up on all known users with a history of violence — where they were between nine and eleven last night when Cornish was being killed.'

As he waited for Webster to finish the phone call, his internal phone buzzed. Control to report that the allegedly stolen Jaguar owned by Roger Miller had been found. Charlie Alpha had located it in a clearing to the east of Denton Woods. There was no doubt it had been involved in an accident. The near-side headlamp was missing, as was the front licence plate, and there were traces of blood all over the wing. Control had arranged for the vehicle to be towed in for a detailed examination. Frost thanked Control, then scribbled a note to remind himself to check whether or not the plastic screws from the Jaguar's licence plate had been recovered.

That done, he had a quick look into the Crime Statistics file in the vain hope that someone might have crept in during the night and finished it off for him. No such luck, so he dropped it back in the filing cabinet.

Webster finished his call to the drug squad. They were aware that two new pushers were operating in the district but had no details on them yet. They would also check on addicts with a history of violence but pointed out that all addicts could be driven to extreme violence when they were desperate.

Frost received the news gloomily. 'Trust them to complicate matters.' He pushed himself up from the desk. 'I think we'll sneak out and have some lunch now, son.'

Before they could move, Johnny Johnson looked around the door. 'You do know Roger Miller and his solicitor are waiting for you in the interview room, don't you, Jack?'

'Of course I know,' said Frost. 'We were just on our way to them, weren't we, son?'

It should have been possible to get from Frost's office to the interview room without a diversion, but Frost thought of one. They were turning the corner from the passage when he stopped, looked cautiously around to make sure they weren't being observed, then told Webster his suspicions about Dave Shelby. 'I'd like to know what he was doing, poking around those toilets, son. He said he saw the broken gate from his motor, but that's impossible. I spotted him stuffing something into his locker last night.'

Webster was unimpressed. 'It could have been anything.'

'Yes,' nodded Frost, 'but wouldn't it be interesting if it was Ben Cornish's plastic bag crammed full of heroin?' He plunged his hand into his jacket pocket and pulled out a large bunch of assorted keys. 'We could take a little look — just to satisfy our curiosity.'

Webster was horrified. 'You're going to search an officer's locker behind his back — without his permission? The Police Federation will go berserk.'

'I'm hoping they won't find out,' said Frost, sorting through the bunch for a suitable key.

Webster took a step back as if distancing himself from the insane act Frost was proposing. 'This is a murder inquiry. Even if you found any evidence, the court would tear you to pieces.'

Frost brushed these objections aside. 'If there's nothing there, then no harm's done. But if I do find something, I leave it where it is, I don't tell a soul what I've done, and I apply for a search warrant.' He moved toward the locker room, the bunch of keys jangling in his hand.

Webster didn't budge. 'I'm sorry, but I want no part of this.'

'Oh,' said Frost, crestfallen. 'I was hoping you'd be my lookout man.'

'No way,' said Webster firmly.

Frost's shoulders sagged. 'Fair enough, son. Can't say that I blame you. You don't want to get into any more trouble. Stay here, I shouldn't be long.' And he was off down the passage.

You'll be caught, you bloody fool, thought Webster. You'll be caught, and you'll be kicked out of the force, and it will serve you bloody right. 'Wait for me,' he called, hurrying after him.

Frost paused by the locker-room door, a relieved grin on his face. 'Thanks, son. All you have to do is stand outside. If anyone comes, just whistle.' A quick look up and down the passage, and he opened the door and slipped inside.

It was a room full of dove-grey metal lockers, standing shoulder to shoulder in rows. The locker with Shelby's name on it was about halfway down the left-hand wall. Ever the optimist, Frost tried the handle, but it was securely locked. He offered his selected key. It was too big even to fit into the lock. He tried another. This one slipped in easily enough, but it wouldn't turn. It was taking far longer than he'd thought. He sorted through the key ring and tried another.

Outside, leaning against the wall, his heart steam-hammering, Webster felt like the lookout man for a smash-and-grab job. He tried to look inconspicuous, but there was no reason for him to be there. The swing doors at the head of the corridor parted suddenly, and two uniformed men marched purposefully through, heading directly for the locker room. He puckered his lips and tried to whistle the warning, but his mouth was too dry. And the men were getting nearer. He fumbled at the door handle and jabbed his head inside the locker room. Frost was kneeling on the floor in front of Shelby's locker, working at one of his keys with a nail file, then testing it in the keyhole. He was unaware the door had opened.

'Inspector!' hissed Webster urgently.

Frost jumped up, and cracked his head painfully on the

protruding locker handle; the sound of the impact boomed like a drum, echoing on and on around the room.

Webster spun around. The two uniformed men walked straight past the door and out the back entrance to the car park.

'I don't think we're cut out for a life of crime,' said Frost, rubbing his head ruefully as Webster returned to his lookout post. He pushed the filed key into the lock. It clicked home. Carefully, he rotated it. Two more clicks. He turned the handle and pulled: the locker door swung open.

Shelby's overcoat swung from a hanger. His street shoes were on the locker floor. Next to the shoes, in a leather case, was an expensive Polaroid instant camera with auto-focus, flash, and delayed action. Frost patted the overcoat pockets. Something bulged. He dived his hand in and pulled out Shelby's driving gloves. Beginning to think it was all a waste of time, he poked his hand around the back of the overcoat to feel for the metal shelf at the rear of the cabinet. His fingers scrabbled blindly, exploring by touch. Nothing . . . nothing . . . something! A packet of some kind. Of heroin? He pulled it out so he could examine it.

A plastic wallet secured with an elastic band. He looked inside. Photographs. A wad of coloured photographs taken with the Polaroid and making full use of the flash and the delayed action. Shelby and various women. In various bedrooms. In various positions of the sexual act. Shelby liked to keep permanent records of his conquests.

A spluttering attempt at a whistle from outside. The door opened. 'Someone's coming,' hissed Webster. With fingers that didn't seem to want to act quickly, Frost stuffed the photographs back into the wallet. One fell to the floor. He snatched it up, then looked at it again. A bedroom like all the others. Shelby lying on the bed, facing the camera. A woman poised over him, back to camera. Both were naked. There was no way the woman could be identified, but something in the room was familiar.

No time for further study. Back it went into the wallet, and the rubber band was slipped over. Hastily, even as voices were raised outside, he rammed the wallet back on the shelf and slammed the door shut. It clanged as if hit by a hammer. He hadn't time to move away from the locker before Johnny Johnson came in. Johnson looked at Frost, looked at the locker then closed the door behind him.

'What are you up to, Jack?'

'Nothing,' said Frost, feeling like the window cleaner caught with trousers down by the husband.

'Mr Mullett has ordered me to find you and take you by the scruff of the neck to the interview room.'

'On our way,' said Frost.

When the inspector had left, the sergeant read the name tag on the locker. He tried the handle. It was locked. Frost was up to something, and Shelby was involved. Right, Jack Frost, he thought. You've got some explaining to do.

'Well?' asked Webster as they quickened their pace to the interview room.

'Nothing,' replied Frost. 'Not a bloody thing.'

WEDNESDAY DAY SHIFT (4)

Roger Miller was sprawled on one of the chairs in the interview room, dragging silently at a cigarette. At his solicitor's suggestion he had discarded his trendy gear and was wearing a quiet grey business suit to present an illusion of soberness and responsibility.

Next to him, sitting bolt upright, was his solicitor, Gerald Moore, fat, pompous, and humourless, conservatively dressed in black. For the umpteenth time Moore sifted through his briefcase and rearranged the order of his papers.

Roger pushed himself up from the chair. 'I'm not prepared to wait here any longer. I'm going.'

Gerald Moore raised an eyebrow in mild reproach. 'Your father would wish you to stay.' The solicitor returned to his briefcase sifting.

Roger tore the cigarette from his mouth and hurled it on

the floor. He'd been stuck in this miserable little room for nearly two hours. He wasn't used to people keeping him waiting. Usually he only had to mention that he was Sir Charles Miller's son and doors were flung open.

The door of the interview room was flung open, and a dishevelled character in a crumpled suit slouched in, immediately followed by a smartly dressed, younger, bearded man. Obviously a plainclothes man and his prisoner, concluded the solicitor, frowning at the intrusion and wondering if the scruffy prisoner was dangerous. He was about to point out they had come to the wrong room when the criminal dragged a chair over to the table, flopped down opposite his client, and introduced himself as Detective Inspector Frost.

A detective! thought Moore. This tramp! No wonder the crime rate is soaring.

'Sorry to keep you waiting, gents,' said Frost, 'but a murder inquiry was taking our attention. I understand you've got something to tell us, Mr Miller?'

Miller started to speak, but Moore cleared his throat loudly to remind his client that he was to be the spokesman. You had to watch every word you said to the police. 'My client has prepared a statement. This is it.' He removed a neatly typed sheet of paper from his briefcase and slid it over to the inspector. Frost let it lie on the table.

'Before I read it, sir, spot of good news. We've found your Jag, Mr Miller. It was parked in a lay-by near Denton Woods. Fairly undamaged — once the blood and bits of brain have been washed off it, it should be as good as new.'

The solicitor tightened his lips.

'Naturally we are pleased at the recovery of the car,' he said, making it absolutely clear that he was the one who was going to do all the talking, 'but we are most distressed that while it was stolen and out of my client's possession, it was involved in a death.'

'Stolen?' said Frost. 'Is that what's supposed to have happened to it?'

Roger Miller thrust his face forward. He didn't like the

attitude of this nondescript little pip-squeak. 'I'm here to answer questions, not listen to your cheap insinuations.'

'Right,' said Frost, blandly, giving the twenty-year-old youth a twitch of a smile, 'I'll read your statement and then ask my questions.'

The statement read:

I returned home from the office at 6.25 p.m. I had brought some work back with me and I worked on it in my flat until 11.15 p.m., at which time I realized that some papers I needed to complete my work were still in my briefcase in my car. At 11.20 p.m. I left the flat and walked around the corner to Norman Grove, where I had left my car, a Jaguar, registration number ULU 63A. To my concern, the car was not there. I presumed it had been stolen so I immediately phoned Denton Police Station to report this fact. I then returned to my flat and went to bed. The first I knew about the tragic accident which caused the sad death of Mr Hickman was when a reporter from the Denton Echo phoned me at my office at two minutes past nine this morning. I was extremely distressed to learn that my car was apparently involved, and I immediately contacted my solicitor and arranged to come to the police to help them in whatever way I can.

'Beautifully typed,' commented Frost when he finished reading it. He let it fall to the table. 'You work for your father, I understand, Mr Miller?'

It was the solicitor who confirmed for his client. 'That is correct. In the head office of Miller Properties Ltd., the holding company.'

'I see,' said Frost, his head swinging from one man to the other. 'And you've approved this statement, Mr Moore?'

'Yes, and my client is now prepared to sign it.'

'I want to sign it right now,' said Roger Miller, pulling a rolled-gold Parker pen from his pocket. 'I've wasted two hours already and I've got better things to do with my time than hang about here.'

'And I'm sure Mr Hickman would have had better things

to do with his time than having to hang about on a slab in the morgue,' murmured Frost, 'but we can't always choose what happens.'

'For a public servant you're bloody insolent,' snapped the youth hotly, his pen scratching his signature across the foot of the page. He thrust the paper at Frost. 'Can I go now?' He jerked his head at his solicitor, implying that whatever the inspector's answer, they were leaving.

'Just a few minor points if you don't mind, Mr Miller,' said Frost, whose finger had directed Webster to stand in front of the door, blocking their exit. 'Please sit down. It shouldn't take long.' He gave them a disarming smile as they returned to their chairs. 'My trouble is, gentlemen, I'm not very bright. There are a couple of things in your statement that don't seem to add up. I'm sure it's my stupidity, so if you could see your way clear to explaining . . .'

'I'm sure it's your stupidity, too,' said Miller condescendingly, 'but try to be as quick as you can.'

Frost scratched his head as if completely out of his depth. 'The first thing that puzzled me, sir, is the question of your leaving your briefcase in the Jag.'

Miller gave Frost a patronising smile. 'And why should that puzzle you, Inspector?'

'According to all the witnesses we've spoken to, sir, you never drive the Jag to your office. You always use the firm's car, the Porsche. So how did your briefcase get in the Jag?'

The solicitor confidently turned a questioning face to his client, then realized to his dismay that the youth was floundering, trying to think of an answer. Roger shook his head helplessly. Quickly, the solicitor said, 'If you don't mind, Inspector, I'd like a word with my client in private. I may have misunderstood his instructions.'

Frost and Webster trooped outside and waited. After five minutes they were called back in again.

'A lapse of memory,' explained Moore, removing the cap from his fountain pen, ready to amend the statement. 'My client intended using the Jaguar car the following day, so he transferred his briefcase from the Porsche.'

'Let me get this straight,' Frost said, his finger drawing circles around his scar. 'Your client drove the Porsche from his office, parked it in the basement car park at the flats, took out the briefcase and walked with it round the corner to Norman Grove, where he put the briefcase in the Jag, and then walked back to the flat?'

'Yes,' said Moore weakly. It didn't sound at all plausible to him now the inspector queried it.

'Very logical, sir. So if you'd like to alter the statement to that effect we can all get on to more important matters.' Moore's pen began drafting a suitable amendment. The words wouldn't flow, and he had to keep crossing out and altering the text. 'Oh, just one other thing,' Frost added. 'As I said, we've recovered the Jag — but the briefcase wasn't in it.'

Miller gave a superior sneer. 'I imagine the thief took it.'

Frost seemed to receive this suggestion with open arms. 'Of course, sir, I hadn't thought of that. Briefcases full of office papers must be a very valuable commodity.' He paused, then said with studied casualness, 'Just one other thing . . .'

Moore's pen stopped in midstroke, and he tried not to show his anxiety. What bombshell was going to be dropped now? He wasn't used to criminal work and was no longer positive that his client was telling the whole truth. He waited apprehensively, his eyes moving from the inspector to his client.

'You say in your statement, Mr Miller, that you reported the theft to the police, then went straight to bed in your flat.'

'That's right,' answered Miller.

'You may not be aware of it, sir, but in the early hours of this morning we had an anonymous phone call reporting that a man had been seen trying to break into the balcony window of a fourth-floor flat at Halley House. We investigated. On getting no reply from your flat and fearing for your safety, we used the caretaker's passkey to enter. Happily, there was no sign of an intruder. But the puzzle is, there was no sign of you, either, sir — and your bed had not been slept in.'

Miller sprang to his feet, sending his chair skidding across the floor. His face was brick red with anger. 'You impudent swine! Are you telling me you had the temerity to sneak into my flat — to check up on me behind my back?'

His solicitor stood up, hissing at Roger to calm down. Miller, fists clenched, chest heaving, fought to gain control of himself. At last he nodded to his solicitor, then sat down. But if looks could kill, Frost would be stone-cold dead.

Moore capped his fountain pen and scooped up the statement, which he replaced firmly in his briefcase. 'My client and I wish to reconsider our position, Inspector. At this stage we have nothing further to say.'

But Frost hadn't quite finished. He addressed the youth. 'Sorry to be a nuisance, but there is one more thing. I think it's only fair to mention it so you can clear up all the lies in one hit. We have a witness who saw you driving the Jaguar away from Norman Grove yesterday evening.' Frost caught Webster's puzzled look and beamed at him. It wasn't true about the witness, but why should Miller be the only one allowed to lie?

With an unsteady hand, and feeling quite battered by the past few minutes' experience, the solicitor zipped up his briefcase and led his client to the door. 'We hope to be back to you within the hour,' he announced.

'I don't think we can allow your client to leave,' said Frost. 'This is a very serious charge.'

'Then I demand some time alone with my client.'

'Fair enough.' Frost gathered up his cigarettes and his matches. He was reaching for the door handle when Miller's resolve broke.

'Wait, Inspector.'

Frost dropped his hand and slowly turned around.

Miller, the arrogance completely drained out of him, fumbled in his pocket for a slim, gold-and-black-enamelled cigarette case. He removed a cigarette which he kept tapping on the case. 'I think I'd better tell you the truth.'

Moore pushed in front of him. 'Not until you've discussed it with me.' He moved to Frost. 'We have nothing to say until we have reconsidered our position.'

'I didn't park the Jag in Norman Grove,' continued Roger doggedly. 'I wasn't at my flat at all last night.'

Moore was shaking with rage. He grabbed his client's shoulder and spun him around. 'If you wish me to continue representing you, Mr Miller,' he spluttered, 'you will remain silent until we have talked together.'

'If you want to continue being my father's solicitor, then shut up, you fat slob,' snapped Miller. 'And take your greasy hands off of me.' The solicitor collapsed heavily onto a chair and dabbed at his forehead with a white handkerchief.

Making sure that Webster had his notebook open and his pen poised, Frost asked, 'So where were you last night, sir?'

'I was with a girl . . . I couldn't mention her before — she is someone my father would strongly disapprove of.'

'In that case I'm beginning to like her already,' said the inspector. 'How long were you with her?'

'From seven yesterday evening until a little after eight this morning. The car was stolen from outside her flat. Damn it, Inspector, I couldn't let my old man know where I was, so I pretended it had been taken from Norman Grove. Obviously, I had no idea it had been used in a hit-and-run when I phoned the police, otherwise I would never have tried it on.'

Frost said nothing. Webster's pen sprinted across the page. Moore took off his glasses and held them to the light so he could better examine the dirt on the lenses. Then he put them back on his nose. 'You were with her all night, from seven until eight this morning? You didn't go out?'

Roger nodded.

'Would the girl corroborate all this?'

'Of course.'

The solicitor's deep sigh of relief was followed by a smile of triumph. 'In that case, Inspector, there is no way my client could have been involved in the death of that unfortunate man. He has an alibi.'

Frost's deep sigh was one of regret. He was hoping for a confession, not more flaming checking up to do. 'Would you mind giving us the lady's name and address, sir?' he asked the young man sweetly. 'Just in case we wanted to check your story.'

Her name was Julie King. She lived in an older-type house that had been divided up into six single-bedroom flats. It was situated in Forest View, a quiet backwater overlooking Denton Woods. The unlocked front door allowed access to a small hall containing a letter rack, a pay telephone, and a fire extinguisher. Julie King's flat was on the first floor.

A flight of stairs took them up to a landing where two doors stood side by side. On the first, a card attached by a drawing pin read 'J. King'. The door to the other flat still had a morning newspaper poking through the letter box and a pint bottle of semiskimmed milk lurking on the step.

'Flats of a couple of prostitutes,' observed Frost, making one of his ill-considered judgements. 'One works days, the other nights. Let's call on the day shift.' He thumbed the bell to Julie King's flat.

'This isn't a bad neighbourhood,' remarked Webster as they waited.

'As long as you don't mind being raped,' said Frost. 'The woods are only a couple of streets away.'

The door, held firm by a strong chain, cautiously opened a few inches. A female voice demanded, 'What do you want?'

'Police,' said Webster, holding out his warrant card to the gap. A hand with long orange fingernails took it, then withdrew. The door slammed shut, then there were sounds of the chain being unhooked before the door opened fully.

A sexual fantasy of nineteen or twenty throbbed and vibrated in the doorway. Her jeans were powder blue and skintight, and her lemon T-shirt was a second skin over a pair of primed, highly explosive breasts with the safety catch off. Her hair was golden blonde and her figure strictly X certificate.

'Yes?' she asked huskily.

Frost's voice sounded a trifle high-pitched so he cleared his throat and tried again. 'Miss Julie King?' She nodded. 'A few questions, miss. Do you think we might come in?'

She ushered them into a sparsely but adequately furnished

room. It was a flat for people who didn't stay very long and it
echoed none of its tenant's personality. A green leather-cloth
settee that had seen better days, and had long since forgotten
them, lolled lumpily in front of a two-bar electric wall fire.
Next to the fire, screwed firmly to the wall, was the landlord's
coin-in-the-slot electricity meter, finished in tasteful ex-
Government surplus olive green. On the far wall, a door was
slightly ajar and allowed a glimpse of sink, refrigerator, and
cooker. A closed door next to it would lead to the bedroom.
The thought of Roger Miller going through that door and
taking this sizzler to bed made Webster hate the man all the
more.

'Nice and compact,' observed Frost, perching himself on
the arm of the settee and taking out his cigarettes. 'Perhaps
you'd question the lady, son. I seem to have done nothing
but ask questions all day.'

Julie took one of Frost's cigarettes, leaning over to give him
a bird's-eye view of deep, inviting cleavage as he lit it for her,
his hand none too steady. She dropped down on the settee,
patting the cushion for Webster to sit next to her. He sat. It
was a very small settee and they were close together. He could
feel the radiated animal heat of her body and was getting the
full blast of her perfume. His hatred of Roger Miller was
increasing by the minute.

He cleared his throat. 'Would you mind telling us exactly
what you did last night, Miss King. From, say, six o'clock
onward?'

She smiled at him. The sort of smile that crept under his
shirt and gently stroked the pit of his stomach. 'Nothing
much to tell. I was here all the time. In the flat.'

Webster scribbled away in his notebook. 'On your own?'

She pursed her lips, and kissed out a tiny puff of smoke.
'No. With a friend.'

'Could I have his name please . . . assuming it was a
"he", of course?'

'Miller. Roger Miller.'

'Master Miller, the MP's son?' chimed in Frost, who had

now wandered over to the kitchen. 'Just like in Happy Families. Where did he park his car?'

Webster scowled. He thought he was supposed to be conducting this interview. 'Are you taking over the questioning, Inspector.'

'Me? Good heavens no, son. You carry on, you're doing fine.' He had now edged over to the bedroom door and was silently turning the handle.

Back to the girl. 'What time did Mr Miller arrive?'

'Five and twenty past six. I remember looking at my wristwatch as he rang the bell.' Her hand moved to show Webster her watch, a ridiculously tiny thing in gold and black with what looked like real diamonds at every quarter hour.

'And how long did he stay?'

She pouted out a smoke puffball. 'He left about eight o'clock this morning. I was still in bed.'

Behind the girl's back, Frost had quietly opened the bedroom door and had disappeared inside. Webster tried hard not to stare in that direction. He didn't want the girl following his gaze. 'Did Mr Miller come by car?'

'Yes,' she answered. 'His blue Jag. He was going to leave here about twenty past eleven, but when he went out he found someone had stolen it. So I said he might as well stay for the rest of the night.'

Frost had now emerged from the bedroom, carefully closing the door behind him.

'Where was the car parked?' continued Webster.

'Just across the road.'

'I wonder if I can ask a personal question?' said Frost suddenly.

Webster groaned in exasperation. How could he possibly conduct an interview with this idiot butting in every five minutes. 'It is important, Inspector?' he asked resignedly.

'Vital,' said Frost, disarming the girl with a friendly grin. 'Tell me, miss, do you have a little mole on your right buttock?'

Webster could only stare dumbfounded. The man had

gone mad, there was no other answer. The girl just looked stunned.

'A little mole, like a beauty spot — just about here?' prompted Frost, jabbing his thigh.

She stood up and crushed out her cigarette in a tiny ashtray on the mantlepiece. 'What if I have? What the bleeding hell has it got to do with you, you dirty old git?'

I couldn't have put it better myself, thought Webster, noticing that in moments of stress the girl's accent became pure cockney.

Frost pulled a postcard-size photograph from his mac pocket. 'Just being curious. I couldn't make up my mind whether it was a fly or a mole.' He displayed the photograph. A nude study. A girl in thigh-high jackboots, carrying a whip. The face was covered by a leather mask, the breasts by nothing at all. Behind the girl a full-length mirror reflected the full glory of her rear view. It also reflected a dainty mole like a beauty spot on the right buttock.

She snatched the photograph from him. 'Where did you get that?'

'I was looking for the bathroom,' Frost explained unconvincingly. 'I went into your bedroom by mistake. One of the chests of drawers was open, and this photograph was on the top. I just happened to spot it.'

'You just happen to be a bloody liar,' she retorted. 'That drawer was shut tight, and the photographs were right at the bottom. If you must know, they're my publicity stills.'

'Publicity stills?'

'I'm in show business — a specialty dancer. I work at The Coconut Grove.'

'The Coconut Grove?' repeated Frost. Then the penny dropped. 'Of course. You're one of Harry Baskin's strippers. Then you must know that other bird . . . Paula Grey . . . the one who nearly got herself raped.'

'Of course I know her,' said the girl. 'She lives in the next-door flat. Your lot were all over the place this morning asking if I'd seen anyone suspicious hanging about. The stupid cow.

She was just asking for trouble cutting through those woods — you get flashers and God knows what in places like that.'

'She was late for work so she took a shortcut,' explained Webster. 'She was afraid Baskin would give her the push.'

'Yes.' She nodded. 'That's just the sort of thing the rotten bastard would do.'

'The rotten bastard got himself robbed last night, did you know that?' asked Frost.

'Robbed? Harry Baskin robbed?' She threw back her head, her body shaking and her breasts jiggling as she laughed. 'That's made my day!'

You've made my day as well, thought Webster, wishing she would laugh more often. But they weren't here about the robbery or the rape, so why couldn't Frost stick to the point? 'We came about the hit-and-run,' he reminded the inspector.

'So we did, son,' agreed Frost, looking about the room. 'Where's your television set, miss?'

She blinked at the pointless question. 'I haven't got one.'

'And you're asking me to believe that you and Master Roger were stuck in this prison cell of a flat from half past six yesterday evening until eight o'clock this morning with no telly to keep you amused? I can't even see any books to read. So what do you do to keep yourselves amused?'

'We happen to love each other,' she said simply. 'What do you think we did?'

But Frost wasn't having any of this. 'Come now, miss, there are limits. If it were me, I could stare all night at your mole and want nothing more than a dripping sandwich and a cup of tea. But Master Roger isn't the stay-at-home type. He couldn't sit still for hours in a pokey little hole like this. He'd want to get out, go somewhere, knock some poor wally down with his expensive motor and then get some silly little tart to provide him with an alibi.'

Her eyes spat fire. 'I find you offensive.'

'Then you're in good company, Miss King. Mind you, I find it offensive that rich men's sons can kill innocent people and get away with it.'

The girl caught her breath and looked frightened. Very frightened. 'Killed? You mean the man's dead?'

Frost looked up in surprise. 'You didn't know he was dead? Surely your boy friend didn't keep that tidbit of news from you before asking you to fake his alibi?'

She stared unbelievingly at him, then looked pleadingly at Webster for him to tell her it wasn't true.

'He died late last night, miss,' the constable confirmed.

She dropped heavily onto the settee, hands twisting her handkerchief into a tight silken rope, her face as white as a hospital sheet.

'So you see, miss,' said Webster quietly, 'it's a very serious matter.'

'He's not worth lying for,' added Frost. 'He wouldn't lie for you.'

She tugged at the handkerchief as if she were trying to rip it in two, then jerked her head up defiantly. 'I'm not lying. Roger arrived here yesterday evening. He stayed with me until eight this morning. We did not go out. We couldn't have gone anywhere even if we wanted to. Roger didn't have any money. He was broke.'

'Broke? Come off it, love. He's rolling in it.'

'He had some debts to pay off — to Harry Baskin, as it happens. If you don't believe me, you can ask him. Which is why we had to stay in . . . all bloody night. Are you satisfied?

There's only one way you could satisfy me, love, thought Frost, and that involves showing me your mole. His eyes held hers. She tried to meet his gaze, but her head dropped. I know you are lying, he thought, but I just can't prove it. He expelled a sigh. 'All right, miss. We'd like you to drop in at the station sometime today to give us a written statement. It shouldn't take long.'

He straightened his aching back and buttoned up his mac. A loose button was hanging by a single thread. He would have to find someone to sew it on for him before he lost it. Julie King didn't look the sort of girl who knew what a needle and thread were for.

.   .   .

'If you want my opinion, she's lying,' announced Webster when they were back in the car.

'Probably,' said Frost, who had just found the note in his pocket that he had scribbled earlier, 'but there's something else that worries me, something that makes me wonder if the girl might, perhaps, be telling the truth. It's that bloody licence plate. It was too damn convenient, our finding it. It's like a crook leaving his name and address, or a rapist leaving a photograph of his dick.'

'The plate fell off when the Jag crashed into the dustbins,' said Webster, who saw nothing illogical about that.

'How many licence plates have you known to fall off?' asked Frost, reaching for the handset so he could call the station.

Johnny Johnson was delighted to hear from him. 'Mr Frost! We've been trying to reach you. Mr Mullett wants to see you. Something about the crime statistics.'

'Sorry,' said Frost, 'can't hear you. This is a very bad line.'

'I can hear you perfectly,' the sergeant told him.

'Good. Then tell me something. I asked for someone to check the spot where we picked up that licence plate to see if they could find the plastic screws. Any joy?'

'No, Jack. Charlie Bravo did a thorough search of the area. Couldn't find anything. Now, about Mr Mullett . . .'

'Still can't hear you,' said Frost quickly. 'Over and out.' He switched off the radio in case the station tried to call back, then rubbed his chin thoughtfully. 'If the licence plate fell off, the screws holding it to the car would have had to come off just before it dropped. So where are they?'

'No idea,' shrugged Webster.

'Secondly,' Frost continued, 'we've got to suppose that both screws came out simultaneously.'

'Why?'

'If only one screw fell out, the other would hold it, causing the plate to pivot down. It would have dragged along while the Jag was still going at top speed. But the plate was undamaged.'

'It wouldn't necessarily drop down,' said Webster. 'The remaining screw could have been holding it so tightly it stayed in position.'

'If it was holding it as tightly as that, son, there's no way it could have unscrewed itself to let the licence plate drop off. No, that licence plate was deliberately removed, carried in the car, then chucked out near the accident so the dumb fuzz could find it.'

Webster looked at Frost pityingly. 'I imagine the last thing Roger Miller would have wanted to do was leave his licence plate behind.'

'If he was driving, I agree. But supposing it was someone else who wanted to get him into trouble?'

The detective constable could only shake his head in despair. This was getting beyond him.

Frost settled back in his seat. 'Try this out for size, as the bishop said to the actress. The girl told us that Miller bets with Harry Baskin and that he's short of money. Let's suppose he's run up a dirty great gambling debt and he can't pay. Like I've told you, Harry has his own roguish little ways of speeding up slow payers — he sets their car alight, or cuts their cat's head off. Suppose Harry decides to put the screws on Roger by getting one of his minions to nick the Jag, drive it around at speed, knocking a few dustbins over in the process, and drop off the licence plate so there's no doubt as to whose car it was . . . a warning to Miller that there's worse to come if he doesn't cough up. That's the plan. But it went wrong. The minion knocks an old man down and kills him. He has to abandon the Jag and leg it back to The Coconut Grove — the car wasn't found all that far away from the club if you recall.'

Webster chewed this over. 'There's a lot of loose ends, but I suppose it's possible,' he grudgingly admitted.

'Yes,' said Frost. 'The only trouble is, if I'm right, then Master Roger is innocent, and that would be contrary to natural justice.' He tugged at the seat belt and fastened it across his lap. 'Ah well, we have other cases to occupy our fertile minds. Let's go and see Old Mother Wiggle-Bum.'

Webster turned the key in the ignition. 'I presume you mean Mrs Dawson?'

The inspector nodded, chewing his lower lip as another nagging doubt rose to the surface. 'She worries me, son. It was bloody windy in the town yesterday afternoon.'

With a grimace, Webster said, 'Was it?' He wondered what the old fool was drivelling on about now.

Frost looked out on the trees of Denton Woods as the car cruised along the ring road. 'Near gale force. It would have blown your beard all over the place. If you were a woman who wiggled her bum and you had just had your hair done for a very important do, would you risk walking in the wind for a couple of hours?'

'No,' said Webster.

'Old Mother Dawson did,' said Frost. 'Before we see her we'll nip into the town and call on a few hairdressers. We might even let them give your beard a blue rinse.

WEDNESDAY DAY SHIFT (5)

Max Dawson gave the barrel of the rifle a final polish with a soft duster, then carefully rested the butt against his shoulder, and lined up the sights to the exact centre of his sleeping wife's forehead. Then, very gently, he squeezed. A metallic click. She stirred a little and slept on.

He lowered the rifle, almost wishing it were loaded. How could she sleep? Her own daughter missing, possibly even lying dead somewhere, and all she could do was sleep.

The rifle was replaced in its leather case and zipped in. He carried it out to the metal cupboard which, in compliance with his firearms certificate, was fixed to the wall beneath the stairs by bolts set in concrete. He was turning the key in the security lock when the phone rang.

It was Karen. It had to be Karen.

He raced back to the lounge, scooped up the phone, and croaked, 'Yes?'

The ringing had woken up Clare. 'Is it Karen?'

An impatient flick of his hand ordered her to silence. He listened, his face red-hot with anger. He turned his head incredulously to his wife. 'Would you believe it? It's the bloody office with some piddling little query.' Enraged, he yelled into the phone, 'Get off this bloody line, you bitch. Don't you dare phone me at home again.' He slammed the receiver down with such force he feared he might have broken it. He checked, and heard the reassuring purr of the dial tone. His hand still shaking, he replaced it carefully this time.

Clare pushed herself from the armchair, where she had been huddled in an uneasy sleep, and stretched to straighten out the kinks in her back. A quick glance in the mirror over the mantlepiece while she fluffed up her hair, then she padded across to her husband and gently squeezed his arm.

'Shall I make some coffee?'

He jerked his arm away. He didn't want her touching him. He blamed her for Karen's disappearance. If she had been here yesterday afternoon when Karen came home early from school, none of this would have happened. 'I don't want any coffee.'

Shrugging off the rejection, she knelt on the padded window seat and looked out across the landscaped garden. Thin sunlight trickled down and an edgy wind ruffled the shrubs and the water of the ornamental fish pond.

The bray of a horn as a car turned off the road and into the drive. She went cold. 'Max, a car!'

He almost leaped across the room to join her at the window. He recognized the Ford Cortina. 'It's the police,' he told her. 'Those two idiots who were here last night.' She reached out for the comforting reassurance of his hand, but he drew away, watching the Ford pull up at the front door, watching the two policemen get out, both looking grim.

The door bell chimed. He couldn't move. He didn't want to move. If he didn't open the door, he wouldn't have to hear their awful news and Karen wouldn't be dead.

A second ring, longer this time.

Clare again examined herself in the mirror, adjusted the

hem of her sweater, then went to the front door. His eyes followed her. Look at her! Her only daughter dead and she's preening herself.

He heard the front door open, then voices. Quite loud voices, not hushed as if they were breaking bad news. A spark of hope flickered. And in they came, first the scruffy one, his voice booming. 'Morning, Mr Dawson. No news yet, I'm afraid. I take it your daughter hasn't been in touch?'

'If she had, Inspector, I would have contacted you,' snapped Dawson, his relief now making him resentful that they frightened him.

'Of course, sir,' said Frost, blandly. 'Anyway, we've circulated Karen's photograph and we've asked everyone to keep their eyes open, so we might strike lucky soon.'

'Circulated her photograph?' shrilled Dawson, his mouth agape in exaggerated astonishment. 'Is that all you've done? Good God, man, if Karen were walking about where people could see her, don't you think she would have phoned me? Face up to facts. She's being held against her will somewhere, or she's injured, or even worse . . . what about the woods where that woman was attacked? Karen could be lying there, helpless.'

'We've got men searching every inch of the woods,' Webster told him.

'I've put one of my best men in charge,' added Frost. 'Detective Inspector Allen. Not very bright, but thorough.'

'Actually, Mr Dawson,' announced Webster, 'we'd like to search the house and grounds. Purely routine, but children have been known to hide and accidentally get trapped. This is quite a rambling building.'

Dawson thought it would be a complete and utter waste of time. He himself had already gone over every inch of the house and outbuildings.

'No harm in being one hundred percent sure,' said Frost, suggesting that Webster and Dawson work down from the attic while he and Mrs Dawson covered the ground floor.

Waiting until he could hear the two men's footsteps overhead, Frost gave Clare a friendly smile. That should have put her on guard. But it didn't. She smiled back. She was wearing an orange angora-wool sweater with flared lemon slacks. The sweater seemed to be moulded on, but she managed to pull it down and wriggle about until it fitted even tighter. 'Where shall we start?'

Frost lined up the ends of his scarf, then worried the living daylights out of his scar. It was time to dive in without knowing how deep the water was.

'Mrs Dawson, if your daughter came back to an empty house yesterday, and if there was a man hiding inside, then I am extremely concerned for Karen's safety. I would want to organize a full-scale police investigation, probably drafting in men from other divisions to help. That would take up a lot of people's time and cost one hell of a lot of money, but if a girl's life is at stake it would be worth it.'

She reached up to the mantelpiece for the knight-in-armour table lighter and sank down in the armchair, hunched up small, clicking the lighter on and off, the flame flaring and dying.

'Before I take such a step,' continued Frost gravely, 'I would like to satisfy myself that the unworthy thought that keeps springing to my mind isn't correct.'

'Unworthy thought?' she stammered.

'Let me be blunt, Mrs Dawson. It will save time. You're a sexy bit of stuff. You're a lot younger than your husband and you're all alone in the house for most of the day. Women in such circumstances have been known to wile the time away with a bit of spare on the side.'

She was up, facing him, her breasts quivering with indignation. 'How dare you . . . !'

He gently pushed her back down into the chair. 'If it helps to find your daughter I'll dare as much as I like. All I'm trying to do is see if we can't eliminate this mystery man from our inquiries.' The lighter clicked on, off, on, off. He felt like doing what her husband had done the night before — take it away from her. 'I'm asking you, point-blank, can I eliminate him or not?'

She found the lighter of consuming interest.

'I promise you, Mrs Dawson, if he was just here for a bit of spare, I'll keep him out of it. Can I eliminate him?'

'Yes, damn you, you can.'

Frost heaved a sigh of relief. The first hurdle safely over. 'I checked with your hairdresser. Your appointment was originally for two o'clock, but you phoned yesterday morning and put it back until five. Is that correct?'

'If you've checked with the hairdresser, then it must be,' she answered defiantly.

'OK,' said Frost. 'So we take it that you altered your appointment because your boy friend was popping in to see you.'

'Yes.'

'And you were both here when Karen came home?'

'Yes.'

'Tell me about it.'

'We were in here, on the settee. We were kissing . . . my dress was unbuttoned. We didn't hear Karen come in. We didn't expect her. That bloody school should have phoned. Karen saw us. She ran out of the house.'

'Any idea where she is?'

'No. But I'm sure she'll be back. My husband doesn't know it, but she's been off like this before. Karen's not quite the innocent he thinks she is.' She put the lighter on the floor then walked to the bar where she slopped a shot of vodka into a glass. Staring defiantly, she raised the glass to her lips. Then she crumpled. 'You won't tell my husband? He'll kill me if he finds out.'

Frost shrugged. 'If it's not necessary for him to know, then I won't tell him. But your daughter is bound to spill the beans when she comes back.'

'I can take care of Karen,' she said significantly.

'Right,' said Frost, rewinding his scarf. 'We'll keep an eye open for her, but we won't worry too much for a day or so. If you get any news, let us know.'

The lounge door opened for the return of Max Dawson and a dusty, cobwebby Detective Constable Webster.

'She's not down here,' said Frost. 'We've looked everywhere.'

When they got back to the car, Frost took a chance and switched the radio on. Control was calling him. Charlie Bravo had gone to Tommy Croll's place to pick him up. No sign of Croll, but his rooms had been broken into and all the furniture systematically ripped and smashed. 'We're on our way,' said Frost.

Detective Inspector Allen rapped at the door of the Divisional Commander's office and went in. Mullett, sitting ramrod-stiff behind his satin mahogany desk, smiled and indicated the inspector should sit.

'You look worn out, Allen.'

Allen sat down wearily and stretched tired muscles. 'Thought I'd better put you in the picture with the rape investigation, sir. I'm sorry to say we've made no progress at all. A mature woman dressed in schoolgirl clothes walks from her home to the woods and we haven't been able to turn up a single witness who saw her. We've knocked on doors, we've asked everywhere. I've been thorough —'

'I'm quite sure you have, Inspector. That goes without saying,' smarmed Mullett.

'I've put our usual circus of known sexual offenders through the hoop . . . still some more to question, but nothing positive up to now.'

'Any joy from your radio and television appeals to the public?'

'We've had a fair amount of response, which we're following up, but most of it useless — old maids who reckon the man next door must be the rapist because he always looks over the fence when she hangs her knickers on the line, that sort of thing. I hate to have to say it, sir, but at the moment it looks as if we'll just have to wait until the rapist strikes again and hope that this time he might leave the odd clue behind.'

Mullett pulled a face. 'We can't leave it like that, Inspector. He must be stopped before he claims another victim. Have you traced the anonymous phone caller?'

'No, sir. We've appealed for him to come forward, but he hasn't obliged yet. I do have one suggestion, sir.' He looked hopefully at the Superintendent.

'Yes?' asked Mullett uneasily, feeling he was about to be forced into making a decision.

'We set a trap, send in a decoy — a policewoman tarted up to tempt the rapist into having a go at her.'

Mullett readjusted his moustache and smoothed the bristles down 'I don't like this, Allen. It could be dangerous.'

'Let me show you the plan, sir.' Allen left his chair and moved to the large-scale wall map behind the Superintendent's desk. 'We would have men hiding here, and here. Also a couple of radio cars on the surrounding roads. I'd have more men back here, and two more staked out here.' He jabbed at the map. 'The woman decoy —'

'Only one?' Mullett queried.

Allen nodded. 'It's safer that way. We want to keep the operation confined to as tight an area as possible, so we can get to the decoy before he can harm her.'

Mullet studied the map over Allen's shoulder. 'You're pinning all your hopes on him operating in the same area as last night. Those woods are vast. You could all be over the west side while he's raping victims to the east.'

'To cover the entire area, sir, would require so many men there wouldn't be room for the rapist to get in. If the bait's attractive enough, I'm hoping he will come to us.'

'How many men are you talking about?' asked Mullett.

'About fifteen or twenty.'

'I don't know,' said Mullett evasively as he returned to his chair. 'There's too much left to chance. And the overall cost would be terrific — fifteen or twenty men, all on overtime. I'm under severe pressure from County to cut down on our manpower costs. Let me show you the memo they sent me.' He unlocked his desk drawer and pulled out the memo with 'Strictly Confidential' typed in red capitals across the top.

Allen barely gave it a glance. He didn't want to see these stupid pieces of paper. 'Then you're saying we do nothing at all, sir? We simply sit back, twiddle our thumbs, and wait for our man to pick his next victim. Is that what you're saying, sir?'

Mullett could feel the wall pressing hard against his back. 'What can I do?' he said weakly, waving the memo like a flag of truce. 'We've got to cut down on expenditure. I mean I could authorize it, and you could waste night after night, fifteen men all on overtime, expenses soaring and nothing to show for it. County would crucify me.'

'Let's restrict it to five nights only, then, sir.'

'Three,' countered Mullett, feeling he was scoring a victory.

'Fair enough, sir. Three,' agreed Allen. 'And then we can decide whether to extend it or not.'

'But let me see a costing first,' called Mullett as Allen made for the door.

'Of course, sir,' smiled the inspector. 'I'll have it on your desk in half an hour. I've already started working it out.'

'This is how we found it, Inspector,' said PC Kenny, leading Frost and Webster into Tommy Croll's rooms.

The two rooms were a chaotic mess with upholstery slashed, drawers pulled out, cupboards yawning open and their contents strewn all over the floor. The mattress in the bedroom had been dragged from the bed and knifed, its lacerations bleeding horsehair. A heap of clothing tumbled from the wardrobe had a snowy coating of feathers from ripped pillows. In the kitchen the contents of packets of soap powder and corn flakes had been spewed all over the floor where they scrunched noisily underfoot.

'It's been done over, sir,' said PC Kenny.

'Funny you should say that,' said Frost, 'I was thinking the same thing myself.' He kicked at a tin of baked beans which rolled to rest against some broken slices of bread. 'No sign of Croll, I suppose?'

'No, sir. His landlady downstairs didn't even know he was out of hospital.'

'Does she know who did this?'

'No, sir. Says it happened while she was out.'

Frost picked up a battered transistor radio from the floor. 'Well, there's no mystery about who did it — a couple of Harry Baskin's heavies searching for the stolen money and putting in the frighteners at the same time.' He plugged in the radio and clicked it on. An angry crackle followed by a blue flash. He switched it off. 'We'll have to find Tommy before Baskin's boys get hold of him. We don't want him ending up like his mattress, with his innards poking out.' He told Kenny to ask Control to put out a priority signal that Croll was to be found and brought in immediately for questioning in connection with the robbery at The Coconut Grove.

Their next stop was at the house of the other security guard, Bert Harris, who lived in one of the newly built houses east of the main Bath Road. Harris, a cropped-haired, thickset man in his late twenties, sported a black eye and a bruised nose, souvenirs of his reprimand from Harry Baskin the previous night. He didn't seem at all pleased to see the two policemen.

'It's not really convenient, Mr Frost,' he protested, but the inspector pushed past him.

'We don't mind if it's a bit untidy, Bert.' He opened the lounge door and peeped inside. A carbon copy of Croll's place with slashed upholstery and emptied cupboards. 'Looks like my house on a good day,' commented Frost as he managed to find a dining chair with its seat intact so he could sit down. 'I take it some friends of Mr Baskin's have paid you a visit.'

'I've got no comment to make on that,' said Harris.

Frost lit up a cigarette. 'Did they find the money before they left?'

Harris laughed hollowly. 'They couldn't find it because I haven't got it. I had nothing to do with that robbery.'

'It had to be an inside job, Bert, which has got to mean you and Tommy Croll.'

Harris pulled a tobacco tin from his pocket and began to roll a hand-made. 'We're talking about five thousand lousy quid, Mr Frost. If me and Tommy split it down the middle, that is two and a half thousand apiece. Do you seriously think I'd risk Harry Baskin's boys ripping me open for a lousy two and a half thou? Look at this bloody mess!' He indicated the rubble of his lounge. 'There's at least a thousand quid's worth of damage. If I was going to stitch Harry Baskin up, I'd pick a night when there was at least ten thousand quid in the office, and when I'd nicked it, you wouldn't see my arse for dust. I wouldn't hang around so Harry could use me as a punching bag.'

Frost was forced to admit that this made sense. 'So who do you reckon took the money . . . Tommy Croll?'

'It's not for me to say, is it, Inspector? But he's stupid enough, and it's bloody funny he's done a runner from the hospital.'

The radio was talking to an empty car. 'Control to Mr Frost. Come in, please.'

Frost picked up the handset and in a mock, quavering baritone, sang, 'I hear you calling me.'

A pause from the other end, then a reproving voice sniffed, 'Please observe the correct radio procedure, Inspector.'

It was Mullett!

'Sorry, Super,' said Frost. 'We seem to be on a crossed line.'

County had been on to Mullett about the nonarrival of the crime statistics, and Accounts had contacted him, wanting to know where the overtime returns were. Frost breezily told Mullett that both returns would go off that day without fail, then signed off quickly.

'Next stop The Coconut Grove, son. I think we should have a little talk with lovable Harry Baskin.'

Like an ageing prostitute who'd had a rough and busy night, The Coconut Grove didn't look its most seductive in the harsh glare of daylight. Shafts of gritty sunlight grated in through grimed windows, spotlighting every blemish. On asking for Baskin, Frost and Webster were directed through a back door, across a yard piled high with crates of empty beer bottles, and on through to another building from which the sound of a misused piano floated out.

Pushing through a side door marked Staff Only — Keep Out, they found themselves in a darkened hall. At the far end of a well-lit stage a long-haired blonde girl, wearing nothing more than a bright red bra and matching G-string, was twisting and gyrating to the repetitive thump of Ravel's *Bolero*, which a pretty, golden-haired man in a floral shirt was bashing out on the stage piano.

'Are you sure we're in the right place?' asked Webster.

'Definitely,' replied Frost.

They were halfway down the aisle when the music reached a climax and the girl suddenly twisted around, whipped off the bra with a flourish and stood bare-breasted, nipples quivering, arms triumphantly outstretched, panting with exertion, and smiling into the dark of the auditorium.

'No, no, no,' yelled a man's voice from the front row.

'Yes, yes, yes!' cried Frost, thudding down the aisle.

'Oh, it's you, Mr Frost,' said Baskin. The girl looked startled, then embarrassed, and immediately covered her breasts with her hands.

'Get those bloody hands off,' called Baskin. 'You've got to get used to people seeing you stripped. Flaunt them, darling, flaunt them.'

Baskin was slouched in one of the front-row-centre seats, an enormous cigar in his mouth pointing almost vertically upward like a Titan rocket ready for launch. 'Breaking in a new girl,' he explained as Webster and Frost filled the seats on either side of him. 'She's still a bit shy.'

'I reckon it's your cigar that's frightening her,' said Frost.

'From the beginning,' yelled Baskin. The girl put the bra back on and the pianist started butchering Ravel all over again.

'You got my money back yet?' asked Baskin.

'Not yet,' said Webster.

The three men sat side by side, talking to each other but looking straight ahead, their eyes glued to the stage where the blonde was working herself up into a fair simulation of erotic frenzy. The building reeked with the aphrodisiac combination of cigar smoke and female sweat.

'You've been up to your old tricks again, Harry,' reproached Frost, eyes dead ahead. 'Putting your frighteners on people. Wrecking their rooms.'

'Now don't take the bra off so quickly,' pleaded Baskin. 'Get the audience drooling for you to unpack your goodies. Tease them, just like you teased me last night.' He turned his head to Frost. 'Don't know what you're talking about Inspector. I don't put the frighteners on people. I'm a respectable businessman. She's got terrific knockers, hasn't she?'

'Has she?' said Frost vaguely. 'I was so engrossed in the music, I didn't notice. Tell me something, Harry. Do you know Roger Miller?'

Baskin flicked about half a pound of ash from the end of his cigar. 'The MP's son? Of course I know him. He plays the gee-gees. Knocks around with one of my show girls.'

'How's his luck with the horses?'

Baskin shrugged. 'Sometimes he wins, but not often. Usually he loses. His trouble is he doesn't know when to stop. He burned his fingers last month doubling up. Would have cost me a packet had he won, but, thank God, he didn't.'

'Does he owe you any money?'

Baskin waggled his cigar reproachfully. 'My clients' personal affairs are strictly confidential.'

'Very reassuring,' said Frost. 'You should be a doctor at a VD clinic. Gawd, look at that!' The girl had reached the end of her routine and stood stark naked in the centre of the stage, the spotlight sparkling on tiny dewdrops of sweat which glistened on her body like jewels. Frost nudged Webster heavily in the ribs. 'The Intimate Bikini Styler Strikes again!' he commented coarsely.

Applauding loudly, Baskin leaped from his seat, then he made a circle with his forefinger and thumb and kissed it wetly. 'Perfect, darling, absolutely perfect . . . take a breather.' She draped a red bathrobe over her shoulders, straddled a rickety chair, and began talking earnestly with the pianist, looking even more erotic half covered than she did when she was naked.

'You know Roger Miller's Jaguar?' asked Frost, reluctantly tearing his eyes away from the girl.

'Concorde on four wheels? Yes, I know it. Why?'

'It knocked down an old man last night,' said Frost, watching Baskin closely.

'Oh yes?' murmured Baskin, apparently more concerned with getting his cigar to draw properly.

'The old man died,' continued the inspector.

A streamer of smoke drifted from Baskin's mouth and lazily twisted and turned as it hit the beam of the spotlight. 'I always knew he'd end up killing someone. He drives like a bloody maniac.'

'Is he a good customer?' asked Frost.

'He's a good customer when he wins,' Baskin replied. 'Trouble is, when he loses he don't want to pay. You have to give him a little nudge.'

'Put in the frighteners, you mean?'

Baskin laughed out a cloud of smoke. 'Frighteners? You're becoming obsessed with that word, Inspector. I sent one of my accounts executives round to his flat to remind him of his obligations. Mr Miller apologized for his regrettable oversight and immediately gave him a cheque in full settlement.'

'When was this?' asked Webster.

'Two days ago. Why? How come it's of interest to you?'

It's of no bloody interest at all, thought Frost dejectedly. Another of his theories had been well and truly booted in the groin. If Miller didn't owe Baskin any money, then Baskin had no cause to nick Miller's Jag for a joyride. 'Come on son,' he told Webster, 'time to go.'

They were out amongst the beer crates when Frost stopped dead in his tracks. He looked back at the rehearsal hall and a smile crawled across his face. He jabbed a finger at Webster. 'Do you know what we are, son, you and me? Do you know what we are?'

What now? thought Webster, shaking his head wearily and asking, 'What are we?'

'A couple of stupid twits, that's what we are, son. Under our bleeding noses, and we missed it. The bikini line, son, the sleek bloody bikini line!'

Webster leaned resignedly against a tower of crates to listen to Frost's latest output of garbage. The old fool had been obsessed about this ever since they'd found that shaver in Karen's bedroom. He was like an overgrown, sniggering schoolboy.

Realizing the constable still hadn't twigged, Frost took the coloured photograph of Karen Dawson from his pocket and passed it to Webster. 'Forget the blonde hair, son, it's been bleached. Look at the face. Look carefully at the face.'

Webster stared at the photograph. He still didn't know what Frost was getting at. Then it hit him. He took the photograph and stared again. The blonde stripper they had been watching on the stage was fifteen-year-old Karen Dawson. The girl that Harry Baskin had mauled with his greasy hands, kissed with his fleshy lips, boasted of taking to his bed, was a kid, an underaged schoolgirl. The swine. The dirty, stinking pig. He was running back to the hall, Frost at his heels, trying to keep up with him.

Baskin was at the door of the hall, lecherousness all over his filthy face. Webster's feet hammered the ground as he thundered toward him, his hands already balled into fists. Too late Frost realized what was going to happen. 'Hold it, Webster!' he yelled, but nothing could hold him now. He seized Baskin by the lapels and slammed him hard against the wall.

'You bastard! You dirty, lecherous bastard!' Before Frost could pull him off, his fist had smashed into Baskin's face and there was blood everywhere.

'You stupid sod!' cried Frost, pushing between the two men and shoving Webster away. Baskin's face was dead white in contrast to the vivid red of the blood pouring from his nose, splashing down his suit and on the ground. One of Baskin's heavies came thudding around the corner. Frost held out his warrant card and yelled, 'Police. Piss off!' The heavy faltered, then turned back.

Webster was still shaking with rage, his shoulders heaving up and down as he fought to gain control of himself. A trembling Baskin stared incredulously at the blood that still cascaded down. He fumbled in his top pocket for a handkerchief and tried to stem the flow. 'My God!' he croaked, as the handkerchief rapidly changed colour, 'I'm bleeding to death.'

'Hold your head back,' ordered Frost, then, taking him by the arm, steered him toward his office. Webster moved as if to join them. 'You stay here,' hissed Frost. 'And don't move an inch — not one bloody inch.'

Inside the office he sat Baskin in a chair, his head well back, the now sodden handkerchief held to his nose. Frost's fingers gently explored the swollen area. 'Nothing broken, Harry.'

'No bleeding thanks to that pig out there,' snarled Baskin. 'Get me a drink.' Feeling he deserved one himself, Frost poured two drinks.

Baskin was now pulling himself together. He gulped down the whisky, hurled the sodden handkerchief into the wastepaper basket, and found himself a clean one in his desk drawer. 'You bastards will pay for this. I'm suing you, I'm suing that sod outside, and I'm suing the whole bloody police force from the Home Secretary downward.' He picked up his phone and began dialling the number of his solicitor. Frost reached out and pressed down on the cradle, cutting him off.

'Forget it, Harry.'

'Forget it?' shrieked Baskin. 'No bloody way!' He dragged a mirror from his desk drawer and examined the damage to his face. 'Look what that bastard has done to me.'

'No worse than what you did to your security guard last night,' murmured Frost. 'So let's say this evens the score.'

Baskin shook his head so firmly it started his nose bleeding again. 'No way, Inspector. That gorilla of yours has gone too far this time.' He moved the phone from Frost's reach. 'I am now going to phone my solicitor and instruct him to institute proceedings.'

Now it was the inspector's turn to shake his head. 'No you won't, Harry. If you attempt to sue my detective constable for assault, I shall be reluctantly forced to lie my head off. I'll swear on oath that you attacked him first and that he was compelled to act in self-defence. It'll be my word against yours — the word of a heroic police officer with the George Cross against the word of a strip-club owner who deflowers fifteen-year-old schoolgirls.'

Baskin stared at Frost as if the man had gone mad. 'Fifteen-year-old schoolgirls? What the hell are you going on about?'

In answer, Frost produced the coloured school photograph, pushed it, facedown, across the desk, then flipped it over as if it were the final ace to complete his running flush. 'That stripper you've been bedding, Harry — her name is Karen Dawson. She's a schoolgirl, and she's fifteen years old.'

Baskin jabbed a finger at the photograph, then snatched it back as if it had come into contact with something red-hot. He looked pleadingly at Frost for some indication that it was all a mistake. 'Fifteen? I don't believe it.'

'A week ago today she was only fourteen, Harry. I reckon you're good for at least seven years. The courts hate child molesters. But from what I saw this afternoon, I've no doubt she was worth it.'

Harry found a clean section of his handkerchief and used it to mop the sweat from his forehead. Refilling his glass, he downed the contents in one gulp. 'You've got to believe me Mr Frost, I had no idea. Blimey, who could tell by looking at her? I've seen twenty-eight-year-old women with smaller knockers than she's got.'

'You don't tell a lady's age by the size of her knockers, Harry. That's a fundamental principle of English criminal law.' As the whisky bottle was handy, Frost topped up his own glass. 'Cheers.'

'Look,' said Baskin, 'this is all a silly misunderstanding. I'm sure there's some way of clearing it all up.' As he spoke, he brought out a fat, bulging wallet and riffled his thumb significantly through a hefty chunk of fifty-pound notes.

Frost stiffened. 'Aren't you in enough bloody trouble, Harry?'

The wallet was hastily replaced. 'You've got to get me off the hook, Mr Frost.'

Head on one side, lips pursed, Frost pretended to give it some thought. 'There's the question of this assault charge you're going to make against my constable.'

'What assault charge?' asked Baskin, sounding sincerely puzzled. 'I tripped and banged my nose on the wall.'

'No more taking the law into your own hands with your security men? We want Tommy Croll in one usable piece.'

His palms spread upward, Baskin said, 'On my word of honour.'

'And lastly,' said Frost, 'that poor slag of a stripper who got herself beaten up in the woods. It would be a noble gesture if you kept her on your payroll until she was well enough to work again.'

'Now hold hard,' Baskin protested. 'That could take ages . . . months.'

'But nowhere near as long as seven years,' Frost pointed out.

A deep sigh of total surrender. 'All right. I'll pay her.'

Frost drained his glass, wiped his mouth with the back of his hand, and stood up. 'I can't make any promises, Harry. I shall simply tell the girl's parents that she applied for an audition here as a dancer and that's where we picked her up. I've got a pretty shrewd idea the girl will keep her mouth shut, but there's no way I can force her.'

'I owe you one,' said Baskin.

'Where do I find the girl?' asked Frost.

'In her dressing room, first left, the end of the corridor.'

Webster was waiting outside, still glowering but inwardly feeling sick in the knowledge that this was the end of his career in the force. Why, oh why, couldn't he learn to control his temper? As Frost approached he glared at him with all the bitter resentment of a man who knows he is completely in the wrong. Let him say one word, just one bloody word, he thought.

With a curt jerk of his head, Frost ordered the constable to follow him. When at last he spoke, the rebuke was fairly mild. 'That was bloody stupid, son.'

'Thank you, I've worked that out for myself,' snarled Webster. 'I suppose you can't wait to report me to Mullett?'

'Report what to Mullett?' asked Frost. 'I saw nothing. Baskin tells me he tripped and banged his nose against the wall. From the size of his hooter I'm inclined to believe that's more than possible.'

At first he couldn't take in what the inspector was saying. In that one punch he was sure he had thrown everything away, but suddenly, with his feet on the gallows trap, the last-minute reprieve. Relief made sweat trickle coldly down his back. He wanted to thank Frost but couldn't bring himself to do it. 'How did you get Baskin to agree to that?'

'By telling him we wouldn't bring any charges in respect of the girl.'

Webster stopped dead in his tracks. 'No charges? After what he's done? He's corrupted a juvenile.'

'Corrupted?' repeated Frost. 'Do you really think Baskin was the first? Your sweet, innocent fifteen-year-old virgin has been on the pill for God knows how long . . .'

Webster stared at him blankly. 'On the pill . . .'

'Yes, son. I found the packet in her bedroom last night. They were prescribed for the mother, who must have passed them on to Karen.'

Webster was stunned. 'You never told me?'

'I didn't think it had anything to do with the case, son. The kid was missing. We were called in to find her. Anything else was between her and her mother. Ah, this must be her dressing room.'

They had turned the corner and were in a short corridor with three doors leading off it. One door was marked Staff Toilets — Men, another Staff Toilets — Women and the door in between, Artists' Dressing Room. The glamour of show business, thought Frost. 'Right, son. She's inside. Go and get her.' He stepped back.

Webster rapped on the door.

'Yes,' called a girl's voice.

'Karen, it's the police.'

Frost groaned. Webster shouldn't have given the game away. He should have barged straight in and grabbed her. His fears were confirmed by a scuffling sound from inside the dressing room, then two loud clicks as the door bolts were rammed home.

'It's the police, Karen,' repeated Webster, banging on the door. 'Open up.'

'Piss off,' screamed the young schoolgirl.

'Kick the door in,' ordered Frost. 'Harry Baskin won't mind.'

Webster stepped back and kicked, his toe landing just below the door handle. One kick was enough. The door crashed back. He stepped inside a cheerless room with a long, greasy fingermarked mirror above a Formica ledge that ran the length of one wall. He couldn't see Karen. Then someone in the mirror moved. He spun around and there was the girl, stark naked, her clothes bundled in her hand, moving quickly to the door. He reached forward to grab at her. She hurled the clothes in his face, then her knee came up savagely. He doubled up, breathless, almost screaming with pain. Sweet, innocent Karen certainly knew how to hurt a man! He reached out blindly and touched naked flesh, then jerked his head back as long red fingernails clawed bloodied lines down his face. He clutched her wrists, pulling her hands away, finding enough breath to yelp in agony as her teeth sank into his arm.

'I could do with some help, Inspector,' he roared, shaking his wrist free of teeth.

Frost's head poked around the door, saw the problem, and hastily retreated. 'Stand guard outside, son. I'll send for a woman officer.'

Some fourteen minutes later Dave Shelby's patrol car nosed its way to the club entrance, and Shelby, followed by detective constable Susan Harvey, climbed out. They sauntered across to the reception lobby where Frost was waiting.

'Here we are, Inspector,' Shelby announced. 'One lady police officer delivered safe and sound, as requested.'

'Thank you, Constable,' said Frost coldly, not responding to Shelby's jocular manner. He was going to have a few quiet words with him when he got him on his own, words that would knock the cockiness out of him.

Unabashed, Shelby asked, 'You're not on this rape inquiry, are you, sir?'

'No,' replied Frost. 'If you want to confess you'll have to see Mr Allen.'

Shelby flipped open his notebook. 'Can I give you the details? I know who made that anonymous phone call last night. I've just interviewed him.'

Frost waved the notebook away. 'Give it to Mr Allen. I'm up to my armpits in naked fifteen-year-old girls at the moment.'

'Some people have all the luck,' called Shelby, quickly walking back to his car.

Frost watched him go. 'He's in a hurry. I'd have thought naked fifteen-year-olds were right up his street.' He turned to the woman constable. 'Did he manage to keep his hands off you, Sue?'

She smiled. 'He knows better than to try anything with me.'

Frost raised his eyebrows in mock surprise. 'I've summed you up all wrong then, Sue girl. I'd have thought one tickle of his Errol Flynn moustache on your cheek and you wouldn't be able to get your knickers off fast enough.'

Susan grinned. 'What's the problem, sir?'

He filled her in on the details, then took her back to the dressing room where the wounded Webster, patiently mounting guard, managed a grin of delight when he saw Susan. 'Karen's wedged the chair against the door handle,' he told them.

Susan tried the handle and banged on the door. 'Karen, I'm a police officer. Open up.'

'Piss off,' called the girl.

'That's French for "go away",' explained Frost. 'Boot it in again, son.'

The door crashed back from the onslaught. Karen, her

eyes blazing, fingernails clawed, was crouching, ready to meet them, like a karate fighter. She was still stark naked and was not going to let them take her without a fight.

Sue moved into the room; the girl lunged foward to meet her. At the last moment, the woman officer sidestepped and stabbed out her foot to catch the girl on the ankle, sending her sprawling to the floor. Then Sue was down on her, her knee in the girl's back, her hand forcing the girl's arm high above her shoulder blades. All Karen could do was scream obscenities and pound the floor impotently with her free hand.

'You can either get dressed,' said the woman detective pleasantly, 'or I can handcuff you and take you out to the car as you are. Which is it to be?'

To Frost's disappointment, Karen agreed to get dressed.

A quick phone call to Clare Dawson before the runaway was returned. Frost was hoping she could get her husband out of the house so mother and daughter could get their stories sorted out. When they arrived Max Dawson was out, cruising the streets, looking for his daughter, and wouldn't be back for half an hour. Apparently his wife hadn't yet passed on the good news, wanting to surprise him on his return.

With sulky defiance, Karen shrugged off her mother's attempts to make a fuss of her and just stood staring, with a sly, superior, knowing smile on her face, the smile of one who has power over another. Just wait until my daddy comes home, the smile said. Just wait until I tell him why I ran away.

But Clare, from long practice, knew just how to handle her daughter. 'Do you still want to go to ballet school, darling?'

Instantly, Karen changed back to the fifteen-year-old, the dance-mad schoolgirl, her eyes bright with excitement. 'It's what I want more than anything, Mummy.'

'I think it can be arranged,' said Clare confidently.

'But Daddy has always said no.'

'You leave your father to me,' replied her mother. 'But first we'd better have a little chat so we can explain to him what's been going on.'

Clare showed them to the front door. 'Thank you so much,' she gushed. Frost grunted his acknowledgement and walked with Susan to the car. As Webster followed, Clare took his hand and gave it a gentle, conspiratorial squeeze, her finger caressing his palm. 'I'm alone here most afternoons,' she whispered. 'Always glad of a bit of company.'

As he joined the others in the car, Webster didn't know whether to feel annoyed or flattered. But he did know it was the best offer he'd had since he arrived in Denton.

'You look happy, son,' commented Frost as Webster slid in behind the steering wheel. 'Your beard's gone all stiff.'

WEDNESDAY DAY SHIFT (6)

The time had wormed its way around to three o'clock. None of them had eaten, so they took a meal break at a little back-street café. The food wasn't up to much, but it was a happy time for Webster, who found he was hitting it off with Susan Harvey.

It was ten past four as they climbed back into the car. Webster, hoping the woman detective would sit next to him, was disappointed when she and Frost settled themselves down in the back seat. 'The cop shop please, driver,' said Frost grandly, 'and go the pretty way round via the gasworks.' Webster acknowledged the order with a petulant grunt. Frost's pathetic attempts at humour had long worn paper-thin as far as he was concerned.

'Control to all units in the Denton area.'

Webster turned up the volume.

'Armed robbery at Glickman's pawnbrokers, 23 North Street. Owner reported shot. Charlie Alpha in attendance but assistance urgently required.'

Frost leaned over to snatch up the handset. 'Hello, Con-

trol. Frost here. We're within two minutes of North Street.
On our way. Over.'

Webster slammed the car around corners and in and out of
back streets as he tried to meet the inspector's rash and impossible estimate of two minutes. Frost and the girl were sent
sliding from one side of the car to the other, their movements
echoed by Frost's spare pair of Wellington boots on the back
ledge. Reaching the High Street, they slowed down to let
Susan off, then roared away to North Street, a side-turning
off Bath Road.

'Left here,' barked Frost. The Cortina nosed into North
Street and pulled up abruptly behind area car Charlie Alpha.

The monotonous shrill of an alarm bell cut through the
air. A small crowd of sightseers was being pushed away from
the entrance to a shuttered shop by a uniformed police constable. Above the shop door a stout iron bracket supported
the universal pawnbrokers' trademark, three brass balls. A
fading painted wooden sign announced S. GLICKMAN, JEWELLER
AND PAWNBROKER. The premises had a shabby, down-at-heel
appearance and didn't look nearly prosperous enough to warrant the attention of an armed robber.

They darted from the car to the shop, the uniformed man
giving a nod of recognition to the inspector. Inside, their feet
scrunched over shards of broken glass that powdered the carpet.

It was a tiny, dingy shop. A couple of paces and they were
at a glass-fronted counter, its shelves stripped bare of the
jewellery it once held. On the wall, to the left of the counter,
a shattered glass showcase containing a mess of broken glass,
cheap watches, and cigarette lighters. The wall showcase to
the right of the counter contained nine-carat gold chains and
pendants and appeared to be untouched.

The fat man in the shiny blue-serge suit dabbing blood
from his face was Sammy Glickman, the owner. Balding,
middle-aged, tiny shifty eyes behind thick-lensed glasses, and
a few more chins than the usual allowance, Glickman was
slumped on a chair in front of his counter. A police officer,

PC Keith Sutton, was questioning him, jotting down his replies.

The sound of the alarm bell was magnified in the enclosed space of the shop. 'Can't someone turn that bloody thing off?' pleaded Frost.

Holding his now crimson and soggy handkerchief tightly against his forehead, the pawnbroker fished a bunch of keys from his pocket, sorted one out, and offered it to Webster. 'There's a switch under the counter . . . left-hand side.'

Webster killed the alarm. It died immediately but the ghost echo of its high-pitched ringing still scratched at their ears.

The shop was too small to hold four men comfortably, so Frost instructed Webster to go with the other officer and start knocking at doors to find out if anyone saw anything. 'Have a look in the road for a licence plate,' he called. 'You never know your luck.'

There was now room to move and Frost was able to get close enough to the pawnbroker to examine his injuries. The forehead wound was little more than a deep cut. 'The radio reported you were shot, Sammy,' said Frost, sounding disappointed. 'I was expecting to find you with your head blown off.'

'Another couple of inches and it could have been, Mr Frost,' Glickman replied.

'I've sent for an ambulance, Inspector,' said Sutton, 'but it's not very serious.'

The eyes behind the thick lenses focused indignantly on the constable. 'Not very serious? I'm bleeding like a stuck pig. It's a miracle I'm still alive. He fired straight at me.'

'He missed you, though, didn't he?' observed Frost, moving behind the counter to poke at the damaged showcase. 'And you're hardly a small target.' Amongst the fragments of shattered glass and the cigarette lighters he spotted some flattened lead pellets. He picked one up with his finger and thumb and displayed it to the constable.

'Yes, sir, I did notice,' said Sutton, sniffing. These damn plainclothes men seemed to think the uniformed branch was blind. 'Shotgun pellets. The man fired a warning shot as he was leaving. A splinter of flying glass caused the damage to Mr Glickman's forehead.'

'It could have gone in my eye,' moaned Glickman. 'Blinded me for life.'

'It could have gone up your arse,' snapped Frost, 'but it didn't, so let's stick to what actually happened.' He dug out his cigarettes and offered the packet around, then had a nose around the shop, pulling at drawers, prodding at showcases. He opened a door behind the counter, and his nose wrinkled at the musty smell of old clothes. Clicking on the light, he faced dusty shelves piled with brown-paper parcels, old suitcases, and hangers full of outdated garments. He returned to the shop, where he examined the security bars and locks fitted to the inside of the main door and shop window. 'He got nothing from the window display, then?' he asked.

'Only from the counter,' said Sutton. 'Mr Glickman said he was in and out in a flash.'

Frost nodded, then sat on the corner of the counter, swinging his leg. 'Right, Mr Glickman. Tell me what happened.'

'What's there to tell?' asked Glickman. 'I'm in my shop, the bell on the door rings, telling me a customer has come in. I raise my head to greet him and I'm looking straight down the barrel of a shotgun. Behind it is this great hulking brute of a man wearing a stocking mask.'

As Glickman was talking, Frost studied the pattern of the shotgun pellet pockmarks on the wall. The spread seemed fairly concentrated and not widespread as would be the case if the gun barrel had been sawn off.

'This gun, Sammy. Was the barrel full-size or had it been sawn off?'

Glickman shrugged. 'When a man pokes something like that at you, Mr Frost, you don't get down and measure it.'

'That's what the girl who was raped said,' murmured Frost.

PC Sutton's shoulders shook as he tried not to laugh. 'It's pretty certain the barrel wasn't sawn off, Inspector — the damage is too localized. Someone from Forensic should be here soon. They'll be able to tell us.'

'Yes, they're such clever bastards,' commented Frost, who had little time for the geniuses of the forensic section. He nodded for Sammy to continue.

'He don't say a dicky bird, just prods me in the gut with the shooter and indicates I should come around the front and lay facedown on the floor. I don't need to be told twice. Down I go and I hear him sliding back the counter doors and scooping the cream of my stock into a plastic bag.'

'What sort of stuff, Sammy?'

'Rings, bracelets, brooches, all exquisite items — twenty thousand quid's worth.'

Frost snorted out a lungful of smoke. 'Twenty thousand! Do me a favour, Sammy. We're the police, not the insurance company.'

'All right,' said Sammy reluctantly, 'perhaps it might have been nearer six thousand. Anyway, he then rams the gun in the back of my neck and says I'm not to move a muscle for ten minutes, otherwise he'll blow my head off. So I lie there all still, but as soon as I hear the door close, I'm up in a flash and I'm out the street yelling, "Stop, thief".' He dabbed his forehead again and was disappointed to see that the flow of blood had stopped. 'Picture the scene, Mr Frost. I'm out in that street yelling, "Stop thief," and who's there to hear me? Not a bloody soul! The only person in the street is the robber, climbing into his motor and yanking the stocking mask off his head.'

Frost slid down from the counter. 'You saw him with the mask off? Did you see his face?'

'It was the only bloody face in the street. Of course I saw it.'

'Would you recognize him again?'

Glickman folded the handkerchief carefully and put it in his pocket. 'Listen, Mr Frost, when a man robs me of thirty thousand pounds' worth of prime stock, I promise you his face becomes memorable.'

'I suppose you didn't get the registration number of the car?' asked Frost, not too hopefully.

'Of course I got the bloody registration number. It was a red Vauxhall Cavalier, registration number CBZ2303. They're nice little motors — my brother-in-law has one.'

Frost couldn't believe his luck. Licence plates falling off Jags, and now an armed robber seen without his mask, his car details noted. He instructed Sutton to buzz Control and get the car's particulars circulated.

'Already done, sir,' said Sutton flatly. He didn't need to be told to do something as basic as that.

'And you've warned Control that the man is armed and dangerous?'

'Of course, sir.' Or as basic as that, either.

Glickman, piqued that he was no longer the centre of attraction, said peevishly, 'Do you want to know what else happened, or am I of no further interest now I've done half your work for you?'

Frost hitched himself back up on the counter and waved for Sammy to go on.

'Like I said, I'm screaming to an empty street. He must have got fed up with me yelling at him because he swings his shooter round and fires — point-blank range. But he misses me and hits that showcase.'

Frost looked at the showcase and lined up the angles. 'Either he was a rotten shot, Sammy, or he only meant to frighten you.'

'He certainly frightened me, Inspector. I'll be putting the biological washing powder to the test tonight, I promise you. Anyway, I fling myself facedown on the pavement until I hear the car roaring off. Then everyone comes running out to see what's up. When I'm screaming, "Stop thief," and being fired at, the street is empty. The minute he's gone they're standing eight deep on the pavement.'

The shop door opened and Webster, with the other uniformed man, returned to report that they hadn't come up with a single witness who had seen anything other than a red, or a blue, or a black car roaring off in the distance. Plenty of people said they had heard the gunshot but thought it was a car backfiring.

'If it was an atom bomb going off, they'd say it was a car backfiring,' muttered Glickman.

Frost's cigarettes were passed around again, and soon the little shop was thickly hazed with smoke. 'One thing for sure,' said Frost, 'whoever did this was either a small-time crook or a first-timer.'

'How do you make that out?' asked Webster.

'Well,' said Frost, adding a salvo of smoke rings to the already murky atmosphere, 'if you go in for armed robbery it's a minimum of seven years, for starters. So why risk seven years robbing a little shithouse like this when, for the same risk, you could rob a bank or a decent jeweller?'

'Thank you very much, Mr Frost,' said Glickman, sounding offended.

'My pleasure,' replied Frost. 'Secondly, he didn't saw off the barrel, as any self-respecting gunman would do. This means he couldn't keep the gun concealed in a deep pocket. He'd either have to tuck it inside his coat as he crossed from the car to the shop or blatantly wave it about. Finally, what does he do when he gets in here? He dashes in, sweeps odds and ends of Mickey Mouse jewellery into a dustbin sack and is out again in seconds. He could have taken his time and nicked all sorts of things of value, but he was in too much of a hurry. Why?' Like a schoolmaster, he looked around for an answer.

'Because he was bloody scared?' suggested Sutton.

Frost nodded his agreement. 'Exactly what I think, young Sutton. It was all so amateurish.'

'It wasn't amateurish the way he fired that gun at me,' objected Glickman. 'He missed me by inches.'

'Thirty-six bloody inches,' said Frost. He pushed himself off the counter and wandered behind it to the till. 'I suppose he didn't touch the takings?' He pressed the No Sale key and the drawer shot open.

'Only the jewellery,' said Glickman, craning his neck to keep an eye on Frost. Some policemen had very sticky fingers.

The till drawer held about seventy pounds. Not rich pick-ings, but it would have increased the gunman's haul by about ten percent. Frost was pushing the drawer shut when he saw the small envelope tucked behind the bank notes. He had seen envelopes like that before. Exactly like that. Taken from a drug addict, newly purchased from a pusher and full of heroin.

Sammy Glickman had been mixed up with a lot of shady dealings in the past, but never with drugs. Frost pulled the envelope out. It was far too heavy for heroin. The flap was sealed. He stuck a finger beneath it and ripped it open, then tipped the contents into his palm. Gold. Gold coins. Five golden sovereigns each bearing the head of Queen Victoria.

'I'm waiting to hear the ding of the till drawer being closed,' called the pawnbroker anxiously, finding it difficult to see what Frost was up to through the thickening smoke screen. Frost obliged him and firmly closed the drawer with a satisfying ding. But he didn't put the sovereigns back. He walked back around the counter and held out his hand.

'What are these, Sammy?'

The eyes behind the thick lenses blinked furiously as they focused on the coins. 'I buy all sorts of precious metal . . . coins, lockets, gold teeth. You can see the sign outside . . . Best Prices Paid . . . there's no crime in it.'

'I didn't say there was, Sammy.'

Webster craned his neck so he could see what the inspector had found. At first he didn't realize what the coins were. They looked small and insignificant, not much bigger than a new penny. Then he saw the George-and-Dragon pattern on the reverse. Of course! The stolen Queen Victoria sovereigns. 'Where did you get these?' he demanded.

The pawnbroker wriggled in his chair. 'I've been robbed, I'm wounded, I'm in a state of shock. I demand to go to hospital.'

'Where did you get them?' repeated Webster.

'I bought them this morning. It's all legitimate.'

If it's legitimate, then why are you looking so bloody

guilty? thought Frost to himself happily. 'Who did you buy them from, Sammy?'

'A young bloke about twenty-five, dark hair cut short, black leather jacket. I've never seen him before. What's this all about, Mr Frost? I'm the innocent victim of a brutal crime. I'm entitled to sympathy, not harassment.'

The summonsed ambulance pulled up outside the shop. Sammy gave a sigh of relief. It would take him to the peace and quiet of the hospital and away from these searching questions.

'Send the ambulance away,' Frost instructed the two policemen, 'then get back on patrol. Webster and I can handle it from here.'

Glickman's face fell. 'I need hospitalisation, Mr Frost. I'm feeling bad. It's delayed reaction from the shock.'

'I'll get the police surgeon to have a look at you when we lock you up,' said Frost. He said it so matter-of-factly that at first Glickman couldn't believe what he had heard. Then he did a double take as the import struck home.

'Lock me up? What are you talking about?'

'Terribly sorry, Sammy,' said Frost, 'but the sovereigns are stolen property. We'll have to book you for receiving.'

Glickman's eyes, magnified behind the lenses, opened wide with feigned amazement. 'Stolen property in my shop? I can't believe it. He said they were family heirlooms.'

'So they were,' said Frost. 'Heirlooms of the family he nicked them from.'

'On my dear mother's funeral plot, Mr Frost, if I had the slightest idea they were stolen, I would never have touched them.'

'How much did you give for them?' asked Frost.

The pawnbroker's tongue crawled around his lips which had suddenly become very dry. 'Thirty pounds each . . . one hundred and fifty nicker the five.'

'Thirty lousy quid!' scoffed Frost. 'And you didn't know they were stolen? That's less than half of the market value.'

'I offered him a low price, Mr Frost, expecting he'd push it up higher. That's business. But he said, "Provided it's in used fivers, you've got yourself a deal." So, if he was happy I was happy. I gave him the fivers, and he gave me the sovereigns — all fair, square and aboveboard.'

'Tell me the rest, Sammy.'

'The rest, Mr Frost?'

'Thirty quid is a bulk price. He must have told you he had a lot more.'

'Really, Mr Frost. I'd have known it wasn't aboveboard if he said he had a lot.'

Frost shook his head in disappointment. 'OK, Sammy, we're booking you for receiving stolen property.'

'Now hold on, Mr Frost . . .' Suddenly his shoulders drooped. 'All right. He said he had about fifty more. They were mine at the same price providing it was in used fivers. I didn't have fifteen hundred quid in cash. I said I'd get it from the bank. He said he'd be back tomorrow.'

Frost grinned broadly. 'Then I'll tell you what's going to happen, Sammy. The minute he puts his foot inside that door, you will phone the station and you will make certain he doesn't leave your shop until the fuzz arrive. If we catch him, I'll drop the receiving stolen property charge, if not, you'll be eating Her Majesty's porridge for a very long time.'

'I'll co-operate with you in every way I can, Mr Frost.'

'I knew you would, Sammy. Now put your coat on. We're going walkies to the cop shop.'

The pawnbroker was crestfallen. 'The station. But you said . . .'

'To look at some mug shots,' explained Frost. 'To see if you can't pick us out the bloke with the shooter. It's part of co-operating with us every way you can.'

Glickman sat in Frost's office hunched over yet another book of photographs that the bearded detective constable had dumped on the desk. His head was aching and the cup of stewed tea they had reluctantly provided to help him swallow the aspirins for his headache was sending acid ripples across his stomach. He wished he'd never admitted he could identify the gunman so he could now be indoors, in his cosy little flat above the shop, filling in his insurance claim form.

He sighed at the unfairness of life and opened the latest book, screwing his eyes as the monotonous rows of criminal faces shivered in and out of focus. He had looked at so many photographs he was now beginning to doubt his ability to recognize the man with the shooter even if he saw him face to face. A cough from the bearded detective prodded him to hurry so the current album could be replaced by yet another. The world seemed to be jam-packed with photographed criminals.

A creak as the door opened slowly, and Inspector Frost backed in carrying three more lethal mugs of stewed police tea. Dumping one in front of the pawnbroker, he asked, 'Any luck yet?'

Glickman's head shook from side to side. 'I've never seen so many ugly faces in all my life.'

'You wait till you see Mr Mullett's wedding photos,' said Frost.

Glickman couldn't even manage a polite laugh. He turned the page and scowled down on rows of faces all scowling back at him. Didn't crooks ever smile? They were probably photographed after drinking this awful tea!

It was a job to concentrate with so much going on, so many people coming into and going from Frost's tiny office. First there was a panic about a missing girl. It appeared that a neighbouring division had picked up a schoolgirl believing her to be a teenager called Karen Dawson who Frost had advised them was missing. As far as Glickman could gather, the trouble was that Frost had already found the girl but neglected to let the other divisions know. And then a little fat detective sergeant called Arthur Hanlon had been in to report on the interviews with various down-and-outs. It seemed that Frost was interested in the last hours of someone who was found dead, smothered in sick, down a public convenience. Glickman, shuddering at all the unpleasant details, felt like being sick himself.

Hanlon was sent out to find more tramps to talk to, and

no sooner was he gone than there was a commotion about a
return the inspector was supposed to have sent off the previous night, but hadn't. And between all these interruptions,
Glickman was expected to concentrate on page after monotonous page of faces that were all starting to look the same. He
flicked over a page with barely a glance. A sharp tap on his
shoulder from the frowner with the beard.

'You didn't look at that page,' Webster admonished
sternly.

Damn police. He felt like identifying anyone, whoever it
was, just to end the ordeal. He turned the page.

Frost drained his tea, wiped his mouth, and poked in a
cigarette. He clicked his lighter, but it failed to flame, so he
rummaged through his desk for a box of matches.

'I can do you a nice automatic gold-plated lighter with
your name engraved for only £29.95,' Glickman offered.
'That's cheaper than wholesale.'

'But a damn sight dearer than a box of matches,' said
Frost. 'You keep your big nose stuck in that book, Sammy,
and stop trying to make a profit out of poor, overworked
policemen.' He slouched back and stuck his feet up on his
desk, knocking his mug over in the process. The phone rang.
He picked it up and listened. 'I've already told you, the crime
statistics will go off tonight, definite . . . unless you keep
interrupting me with these stupid phone calls.' He thumped
the phone down.

No sooner had Frost disposed of that call than the door
opened and a tall, important-looking policeman in a tailored
uniform, all teeth, moustache, and buttons, marched in. The
frowner stiffened to attention. Frost swung his legs off the
desk, scrabbled for a file, and pretended to be adding up
columns of figures.

'I was expecting your further report on the hit-and-run
investigation,' said Mullett stiffly.

'Sorry about that, Super,' said Frost. 'Lots of things have
happened. We found that missing girl.'

'Yes, I heard, and apparently you failed to let other divisions know.'

'I got tied up with this armed robbery,' explained the inspector, who had hoped the Commander wouldn't have heard about that little faux pas.

'I don't want you to take on extra cases, Inspector,' Mullett told him. 'I want you to concentrate on the hit-and-run. I get phone calls every five minutes from the House of Commons asking what progress we're making. What about Julie King? I understand she confirms that Roger Miller was with her all night.'

'She looks the sort who would say anything, or do anything, for a couple of quid,' said Frost, failing to locate his ashtray and shaking ash over Mullett's shoes.

Mullett stared down at his shoes and flicked them distastefully. 'If, as he claims, the car was stolen from outside the girl's flat, have you made house-to-house inquiries in the area in case anyone saw something?'

Flaming hell! thought Frost, I never gave it a thought. 'The very next item on our agenda, Super,' he lied. 'Just as soon as we've finished with this gentleman here. He's the victim of the armed robbery.'

'The bullet missed me by inches,' said Glickman, putting in his two-penny-worth.

'And we've got a lead on those sovereigns,' added Frost, determined to throw in all the pluses.

Mullett drew in his breath. 'All I am interested in, Frost, is the hit-and-run. I must have something positive to tell Sir Charles Miller. Put the house-to-house inquiry in hand right away.'

'Right away, sir,' Frost assured him, putting his thumb to his nose and waggling his fingers as soon as the door closed behind his Divisional Commander. Then he stood up and declaimed dramatically: 'She was only a stripper's daughter, so very good and kind/No stain upon her character, but a mole on her behind.'

Webster's scowl deepened. How childish could you get? He squinted at his wristwatch. Nearly five past seven. He smothered a yawn and felt tiredness creeping over him. Hardly any sleep last night, already on duty for ten hours solid and they still had the house-to-house inquiries about the stolen Jaguar to make. He wouldn't see the inside of his rented room much before midnight. Later he would realize what an optimistic estimate that was.

The phone rang. Frost listened and frowned. 'Thanks,' he grunted, 'I expected as much.' He hung up. 'The red Vauxhall Cavalier,' he told Webster. 'It was reported stolen at three o'clock this afternoon.' He stretched out his arms and yawned openly. 'As soon as Sammy has identified the man with the golden gun, we'll go home. I could do with an early night.' Webster reminded him of the house-to-house, but Frost wasn't interested. 'That can wait. We've got more important things to do than waste time trying to clear that little snot. No, we'll have an early night.' He stared pointedly at Webster's beard, then began to sing 'Does Santa Claus sleep with his whiskers over or under the sheets . . . ?'

Glickman's shoulders quivered with suppressed laughter. He thought the inspector was a real card. The bearded one had no sense of humour and was so easily riled. Glickman's eyes travelled over a page filled with sneering punks and scowling skin-heads. He licked his finger and turned the page.

He stared. He blinked. Then stared again.

'It's him!'

Frost and Webster leaned over his shoulder. 'This one!' insisted Glickman, jabbing a pudgy finger on the glossy black-and-white.

'Are you sure?' Frost asked doubtfully.

'I'm one hundred fifty percent sure,' claimed the pawn-broker. 'You can't get any surer than that.'

The photograph was of a rather hopeless-looking individual with tight curly hair and a mournful expression. Webster read out his details. 'Stanley Eustace, aged forty-seven . . .'

'I know who it is,' cut in Frost, who had found his matches but seemed to have lost his cigarettes. 'Useless Eustace. He's a petty crook, shoplifting, breaking and entering, nicking cars, stripping lead from church roofs. He usually gets caught because he's so bloody stupid. But he's never used a shooter in his life.'

'Well, he used one this afternoon,' Glickman said positively. 'Can I go home now?'

No spare cars were available, so Glickman, bitterly complaining, was left to find his own way home. Frost then asked Webster to bring the Cortina around to the front. They were off to pick up Stan Eustace.

Webster hesitated. 'He's armed and dangerous. Hadn't we better take some reinforcements with us . . . and a couple of police marksmen?'

But Frost scorned this suggestion. 'I know him, son. I've nicked him enough times. He's harmless. The gun was only for show.'

'For show!' exclaimed Webster. 'He nearly blasted that showcase from the wall.'

'Probably got his finger caught in the trigger,' said Frost airily. 'You can stay in the car if you like. I'll go in the house and drag him out.'

He was slipping on his mac when an agitated Johnny Johnson poked his head in. 'Sorry to interrupt you, Inspector, but you haven't seen Dave Shelby on your travels, have you?'

'No,' replied Frost, 'not since he delivered sexy Sue to us at The Coconut Grove round about two o'clock. Why?'

The station sergeant rubbed a hand wearily over his face. 'I'm dead worried, Jack. Since he left you he hasn't made any routine calls, hasn't contacted us or answered his radio. He was supposed to report to me, here, at seven — he's only doing a part-shift — but he didn't show up.'

Frost didn't think there was any cause for concern. 'He's probably in bed with some woman somewhere and forgotten the time.'

'I'm really worried, Jack,' insisted Johnson, and he looked it. 'For all Shelby's faults he's never once failed to report in.' He waved away Frost's offer of a cigarette.

'Have you had a word with Mr Allen, Sergeant?' inquired Webster. 'Shelby said he was going to see him about the anonymous phone call.'

'There's your answer,' said Frost, tucking his scarf inside his mac. He sent Webster out to ask Allen. Within a couple of minutes Allen, accompanied by Sergeant Ingram, marched in.

'What's this about Shelby?' snapped Allen. 'I haven't seen him all day.'

'I saw him this morning,' said Ingram, 'but I've been off duty all afternoon.'

'He's gone missing,' said Frost, giving brief details. 'Johnny's worried about him.'

'He hasn't reported in for nearly five hours,' added the station sergeant.

'Five hours!' exclaimed Allen in disbelief. 'Why have you waited five hours before telling anyone?'

The station sergeant looked embarrassed. 'He was doing a job for Mr Frost taking a WPC over to The Coconut Grove. I thought Mr Frost might have commandeered his services and told him not to answer his radio.' It was Frost's turn to look embarrassed. It wouldn't have been the first time he had cut corners by doing that.

'For heaven's sake,' said Allen, 'he's in a patrol car. You can't lose a police officer and a patrol car.'

'I've asked all patrols to look out for him,' said Johnson. 'No sightings yet.'

'Have you tried the hospitals?' asked Frost. The sergeant nodded. 'Then what about his home? He might have gone straight there.'

'He would have signed off first,' said Johnson.

'Try his home anyway,' ordered Allen, 'but be tactful. We don't want to get his wife worried.'

Anxiously watched by all the others, Johnson dialled Shelby's house.

'No, he's not back yet,' replied Mrs Shelby. 'I'm expecting him soon. Any message?'

'Not really,' said Johnson, trying to sound unconcerned. 'He's probably on a job for Mr Frost, but I wanted to grab him before he left. Ask him to ring me when he gets in, would you?' He replaced the receiver slowly, his head bowed. 'I'm worried,' he said. 'Bloody worried.'

Ingram walked across to the wall map behind Frost's desk. 'I've had a nasty thought,' he said, and he pointed to the wall map. 'North Street is here. The armed man in the getaway car was heading off in this direction . . . which would take him smack bang into Shelby's patrol area.'

Allen squeezed past Webster to study the wall map himself. 'You're suggesting that Shelby could have spotted the getaway car and tried to intercept it?'

'It's possible, sir,' answered Ingram, 'The gunman's armed. Shelby could have got himself into trouble.'

Allen tugged at his lip, then turned to Frost. 'What do you think?'

Frost stuck his hands in his mac pocket and drew hard on his cigarette. 'If Shelby spotted the car, he wouldn't have gone after it off his own bat. He'd have radioed in.' Johnny Johnson nodded his agreement.

'But his radio might be on the blink,' said Allen, 'which is why we didn't get any calls earlier. He could have tried to stop the getaway car and the gunman could have turned nasty . . . wounded him, or taken him hostage.'

'The gunman,' interjected Frost, 'is Useless Eustace — Stan Eustace. Glickman identified him. Stan would never hold a gun to a copper in his life.'

'And he would never have committed an armed robbery in his life,' retorted Allen with a sarcastic smile, 'but he did this afternoon.' He looked once more at the wall map. 'It's pointless wasting time speculating. A police officer has gone missing, so we take no chances.' He moved his head to the station sergeant. 'All leave is stopped, Johnny. You'd better start calling the off-duty men in. We'll have to get a full-scale search organized.'

'While you're getting it organized,' said Frost, edging toward the door, 'me and Fungus Face will pay a visit to Stan Eustace's house. If he doesn't know he's been identified, we might be able to pick him up with only minimum loss of life.' He beckoned for Webster to follow him and was away.

'Get the search organized,' Allen instructed Ingram. 'I'll go and break the news to Mr Mullett.'

WEDNESDAY DAY SHIFT (7)

The tiny garden in front of Stanley Eustace's semi-detached house in Merchants Lane was overgrown with weeds, and the lawn had as fine a crop of thistles as Frost had ever seen. Lights were on downstairs and a radio was playing. There was no escape route from the back of the premises, so there was no need for the two detectives to split up.

Frost pushed the door bell. It wasn't working, so he had to bang on the door with his hand. He tapped gently, hoping it might sound like an insurance salesman and not a visit from the fuzz.

Webster made a point of hanging back, expecting any minute to see the barrel of a shotgun break through a window. Frost could prattle on about Eustace being harmless until he was blue in the face. Webster remembered the story Johnny Johnson had told him only that morning of how Frost thought the Bennington's Bank gunman was harmless and got himself a bullet in the face to prove him wrong.

No-one seemed to want to open the door, so Frost banged again, a little harder this time. He lifted the flap of the letterbox and peeked through. He was rewarded by a Cinemascope view of a white-slacked crotch approaching. He straightened up smartly as the door opened and Sadie Eustace, Stanley's well-padded, tough little brunette wife, in white slacks, black jumper, and enormous blue doughnuts of dangling earrings, put her hands on her hips and demanded to know what they wanted.

'Stan in, Sadie?' asked Frost, pushing past her and jerking his head to the stairs for Webster to search the upper rooms.

'Where's your warrant?' screamed Sadie, following behind the inspector as he opened and shut doors, looking for her husband.

'Warrant?' said Frost, going through the elaborate panto-mime of patting his pockets as if trying to locate it. 'I've got it here somewhere.' By the time he had patted the last pocket he had looked in every downstairs room.

There was a crashing of doors from above. 'What's that hairy bastard doing up there?' cried Sadie, frowning up the stairs where Webster, fearing a stomachful of lead shot, was flinging open doors, then pressing himself flat against the wall à la Starsky and Hutch. The last door he crashed open was the bathroom, where the shock waves sent a mirror tumbling down from a shelf to shatter on the floor. That was when Webster actually did fling himself flat on his face, hugging the carpet and inhaling dust.

'You all right, son?' called Frost up the stairs.

'Yes,' said Webster curtly, standing up and brushing dust from his clothes. 'I slipped.' He thudded downstairs to the kitchen where Sadie, her arms folded, her earrings quivering angrily, was glaring at the inspector.

'You come bursting into my house without a warrant —'

'I thought I had it on me, Sadie,' said Frost, not in the least shame-faced. 'My mistake. So where is Stan — out selling the loot?'

'Whatever you want him for, he didn't do it. He hasn't been out of the house all day. What's it about?'

'Armed robbery,' Webster told her. Behind her he could see a stripped pine-wood paper-towel dispenser that Stan had fixed to the wall. It was hanging lopsidedly from one corner.

'Armed robbery? My Stan?' She laughed derisively. 'Do me a favour! You're out of your tiny minds.'

'No doubt about it, Sadie, I'm afraid,' said Frost, trying to fix the paper-towel dispenser in place, then giving it up as a bad job. 'It's got your Stanley's fingerprints all over it — it was a balls-up from start to finish.'

The phone in the hall rang. Sadie stiffened. 'Excuse me,' she said, trying to sound casual, but Frost barred her way. 'Answer it, son,' he told Webster.

The phone was on a telephone table under the stairs. Webster picked it up and listened. The sound of payphone pips, which stopped when the money was inserted. 'Hello . . . is that you, Sadie?' asked a man's voice. In the background, Webster could hear traffic rumbling past the kiosk. 'Sadie, it's me, Stan. I'm in a spot of bother. I need your help.'

'Stan, it's the bloody police,' Sadie screamed from the kitchen. Immediately there was a click, then a splutter of the dial tone. Webster hung up and returned to the kitchen.

'Stanley?' asked Frost. Webster nodded. 'Well, he knows we're on to him now, son.' He turned to Sadie. Her bosom was heaving and her eyes were ablaze with defiance. 'Nice one, Sadie, but what's the point? He can't keep running all his life.' She said nothing. Her lethal expression said it all.

They let themselves out. As they closed the door behind them they could hear her crying.

Back in the car Frost was wondering whether to tuck it around a side-turning and wait a while in case Stanley returned, but he decided against it. Even Useless Eustace wasn't that stupid.

Then the radio called him. Johnny Johnson, sounding grim.

'Yes, Johnny?'

'We've just had a phone call, Jack. A Mr Charles Fryatt. He reports seeing an apparently abandoned police car.'

Frost stiffened. 'Where?'

'In Green Lane, the cut-through to the main road.'

Frost felt his heartbeats quicken. 'And Shelby?'

'Mr Fryatt says he saw no sign of a driver, not that he looked very far. He thought he'd better get straight to a phone and tell us. Can you get over there?'

'On our way,' said Frost. 'Over and out.'

Green Lane was little more than a bumpy dirt track turning out of Bath Road and almost petering out before it reached Denton Road. The Cortina jolted and shuddered as it picked its way over the potholes and followed the twisting lane down into a depression completely hidden from both main roads.

'Look out!' called Frost and Webster braked abruptly as

the headlights swooped down on the bulk of something directly in their path. It was Shelby's patrol car, the Ford Escort, looking lost and miserable in the darkness.

Cautiously, they approached. The driver's door gaped open; a stream of police-channel chatter flowed from the radio. Frost's torch beam pried inside. The keys swung from the ignition, a clipboard with the day's standing instructions lay on the passenger seat. He picked up the handset and radioed through to Control to report they had arrived at the scene.

'Any sign of Shelby?' Johnson asked anxiously.

'Not yet,' replied the inspector.

'Don't move!' called Webster urgently. 'Just look down, by your feet.'

About an inch or so from where Frost was standing the beam of Webster's torch glinted on something. The ground was wet. Stained with red. Frost dropped to his knees to examine it closer. He dabbed it with his finger. It was blood. A lot of blood.

'And look there!' called Webster, swinging his torch up to the rear-door window of the patrol car.

The window was a crazy paving of shattered glass, milkily opaque. Embedded in the glass, also held in the paint work of the door, were tiny flattened pieces of metal. Lead pellets, identical to the pellets found in the wall at the pawnbroker's. Ingram's theory wasn't looking so farfetched now.

'Shit!' said Frost. He returned to the handset. 'Johnny. It doesn't look too happy, I'm afraid. There's blood and shotgun pellets all over the place. You'd better send a full team down here right away.'

Within twenty minutes the area was cordoned off and was droning with mobile generators that fed the many floodlights illuminating the scene. Men from Forensic were crawling, inch by inch, over the car. Scene-of-crime officers were taking photographs with blinding blue flashes, dusting for prints and circling blood splashes and lead pellet pockmarks with white chalk. A group of off-duty men who had spent most of the previous night and this morning combing Denton Woods on their hands and knees now scoured the scrubland on their hands and knees.

Frost, leaning against his Cortina, watched gloomily, the smoke from his cigarette spiralling upward. This was the time for experts and specialists and for attention to detail, so he kept well out of the way. Webster, who had been talking to a couple of the Forensic men, came over to join him.

'Forensic says the ground's too hard to leave any proper impression, but there are traces of a second car. The other vehicle was ahead of Shelby's patrol car, probably blocking the road. It looks as if Shelby stopped, got out, and was fired on as he walked toward the other car.'

'Then where is he?' asked Frost.

'Probably been taken away in the other car. There are marks where something was dragged.'

'Why?' said Frost, scratching his head. 'Why not leave him?' He looked up. 'Hello . . . what does that toffee-nosed git want?' One of the Forensic team, a man with long grey hair, was waving Frost over to the abandoned car.

'Preliminary report, Inspector,' he announced briskly. 'The blood on the ground and the blood splashed on the car is group B, which is Police Constable Shelby's group. The quantity of blood spilt suggests the wounding must have been extensive. Obviously, without knowing the area of the wounding, we can't be more specific. From the quantity of pellets we have recovered it seems pretty definite that only one cartridge was fired, and from the flattening of the pellets and the spread, I think we can safely say that the gunman was not much more than nine feet away from the patrol car. In other words, he would have been standing about . . . here.' He moved to a point some nine feet away and marked it with his heel. 'Our reconstruction is that the other car had already stopped. Shelby got out of his vehicle and walked toward the other car. The gunman climbed from his car and shot your policeman, who fell to the ground, bleeding extensively. The gunman then dragged Shelby to his own car and drove off with him.'

Frost looked down at the darkening pool which sluggishly reflected the overhead lights. 'Any idea how long the blood has been there?'

'I'm sorry, Inspector, I should have said. About four to five hours.'

Frost nodded gloomily. This would tie in with the time Stan Eustace was speeding away from the pawnbroker's.

'We'd like to take the car back for detailed examination,' said another of the Forensic team.

'Sure,' agreed the inspector, trying to work out what he should do next. Everyone was looking for the red Vauxhall Cavalier, and until that was sighted all he could do was wait.

Two more cars pulled up. Mullett emerged from his silver grey Rover at the same time as Allen and Ingram climbed out of their black Ford. Like an army detachment, all keeping perfect step, they marched purposefully toward Frost.

'Nasty business,' said Mullett after peering into the abandoned Escort and examining the blood puddle. Allen, not trusting the garbled version he would get from Frost, took the situation report direct from Forensic before bustling back to join the Divisional Commander.

'Anyone who has lost that amount of blood is going to need medical treatment, and damn quickly,' Allen snapped. 'I take it you've warned all doctors and hospitals, Frost?'

'Yes, I did manage to think that out for myself,' said Frost. 'Hospitals and doctors all advised.'

Missing with his first barrel, Allen fired the second. 'And you've got a car watching Eustace's house? He's bound to try and sneak back.'

Bull's-eye! thought Frost ruefully. 'Actually we were just on our way there.' He began to move toward the car.

'No. You stay here,' said Allen, thinking what a feather in his cap it would be if he were the one who arrested Eustace. 'This requires a police marksman, like Sergeant Ingram.' He swung around to Mullett. 'We'll need to draw a revolver from the armoury, sir. Would you arrange the necessary authorisation?' And with the Divisional Commander's agreement, he yelled for Ingram to join him and trotted off to his car.

Good bloody riddance, thought Frost, watching them drive away.

'Nasty business,' said Mullett again.

A squawk from a car radio. One of the uniformed men picked up the handset and answered the call, then waved and yelled, 'Mr Frost. Control wants to speak to you urgently.'

'Right,' said Frost, leaving Mullett with Webster, neither of whom could think of a thing to say to the other. Mullett dredged his mind for some innocuous small talk. 'Getting on all right?' he said at last.

'Yes, thank you, sir,' replied Webster tonelessly, his eyes fastened on Frost, who was leaning against the car, the handset to his ear, his expression revealing that something was terribly wrong.

Frost walked slowly back to the Commander, his face grim. 'Mr Mullett,' he said.

Mullett felt the cold of approaching bad news and shivered. 'Yes, Frost?'

'PC Shelby, sir. They've found him — in a ditch about three miles from here, just off the new Lexington Road.'

'Is he all right?' whispered Mullett. A silly question because he already knew the answer. The expression on Frost's face simply screamed it out.

Frost looked down at the blood on the lane. 'No, sir. He's dead.'

'That must be him,' said Webster as the car headlights picked out the figure of a man flagging him down. The man in a thick overcoat and muddy boots was a farm labourer. He had found the body.

'He's down here,' said the man, his boots clomping as he took them down a winding lane that snaked back to the farm where he worked. They followed in silence. Tall boundary hedges on each side made the lane very dark. A little way down, and they could hear the gurgle of water. It reminded Frost of the previous night when he'd followed Dave Shelby down those steps to the body of Ben Cornish. The clomping of boots stopped. The man pointed to where the lane started to make a lazy curve and where a drainage ditch, some two feet deep, hugged the side of a hedge-bordered field. From behind the hedge the plaintive lowing of cattle quivered gently in the darkness.

'He's in there,' said the farm labourer. 'In the ditch.' He wasn't going any farther. He had seen it once. He didn't want to see it again.

The two detectives moved forward. A narrow verge, overgrown with lank grass, separated the ditch from the lane. Flattened grass lurched over and combed the surface of muddied water which overflowed slightly at that point because of some obstruction. Webster fumbled for his torch and clicked the button.

A waxen hand, bobbing gently up and down, poked through green slime. The body was sprawled facedown in the stagnant murk. The water made the police uniform look jet black.

'I tried to pull him out,' called the labourer from the other side of the lane. 'I thought he might still be alive. But when I saw his face . . .'

Frost knelt on the wet grass and plunged his hand through the slime to grab Shelby's hair so he could lift the head. As it broke through the surface, Webster stifled a cry and Frost felt his stomach writhe in protest.

The head, dripping water and blood, had only half a face. The left-hand side was bloodied pulp with part of the cheek and lower lip flapping down, showing teeth and bone. There was no left eye, only a spongy red socket, and the forehead was pocked with embedded lead shot. Frost couldn't look any more. He released his grip, letting the head fall back in the ditch with a hollow plop. He dried his hand by wiping it on his mac.

Webster was the first to speak. 'Shall we get him out?'

'No,' said Frost, staring into the distance. 'Not until the police surgeon has seen him. You know what a fussy little bastard he is.' What is this, he thought, a rerun? I said all this last night.

After taking a few details, they let the farm labourer get off home. Then a scene-of-crime officer arrived with his expensive Japanese camera and his ultrafast colour film and took flash photographs of the ditch, the grass, and the bobbing white hand. Nothing else to photograph until the arrival of the police surgeon.

'There he is,' called Webster, watching a car gingerly nose its way up the lane, pulling up a few feet away from the two detectives. Slomon climbed out, nodded briefly to Frost, then peered into the ditch. 'Have I got to get down there?' he asked.

'Yes,' said Frost, 'you bloody well have.' Just let Slomon try to skimp this examination.

The doctor returned to the car for his Wellingtons. He pulled them on, removed his coat, and rolled up his shirt sleeves. Then, very carefully, he stepped down into the ditch. 'I'd like some light, please.'

Three torch beams homed in on him as he busied himself with his instruments and thermometers. In spite of the difficult working conditions, Slomon took his time, determined not to repeat the fiasco of the previous night. He explored the body very carefully before clambering out.

'At a guess, he's been dead between four to six hours,' he reported, drying his hands on a towel from his car. 'Impossible to be precise in these conditions, but the post-mortem will pin it down.' He rolled down his sleeves and shrugged on his jacket. 'Again, the post-mortem will confirm, but I'm pretty certain he was dead before he was dumped in the ditch. He wouldn't have survived long with those injuries, anyway.'

The poor bastard wouldn't have wanted to live with his face looking like that, thought Frost. 'Can we move him, Doc?'

'I don't see why not. The pathologist won't be able to do much with the body as it is.' Slomon went back to his car promising his written report within the hour.

The scene-of-crime officer seemed too busy with his camera to help, so Webster and Frost pulled off their shoes and socks, rolled up their trouser legs, and stepped into the ditch. The water was as cold as death as it lapped around their bare legs, and their feet sunk into squelchy black mud. With Frost taking the shoulders and Webster the legs, they heaved. Shelby was heavy and stubborn. He clung to the bottom. They gritted their teeth and pulled. Suddenly, the body tore free from the grip of the thick mud and emerged through the slime, the head with its hanging flaps of flesh flopping down, streaming dirty stinking water. The proceedings were punctuated by blinding blue flashes ripping into the darkness as the scene-of-crime officer took photograph after photograph.

They laid Dave Shelby on the grass verge, well away from the flattened grass that Forensic would want to crawl over and examine. The scene-of-crime officer brought a plastic sheet from the boot of his car and they draped it over the body.

From the dark distance they heard the plaint of an ambulance siren, then saw its flashing blue light bobbing over the top of the hedges as it picked its way through the winding lane. But before it reached them, other car headlights flared. The Rover and the Ford. Mullett, Allen, and Ingram approached, their faces set.

Frost stepped back from the covered body. Mullett bent over and lifted a corner of the plastic sheet, then, his face screwed up as if in pain, turned his head. 'Such a waste. A fine young officer. Such a wicked waste.'

He moved away, his place taken by Allen, who knelt by the body, a torch in hand, peering at the horror of the shattered face as if examining a suspect piece of steak from the butchers. At last he replaced the sheet and straightened up.

Mullett was finding it difficult to control his emotions. 'Whoever did this,' he said, 'I want him. I don't care how many men it takes, I want him.' To Frost he said, 'I'm putting Mr Allen in charge. You will take over his cases.'

'Right,' acknowledged Frost, who hadn't really expected Mullett to allow him to handle an investigation of this importance.

Mullett cleared his throat and shuffled his feet. He spoke to Frost but didn't look at him. 'Someone's got to tell Shelby's wife,' he said.

His wife! Young Mrs Shelby, not much more than a teen-

ager, with two kiddies, one three, the other eighteen months,
and a third on the way.

'I thought you'd be doing that, sir,' said Frost.

Mullett stared straight ahead and slapped his palm with
his leather driving glove. 'I want the news broken gently,' he
said. 'If she sees the Divisional Commander turning up on
her doorstep . . . I understand she's pregnant . . . the
shock . . . It might be better if you . . .' He let the rest of
the sentence hang.

'You're ordering me to do it, then?' asked Frost, determined not to volunteer.

'Er, yes,' muttered Mullett, wishing the inspector wouldn't
drive him into a corner like this. 'It would be best.'

For you, you bastard, but not for me, thought Frost bitterly. 'All right, Super. If you say so.'

Mullett, relieved to have wriggled out of the unpleasantness, put on his sincere expression. 'And tell Mrs Shelby that
if there is anything at all I can do to help in her moment of
sorrow, she has only to ask. Her husband was one of my finest
officers.' As Frost moved off, he called after him, 'And tell her
we're going to get the swine who did it.'

'Yes, that should cheer her up no end,' muttered Frost as
he called Webster over and opened the door of the Cortina.

Lying back wearily in the passenger seat, he shook the last
cigarette from the packet. 'This is one bloody job I hate, son.
I've done it enough times, so I ought to know.' A stream of
smoke hit the wind-screen and spread out. 'Back to the station, first. There's something I've got to do.' He had remembered the candid photographs in Shelby's locker. He didn't
want some well-meaning person parcelling them with the
dead constable's effects and sending them to his widow.

The mood at the station was one of cold shock and white-hot
anger. 'He was a bloody good bloke, Jack,' said Bill Wells.
'One of the best.' Frost said nothing. Shelby's death had upset
him as much as it had anyone, but Shelby wasn't a bloody
good bloke. He was shifty, lazy, a lecher, and a liar.

He made his way to the locker room. It was empty. He

found the key that worked before and opened up Shelby's locker. The camera was there but the photographs were not. He swore softly and locked up, then went to rejoin Webster in the car.

They sped through the main roads, all traffic lights with them just when Frost wanted delay, wanted to put off as long as possible the moment when Shelby's wife opened that door.

Shelby's two-storey semi was on a corner — its downstairs lights behind bright-red curtains glowed welcomingly. Webster slid the car into an empty parking space on the other side of the road and switched off the engine. Frost made no attempt to move. He found a fresh packet of cigarettes and slowly stripped off the cellophane. He took his time lighting a cigarette to his satisfaction, then crushed it out in the car's overfilled ashtray. 'Damn and sodding blast!' he cried. 'This is what Mullett's paid his inflated bloody salary for, to do lousy jobs like this.' He scrubbed at his face with his hands and seemed to cheer up now he had got that off his chest. 'Come on, let's get it over and done with. You go and find a woman neighbour who can stay with her, and I'll break the news.'

Through a red-painted gate and up a small path to the front door, where he thumbed the buzzer. Excited voices from inside. Quick, light footsteps, then the door opened slowly. A child, a three-year-old boy in light-blue pyjamas and smelling of Johnson's bath soap, regarded him with a puzzled frown. 'I thought you were my daddy,' he said.

'Is your mummy there?' Frost asked, again mentally cursing Mullett for being a cowardly bastard. This was going to be harder than he thought.

A young woman opened a door at the end of the hall. When she saw Detective Inspector Frost standing there, and not her husband, the colour seeped from her face and she briefly held the doorframe very tightly to steady herself. 'Go in the other room and play for a bit, Tommy,' she told the child, doing her best to keep her voice sounding normal. As the boy pushed past her, she walked slowly to the front door.

'Hello, love,' said Frost, realizing he had forgotten to check at the station to find out what her first name was. 'Do you think I could come in? I've got something to tell you.'

She took him to the kitchen, looking in at the lounge on the way through to make sure the children were all right. A small, warm, friendly kitchen. Frost could smell something cooking — the appetising aroma of a casserole, a meal that could be kept in the oven on a low heat for ages without spoiling. Ideal if your husband was inclined to come home late. On the small kitchen table, which was laid with a white tablecloth, were two place settings. She invited Frost to sit, then went over to the hob to stir something in a saucepan, her back to him. He remained standing.

Very busily engaged in stirring what didn't need stirring, she asked, 'Is he hurt?'

'He's dead, love,' said Frost bluntly. Her back stiffened. She carried on stirring, the spoon clack, clack, clacking against the side of the saucepan.

'I knew something was wrong when I phoned the station. They kept saying he was working late, but I knew.'

'I wish you'd cry,' said Frost. 'I wish you'd bloody cry.'

And then her face crumpled and her body was racked with sobbing.

Frost held out his arms and gripped her tightly. 'That's right, love, just cry.' He could feel her scalding tears running down his face, trickling on to his neck. He held her, saying nothing, sharing her grief. Then she was still. 'How did it happen?' she whispered.

'He was shot, love. He was trying to stop a cowboy with a gun.'

She moved away from him and rubbed her face dry with her apron, then she turned off the oven and the hob and slumped down heavily in one of the chairs at the table. Frost pulled out the other chair and sat next to her, his face wet and stinging from her tears.

'Are you all right?' she asked him.

'Me?' said Frost in surprise. 'I'm fine, love.' But his hands were shaking.

'He was a marvellous husband,' she said, 'really marvellous. He idolized me and the kids. We were all he lived for. He would never look at another woman, although they kept looking at him. They all fancied him, he was so good-looking, you see; but he was mine. We loved each other.'

'I know,' said Frost. The phone rang. 'I'll get it,' he said.

The voice at the other end said 'Denton *Echo,* here. Could I speak to Mrs Shelby, please?'

'Piss off,' said Frost, hanging up. It rang again. He disconnected it from the wall. She was bound to be plagued by the media, all eager to know what it felt like to be the widow of a policeman who had had his face blown off. He made a note to get her calls intercepted and to ask the station to place a man on guard outside the house. That was the least Mullett could do for her.

'People will have to be told,' she was saying. 'His parents. It will break their hearts.'

Frost nodded. She was trying to sound calm, but he could see she was on the edge of hysteria. Where the hell was Webster with that woman neighbour?

An excited shout, followed by a fit of giggles, came from the other room. 'Will the kids be all right?' he asked.

She nodded. 'I'll put them to bed in a minute.'

The door buzzer sounded. At bloody last, he thought. 'My colleague with your neighbour,' he told her. 'We thought you might need company.' As she started to protest, he added, 'You can always send her away if you don't want her.'

'Thanks for coming,' she said. 'I'm glad it was you.'

He gave her a hug, then made his way to the front door. Coats and hats were hanging from hooks in a recess under the stairs, and on the end hook was Dave Shelby's police greatcoat. Looking back to ensure the kitchen door was shut, he quickly went through the pockets, heaving a sigh of relief as his fingers closed around the packet of photographs. He slipped it in his mac pocket, then opened the front door to Webster and a fat, motherly-looking woman from next door. 'She's in the kitchen,' he whispered, letting the woman squeeze past.

'How did she take it?' Webster asked when they were back in the car.

'Bloody badly,' said Frost. 'It seems Shelby was the world's greatest husband — never even looked at another woman in his life.' He didn't tell Webster about the photographs.

Webster turned the key in the ignition. 'Back to the station?'

Frost shook his head. 'I don't think I could stand it, son. All the bloody gloom. We've had all of Inspector Allen's cases dumped on us, so let's nip over to the hospital and chat up that poor tart who didn't get raped last night.'

By now Webster needed no directions to find his way to the hospital. Indeed, so automatic was his driving that he suddenly realized his head was dropping and had to jerk it up to stop himself from falling asleep. He wound down the window and let the slap of cold air keep him awake.

Inside the hospital it was the same round of long, lonely corridors, the same smell of antiseptic and stale cooking. They passed a young nurse, a stray wisp of hair over her forehead, scurrying off on some errand. She was the same nurse Dave Shelby had been chatting up the night before. She had now lost forever her chance of appearing in his photographic collection.

Paula Grey was in Sinclair Ward. Frost didn't need to ask the way. His wife had been in Sinclair Ward. His wife! He felt guilty that he couldn't honestly mourn her death. Everyone should have somebody who would grieve at their passing. Even poor Ben Cornish.

The night sister was expecting them and pointed to a bed by a window. Paula Grey was sitting up, propped by two stiffly starched hospital pillows which crackled as she moved. The flesh around her eyes was purple and puffy. Below the eyes, her face was encased in a mask of bandages with a slit for her mouth. A cigarette poked through the slit and she puffed away at it greedily. Her bedside cabinet was loaded with a bowl of fruit and a vase of bronze-coloured chrysanthemums which propped up a card reading *Get well soon, Paula — from the girls at The Coconut Grove.* The blackened eyes narrowed suspiciously as the two men approached.

'Present from Mr Baskin?' asked Frost, nodding at the fruit as he drew up a chair to the side of the bed.

The cigarette waggled furiously. 'Baskin? That lousy git? He wouldn't make you a present of the time of day. So who the hell are you?'

'Frost, Detective Inspector Frost. Old Father Time at my side is Detective Constable Webster. You're not going to be able to eat that fruit with a broken jaw are you, Paula?'

She waved a hand toward the dish. 'Help yourself.'

Webster didn't want anything. Frost took a banana and began peeling it. 'We'd like to ask you a few questions about last night.'

'I've already told everything to Old Misery Guts.'

'Old Misery Guts is off the case. It's mine now,' explained Frost. 'Tell me what happened.'

'There's nothing to tell. I walked through the woods, I got jumped on. But I'll tell you this. The bastard had better not try it again. I'll be ready for him.' She reached for her locker and took out a flick knife. 'I'll rip the bastard to pieces! I'll emasculate him!' She said it with such vehemence that Frost was quite prepared to believe her.

'Did you see him? Would you know him again? It would be a pity if you cut the wrong man's dick off.'

'That's the trouble: I never saw the sod. He jumped me from behind.'

'But you must have some idea,' insisted the inspector. 'Was he young and well built like me, or old and decrepit like George Bernard Shaw here?'

Not more bloody beard jokes, fumed Webster, refusing even a token smile. The blackened eyes turned toward him and a long stream of smoke was ejected from the slit in the bandages.

'He's nice, isn't he?' said Paula.

'If you like them hairy,' said Frost, hiding the banana skin behind the flower vase. 'But you've got to help us, Paula love. You're his sixth victim, and we haven't had one decent description. For all we know he's a one-legged Chinaman. Now think, love. Any little clue?'

She bowed her head in thought, then shook it negatively. 'Sorry.'

'Then tell us, in detail, what happened. It might bring something back.'

'I'm late for my spot at the club. I'm legging it as fast as I can, taking the shortcut through the woods. Suddenly, something black is chucked over my face.'

'A cloth?' asked Frost.

'No, plastic of some sort. I can't see. I can't breathe. I try to scream but hands go round my throat and start squeezing. I reach up to his face, ready to claw his bleeding eyes out, but he squeezes harder and I'm choking. Then I passed out.'

'You say you reached for his face?' asked Frost excitedly. 'Was he hairy like my colleague, or nice and clean-shaven like me?'

'He had a mask on — plastic of some kind. All I could feel was plastic. He even had plastic gloves on his hands.' She sunk back on the pillow. 'They won't let me have a mirror. How bad is my face?'

'It looks like a baboon's backside,' said Frost, bluntly, 'but it will heal. Now what about your attacker? Did he have any minor blemishes that might help us identify him, such as a wooden leg, or a plastic dick, or a mechanical appliance?'

The cigarette was threatening to set fire to the bandages. She took it from her mouth and dropped it into the flower vase. A woman after my own heart, thought Frost.

She thought for a while. 'His trousers,' she said. 'There was something about them.'

'What about them?' asked Frost quickly.

'I could be wrong. It was as I was passing out. I reached down . . . to grab him, you know. I got the impression his trousers were made of some sort of towelling.'

Frost sat up excitedly. This was something new. 'Like jogging trousers, or part of a track suit?'

'Could be,' she said.

'Anything else?'

'Sorry,' she said, sounding tired. 'I can't help any more. You wouldn't have a fag on you by any chance?'

Frost located her mouth through the slit and pushed a cigarette in. He lit it for her. 'You know he didn't rape you?'

'Yes. That's the final bloody insult, that is.' She inhaled deeply and coughed, her head banging on the pillow. 'I can't tell you anything else.'

'You've been a big help,' said Frost, standing up. 'If anything comes to mind, here's my card.' He laid a grimy card next to the one from the girls at The Coconut Grove. 'And here's some fags.' A fresh packet was pressed into her hand. He waved goodbye and was halfway down the ward when he remembered something else he had wanted to ask her. Telling Webster to wait, he ambled back to the bed.

'Quick,' she said, pulling back the clothes, 'get in before Sister comes back.'

He grinned. 'If only I had the time, love, I'd be in there like a ferret up a rabbit hole. Couple of quick questions. You live in the same flats as Julie King, don't you?'

'That's right. Why?'

'Happen to know if she was in last night?'

'Yes. She had her posh boy friend with her — that MP's stuck-up son. I happened to look out of my window about sixish and saw his car pull up.'

'What time did you leave for The Coconut Grove?'

She tapped her chin as she thought. 'About ten to eleven.'

'And was Roger Miller still there when you left?'

'As far as I know.'

'Oh,' said Frost, sounding disappointed.

'Julie went out, of course, but Roger didn't.'

Frost felt his heart misfire a couple of times before it started beating faster. If Julie had gone out, she could no longer alibi her boy friend. 'How do you know she went out?'

'I saw her, didn't I? I was dashing off down the street, worried about being late and what bastard Baskin would say, when Julie roared past in that Jag.'

'Roger's Jag?'

'Yes.'

'Was Roger with her?'

'No, only Julie. I yelled after her, hoping for a lift, but she didn't hear me. If she had, I wouldn't be in this lousy place.'

'You saw Julie driving off in Roger Miller's car about ten to eleven last night?' repeated Frost, anxious there should be no misunderstanding.

She nodded. 'How many more bleeding times?'

Frost beamed with delight. 'Paula, my love, if ever you feel like being raped again, any hour of the day or night, just give me a ring and I'll be right over.'

He clattered off down the ward and grabbed Webster's arm, urging him to move faster as he explained the latest development. As soon as they were back in the car he radioed through to Control, requesting that Julie King be brought in for questioning immediately.

WEDNESDAY NIGHT SHIFT

Frost could smell her loin-tickling perfume the minute he entered the lobby. It made him forget the misery of the previous few hours.

'She's in the interview room,' called Bill Wells, ruling a line under the previous entry in the Incident Book. 'Jordan and Simms have just brought her in.'

Webster was sent to relieve the two uniformed men from their arduous task of keeping an eye on Julie King while Frost shuffled over to the station sergeant.

'She's a nice bit of crumpet,' commented Wells.

'Yes,' agreed Frost. 'So long as you don't mind getting run over. Any progress with the murder investigation?'

Wells shook his head sadly. 'That was a lousy business, Jack. A damn fine officer.'

'Yes,' muttered Frost flatly. 'Pity he wasn't so bloody good while he was still alive. So Allen hasn't got anywhere yet?'

'He's put an all-stations alert out for Stan Eustace. We'll get him.'

'Assuming he did it,' said Frost, sounding doubtful.

Wells looked surprised. 'Mr Allen is convinced of it.'

'Ah, well,' sniffed Frost, 'that's the end of it, isn't it? We needn't bother with a trial.'

'The men were asking about their overtime,' said Wells, abruptly changing the subject.

'It's my number-one priority,' said Frost, swinging his scarf around his head like a lasso and heading for the interview room and Miss Julie King. He almost made it.

'Mr Frost!' It was Mullett, his face sombre.

What now? thought Frost. He dived in first with the good news. 'We've learned Roger Miller wasn't driving the hit-and-run car, sir. It was his girl friend. We've brought her in for questioning.'

Mullett twitched a smile. 'That's excellent news, Inspector. Sir Charles will be delighted.' The smile twitched off. 'Did you see Mrs Shelby?'

'Yes, sir. I broke the news.'

'How is she taking it?'

'She's shattered, sir. I've arranged for a man to stand guard outside the house to keep the TV and press away.'

Mullett's lips tightened. 'Of course, Frost, quite right.' He bowed his head sadly and studied his shoes. 'We'll miss him, Frost. A damn fine officer.'

'So everyone keeps telling me, sir,' said Frost, thinking of all the colour photographs, most of which were taken when Shelby was supposed to be on duty. He turned to go, but he wasn't quick enough. Mullett still had one more bullet left to fire.

'Did the crime statistics go off?'

'Yes, sir,' replied Frost, instantly regretting the lie. Mullett was in such a good mood about Roger Miller he might well have overlooked the truth.

In the interview room Julie King, wearing orange slacks, a yellow jumper, and a white beret, sat on the edge of one of the hard chairs, her fake leopard-skin coat slung over the back. She smouldered, her cigarette smouldered, and her orange-painted nails seemed ready to claw at the slightest provocation. And provocation was the only thing not denied her. They wouldn't let her phone Roger, they wouldn't tell her what it was about, and this bearded wonder wouldn't even talk to her. He just stood leaning against the wall, his eyes half closed, ignoring all her questions. She was all ready to explode when in came Scarface, as scruffy as ever, a long scarf sweeping the floor as it trailed behind him.

'Why am I here?' she demanded. 'No-one's said a damn word. What is this, the bloody Gestapo?'

'A few questions, fräulein,' said Frost, settling himself down at the table and arranging his cigarettes and matches within easy reach.

She consulted her jewelled wristwatch. 'I'm due at the club in thirty-five minutes.'

Frost flicked a match into life with his thumbnail and lit up. 'I don't think you're going to make it, Miss King. We've found out you've been telling us fibs.'

She dug into her handbag for a nail file and began rasping away a couple of inches of orange nail. 'Everything in my statement was true. Roger was with me all the time.'

A theatrical sigh from Frost. 'You'd better tell her, Constable. I don't like breaking bad news to girls with moles on their behinds.'

Webster dragged a chair over and sat beside her. 'You were driving the Jag, miss, not Roger Miller.'

She studied her nails and decided some minor adjustments were necessary. She filed carefully. 'I don't know what you're talking about.'

'You were seen driving the Jaguar.'

'Was I?' She blew away a puff of orange dust.

'Yes,' said Webster.

She gave him a sweet, pitying smile. 'You must think I'm bleeding stupid. No-one saw me getting in the car for the simple reason I wasn't in it.' She dropped the file in her handbag and snapped it shut. 'I'm not obliged to stay here, and you have no right to keep me.' She stood up. 'I'll find my own way out.'

Frost stuck out a leg, barring her way. 'We haven't got time to sod about, miss,' he snapped. 'You were seen by your next-door neighbour, Paula Grey. She yelled out, hoping for a lift. But you couldn't have heard, because you roared straight off. I'm not bluffing. She's given us a signed statement.' To prove it, he waved a piece of paper at her. It was only a typed request from County for the crime statistics, but it looked important.

Slowly, she sank back in her chair. Her mind seemed to be racing. 'That's right,' she said at last, 'I remember now. I went out for some cigarettes. I bought some and came straight back.'

Frost was doing a trick with his chair, rocking it and making it balance on its two back legs. He beamed her a paternal smile of complete understanding. 'I knew there would be a perfectly logical explanation. Where did you go for the cigarettes?'

She hesitated. 'A pub. The Black Swan.'

'A twenty-minute round-trip,' said Frost. 'Ten minutes there, ten minutes back . . . plus the time it took for you to get served.'

'So?' she said warily.

'I'd have thought it was bloody obvious,' said Frost. 'During those twenty minutes, the hit-and-run took place. It was you who knocked Hickman down. It was you who killed him.'

She shivered and rubbed her arms, then pulled the fur coat over her shoulders. 'It's cold in here.'

'It's colder in the morgue,' said Frost. He dribbled smoke through his nose. 'Why prolong the agony, love? There's no way you can wriggle out of this. Get it off your lovely chest. Tell us the truth.'

He settled back in his chair while Webster took it all down in his notebook.

'I had never driven a Jag before. I asked Roger if I could take it for a thrash down the Bath Road. He said yes and gave me the keys. At about ten minutes to eleven I left. Roger stayed behind in the flat.

'I might have been going a bit fast round the old people's flats, but I'm sure I was within the speed limit. It was dark, and as I turned a corner I felt a bump. I never saw anything and didn't know I had hit anyone.

'When I got back to the flat Roger started moaning because the headlamp was broken. Then we saw the blood on the wing. I got frightened. Roger said he would report the car as stolen, so we hid it down a side street and then went back to the flat, where Roger phoned the police. I never knew at the time I had hit anyone, otherwise I would have stopped. And I hadn't been drinking. I didn't have a drink all night.'

When she had finished, she looked to Frost for his reaction. He showed none.

'Is that it?' he asked.

She nodded.

'Right, we'll get it typed, then you can sign it. In the meantime, I'm afraid you'll have to wait in the cells.' Seeing her dismay, he added, 'Not for long, only until we fix bail.'

After the girl was taken out, he yawned and stretched. 'Right, son. Let's go and pick up Master Roger and see if he confirms her story.'

At first Roger Miller blustered, demanded to be released, and threatened all kinds of lawsuits that would leave Frost and Webster jobless, penniless and prospectless. But when they told him that Julie King had made a statement admitting she alone was driving the Jaguar, he calmed down and without further prompting gave them a statement that confirmed the girl's story in every detail.

Webster borrowed the station Underwood from Collier, dumped it on his desk on top of the crime statistics, and started pecking out the statements. Frost, who had found some salted peanuts left over from the previous night, was slouched in his chair, his crossed feet up on his desk, hurling peanuts in the air and trying to catch them in his mouth.

Mullett swept in without knocking. Frost flung his feet off the desk, managing to knock a file on the floor, splashing papers everywhere. But there were no frowns from the Divisional Commander, who was in a most affable mood. 'Well done, Frost. I've just put the phone down after speaking to Sir Charles. He is absolutely delighted to learn that you have been able to clear his son. In fact, he's coming over to see me right away. Are the statements ready yet?'

'On the last one now,' said Webster, rubbing out a mistake and blowing away the rubber dust.

'Excellent,' said Mullett, smiling, 'I'll take them with me.'

The warning light at the back of Frost's brain blinked on and off. What was the sly old sod up to now? 'Take them with you, Super?'

Mullett's insincere smile blinked on and off. 'I'd like to show them to Sir Charles. He's bringing his solicitor with him.'

He hovered over Webster, completely putting him off, causing him to hit the wrong keys repeatedly. But at last the final page was typed. Mullett snatched it from the machine and bore the statements away.

It was an hour later that Frost was summonsed into Mullett's office, an hour spent grappling with the crime statistics that had supposedly already gone off. Webster, frowning and scowling more than ever as he tried to make some sort of sense out of the inspector's hopeless jumble of figures, decided he had had more than enough. As soon as the door closed behind Frost, he hurled down his pen and stuffed the papers back into their folder.

He was dead tired, it was past one o'clock in the morning, and there were limits to the number of hours he could work without sleep. If it were something important, he'd have stuck it out, but not for the lousy crime statistics. It was Frost's incompetence that had caused the trouble, and if he wanted them done tonight, he could damn well do them himself.

Webster grabbed his overcoat from the hat stand and put it on. Through the grime of the windows the night looked cold, windy, and unfriendly. He turned up the collar of his coat and awaited the inspector's return. It was time to assert himself.

·   ·   ·

Frost tapped at the door of Mullett's office and went in. As soon as he was inside he started coughing and his eyes stung. The room, blue-fogged with smoke, stank of cigars and an overpowering after-shave, a legacy of the now-departed Sir Charles Miller.

'Come in,' boomed Mullett, valiantly drawing on a Churchillian cigar. Frost shuffled over to the desk and lit up a cigarette, his nose twitching as he sampled the air. 'Smells like a Limehouse knocking shop in here, Super.'

'It's very expensive after-shave,' rebuked Mullett, pushing out the tiniest of smoke rings and coughing until his eyes watered.

'You'd be surprised what gets shaved these days,' began Frost, but Mullett didn't let him expand.

'Thought I'd put you in the picture, Frost. First of all, allow me to pass on Sir Charles's congratulations. He's absolutely delighted that we have been able to completely clear his son.'

'Not completely,' corrected the inspector. 'We've still got him on conspiracy to pervert the course of justice, making false statements, falsely reporting his car was stolen . . . and that's just for starters.'

Mullett took off his glasses and began to polish them, slowly and deliberately, so he wouldn't have to look at Frost. 'I was wondering whether it was absolutely necessary to involve the son? It's entirely up to you, of course.'

'I don't see what you mean,' said Frost, adding his cigarette ash to the corpses of two fat cigars in Mullett's large ashtray.

'The girl's admitted everything. Roger was only trying to help her. Should he be punished for that?'

'Yes,' said Frost.

Mullett sighed a mouthful of cigar smoke. The inspector wasn't being at all understanding. He readjusted his smile and pressed on. 'I wouldn't dream of interfering, of course, but I can't help feeling that everyone's interests would be better served if we didn't make it known that Roger Miller falsely claimed his car was stolen. It can only complicate things.'

'Oh?' grunted Frost.

'Yes,' said Mullett, bravely plunging on to deeper and more dangerous waters. 'If we remove that element we remove Roger from any official involvement in the hit-and-run. We could say the girl drove the car, had the accident, but didn't tell Roger what had happened as she didn't want to get him involved. That would completely eliminate him from any charges.' He clapped his hands together and smiled at Frost, certain he would see the sense of all this.

Frost laid his cigarette to rest alongside the two cigar corpses. 'It's a nice fairy tale, Super, but it's not the truth and it's not what they say in their statements.'

Mullett cleared his throat. 'Not in their old statements, no.'

There was an almost audible click as Frost's head jerked up. 'What do you mean, old statements?'

'I have had fresh statements taken.'

At first Frost couldn't believe what he had heard. He stared at Mullett, who suddenly found a paper knife on his desk that required fiddling with. Frost felt like snatching it from his hand and burying it to the hilt in the desk. He could hardly keep his anger in check.

'Am I hearing you correctly?' he shouted. 'Are you trying to tell me that you have gone behind my back and taken fresh statements — different statements?'

Mullett shrunk back from his onslaught. 'It's not quite like that, Inspector. Sir Charles's solicitor had a word with them both, as a result of which they each decided to change their stories slightly.'

Frost was now furious. 'You conniving sod! What bloody business have you got, going behind my back, conspiring with your rich mates to get witnesses to change their statements?'

Mullett's fist pounded down on his desk, making the ashtray jump. 'You will kindly remember whom you are talking to, Inspector.' The look of contempt on Frost's face was unsettling. Surely the man could see this was all for the best. He would try to reason with him.

'Listen to me, Inspector. First, Sir Charles is paying the full costs of the girl's defence.'

'That was her bribe,' hurled Frost. 'What was yours?'

The Superintendent's mouth opened and closed. Rage made him speechless. His entire body quivered. 'How dare you,' he managed at last. 'You've shot your bolt now, Frost. You've gone too far this time!'

But Frost was still on the attack. 'So what do you intend to do?' he snarled back, 'report me to the Chief Constable?' He snatched the phone up and offered it to Mullett. 'Here you are — take it. Report me! Shall I dial the number for you?'

With a halfhearted flutter of his hand, the Divisional Commander waved the phone away. 'Please listen. Not only is Sir Charles paying for the girl's defence, he is also ensuring that sufficient funds will be made available to compensate the unfortunate victim's widow.' He paused, then added significantly, 'But, what I am sure will be of great interest to you is that he has also generously agreed to make a donation of five thousand pounds to start a fund for the widow and children of PC Shelby.' He leaned back, confident that his ace would not be trumped.

'It's not only his bloody after-shave that stinks,' said Frost.

Ignoring this remark, Mullett continued in a voice ringing with belief in the justice of his argument. 'As I said, this is your case. The decision is yours and yours alone. It's only a slight bending of the rules. I'm sure Mrs Shelby and her young family would be very grateful for the money, but if you feel we should deprive them of it, well, as I said, the decision is yours.'

You shit, thought Frost, you utter shit! But he knew he was beaten. Wearily, he stood up. 'All right, sir. Whatever fiddles you've arranged with your mate Sir Charles, you go right ahead. I just don't want to know about it.' The slam of the door as he left rattled everything moveable in the office.

With only a brief frown at the manner of the inspector's exit, Mullett sighed, relieved that the unpleasantness was over. He picked up the phone and dialled the ex-directory number Sir Charles had given him.

'Hello, Sir Charles. Mullett here. That little matter we discussed. I've put it in hand, sir . . . Not at all, Sir Charles . . . my pleasure.' He hung up and tapped the receiver lightly with his fingertips. Most satisfactory. Sir Charles wasn't the sort of man who would forget a favour.

Fuming and desperate for something to kick, Frost stamped back to his office. The wastepaper bin provoked him by standing in his path, so he booted it across the office floor. It bounced off the desk leg and voided its contents all over the feet of the scowling, I'm-going-home-and-just-you-try-to-stop-me Webster.

'Sorry, son,' muttered Frost, crashing down in his chair, 'but there are some rotten shits in this station, and they're all called Mullett. You'll never believe what's happened. Shut the door.'

He told the detective constable of the scene in the Divisional Commander's office. Forgetting for the moment about going home, Webster sank into his own chair and listened with growing incredulity.

'You mean he destroyed the statements we took?'

'Yes, son. I think it's called perverting the course of justice, but if you're an MP with five thousand quid to spare, then it's called a slight bending of the rules for a good cause. Sod the crime statistics, sod the overtime returns, and sod our beloved Divisional Commander. I'm going home.'

That was when the internal phone rang.

Control reporting another rape in Denton Woods.

A seventeen-year-old girl.

Bodies aching, feeling tired, dirty and gritty, Frost and Webster headed back to the car, which seemed to have been their home for most of the long, long day. As usual, Webster was driving too fast, but the dark streets were deserted and they passed no other traffic.

They reached the woods to find the ambulance had beaten

them to it, its flashing beacon homing them into a lay-by alongside Charlie Alpha. The rear doors of the ambulance were open, and already the victim was being loaded into the back.

The wind whined and shook the trees, sending a confetti shower of dead leaves on Frost and Webster as they hurried across to the victim. The girl's eyes were closed and one side of her face was swollen and bruise-blackened where she had been hit. All the time she shivered and moaned. Very carefully, Frost tugged down the blanket to expose her neck. And there they were, the familiar deep, biting indentations of the rapist's fingers.

'Isn't it about time you had a go at catching the bastard?' asked one of the ambulance men, who had a young daughter.

Frost said nothing. What the hell was there to say?

The ambulance lurched forward and sped on its way to Denton Hospital, its siren screaming for the road to be kept clear.

They turned their heads at approaching voices. Along the path came two police constables, Simms and Jordan. Between them was a youth of about nineteen. He had dark hair, tightly curled, and wore a gray jacket with black trousers. There was a swagger about him that reminded Frost of Dave Shelby. As the group came nearer he could see that there was a raw scratch running down his right cheek to below his chin.

Simms pushed the youth forward. 'This is Terry Duggan, Inspector. The girl's boy friend. He found her.'

'Hello, Terry,' said Frost, his eyes noting that in addition to the scratch on his face, there were nail rakes on the back of his wrists.

'The girl's name is Wendy Raynor, she's seventeen, and she works part-time in a shop. They'd been to a disco . . .' began Simms.

'Let Terry tell me,' said Frost.

'We left the disco at about half ten,' said the youth. 'We had to leave early because her parents wouldn't let her stay out late. On the way back we had this row, so she jumps out of the car and stomps off home on her own.'

'Slow down, son,' interrupted Frost. 'I'm not at my brightest at this time of night. What was the row about?'

The youth gave a sheepish grin, blushed, and moved his hand vaguely. 'You know, just trivial stuff — a difference of opinion.'

'And she made you stop the car?' asked Webster.

Terry shifted his gaze to the bearded bloke. 'No, we'd already stopped. We were parked.'

'Where?' This from the down-at-heel one.

'Over there.' Terry pointed into the dark. 'Round the back of that big tree.'

'Why?' demanded the bearded one, another miser with words.

'Why?' repeated Terry in a tone that suggested the answer should be obvious. 'Why does anyone bring a bird to the woods at night?'

'I see,' said Frost, motioning for him to carry on.

'Anyway, we're steaming away through the preliminaries in the back seat, and I'm trying to get her tights off her, when she suddenly goes all stiff and calls me a dirty sod. Then she starts struggling and scratching and pushing me off. I don't reckon she'd ever done it before. Still, I wasn't going to let the money I'd lobbed out on those disco tickets go to waste, so I tried again. This time she panics, jumps out the car screaming blue murder, and goes dashing down that path, pulling up her tights.'

'Did you run after her?' asked Webster.

'No bleeding fear!'

'Seventeen years old,' said Webster, getting angry, 'never done it before, gone eleven o'clock at night, and let her run off in those woods on her own?'

'She was already screaming I was trying to rape her,' said Terry. 'If I'd chased off after her, I reckon she'd have thought I was trying to finish the job.'

The wind stirred, shaking the trees until the branches creaked. Frost shivered and wound his scarf tighter. 'What did you do then?'

'I drove home and got my head down. About half past

midnight, my phone starts ringing. I staggered out of bed to answer it, and it's Wendy's old man screaming and shouting because she isn't home yet. I told him we'd had a bit of a barney and she'd legged it off on her own, but he sounded so worked up I said I'd go and look for her. I drove back here, then followed the path around.'

'Show us,' said Frost.

He took them along a narrow path which narrowed even more as it plunged deeper into the woods. A wall of thick bushes on each side brushed their shoulders as they pushed through. After some forty feet, Terry stopped.

'When I reached here I heard this moaning noise. At first I thought it was a couple having it away, then I realized it was Wendy. I forced my way through those bush things there.' He indicated a gap between the bushes where branches had been bent back and broken. 'It wasn't like that when I first saw it — the ambulance men smashed it down getting their stretcher through. Anyway, that's where I found her, stark naked, her face beaten up, her clothes all over the place. The poor bitch was moaning and whimpering. I piled her clothes all over her to keep her warm, and legged it back to the car. Then I drove round until I found a phone box and called the law.'

Frost pushed through the gap and shone a torch around. A small glade, the grass flattened and trampled, but probably all from the ambulance men, the youth, and Jordan and Simms. A pair of laddered tights, screwed into a ball, was caught in a patch of stinging nettles which hugged the base of a beech tree. There seemed little point in picking them up, so he left them there. He switched off his torch and rejoined the others.

'I suppose I'd better go and tell her father what's happened,' said the youth.

'I wouldn't,' said Frost. 'If I was her father I'd half bleeding kill you.'

Jordan had moved some way down the path and was speaking quietly into his personal radio. He caught Frost's eye and beckoned him down. 'Charlie Bravo has been round the girl's parents' house and taken them to the hospital, sir. It seems there's a bit of a discrepancy. The laddo here says he was home in bed around eleven. The girl's father says he kept phoning him, didn't get a reply, so he took a cab round there. He was at Terry's place just after midnight. Terry's car wasn't outside. The father nearly kicked the door in, but got no reply so went back home. When he phoned at half past twelve, Terry answered the phone on the second ring and didn't sound as if he'd been woken up from a deep sleep.'

'I can well do without complications like this,' muttered Frost gloomily. 'What do you reckon, then?'

'My guess is Terry raped her, sir. He got all worked up in the car, then, when she ran off, he followed, looking for her. I reckon he found her and jumped her. Then he drove home and pretended he'd been in bed since eleven.'

Frost sniffed and thought this over. 'I doubt it, young Jordan, but far be it from me to dampen the enthusiasm of young coppers. Take Duggan back to the station — say it's for a statement — and then get the clothes off him and send them over to Forensic for examination. And tell the police surgeon to give him a going over. I want to know if he's had sex recently.'

They walked back to the others. Frost tried to light a cigarette but the wind kept blowing out his matches, so he gave up in disgust. 'I want you to go down the station with these officers to make a statement, Terry. We'll get the doctor to have a look at those scratches while you're there — they might turn septic.'

He waited until they were out of earshot, then he filled Webster in. Webster listened intently. 'So Jordan reckons Terry raped her?'

'That's the suggestion, son,' said Frost, crouching to windward of a large oak and managing this time to light up. 'It's possible, but I'm not really sold on the idea. I can't see Terry going to the trouble of stripping her off. I see him as a tights down, skirt up, unzip the old Levis and crash, bang, wallop sort of man. I could be wrong, though. He might be the romantic type and like to strangle and strip them first.' He pulled the cigarette from his mouth and frowned at it. The wind was making it burn unevenly down one side, charring the paper. It tasted terrible. 'My money's still on the old Denton rapist.'

'Then hadn't we better make a search of the area?' suggested Webster.

'A search,' said Frost. 'No thanks, son. It's too bloody cold. We'll let Forensic have a sniff round if they want to, but I'm for going back to the station and getting warm.'

'If I were in charge of the case,' said Webster stiffly, 'I wouldn't hesitate to organize a search, just as Mr Allen did last night.'

'And a fat lot of good it did him,' Frost pointed out. 'But if you feel like organizing one, be my guest, so long as you don't expect me to take part.'

Someone's call and the wave of a torch let them know that the experts from Forensic had arrived. Two of them. A miserable man and a little fat jolly man. Frost took them to the clearing where the jolly little one surveyed the scene with delight.

'Plenty of footprints here,' he said.

'Yes,' replied Frost. 'Two ambulance men, two policemen, my detective constable, a suspect, me, and the girl. If you find anything else, let me know.'

Webster's mood showed itself in his driving. He was furious at Frost's refusal to arrange a search. Frost was always looking for shortcuts but there were cases that didn't lend themselves to the inspector's slipshod methods. This was one of them.

'So how exactly do you intend to proceed?' he asked, savagely twisting the wheel as they turned into Market Square.

'We'll get Terry out of the way first, then we'll think about it,' answered Frost. He looked up, startled, as the car bumped the kerb after too wide a turn. 'Careful, son, you're driving like I do.'

The station lobby looked as tired as they did. 'Susan Harvey is waiting for you in your office, Jack,' called Wells. Suddenly Webster felt a lot less tired.

Susan was in Webster's chair, hugging a mug of instant

coffee. She had returned from the hospital, where she had managed to talk to seventeen-year-old Wendy Raynor.

'Fractured jaw and a few bruises,' she told them. 'And she's in a state of severe shock. She's been sexually assaulted. Before the assault she was a virgin.'

Frost sat in his chair and began to swivel from side to side. 'And who does she say raped her?'

Susan put the mug down on the desk. 'Terry Duggan. He tried it on in the car. She ran off, but he followed and raped her.'

Webster's eyes flashed. 'The bastard!'

'He looks lovely when he's angry, doesn't he, Sue?' murmured Frost. He thought for a while, tapping his cigarette on his thumb. 'My money wasn't on the boy friend.'

'Then you were wrong, weren't you?' said Webster with an ill-concealed sneer.

'I'm always wrong,' admitted Frost. He studied his cigarette, decided he had tapped it enough, and popped it in his mouth. 'She's positive it was Terry?'

'She's confused, but she swears it was him. I don't think she actually saw him. He jumped, threw something over her face, and started to strangle her. When she came to, there was Terry staring down at her.'

'But that could have been when Terry came back to look for her,' said Frost thoughtfully. 'And if it was Terry, then he's infringed the "Hooded Terror's" copyright — the cloth over the face, the strangling . . .'

'A copycat crime,' said Webster, determined that Frost should be wrong, 'He read about it in the papers and copied it.'

The phone rang. Webster answered it. The hospital. Swabs taken from Wendy Raynor were on their way to Forensic.

Frost opened the door and yelled to Bill Wells, 'Has the doctor seen Terry Duggan yet?'

'He's with him now,' the sergeant yelled back.

'We'll soon know,' said Frost, once again swivelling from side to side. 'The thing is, she never actually saw him.' Then he grinned. 'Did I ever tell you that old wartime joke about the girl munitions worker who was raped in the blackout?'

Jokes! thought Webster. A seventeen-year-old's been raped and he makes jokes.

'The police asked the girl who did it, and she said she couldn't say because it happened in the blackout. "But I can tell you this," she said, "the rapist was definitely one of our foremen." "How can you be so sure?" asked the fuzz. She said, "Because he kept his bowler hat on all the time and I had to do all of the work." ' He guffawed with laughter as he reached the punchline. Webster maintained a stony silence, but Susan was convulsed and almost choked over her coffee.

A tap on the door, and the duty doctor, a plump little Welshman, came in.

'You've just missed a good joke,' said Frost, wiping his eyes. 'The girl who was raped in the blackout —'

'And the foreman did it,' said the doctor, dumping his bag on Frost's desk. 'You tell me that every time there's a rape.' He knocked some papers off a chair and sat down. 'I've examined this young man, Duggan. There are fingernail scratches down his face and wrists, which I'm sure you've already noticed. I've taken a blood sample, which is on its way to your forensic laboratory, together with his clothes. And he has had sex within the last couple of hours.'

'Which is more than I've had,' said Frost. He pinched his nose. 'Well, young Webster, it's beginning to look as if you might be right. I suppose we'd better see what he's got to say for himself.'

Terry Duggan, wearing only a police-issue red-and-grey blanket and a loaned pair of gym shoes some four sizes too big, leaped up angrily as Frost and Webster entered the interview room.

'What's the bloody game?' he demanded. 'I've been stripped, my clothes have been taken away, I haven't been allowed to leave, and no-one will answer my questions.' He paused for breath. 'And another thing, that bleeding doctor did more than examine my scratches. He got bloody intimate.'

'He gets carried away,' said Frost. He opened a folder and drew out a typed sheet. 'Is this the statement you have just made to the police officer?'

Terry squinted at it. 'Yes.'

'And you're sticking by it?'

The youth jutted out his chin defiantly. 'Of course I am.'

'Then I must ask you to sign it.' Frost borrowed a ball-point pen from Webster and passed it to Duggan, who scrawled his name at the foot of the document. Frost and Webster added their signatures as witnesses.

Frost tucked the statement back in the folder, then shook his head reproachfully. 'You're a silly sod, you know?'

'Why?' asked the youth, staring him out.

'You're in serious trouble, my son, and you make it worse by telling us a pack of lies.'

Terry clutched the blanket closer to his body. 'What do you mean, about me being in serious trouble?'

Frost motioned for Webster to break the news.

'Wendy tells us it was you who raped her, Sonny Jim.'

Duggan looked first at Webster, then at Frost. They both stared back coldly. He tried to laugh, but it wasn't very convincing. 'Rape? Me? Do me a favour. I've never had to fight for it in my life. If they don't give it willingly, then I don't bloody want it.'

'You fought for it in the car,' said Frost.

Duggan shrugged. 'They always put on a show of reluctance at first — they don't want you to know that they're as eager for it as you are. But as soon as Wendy started marking me with her nails, I packed it in.'

'. . . and you drove straight back home,' read Frost from the statement.

'That's right.'

'Parked your motor outside your house and, in a highly emotional but unfulfilled state, you crept into your little bed and went straight off to sleep?'

'That's right.'

'So, by 11.30 you were indoors and in bed and your motor was parked in the street outside?'

A slight hesitation, but again the answer was 'Yes.'

'And yet when Mr Raynor, Wendy's father, called at your house at midnight, there was no car outside, and although he kicked and banged on the door, there was no answer.'

'I didn't know her old man called round my place,' exclaimed Terry.

'Well, he damn well did,' chipped in Webster. 'But you weren't in, were you? You were down in the woods raping his seventeen-year-old virgin daughter. Don't try to deny it, Sunshine, the medical examination you just had proves it.'

Terry sat down heavily in the chair and readjusted the blanket. It was prickly and scratchy and was making him feel itchy all over. 'All right, so I didn't go back home right away. I went back to the disco to see if there was any spare talent knocking about. I didn't want the night to be a complete washout.'

'Any witnesses who saw you back in the disco?' asked Webster.

'No. I never got inside. I met this bird in the car park. She didn't look very tasty, in fact she looked a bit of bleeding rough, but at least she was available, so we got inside the car and we had it away.'

'Her name and address?' barked Webster.

'No idea, squire. I'd never seen her before and I hope I never see her again. If I hadn't been so desperate, I wouldn't have touched her with a barge pole.'

'Didn't you drive her home afterward?'

'Home? That's a joke. She'd been sleeping rough. She asked me to drop her off at the main road so she could thumb a lift up north on a lorry.'

Webster snapped his notebook shut and walked across to the youth. He grabbed the blanket, screwing it tightly in his fist, and jerked him to his feet. 'You must think we're bloody stupid, Duggan. You tried it on with Wendy. She wouldn't have it, which was an insult to your virility, so you chased after her, choked her, broke her jaw, and raped her.'

'I didn't. If there's no bleeding co-operation, then I don't want it,' cried Duggan, trying to pull away, but the detective constable's grip was viselike.

'Before you leave this room you are going to give us a signed statement admitting everything.'

'I want a lawyer,' said the youth.

Webster snatched away the blanket. 'When you've given us a statement, you bastard.'

The phone rang. As Webster had taken over the questioning, Frost had to answer it. He listened, thanked the caller, then hung up.

Webster, his fists clenched, was standing toe to toe with the naked Duggan, his face red and angry. The youth looked terrified.

Frost stood up and pocketed his cigarettes and matches. 'That was Forensic, son,' he said casually, 'with the results of their tests. The man who raped Wendy has blood group O, and young Terry here is blood group A.' He gave Webster a sweet smile. 'I'll see you back in the office.'

And he went out, leaving the constable to make his apologies to the suspect.

When Webster returned to the office he was fuming. He had been made to look a proper fool in front of a suspect, forced to offer grovelling apologies to a sneering young bastard.

Frost was at his desk shuffling through papers. Webster was all ready to give him a mouthful when Susan Harvey came in.

'Hello, Sue,' said Frost. 'You still here?'

She looked inquiringly at Webster. 'I said I'd drive her home,' he told Frost.

'Home?' said Frost in surprise. 'It's not time to go home yet, is it?'

'It's nearly two o'clock in the morning, Inspector. I've been on duty for more than sixteen hours on the trot. I'd fill in an overtime claim if I thought it stood the remotest chance of getting to County accounts.' Immediately he said it he wished he could have bitten his tongue because Frost's head moved to the Overtime Return file still in the centre of Webster's desk.

'Thanks for reminding me, son. I promised Bill Wells they'd go off today.' He scratched his chin. 'Tell you what. We won't bother adding them up. They've got dirty great computers at County that can do that for us. We'll just scribble down the figures and send them off like that.'

'But it will still take hours,' protested Webster wearily.

'Not if we split it three ways,' said Frost. 'You'll help, won't you, Sue?' And he dealt out three heaps of returns from the file as if dealing hands of cards.

So they pulled up their chairs and filled in page after page of figures copied from the men's claim forms, allocating them to various categories of crime. Frost did a lot of groaning and smoking and seemed to be tearing up more forms than he filled in. Time hobbled along. Webster was finding that the figures had a tendency to blur into indistinctness. He staggered out and made some instant coffee, which helped a little. Then he realized he had been staring at the same column of figures for five minutes. He reached for another claim form. There were none. He had finished. Within another couple of minutes Susan, too, had finished her stint.

'Marvellous,' beamed Frost, dealing them out some more from his own pile. But in ten minutes the return, folded in its official envelope marked 'Overtime Figures — Urgent,' was all ready for transmission to County for inclusion in the next batch of salary cheques.

'We all deserve a pat on the back for that,' said Frost, looking at the envelope as if he couldn't believe his eyes.

'Yes,' grunted Webster, slipping on his overcoat, all ready for the off before Frost remembered the crime statistics.

Frost clicked his fingers. 'Flaming hell, son . . . we forgot something!'

'What's that?' grunted the constable, taking Susan by the arm and steering her to the door.

'The anonymous telephone caller who phoned about the girl in the woods last night. Dave Shelby said he knew who he was.'

Freedom only half a turn of the door handle away, Webster said, 'But Shelby's dead.'

'My memory's not that flaming bad,' retorted the inspector. 'Shelby said he'd seen the bloke. In which case he would have made an entry about it in his notebook.' He moved Webster's hand, opened the door, and yelled, 'Sergeant Wells!'

Wells approached and gave a mocking bow. 'You rang, my lord?'

'Don't ponce about when addressed by a senior officer,' rebuked Frost sternly. 'Where's Dave Shelby's notebook?'

'I thought you knew,' said Wells. 'It's missing.'

Thank God for that, thought Webster. Now we can all go home.

Frost frowned. 'Missing?'

'It wasn't on the body, Jack, and it wasn't in the car. Mr Allen's made a search, but no trace of it. He reckons it might have fallen from Shelby's pocket when he was in the getaway car.'

'So what news on the getaway car? Someone should have spotted the Vauxhall by now.'

'Stan Eustace was always good at finding places to dump his stolen motors, Jack.'

'About the only thing he is good at.' He took the brown envelope from his desk and handed it to Wells. 'I'm off home. Here's your lousy overtime returns. Stick them in the post bag.'

Wells looked at the envelope, his eyebrows arched. 'It's gone three o'clock in the morning, Jack. The County collection was ages ago. If this doesn't reach them first thing today it'll miss the salary cheques and we'll have a bloody mutiny on our hands.'

Frost waved an airy hand. 'Don't get excited. Webster can drop them in the County letter box.'

Webster's beard bristled. 'I can do what? It's an hour's drive each way.'

Another airy wave from Frost. 'Fifty minutes at the outside — a lot less if you're not too fussy about obeying traffic lights. Use my car. You can take Sue with you and drop her off on the way back.'

As he crawled into the car, Webster realized that he wasn't going to be able to do it. He was too tired. He'd fall asleep at the wheel. Susan got out and moved around to the driving seat. 'Slide over,' she said. 'I'll drive. You'd better spend what's left of the night at my place — you're in no fit state to drive back.'

Webster did a mental inventory of Susan's tiny flat — no sofa and only one bed. He felt his tiredness slipping away but didn't make it obvious. He stuffed the envelope into the dash compartment. 'I didn't bring my pyjamas,' he said.

'And I haven't got a nightdress,' murmured Sue, turning the ignition. Webster leaned back in his seat and purred. The night wasn't going to be a total disaster after all.

On the way back from County Headquarters he could fight sleep no longer. When he opened his eyes the sky was dawn-streaked. 'Where are we?' he asked.

'Nearly there,' she told him. 'I'm taking a shortcut.'

The shortcut was a narrow lane joining two side roads. A short, bumpy ride.

'Look out!' cried Webster. Something loomed up in front of them.

The headlights had picked out a car. A car parked bang in the middle of the lane, no lights showing. They could have run straight into it.

Carefully, Sue manoeuvred the Cortina to squeeze past. Webster twisted his head to look back. The lunatic who parked it so dangerously deserved to be booked. Then his heart sank.

The car was a red Vauxhall Cavalier.

The registration number was CBZ2303.

'Oh no!' croaked Webster in disbelief.

'What's up?' asked Sue.

'Every bloody thing is up,' he said despairingly as he reached for the handset. He called Denton Control to report he had found Stan Eustace's getaway car.

THURSDAY DAY SHIFT

Webster sat in the car with Sue and waited. Within twenty-five minutes Detective Inspector Allen had arrived on the scene. He must have been asleep in bed when the call came through, but in those twenty-five minutes he had managed to shower, shave, and put on a freshly pressed suit. He looked immaculate. By contrast, Detective Sergeant Ingram, sour and crumpled at his side, looked as if he hadn't slept properly for a week, which tended to underline the whispered rumours of his marital troubles. He looked even more sour when Allen doled out a few begrudging crumbs of praise to Webster.

'Well done, Constable. Good piece of observation.'

The obligatory acknowledgement over, Allen and Ingram approached the Vauxhall and sniffed gingerly around, looking but not touching. Webster had hoped he and Sue would now be allowed to drive off and get to bed but Allen didn't seem ready to dismiss them yet.

Allen was standing on tiptoe to see over the hedge that bordered the lane. Behind it was a field of tall grass, heavy with early-morning dew. He dragged back his cuff to consult his watch. If he could do it in twenty-five minutes, what was holding up the forensic team?

Then the brittle early-morning quiet was shattered as carloads of hastily summonsed off-duty men and the team from Forensic arrived. Soon the area swarmed with men crawling over every inch of the Vauxhall and its surroundings. The car was dusted for prints inside and out, the interior was given microscopic scrutiny for traces of blood and tissue, and then the seat covers and carpets were removed and vacuumed to retrieve clinging hairs and fibres.

Other men were on their hands and knees, noses almost grazing the road surface as they looked for anything the murderer might have dropped. It was still dark, but the area was floodlit. The first success was the finding of a small patch of oil a few yards up the lane, indicating that another car had recently been parked on that spot for some time. More than likely this car was the backup that Stan Eustace transferred into after he had dumped the Cavalier. Judging from the amount of oil leakage, the other car must have been an old banger.

One team was given the task of knocking on the door of every house in the vicinity to ask if anyone had seen a car parked in the lane during the previous day, or if they had seen the Vauxhall drive up.

'I know it's early and most of the householders are going to be tucked up in bed,' said Allen, addressing the team, 'but that is their hard luck. Today they are all going to see the dawn break for a change. How you wake them, I don't particularly care. Just do it. And if anyone complains that their beauty sleep is more important than finding the murderer of a police officer, let them write to the Chief Constable. Most important, I want you to make sure you speak to everybody in the house, not just the poor sod who staggers downstairs to open the door. Now off you go.'

Another two men went with Ingram to search the section of the field near the hedge. It wasn't expected to yield anything but Allen, unlike Detective Inspector Jack Frost, always did things thoroughly.

Webster tried to catch the inspector's eye to ask permission to leave, but Allen had marched straight past and was at the Vauxhall to talk to the two men dusting it for prints. 'Anything yet?'

One of them looked up from his work and shook his head. 'Not a damn thing so far, Inspector. It's been wiped clean.'

As Allen turned away, Webster moved forward to let the inspector know he was going to make a move.

'Good morning, son. The whole bloody place stinks of coppers, doesn't it?'

Webster visibly cringed at the familiar breezy voice. Where the hell had he come from? It was far too early in the morning to stomach a fresh dose of Jack Frost.

With a grin and a nod to his assistant, Frost, looking as if he had slept in his clothes in a ditch, shuffled over to the immaculate Allen.

'Hello, Frost,' said Allen without the slightest hint of enthusiasm. Events were going quite well and he didn't want Frost's jarring presence messing everything up. 'Bit early for you, isn't it?'

'Bit late, actually,' yawned Frost, rubbing an unshaven chin. 'I haven't been home all night. I fell asleep in the office.' With his head on one side he gave the Vauxhall the once-over, his hands scratching an itch on his stomach through his mac pockets. 'So this is where Useless Eustace switched motors?'

'Yes,' acknowledged Allen curtly. 'Your assistant spotted it.' He was now beginning to wonder if he wouldn't be better served with Webster than with Ingram, who had been getting quite slapdash of late.

'It's the way I train them,' Frost said, moving forward for a look inside the car. The two men from Forensic shifted out of his way as he poked his head inside the driving door. 'I can't see much blood.'

'We haven't found any yet,' Forensic admitted, 'but we're still searching.'

'I wouldn't have thought you'd have to look very hard for it,' said Frost. 'Shelby's head was half blown off. The inside of the car ought to be swimming with blood, brains, and bits of ear hole.'

Allen pulled a face. Frost's crudeness was hard to take at the best of times, but at this tender hour of the morning . . . ! 'Eustace could have wrapped the body in waterproof sheeting. A sheet was missing from the boot of Shelby's patrol car when we went through it yesterday.'

Frost tapped his first cigarette of the day on the packet and lit up. Then he had his first cough of the day. 'I don't care what you say,' he spluttered, 'I just can't see Useless Eustace as a police killer.'

Allen started to reply, but his attention was diverted by a shout.

'Mr Allen!'

He looked up. An arm was being waved from behind the hedge. Ingram had found something. 'Excuse me,' he muttered, hurrying over to see what it was.

Frost took a stroll across to the Cortina, where Webster, slumped in the front seat next to Sue, was fighting hard to keep his eyes open. Sue was talking to him, but he just didn't seem able to take in what she was saying. Wasn't it just his rotten luck spotting that car! If he'd kept his eyes closed, he would now be lying in the snug warmth of Sue's little single bed, his arms locked around her un-nightdressed body, caressing her gorgeous — but why torment himself? He yawned. The thought of yet another long, dreary day muddling through with Frost seemed an unbearable prospect.

Frost spotted the yawn and, of course, with his one-track mind, misinterpreted it. 'Tired, my son? Heavy night with Sue, was it? You should have tried getting some sleep instead.'

Webster was so tired he couldn't even raise a scowl in protest.

'One thing about a beard,' burbled Frost, rasping his chin again, 'you don't suffer from five o'clock shadow.' He turned his head. 'Hello, what's Old Clever Balls looking so happy about?'

Allen was striding over, Ingram trotting at his heels. 'Thought you might be interested to see this, Frost, especially as you can't see Eustace as a police killer.' He held up something in a polythene bag. 'We've found Shelby's notebook.'

Frost took the bag from Allen and turned it over and over in his hands. 'Where was it?'

Ingram pointed. 'I found it in that field, close to the hedge, near where the Cavalier was parked.'

Frost looked puzzled. 'And how the hell did it get there?'

Allen sucked in air, then sighed. How dense could you be? 'I'd have thought that obvious, Inspector. Eustace found it in the car after he dumped the body. It must have fallen from Shelby's pocket. It was incriminating evidence and he had to get rid of it in a hurry.'

'Oh, I see,' exclaimed Frost as if this now explained everything. 'He wipes the car clean of prints, doesn't leave a speck of blood behind, but he gets rid of vital evidence by just chucking it over the nearest hedge.'

'What did you expect him to do with it?' snapped Allen in exasperation. 'Eat it? Stick it up his arse? He daren't keep it on him, it linked him with the killing. What else could he do but chuck it?'

A uniformed man approached and gave Allen a smart salute. 'Lady in the cottage down the lane, sir. Says she saw a black Morris Minor parked down here for most of yesterday afternoon.'

Allen's eyes gleamed with satisfaction. 'Good work. I'll be with you in a couple of seconds to talk to her.' He took the polythene bag from Frost and handed it back to Ingram. 'I want the notebook checked for fingerprints. Odds are it's been wiped clean, but you never know your luck.' He noticed Frost still hovering. 'I'm sure you're very busy, Inspector. Don't let me hold you up.'

'Actually, I want to take a look in the notebook. Dave Shelby was supposed to have interviewed our anonymous phone caller. I'm hoping he kept his mind on the job long enough to write down the name and address.'

Ingram held open the bag so Frost could carefully extract the notebook, holding it by its corners with his handkerchief. An elastic band looped around the unused pages allowed Frost to go directly to the entry, the very last entry Shelby had made before he died. It read *Desmond Thorley, Dove Cottage. Interviewed re rape case phone call.*

'Bingo!' cried Frost, snapping the notebook shut and dropping it into the polythene bag. He trotted across to the Cortina. Neither Webster nor Sue seemed willing to yield their front seats, so he climbed into the back.

'It's all happening, son. I've got the name and address of the bloke who made the anonymous phone call. Drop Sue off, then we'll go and pay him a nice early visit.'

Webster's spirits plummeted to a new low. 'It's barely four o'clock in the morning,' he complained. 'He'll be fast

˙asleep in bed . . .' He yawned conspicuously and added pointedly, 'The lucky bastard!'

'He won't still be in bed after I've kicked his door down,' replied Frost cheerfully. 'Come on, son, hurry up. There's lots to do.'

Even to Webster, punch-drunk through lack of sleep, Dove Cottage looked nothing like a cottage. The shape was all wrong. In the dark of early morning it looked just like a railway carriage, and as they neared it he could see that that was exactly what it was. A dilapidated Great Western Railway carriage of pre-war vintage, dumped on a piece of waste ground situated north of the woods. It stood on brick piers, allowing it to rise proud above islands of stinging nettles in a sea of coarse, waist-high grass. Tastefully dotted around to break the monotony of the landscape were mounds of crumbling oil drums, the rotting hulk of a Baby Austin car body, and odd rust-crusted relics of long-obsolete farm machinery.

Like explorers hacking their way through virgin jungle, they pushed through the wet grass, eventually arriving at the foot of a set of rickety wooden steps that led up to the carriage door with its brass turnkey handle.

'I think this is our train,' murmured Frost, risking the climb up the steps. He tried the handle, but the door seemed to be bolted on the inside, so he pounded at it with his open hand. The noise echoed like a drum, but there was no movement from within. He hammered again, much harder this time, making the whole structure shake on its brick foundations.

Inside, a bottle toppled over and rolled. A crash of someone bumping into something, the shout of someone swearing, then a bleary voice demanded, 'Who's there?'

'Two lovely policemen,' called Frost. 'Open up, Desmond.'

The door opened outward, almost sending Frost flying. Desmond Thorley, in his late fifties, very bald and softly plump, ungummed his eyes and squinted at his visitors. He wore a filthy dressing gown the front and sleeves stiff with dirt. Under the dressing gown were a pair of grimy, food-stained pyjamas, the trousers held up by a rusty safety pin. He looked dirty. He smelled even dirtier.

'Meet Dirty Desmond,' said Frost to Webster.

Thorley clutched together his gaping dressing gown to cover his pyjamas. 'Oh, it's you, Mr Frost. I suppose you want to come in.'

'I don't want to,' replied Frost, 'but it's one of the hazards of the job.'

They stepped into thick, greasy darkness that smelled of stale sweat, unwashed socks, and bad food. A match flared as Thorley lit an old brass oil lamp which spluttered and spat out choking black smoke, but at least masked most of the other odours. He cranked up the wick, then replaced the glass chimney. They could now make out, dimly, the camp bed, some upholstered chairs rescued from a rubbish heap, and a card table on which were four food-encrusted plates and various half-finished tins of beans and pilchards. The floor was carpeted with dirty socks, unwashed underclothes, and empty spirit bottles.

'Be it ever so humble,' said Desmond, noting their disapproval.

'Humble?' snorted Frost. 'It's a bloody shithouse.'

'That,' sniffed Desmond, 'is rude.' He fluttered a hand toward the chairs. 'Sit down if you like, but be careful. The cat's been sick somewhere and I'm still trying to find out where.' He flopped himself down, but they opted to stand.

'Did you have a visit from one of our police officers yesterday?' Frost asked him.

He flapped a vague, limp hand. 'I might have done, Inspector, but my memory's not at its best at this unearthly hour.' His tongue flicked along his lips. 'You wouldn't, by chance, have some alcoholic refreshment about your person?' He spoke like a failed actor, which is exactly what he was.

From his mac pocket, Frost produced a miniature bottle of Johnnie Walker, part of the spoils from the party. He held it by the neck and swung it from side to side. Desmond's eyes locked on to it like heat-seeking missiles.

'Information first, drinkie-poos second,' promised the inspector. 'You had a visit from a policeman yesterday?'

A happy smile lit Thorley's face as he recalled the incident. 'A lovely boy, my old darling. His name was Shelby — so good-looking and so macho. He suggested it was I who phoned the constabulary the other night when that poor woman was so brutally used.'

'And was it you?' asked Webster, keeping close to the door, where a thin whisper of air was trickling through.

Thorley's gaze was transferred from the bottle to the constable. 'Oh yes. I confessed all to him. How could I lie to someone with such long eyelashes as he had.' He leaned forward to study Webster's face. 'But not so long as yours, dearie.'

Frost tugged at Webster's sleeve to remind him who was supposed to be doing the questioning. 'Do your courting later, son,' he whispered.

'I couldn't help your constable very much,' admitted Thorley. 'I found the girl. Like any law-abiding citizen, I phoned the police. That was all there was to it.'

'Did you see anyone that night?' Frost asked.

'Not a soul, my dear.'

Frost put the bottle back in his pocket.

'I saw one person only,' added the podgy man hurriedly. 'But not in the woods. As I was hastening to the phone box, there was someone in front of me, walking very quickly.'

The bottle came out again. 'Description?'

'I only saw him from the back. Medium height, dark clothes.'

'What were you doing in the woods at that time of night?' asked Webster.

'Just taking a stroll,' replied Desmond.

'It was a bit more than that,' said Frost. 'You like sneaking around in the dark spying on courting couples, don't you Desmond?'

The podgy man grinned sheepishly. 'A harmless hobby. And that's how I found the girl. I was taking a late-night stroll, ears ever alert for the sounds of casual copulation, when I came across the poor dear all still and naked. I really thought she was dead.'

'Did you see anyone jogging during your prowl around?' Frost asked.

Desmond pushed out his lips in thought. 'No, Inspector, I didn't. You often see knobbly-kneed men in running shorts, or joggers in track suits going round and round the paths, but I don't recollect seeing any last night.'

It was clear he could tell them nothing more, so Frost handed the bottle over and they took their leave. Like a good host, Desmond saw them out.

'I like your friend,' he whispered to the inspector.

'He's not used to the ways of men,' said Frost, steering the scowling Webster out into the clean, fresh-tasting air.

They hacked their way back to the car.

'What time is it?' asked Frost.

Webster brought up his watch. 'Four fifty-six.'

'Drop me off at my place and then let's get some sleep. I'll see you back at the station at noon.'

'Yes,' yawned Webster.

The sky was lightening. Somewhere, way off in the distance, a rooster crowed, then a dog barked. Lights were starting to come on in some of the houses. Denton was waking up. Frost and Webster were going to bed.

Police Superintendent Mullett looked once again at his watch and angrily reached out for the ivory-coloured telephone.

'No, sir,' replied Sergeant Johnson. 'Mr Frost still isn't in yet.'

Mullett replaced the phone and snatched up his copy of the Denton *Echo*. It was open at an inside page where the headline read FLEEING JEWEL THIEF SHOOTS POLICEMAN DEAD. Beneath it a recent photograph of David Shelby smiled across four columns. But it wasn't this story that was causing Mullett's annoyance. It was the story that had relegated it to the second page. He refolded the paper to page one, where enormous banner headlines screamed 17-YEAR-OLD GIRL RAPED. HOODED TERROR CLAIMS 7TH VICTIM. Alongside this story, in bold type, was an editorial which was headed 'What is Wrong with the Denton Police?' The theme of the editorial was that, because of incompetence, after seven attacks Denton police were still without a single clue to the identity of the rapist. It suggested that perhaps an experienced officer from another division should be brought in to take over where the Denton force had so clearly failed.

On first reading the editorial, Mullett had marched with it into Frost's rubbish dump of an office, only to find that the inspector had not yet deigned to report for work. On Frost's desk, unread, was a report from Forensic on the previous night's rape, suggesting that a full-scale search of the area would be advantageous. When he checked with Sergeant Johnson, Mullett was appalled to learn that no search of the area had been made, or planned. And, to cap this catalogue of incompetence, Frost, the investigating officer, hadn't even bothered to interview the rape victim!

He slumped down in Frost's chair, shaking his head in dismay. And that was when he saw, in the middle of the desk, weighted down with an unwashed tea mug, the crime statistics that Frost had assured him had gone off the previous day.

Back to his office, where he scribbled down notes of all the matters he wished to take up with the inspector. That done, he buzzed Inspector Allen and asked him to come to the office.

Inspector Allen, immaculately dressed and coldly efficient, so different from the wretched Frost, drew up the offered chair and sat down.

'Have you seen this?' asked Mullett, pushing the newspaper across, jabbing the offending editorial with his finger.

Allen smiled thinly, thanking his lucky stars that he had dumped the case on Frost before the newspaper story broke. 'Yes, I've seen it.'

'I want you back on the rape case as soon as possible.'

Allen reminded the Superintendent that he had to bring the murder inquiry to a satisfactory conclusion first.

'Yes, of course,' sighed Mullett. 'That must be our number-one priority. What progress so far?'

Allen brought him up to date on the finding of the Vauxhall.

'Any fingerprints?'

'No, sir. No prints and, so far, no bloodstains.'

Mullett looked up from polishing his glasses. 'No bloodstains? But Shelby's wounds would have been simply pouring with blood.'

The inspector explained his theory about the waterproof sheeting taken from Shelby's patrol car.

Mullett looked worried. 'No blood, no fingerprints. But that makes it impossible to link Shelby's body with the getaway car.'

Allen smiled. 'We tie Shelby to the car by his notebook, sir. We found it on the other side of the hedge where the Vauxhall was abandoned.'

'Were Eustace's prints on that?'

'No, sir. Like the car, it had been wiped clean. But that doesn't matter. It's solid evidence. All we've got to do now is catch Eustace, and that shouldn't take long — a day or two at the most. He won't have much money. All he's got are the cheap pieces of jewellery he stole from Glickman, and we've put tabs on all the local fences. We've also put a twenty-four-hour surveillance on his house, and I've arranged for his phone to be tapped. We'll get him, sir, and soon, I promise you.'

Mullett leaned back in his chair and relaxed. He almost felt like purring. How marvellous to have some good news for a change. A speedy result on the murder inquiry would take much of the heat off the rape cases. Thank goodness he had one officer he could rely on. He thanked Allen and sent him out to speed up the hunt for Stan Eustace.

As Allen left the office, Mullett jabbed the button on his internal and again asked if Mr Frost had arrived yet.

The minute hand of the clock in the lobby gave a convulsive twitch and clunked nearer to twelve noon. The tall, thin, angular woman in the green coat, clutching the handbag, shifted her position on the uncomfortable seat and focused hard black eyes on Sergeant Johnny Johnson, who was doing everything possible to avoid her piercing gaze. Come on, Jack Frost, he said to himself. The Super wants you, this old dear wants you, and we all want you, so where the hell are you? He must have murmured this aloud, because the woman was now staring at him suspiciously. He grinned sheepishly. 'I don't think he'll be too long, madam.'

Her sharp chin thrust forward. 'It just isn't good enough. A woman is brutally assaulted and then completely ignored by the authorities.'

'If you'd like to leave details, I'll pass them on to Mr Frost the minute he arrives,' suggested Johnson.

'Leave details?' She pushed herself up from the bench, her voice rising with her. 'Am I hearing you correctly, Sergeant? I demand to be allowed to talk to a senior policeman, and I insist that a woman police officer be present.'

Mullett, crossing the lobby on his way back to his office, paused. This sounded like trouble. He walked over to the sergeant. 'Who is this lady?' he asked.

'A Miss Norah Gibson, sir. She claims she has been raped.' Johnson stressed the word 'claims,' but Mullett failed to take the hint.

'Raped? And you're making her sit out here and wait?' he gasped incredulously. 'Good Lord, Sergeant, where's your common sense? If the Denton *Echo* got hold of this . . .'

'Er, if I could have a quiet word, sir,' said Johnson, lowering his voice so the woman couldn't hear. But Mullett was already on his way over.

'Good morning, madam. I am Police Superintendent Mullett, the Denton Divisional Commander. Do I understand you've been . . .' He hesitated for a second before bringing himself to say the word 'raped?'

Her knuckles tightened on the strap of her handbag. 'That is correct, but it seems no-one wants to know.'

At that moment, Frost breezed in, saw the Superintendent, saw the woman, and quickly backed out. But not quickly enough . . .

'Inspector Frost!' bellowed Mullett.

'Sir?' said Frost, coming in again as if for the first time. He acted surprised to see the woman. 'Hello, Norah. What are you doing here?'

Her eyes iced over. 'Miss Gibson to you,' she spat.

'She's been raped,' said Mullett.

'She should be so lucky!' said Frost.

Mullett's face went red. He had to compress his fists to control himself. He inched his face very close to Frost's and said through clenched teeth, biting off and spitting out each word, 'Get a woman police officer and also someone capable of taking a statement, and join me immediately in the interview room.'

He turned to the woman. 'If you would kindly accompany me, madam?' As he led her to the interview room she turned and beamed Frost a thin, tight smile of smug satisfaction.

Frost looked up at the ceiling for sympathy. 'Why does that stupid, horn-rimmed bastard always want to interfere?' He lowered his head as Webster, engrossed in conversation with Detective Constable Susan Harvey, pushed through the swing doors.

'Hold it, you two,' he called. 'We're wanted in the interview room. A lady's been raped.'

Mullett sat the woman down, phoned for a cup of tea to be brought in for her, stressing that he wanted a cup, not a chipped enamel mug, then looked at his wristwatch to time how long it took Frost to obey a direct order. He didn't have to wait very long. The tea arrived, followed closely by Frost with that reject from Braybridge and the good-looking Susan Harvey. Frost had a blue folder tucked under his arm.

Susan drew up a chair next to the woman to give her moral support. Frost leaned against the wall, a cigarette drooping from his mouth. Mullett wished he would smarten himself up a bit. And he wished the man wouldn't slouch in that slovenly manner. He looked more like a street-corner layabout than a detective inspector.

When Frost was satisfied that Webster was ready with his shorthand notebook he dropped his cigarette end on the floor, then gave Miss Gibson a disarming smile. It failed to disarm her.

'If you'd like to tell us what happened, Miss Gibson?'

She looked down at the floor and blushed. 'I was raped last night.'

'What, again?' asked Frost.

Her head snapped up. 'Yes, again! Some women are natural targets for filthy men, and, sadly, I seem to be such a woman.' She fumbled in her handbag for a handkerchief and dabbed at her eyes.

'Tell me,' asked Frost, striking a match on the wall to light up yet another cigarette, 'how many times have you been raped over the past three months?'

Her lips compressed. 'It's not the sort of thing one keeps count of, Inspector.'

'But we keep count of them, Miss Gibson. Every time your knickers are forcibly removed, the old computer clocks it up. Now let me see.' He opened the blue folder and flipped through its contents. 'Here we are. At the last count it was seventeen times — but each time the doctor examined you he found you were still a virgin. So who raped you, the archangel Gabriel?'

It began to dawn on Mullett that things were not as he had been led to understand. Why hadn't somebody told him? He cleared his throat and studied his watch as if surprised at the time. 'Dear me . . . You must excuse me . . .' And he scuttled out of the room.

'We'll carry on without you then, sir?' called Frost after him. Mullett affected not to hear.

The woman sat straight-backed in the chair, tightly clutching the handbag resting on her lap. 'I might have made mistakes in the past, Inspector, but last night was real.' She dabbed at her eyes again. 'You've got to believe me.'

Frost sat down. 'If you say you were raped, then of course I believe you, Miss Gibson. Tell us what happened.'

She reached out for Susan's hand and clutched at it. 'I was walking through Denton Woods last night, a little after eleven o'clock, when a naked man leaped out on me from the bushes. He knocked me to the ground and savagely raped me.' She stared pleadingly into his face. 'That's the truth, Inspector.'

Frost rubbed his scar. 'I'm sure you wouldn't tell us lies, Miss Gibson.' To Webster's surprise, the inspector's voice was strangely gentle. 'Can you describe this man?'

She dropped the handkerchief back into her handbag. 'No. I'm sorry.'

'Don't let it worry you,' said Frost, patting her hand. 'None of his other victims could describe him either.'

She blinked back her tears and smiled bravely.

'Would you be willing to submit to a medical examination?' Frost asked. 'A lady doctor if you prefer.'

Her eyes widened in alarm and she firmly shook her head. 'Oh no. It would be too humiliating.'

'I quite understand,' sympathized Frost. 'Thank you so much for coming, Miss Gibson. You've helped us a lot. I'm sure we'll catch him now. But in the meantime, stay away from the woods.' He whispered to Susan to drive the woman home, and gave a friendly wave as the door closed behind them.

'The poor cow always asks for me,' said Frost. 'I'm the only one who'll listen to her.'

Webster snapped his notebook shut. 'Stupid bitch. What a complete and utter waste of time.'

'Don't be too hard on her,' said Frost softly. 'Imagine how you'd feel if the nearest you ever got to the real thing was making up stories for the police.' He aimed his cigarette end at the waste bin. 'Let's get a cup of tea.'

Sergeant Johnson was waving frantically as they crossed the lobby. 'Mr Mullett wants to see you right away, Jack. Understand he's worried about your lack of progress with the rape inquiry.'

'Blimey!' exclaimed Frost. 'I only took it over yesterday.'

The phone rang. 'Denton police,' said Johnson. He listened, then smiled. 'Yes, madam, he is.' He held the phone out to Frost. 'One of your lady friends, Jack. Won't give her name.'

Frost thought for a moment. 'It must be Shirley. I think I was supposed to take her out last night.' He sent Webster to collect two teas from the canteen and reached for the phone but, seeing Johnny's ears flapping, decided to take the call in the privacy of his office.

He sat at his desk trying to think of an excuse for Shirley. He saw the report from Forensic and skipped through it. 'If they want to search, let them bloody well do it,' he muttered, pushing it away. He picked up the phone. 'Hello, Shirley.'

There was silence from the other end, then a woman's voice said 'Mr Frost . . . ?' It wasn't Shirley.

'Yes, Frost here,' he said. 'Who is that?'

'It's Sadie — Sadie Eustace.'

Frost slid back in his chair. Sadie! The wife of Useless Eustace! 'What do you want, Sadie?'

'Can I talk to you in confidence?'

'Of course you bloody can't,' said Frost. 'Your old man's wanted for murder.'

'He didn't do it, Mr Frost.'

'Of course he didn't, Sadie. He didn't do any of the jobs he was sent down for. He's a model citizen.'

'But he didn't kill that copper. He swears it. Listen, Mr Frost, this is for your ears only. Stan's been in touch with me.'

Frost sat up straight. 'No, you listen to me, Sadie. First of all, I'm not on this case, so you're wasting your time talking to me. Secondly, whatever you tell me goes straight on the record — every word. If you don't want that to happen, hang up and I'll forget this conversation ever took place.'

'Stan wants to talk to you, Mr Frost. He says you're the only one he can trust.'

'Then let him come to the station and give himself up. I'll talk to him then.'

'No, Jack, please. I don't want to speak over the phone. Can you come over to the house?'

'Just a minute.' He put down the phone and wandered

outside so he could see the lobby. The desk phone was on its rest and Sergeant Johnson was taking details from a woman whose cat had been locked in a neighbour's shed. Satisfied that the sergeant wasn't eavesdropping on the conversation, he went back to his desk. 'Listen to me, Sadie. I can't come to your house. It would be more than my job is worth. I shouldn't even be talking to you now.'

'The cafeteria in Woolworth's in the High Street.'

'What about it?'

'I'll be there in five minutes. Corner table. Meet me.'

'No!' said Frost firmly.

'Please,' said Sadie as she hung up.

'No,' said Frost even more firmly to the dial tone. He hung up, then spun around guiltily as Webster pushed in with the teas. 'Shut the door, son.'

Webster backed against the door to close it. He put one cup of tea on the inspector's desk.

'Ta,' said Frost, stirring it with a pencil, still not certain what to do about the phone call. 'I've just had Stanley Eustace's wife on the phone. She wants me to meet her in five minutes.'

Webster raised his eyebrows. 'Have you told Mr Allen?'

Frost shook his head. 'She doesn't want me to tell anyone. Says it's to be off the record. What do you think?'

Webster drained his cup and parked it on the window's ledge. 'I think you'd be mad to go.'

'That's what I think, too,' said Frost gloomily. 'Stark, staring, bleeding mad.' He stood up and shuffled on his mac. 'If anyone wants me, you don't know where I am.'

With the lunch-time rush the cafeteria was a cacophony of crockery, cutlery, and raised voices. Sadie was hunched up in the corner, staring at the brown plastic tabletop, which was puddled with spilt tea. Frost bought two coffees from the quick-service counter and carried them over.

'Anyone sitting here?' he asked, dropping down on the padded vinyl bench. He slid one of the coffees over. She raised her head, forced a smile, then began to stir her coffee mechanically.

'Thanks for coming, Jack.'

'That's all right,' replied Frost. 'I felt like getting kicked out of the force.' He tore open the little plastic bag of sugar and tipped it into his cup. 'So what have I risked it all for?'

She leaned forward. 'He didn't do it, Jack.'

'The jeweller identified him, Sadie.'

She brushed that aside with a flick of her hand. 'I know he did the jeweller, but he didn't shoot that copper.' She covered her face with her hands. 'I wish he'd never bought that bloody gun. I told Stan right from the start it would only lead to trouble. He said it would only be a prop, a frightener. He said he would never pull the trigger . . . but . . . but I knew different. Stan never meant to hurt the jeweller. He only meant to frighten him.'

'He did that all right,' said Frost. 'He frightened the shit out of him.'

'He panicked,' she said.

'Yes, and he panicked when he was stopped by the constable. He panicked so much he blew half his bloody head off.'

She continued to stir her coffee, then pushed the cup away, untasted. 'Stan swears to me that he didn't do that policeman.'

'If I had killed someone, Sadie, I'd swear I hadn't done it.'

She looked him directly in the eye. 'I believe him, Mr Frost.'

He smiled ruefully. 'My wife used to believe me, love, but most of the time I was bloody lying.' For some reason he was beginning to feel uneasy. As if someone was watching him. He let his eyes wander around the adjacent tables. People were more concerned with their food than with him. Then he realized Sadie had been talking and he hadn't been listening.

'Stan wants to see you, Mr Frost. He wants to arrange a meet.'

'He's been in touch?'

She nodded.

'Listen, Sadie. When he gets in touch again you can tell

him that I don't want to know. I believed him at first, but today we found the dead copper's notebook smack bang next to Stanley's getaway car. Unless he can explain that away, he can forget all about meets as far as I'm concerned.' He was all ready to slide off the bench and get the hell out of there when a shadow fell across the table. Someone was standing there, looking down at them. He slumped back and groaned. No need to raise his head. He knew who it was.

Detective Inspector Allen, his lips twisted into a knowing, superior smile, his eyes glinting with the pleasure of having caught Frost out.

'Well, well, well, and what have we here?'

Shit! thought Frost, his eyes scanning the cafeteria. Plain-clothes men everywhere. No wonder he had felt uneasy.

'We thought she was meeting her husband,' Allen explained. 'We followed her from the house.'

'I'm sorry, Jack,' said Sadie. 'I didn't know the bastards were lurking.'

Frost slouched back on the bench and sought the solace of a cigarette. It gave him something to do while he pulled his thoughts together. 'I should have realized,' he said. 'I'm bloody stupid.'

'I would say criminally stupid,' said Allen, dumping himself down on the bench. 'Just what do you think you are doing here, Frost? A prearranged meeting with the wife of a man who has murdered a young police officer?'

'I asked Mr Frost to see me for a private talk,' snapped Sadie.

'Private?' asked Allen mockingly. 'So, some parts of a murder investigation are suddenly private?' His head snapped around to Frost. 'You had no business seeing this woman without my express permission.'

Frost said nothing. The trouble was that Allen was one hundred percent right and bloody knew it, and was going to squeeze every last drop of advantage from it. But what the hell. He leaned across the table and pressed Sadie's arm. 'Try not to worry, love.' He stood up and pushed past Allen.

'Hey, where do you think you're going?' shouted Allen. But Frost was weaving his way through the tables.

All right, thought Allen. You can walk away from me, Frost, but just wait until Mullett learns about this little caper of yours.

'What joy?' asked Webster when Frost returned to the office and bundled his mac on the hat stand.

'More misery than joy, son. I was caught red-handed by Old Clever Balls.'

Serves you damn well right, thought Webster. 'What did she want?'

'Stanley wants to have a meet. I said no.'

'She must know where he is then.'

'I'm sure she does, son.'

'Did you tell Mr Allen?'

'No. He's so bleeding clever, let him find out for himself.' He chucked himself in his chair and shoved all the incoming post, unread, into his out-tray. 'Any news from Arthur Hanlon on our dead tramp?'

'He was asking for you,' Webster reported. 'He says he's spoken to all the unwashed and flea-ridden in Denton and can't come up with anyone who saw Ben Cornish later than four o'clock.'

Frost uttered a little sigh of disappointment. 'We're not getting very far with that case, are we, son? No-one seems to have their heart and soul in it. Hundreds of flatfeet looking for poor old Stan Eustace and all I've got is little fat Arthur Hanlon looking for the bastard who stamped Ben to death.'

The door handle rattled and someone kicked one of the panels. Webster opened it to admit Sergeant Ingram, his arms full of files.

'I was asked to bring you these,' he said. 'They're Mr Allen's files on the Denton rapist investigation.'

'Put them on Webster's desk,' said Frost, who certainly didn't want them on his. He noticed how tired and drawn the sergeant looked. 'Mr Allen working you hard, is he?'

'Hard enough,' said Ingram. 'Mr Allen said will you please keep his files in good nick.'

'I'll treat them as if they were my own,' said Frost.

Ingram forced a smile. 'That's what he's afraid of.' The smile immediately snapped off. As he went out, he had to push past an agitated Sergeant Johnny Johnson coming in.

Frost jerked his head at the departing Ingram. 'He doesn't look too happy.'

'Wife trouble,' said Johnny Johnson. 'I'll tell you someone else who doesn't look too happy, Jack. Mr Mullett. He's been sitting in his office waiting for you for more than an hour.'

Frost's jaw dropped and he smacked his brow. 'Flaming hell, I forgot all about the old git. I was on my way in to him when Sadie Eustace phoned.'

'He knows all about your tryst with her as well, Jack. Mr Allen has been putting the verbal boot in.'

'He's a darling man,' said Frost as he zipped through the door on his way to the Divisional Commander's office.

He was halfway down the passage when Police Constable Kenny, looking pleased with himself, grabbed at his arm. 'We've got him for you, Mr Frost. He's in the interview room.'

Frost's spirits rose. 'Who?' he asked hopefully. 'The Denton rapist?'

'No, sir, Tommy Croll, the security guard from The Coconut Grove. You said you wanted him picked up.'

'Oh,' said Frost, trying not to sound disappointed. With so much else on his plate the robbery had completely slipped his mind. 'Where did you find him?'

'Sneaking back into his digs to pick up his clothes.'

Frost patted the constable on the back. 'Good work, young Kenny. Hold on, would you. Mr Mullett's waiting all eager to give me a bollocking, so I'd better get that treat over first. Shouldn't be more than ten minutes though.' And he plunged on down the corridor for his tryst with the Superintendent.

.   .   .

'Come in,' growled Mullett, his head bowed over his midday post. He heard the door open and close. He looked up and there was Frost, in that shiny suit with the baggy trousers, out of breath and looking worried. Good. He would give him something to look worried about.

'I asked to see you more than an hour ago, Inspector,' he observed icily.

'Sorry about that, Super,' said Frost, searching his pockets for his cigarettes. Damn, he'd left them in the office. He looked hopefully at the silver cigarette box twinkling in the sunlight on Mullett's desk. Mullett scooped up the box and locked it away in his drawer. Sometimes Frost had the gall to help himself without being asked.

'This is your last warning, Frost. In future, when you receive a summons from me, you will be here, on the double.'

Silence from Frost, who was looking very sorry for himself. He would look even sorrier before Mullett had finished. Mullett produced the copy of the Denton *Echo,* the editorial ringed in blue felt tip. He pushed it over to Frost. 'Have you seen this?'

'Not yet, sir.' Frost gave it the briefest of glances and chucked it back. 'Load of balls.'

'On the contrary, Inspector,' snapped Mullett. 'What they are saying is painfully correct. A girl was raped last night. Have you interviewed her?'

'Well, no,' said Frost, shifting from one foot to the other, 'Detective Constable Harvey took a statement . . .'

But Mullett wouldn't allow him to finish. 'A rape case. A girl raped and the officer in charge of the investigation doesn't even bother to interview her personally.'

'We were busy with her boy friend last night,' retorted the inspector. 'She claimed he raped her. We had to clear him first.'

'Clearing the innocent does nothing to reduce our unsolved crime figures. Catching the guilty does,' snapped Mullett. 'I further understand you haven't yet made a search of the rape area.'

'I was on my way to do it when I got your summons, sir,' said Frost, meeting Mullett's stare of disbelief unwaveringly.

'Make sure you do it, then. And have you interviewed the men on the list of suspects that Mr Allen has drawn up?'

I've not even opened his bloody files yet, thought Frost. 'It's my number-one priority,' he said.

Mullett had plenty more bullets in the chamber. 'What progress with that dead tramp?'

'Not much joy up to now, sir,' said Frost.

Mullett stared hard to show his dissatisfaction. Frost shuffled his feet and looked down to the blue Wilton. It sped things up if you looked contrite, and Frost was dying to get back to the office for a cigarette. 'If there's nothing else, Super . . .' he edged toward the door.

Mullett was opening and shutting drawers. There was quite a lot more, but he had mislaid his notes.

'What about the robbery at The Coconut Grove?' he barked.

'Got a suspect in the interview room right now, Super.'

'Good. Then let me see some action, Frost. Let me see some progress, something that's been sadly lacking up to now.'

He flipped his hand dismissively, remembering too late about the Sadie Eustace business and the crime statistics.

Frost slouched back to his office, where he gave the waste bin a vicious kick. 'Would that that was the reproductive area of our beloved Divisional Commander.' Then he collapsed in his chair and found the cigarettes he had been seeking. He raised his head to Webster, who was regarding his superior's show of childishness with superior disdain. 'Mullett's been rambling on about a list of suspects in the rape case, son. Any idea what the old git's talking about?'

Webster extracted some stapled lists of names and addresses from one of Allen's files and handed it to the inspector. Frost thumbed through the pages, wincing at the sheer volume of names.

'List of suspects?' he snorted. 'It's more like the Classified Telephone Directory. There must be every sex offender in the county down here.' He stopped at a name he recognized. 'Freddy Gleeson! Fred the Flasher? Allen must be off his nut if he thinks Freddy could possibly be the rapist. His dick is for display purposes only, not for use.' He let the list drop to the desk and pushed it away. 'Forget it. It'll take weeks to go through that lot.'

'Couldn't we at least pull in some of the more likely ones?' Webster asked.

Frost thumbed the pages once more and shuddered. 'Waste of bloody time. These are all people with previous form. My gut feeling is that our bloke has never been caught before, so we're not going to find him in lists of known offenders.' He looked up impatiently as someone knocked at the door. 'Yes?'

PC Kenny poked his head in. 'Tommy Croll is still in the interview room, sir,' he reminded the inspector.

'I was just on my way in as you knocked,' said Frost.

Tommy Croll was unshaven and unwashed, his clothes even more crumpled than Frost's. He blinked nervously as the inspector entered with his hairy sidekick.

'Hello, Tommy,' greeted Frost, settling himself down in the familiar hard interview room chair. 'Nice of you to come and see us.'

Tommy said nothing. He had long since learned that the best technique to use with the police was to say as little as possible.

Frost folded his arms, smiled at Croll benevolently, then fished out his cigarettes. He lit one very slowly, dribbling the smoke across the table. 'You're the answer to my prayers, Tommy. I'm in serious trouble with my Divisional Commander. To get back in his good books I need a quick confession and no sodding about.'

'I didn't do it, Mr Frost,' Croll whined.

'Now that's a pity,' said Frost, 'because it means we might have to resort to desperate measures, such as violence.' He jerked his thumb to the door as a signal for the uniformed man to leave.

Croll tried not to show his concern. He was now alone in the interview room with Frost and that thug with the beard, and he'd heard some alarming stories about him. There was even a whisper that he had beaten up Harry Baskin, and you would have to be a real hard case to even contemplate doing anything like that.

'As you probably know,' said the inspector, 'my hairy colleague was drummed out of Braybridge for smashing up prisoners. I'd never allow him to do anything like that to you, Tommy — not in my presence.' He pushed himself up from the chair and stretched. 'So I'll go and take a little stroll around the block.' To Webster he said, 'Try not to leave any marks, son.'

Tommy tried to smile to show he knew it was all a bluff, but the smile wouldn't come. 'You've got to believe me, Mr Frost. I didn't do it.'

'I don't care if you did it or not,' Frost said. 'All I want is a bloody confession.' Then he seemed to have second thoughts and settled down again in the chair. 'I'll listen to one fairy story and one only, Tommy, and then your teeth get knocked out.'

Croll opened his arms in appeal. 'It happened just like I told you, Inspector . . . I heard the right signal. I opened the door and wham, I'm coshed — I'm out cold.'

'Balls!' snapped Frost. 'That little tap you got wouldn't have knocked out a four-year-old.'

Croll chewed his lower lip and his eyes sized up the hairy thug. 'All right, Mr Frost. I'll tell you the truth.'

'Good,' beamed Frost, motioning for Webster to change roles from heavy to shorthand writer.

'It was like I told you before, Mr Frost, right up to the time where I got the signal to open the door. I opens it and there's this geezer wearing a Stan Laurel face mask and holding a cosh of some sort. He clouts me round the nut, but I reckon he hadn't done it before, because he didn't hit me very hard. Anyway, I figured that if I didn't drop down unconscious, he'd welt me a damn sight harder the second

time, so I fakes it and down I go. I lies there, dead still, until
he's grabbed the money and gone.'

'So when he'd gone, why didn't you start banging and
yelling?' asked Frost.

'I was going to, honest. Then I suddenly thought what Mr
Baskin might do to me if he found out I'd been faking and
hadn't put up a fight. So I thought I'd better carry on faking.
I didn't even yell when Mr Baskin booted me in the ribs.'

Frost puffed out the tiniest stream of smoke through compressed lips. 'So tell me about Stan Laurel. Describe him.'

Croll gave a noncommittal shrug. 'Medium height, medium build. I hardly saw him.' His nostrils twitched as the
smoke from the inspector's cigarette wafted over. 'I couldn't
half do with a fag, Mr Frost.'

'You'll have a lighted fag stuck right up your arse if you
can't come up with a better description than that, Tommy
boy,' said Frost.

Blinking hard, Croll gulped as he tried to think of something that would satisfy the inspector. 'Well, he stunk of
scent . . . after-shave, I suppose . . . and he had these
poncey shoes on.'

Frost caught his breath. 'What sort of shoes?'

'Expensive shoes. You could see the quality — they must
have cost a packet. As I lay on the floor he stood near me, his
shoes inches away from my face. I know them off by heart.
Sort of brown and cream with a woven pattern.'

The inspector stretched his arms out above his head, then
massaged the back of his neck. 'You might have helped us
there, Tommy.' He heaved himself up from the chair. 'You
might have helped us a lot. Now, we can either lock you up
or set you free and let Mr Baskin know where you are. What
do you prefer?'

'Locked up, Mr Frost.'

'Well,' smiled Frost as if bestowing a great kindness, 'as a
favour to you.' He shook some cigarettes from his packet and
pushed them over, then he called in the uniformed man and
asked him to lock up the prisoner. That done, he flopped

back into the chair, clasped the back of his neck with his interlocked fingers, and purred contentedly at the ceiling.

'Have I missed something?' asked Webster.

A beam from Frost. 'I've got a feeling in my water, son. One of my hunches.'

'Amaze me with it,' Webster said without enthusiasm.

'Fancy shoes, son. Brown-and-cream fancy shoes. Roger Miller has got a wardrobe full of them; we saw them when we had that little nose around his flat.'

'Thousands of people have got brown-and-cream shoes,' said Webster as he sneaked a look at his watch. He wanted to be in the canteen for lunch at the same time as Susan Harvey and was hoping that this bumbling half-wit of an inspector wouldn't detain him much longer.

But Frost had no intention of being hurried. 'Try this out for a scenario, son. Roger is in Baskin's ribs for a lot of money. He knows Baskin will get very nasty if he isn't paid.'

'We've been through all this,' sighed Webster.

'That was when I thought Baskin had nicked Roger's motor. Just hear me out,' insisted Frost. 'Roger hasn't got the money to settle his gambling debt, so he gets the bright idea of stealing it from Harry Baskin. He gets his girl friend with the mole on her bum to help — she's got all the inside gen and she's the one who phones pretending to be the nurse, while Roger, in his Stan Laurel mask, does the dirty deed.'

'It's a possible theory,' sniffed Webster, patently unimpressed and more concerned with getting this stupid conversation over and done with.

'I haven't finished, son.' Frost stood up and began to pace about the room. 'I've always worried about the way that licence plate came off the Jag. But what if it was meant to come off?'

'I don't follow you.'

'They knew what Baskin would do to them if he ever suspected, so they badly wanted an alibi. An alibi that would put Roger miles away. Everyone knows his flash motor. So the girl friend puts on one of Roger's caps, drives the Jag round and round the old people's flats, bashing into dustbins, trumpeting away at the horn, making sure no-one could avoid seeing the car. And just in case no-one got the registration number, she chucks the licence plate out of the window for the cops to find. When the police followed it up, Roger would say, "Yes, officer, it was I who caused the public nuisance," pay his fine and for fifty quid he's bought himself a cast-iron alibi for the time of the robbery. What went wrong, of course, was the girl knocking down that old man. That sodded everything up. There was no way Roger was going to say he was driving after that.' He sneaked a glance across to Webster to see how this was being received.

It wasn't being received too well. Webster immediately saw the flaw in the reasoning. 'Very ingenious . . . except for the fact that Miller didn't owe Baskin any money. He'd settled his debts two days before the robbery.'

Frost stopped dead in his tracks. 'Damn and bloody blast!' he shouted. 'I'd forgotten all about that.'

The door opened and the sergeant from the motor pool walked in. 'Been looking for you everywhere, Mr Frost,' he said. 'You borrowed a car from the pool this morning.'

'Did I?' said Frost, a nasty feeling of more trouble starting to creep up his back.

'Yes, sir. When that stolen Vauxhall was found you wanted to get over there in a hurry. You told us your assistant was using your own car so you took one from the pool and promised you'd bring it straight back.'

'We came back in your Cortina,' said Webster.

Damn! thought Frost. I must have left the flaming pool car down that lane. He patted his pockets for the keys. He didn't have them. 'I must have left them in the ignition,' he admitted sheepishly. 'Still, no problem. I'll nip over and bring it back. I know where it is.'

'You don't know where it is, Mr Frost,' the sergeant told him grimly. 'At this moment it's being hauled up from the bottom of a canal in Lexington. Lexington police have arrested two joyriders.'

'Bum holes!' said Frost, now feeling very depressed. 'I don't think it's going to be my day.'

THURSDAY DAY SHIFT/NIGHT SHIFT

It wasn't going to be Webster's day either. Before he had the chance to explain about his lunch date with Susan, he was dragged by the inspector out through the back way to the car park. Frost was anxious to make himself scarce before Mullett learned about the pool car fiasco.

First they went to Denton Hospital to interview the seventeen-year-old rape victim, but she could add nothing to the statement she had already given to Susan Harvey. Indeed, she remained convinced it was her boy friend who had assaulted her, despite the medical evidence to the contrary.

That chore out of the way, Frost directed Webster to some appalling little back-seat transport café where they dined on burnt sausages, greasy chips, and tinned peas. To add insult to injury, Webster had to pay the bill for both of them when Frost realized he hadn't drawn any cash from the bank. The deepening scowl on Webster's face was threatening to become a permanent feature.

Sulkily slinging himself back in the car, the acidic stewed tea and the stale chip fat fermenting in his stomach, Webster asked the inspector where he wanted to go. He just didn't care anymore. Life was one long round of chauffeuring Frost, teetering from one crisis to the next while having to endure his unfunny jokes about beards and whiskers.

'Denton Woods,' said Frost. 'Mr Mullett is very cross with us because we didn't search the area for clues last night.'

'It'll take more than two of us,' grunted Webster, slamming the car door too hard and wincing as acid indigestion made its first tentative stab.

'Only if we do it properly,' said Frost cheerfully, leaning back and puffing contentedly at a cigarette. 'Not a bad meal, was it?'

The thin, yellow afternoon sun did little to warm up the

woods, and they hunched up inside their coats as they
trudged along the path. 'You know, son,' said Frost when
they squeezed through the bushes and found themselves in
the clearing with its wet, flattened grass, 'I've got a hunch. I
reckon he's going to try it on again tonight.'

'Oh yes?' grunted Webster. He just couldn't care less. He
had had his fill of Frost and was counting the hours until he
would be off duty and round to Susan Harvey's little flat with
the door bolted and the phone off the hook.

'The weather's getting colder,' Frost went on. 'He's going
to have to grab his opportunities. If he does his stripping-off
act much longer he'll end up with a frostbitten dick.' He
scuffed the grass with his foot, already anxious to be away,
but Webster suddenly bent down and tugged at something, a
scrap of cloth caught on the lower branch of a bush. He held
it out to Frost, who backed away. 'It's not a clue, is it, son?
I'm not in the mood for clues.'

By the look of it, the scrap of cloth had been hanging
around the woods for years, but Webster slipped it into a
small plastic envelope. 'I'd like to send this to Forensic . . .
unless you've any objection?' His tone dared Frost to demur.

'If it makes you happy, son. Now let's get the hell out of
here before you pick up any more rubbish.' He squeezed back
through the gap to the path, while Webster protested that
they hadn't even begun to search the area. 'We haven't got
time,' said Frost, hurrying back to the car. 'We're never going
to nab this sod by sniffing around for clues. The only way
we'll do it is by catching him in the act — in flagrante dick-o,
as the lawyers say.'

'And how are we going to do that?' asked Webster.

'I've got a plan,' said Frost, grateful to be back in the car
after the cold dankness of the forest. 'I'll tell you when we get
back to the office. Next port of call, the bank. I've got to get
some money.'

Webster was turning the key in the ignition when another
car roared up and skidded across to block their path. A plump
little man in a blue mac and a porkpie hat jumped out and
hurried over to them.

'I've been looking for you everywhere, Inspector,' puffed Detective Sergeant Arthur Hanlon, out of breath. 'Mr Mullett's screaming blue murder — something about a wrecked car — and Johnny Johnson says they can't get in touch with you by radio.'

'It's on the blink,' said Frost.

'It's been turned off,' accused Hanlon, clicking the switch.

'I don't understand these technical terms,' said Frost, firmly switching it off again. 'Now speak your piece, Arthur. I've got to go to the bank.'

'I've found someone who was with Ben Cornish on Tuesday evening,' reported Hanlon. 'They call him Dustbin Joe, so you can imagine what he smells like. He was just about coherent, and his breath stank of meths, but if we can believe him, he reckons he saw Ben about eight o'clock Tuesday evening and Ben told him he was on his way round to his mother's to try and tap her for some money.'

'Now that's very interesting,' said Frost, scratching his chin thoughtfully, 'because his family said they hadn't seen him for weeks.'

'The statement's on your desk,' said Hanlon. 'Just sniff, you'll find it.'

'You're a little gem, Arthur,' beamed Frost. 'Now, if anyone asks, you haven't seen me. I'm the man who never was.' He closed the car door. 'Change of plan, son. Let's go straight to Mrs Cornish.'

Mrs Cornish, who had affected indifference to her son's death, was wearing the black woollen dress she had worn at her husband's funeral. Frost didn't comment on this fact. He sat with Webster in the tiny kitchen which reeked of fried onions, a smell that threatened to rouse Webster's stomach to further rebellion. The yapping, snarling mongrel in the yard kept leaping up and banging its nose on the window in its frenzied efforts to rip them to pieces.

She folded her arms belligerently. 'Like I told you, we hadn't seen him for God knows how long. Hadn't seen him and never wanted to see him.'

'Ben met someone Tuesday evening, just after eight, and said he was on his way round here,' said Frost.

'Well, he didn't come,' said the woman flatly, 'and I would have slammed the door in his face if he did.'

A banging as the front door closed, then footsteps along the passage. Danny pushed into the kitchen, stopping dead when he saw the two detectives. 'What the hell?' he exclaimed. For a moment he looked as if he was going to turn tail and run.

'They're asking about Ben,' said his mother quickly. 'They seem to think he was here on Tuesday. I've told them we hadn't seen him for months.'

'Quite right,' said Danny, still hovering by the open door.

'And that's all we've got to tell you,' said Mrs Cornish to Frost. 'I want you to leave now.' To hurry them on their way, she asked her son to let the dog in.

Webster reversed out of the back street and pointed the car toward town. 'So what did that achieve?'

Frost, plunged in deep thought, surfaced with difficulty. 'I reckon they're lying, son. I'll lay odds that Ben did go home on Tuesday.' His watch told him it was a quarter past three. 'Foot down, son. I must get to the bank before they close.'

The nameplate above the cashier's window in Bennington's Bank said the young teller's name was Gerald Kershaw. He took Frost's cheque and clouted it with a rubber stamp. He didn't look very happy.

'Fives, please,' said Frost, watching carefully as the youth counted out the crisp, brand-new notes.

'I've got to call in at the police station tonight, Mr Frost,' said the youth gloomily.

'Been fiddling the books?' asked Frost, taking the money and rechecking it. 'I'd flee the country if I were you.'

The cashier grinned. 'No, not quite as bad as that. I've got to produce my driving licence and insurance details. A traffic cop caught me driving through a "buses only" lane.'

Frost tut-tutted and shook his head at the gravity of the

offence. 'That's a thirty pound fine at least, plus fifteen quid costs. It's cheaper to rob a bank — you'd only get probation for that.'

The youth leaned forward confidentially, keeping his voice low. 'I suppose there's no way the charge could be dropped, Mr Frost. I know the police have discretion, and it was a first offence.'

Frost gasped at the enormity of the suggestion. 'No chance,' he said. He was stuffing the notes in his wallet and about to turn for the door when the idea struck him. He beckoned the youth closer. 'Tell you what, Gerald. I might be able to fix it for you in return for a very small favour.'

'A small favour?' repeated the teller doubtfully.

'It's all right; it's official police business,' said Frost, 'but it's very confidential. I want to know a few minor details about someone's account.'

The cashier looked furtively about him. No-one was watching. 'What's the name of the account?' he asked, moving to the monitor screen and typing in the password for current accounts information.

Outside in the car, which was tucked, well hidden, down a side street in case a cruising police car spotted it, Webster waited impatiently. He felt like the driver of a getaway car in a bank raid. Ten minutes had passed since Frost, coat collar turned up, had sidled into the bank. How long did it take the idiot to cash a simple cheque?

Another minute ticked by and there he was, bounding along, his mac flapping, a broad grin threatening to split his face. He slid in beside Webster and flung out his arms with joy.

'I have a theory, son, that for every bit of bad luck you get compensated by a bit of good. So I deserve a bloody big chunk and I've just had it. Guess what?'

Webster didn't answer. He was in no mood for stupid guessing games.

'When Roger Miller gave Harry Baskin his cheque for £4,865 to pay his gambling debts, he didn't have a penny in his bank account; in fact, he was overdrawn by £32. But the morning after the robbery he paid in a cash deposit of £5,130, just in time for his cheque to be honoured.'

Webster turned slowly in his seat. 'The morning *after* the robbery?'

Frost hugged himself with delight. 'Yes, my son. Let's go and bring the bastard in.'

Through the dull throb of his headache, Police Superintendent Mullett bravely smiled his thanks as his secretary, Miss Smith, brought him a cup of hot, sweet tea and a large bottle of aspirins. His headache was getting worse. He took off his glasses and pinched his nose to ease the strain, then gave his full attention to the station sergeant.

'We've been radioing Mr Frost constantly since one o'clock, sir. He hasn't responded, I'm afraid.'

Grunting his disapproval, Mullett popped two aspirins in his mouth and swallowed them down with a gulp of tea.

'His radio could be out of order,' suggested the sergeant.

'Yes,' snapped Mullett, replacing his cup on the saucer, 'we all know how often and how conveniently Mr Frost's radio breaks down. He's to report to me the second he comes in, Sergeant.'

When the sergeant left, Mullett relaxed enough to take from his drawer the envelope with the House of Commons crest. He drew out the gold-engraved invitation and the short note in Sir Charles Miller's own hand thanking him for his assistance in the hit-and-run case and inviting Mullett and his good lady to a small social gathering at the MP's house the following night at which the Chief Constable would also be present.

Mullett's pleasure at receiving this had almost outweighed his annoyance about the wretched business of the stolen police car. He had already had the press on the phone for his comments and he dreaded seeing the morning's Denton *Echo,* which really seemed to have its knife out for the police these days.

He ran his finger along the gilt edge of the invitation, and the contact made him feel better. Sir Charles Miller's private telephone number was on the letter requesting that the Superintendent phone him personally to confirm his acceptance. He had dialled the number and was holding on while the butler went off to find his master when there was a knock at his door.

'Wait!' ordered Mullett imperiously, but his command was ignored. The door opened and Frost ambled in, grinning from ear to ear.

'I asked you to wait,' barked Mullett. Typical of the man. Never here when you wanted him, but ask him to wait and he comes bursting in regardless.

'Hello, Mullett,' boomed Sir Charles at the other end of the phone.

'I've just arrested Roger Miller,' Frost announced.

Mullett's mouth opened and closed. He looked at Frost, then looked at the phone in his right hand. 'You've what?' he croaked.

'Hello, Mullett, are you there?' asked a puzzled Sir Charles.

'It was Miller who nicked that five thousand quid from The Coconut Grove the other night,' continued Frost proudly. 'His girl friend was his accomplice; she's given us a full confession.'

Mullett forced a barely sustainable smile of commendation and then became painfully aware of the irritated voice barking out of the phone. He took a deep breath. 'Hello, Sir Charles,' he said at last. 'I'm afraid I might have a bit of bad news for you.' With his free hand he dropped the invitation into the waste bin. Its thud as it hit the bottom sounded the death knell of his current social climbing aspirations.

'Well done, Jack,' called Johnny Johnson as the inspector trotted back to his own office. 'How did Mr Mullett take it?'

'Well, he didn't exactly kiss my feet,' replied Frost, 'but at least it distracted his attention from the car I lost.'

Frost had played his usual game of bluff and double bluff, aided by gambler's luck, which was paying him one of its brief visits. First he and Webster had picked up the girl, Julie

King, telling her that Roger Miller had been positively identified and had made a full confession implicating the girl as his accomplice. 'The lousy bastard!' she said. 'He promised to keep me out of it.' She then made a statement giving them everything they wanted. Armed with this, they arrested Roger, and, once he was in custody, Frost was able to issue instructions for his flat to be searched. To Frost's Academy-Award-winning act of stunned surprise, the exclusive handmade brown-and-cream shoes were found. These were later identified by Croll as those worn by his attacker. And tucked away, right at the back of a built-in cupboard, they found a Stan Laurel mask.

Then the uninteresting bit. The paperwork and the tying up of the various loose ends. This was interrupted at one stage by a phone call from Harry Baskin, who had obviously been contacted by Sir Charles Miller. He said he didn't want to prefer charges.

'This isn't a civil case, Harry,' Frost had told him. 'It's a criminal charge, so you've got no say in the matter.' It was another two hours of comings and goings with Miller's solicitor and the director of the Public Prosecutions Office before Frost was able to turn his mind to more important matters.

'The rape case, son,' he informed Webster, 'I want to make a move on it tonight.'

'Tonight?' repeated Webster, hoping he wasn't hearing correctly. He had intended spending the night in the narrow El Dorado of Susan Harvey's single bed.

'Yes. My every instinct tells me that King Dick is still in the area and he's going to have another bash tonight. So let's give him someone to have a bash at.'

'A decoy?'

'Exactly. Someone young and tasty with enormous knockers.' He opened the door and yelled in the general direction of the duty room, 'Sue . . . got a minute?'

Oh no! thought the dismayed Webster. Please, not Sue!

Frost pushed a chair toward her so she could sit down, then asked, 'You doing anything tonight, Sue?'

She hesitated, shooting a little sideways glance at Webster, who could only shake his head helplessly.

'If not, how would you like to be raped?' continued the inspector.

This was one of the inspector's little jokes, of course. She giggled as she waited for the punchline. Then she saw he was deadly serious.

'I need you as a decoy, Sue. For this bloody rapist. I want to nail the bastard tonight.'

For just a second she hesitated, then she said, 'What's the plan?'

'It's Mr Allen's plan, actually. I found it in the file. We fit you up with a two-way radio and we stake out the area. You prowl around, oozing sexual attraction, then, when he rises to the bait, we pounce, and then we all go home and have a cup of tea. How does it sound?'

She smiled. 'I'll do it. After seeing what he did to that kid last night, I'll do anything to get the swine.'

Frost patted her hand. 'Good girl. Now, we know he likes them young, dewy-eyed, and innocent, so no make-up, no bra, sensible knickers, and simple clothes — and take the Karma Sutra out of your pocket.' He consulted his watch. 'It's coming up to half past seven. Get off home. Try and grab some kip because, if we're lucky, it's going to be a busy night. I'll send Webster round at ten to pick you up and bring you back here for a final briefing.'

Webster yawned pointedly. If he could get off now he would be able to drive Sue back to her flat, and to her bed, and they could relax and make up for the disappointment of the night before. 'Perhaps we'd all better snatch a few hours' sleep,' he suggested.

'Sure,' said Frost vaguely. 'But there's a couple of quick jobs we must do first.'

They'd better be quick, thought Webster, whispering to Susan that he'd be round at nine, earlier if he could, which would give them at least an hour before she had to get dressed in her decoy outfit.

'So what are these jobs?' urged Webster when Susan had left.

'Mm?' said Frost, not listening. He had taken out the packet of action photographs from Dave Shelby's collection and was finding one of consuming interest. It showed Shelby and a woman, both naked. Shelby was lying on the bed, grinning. The woman, her back to the camera, showing off gorgeous buttocks, was astride him. The punchline to his old joke came into Frost's head. 'I knew it was the foreman,' he muttered to himself, 'because I had to do all the bloody work.' He caught Webster's eye. 'Something nagging me, son. Why do I feel I should know where this was taken, and why do I feel it's important?'

Can't the old fool keep his mind on one case at a time, thought Webster as he bent to take a look. Wow! Lucky Shelby! The unknown woman looked a right little raver, and the action shot made him even more anxious to get the hell out of the office and into Sue's bed posthaste so he could grin up at Sue as Shelby was grinning up at the woman.

'I'm not sure who the woman is,' said Frost. 'I think it's Mullett's secretary. But I'm sure I know that bedroom. We've been there — and recently.'

Webster tore his eyes away from the woman's bottom and studied the rest of the photograph. Behind the lovers was an out-of-focus yellow background. To one side, also out of focus, a brown fuzzy blur that might possibly be a bedside cabinet and which was topped by something that seemed to glow red. He shook his head. It meant nothing to him.

Then Frost let out a yelp of triumph. 'Got it!' He jabbed a finger. 'That is Mrs Dawson's bedroom.'

Webster picked up the photograph and looked again, trying to compare what he saw with what he remembered. Of course. The out-of-focus yellowish background, the colour distorted by the flash, would be the cream leather headboard. Once that was established the other blurred objects clicked into sharp focus, down to the LED digital clock with its oversized red numerals. There was no doubt about it, Dave

Shelby had been having it off with Mrs Dawson of the buttocks beautiful.

'What if her old man had found out?' said Frost quietly.

Webster whistled softly. Then there would have been hell to pay. Max Dawson had a violent temper, and an armoury of firearms. Then it hit him what Frost was implying. 'Surely you're not suggesting . . . ?'

'Why not?' asked Frost. 'It's much more likely Dawson would kill Shelby than Useless Eustace, and it's always bugged me that there was no blood in the getaway car.'

'But we found Shelby's notebook.'

Frost clicked his Biro on and off. 'There must be some other answer as to how it got there.' He pushed the pen back into his top pocket.

'You'll have to tell Mr Allen.'

Frost tightened his lips stubbornly. 'He wouldn't listen, son. He's already made up his mind that Stan is his murderer. Besides, I don't want anyone to see these photos until I'm sure. We'll have to interview Max Dawson ourselves.'

'But it isn't our case,' insisted Webster.

Frost stuffed the photograph back with the rest and put them in his pocket. 'I promised Stan's wife I'd help if I could.'

'You don't owe her a bloody thing. We've got enough on our plates with this rape case. Besides, Mullett will crucify you if he finds out you've been meddling again.'

But it was hopeless. When Frost was in his stubborn mood, neither logic, common sense, nor appeals to reason would shake him. 'It won't take us long, son,' he said.

Clare, wearing a see-through blouse and white slacks, opened the door to them, but the smile died on her face and she looked startled, as if she was expecting someone else. 'Max is out,' she said. 'He's gone to London for a meeting. He won't be back until the morning.'

'Then perhaps you can help,' said Frost, smiling. It suited him to be able to question the woman first.

They followed the famous photogenic wiggling bottom

into the oak-panelled lounge with its walls covered in weapons, one of which could have been used to kill Dave Shelby. She waited nervously, rubbing the back of one hand, watching Frost as he slowly and deliberately unwound his scarf. It was stifling in the lounge with the pseudo log fire eating up the therms.

'What is it about?' she asked anxiously.

'How's Karen?' said Frost, balling the scarf and ramming it into his mac pocket. He sat down on the settee and unbuttoned his coat.

'She's fine,' Clare told them. 'My husband has agreed she can go to ballet school at the end of this term.'

Frost smiled at her. 'So all secrets are safe?'

'Yes.' She waited for him to come to the point.

Frost opened his wallet and took out the press release black-and-white photograph of Dave Shelby, smiling and alive. He held it up to her. 'Recognize him?'

She gave it barely a glance before shaking her head.

Still holding it up to her, Frost said, 'I think you do, Mrs Dawson. His name is David Shelby, he's a policeman, married with two young kids. He was shot dead yesterday.'

'Oh!' She took the glossy, then pretended to recognize it for the first time. 'Of course. Yes, I read about it in the paper.' She offered Frost the photograph back, but he didn't take it.

'Then you know why we are here, Mrs Dawson?'

Her hands fluttered vaguely. 'I haven't the faintest idea.' Webster wandered over to the rack of guns with their polished stocks and mat black barrels. If weapons of death could look beautiful, then these looked beautiful. From a casual glance there was no way of telling if any of the shotguns had been fired recently, and, in any case, none of these guns would be returned to the rack without being thoroughly cleaned.

Frost took the black-and-white photograph from the woman's hand and replaced it with the Polaroid. The colour drained from her face. 'Why are you doing this to me?'

'Because we are investigating a murder, Mrs Dawson. Debbie saw the man drawing the bedroom curtains, but it wasn't Karen's bedroom — it was the room next door . . . your bedroom. You were in bed with Dave Shelby when Karen came home unexpectedly, weren't you? She burst in on you, saw you together. That's why she ran out of the house?'

She gave the photograph back to the inspector, then slowly walked over to the bar and poured herself a stiff vodka. She offered the bottle to Frost, who refused. With one elbow on the bar counter she emptied half the glass, then set it down. 'All right. So I was in bed with your policeman. But I didn't know he was married, and I didn't know he had children.'

'Would it have made any difference if you had known?' Webster asked her.

She frowned, considering this, then shook her head almost imperceptibly. 'No. I don't think it would. I can't help it: I need men. I met Dave in a pub — I forget which one. I was feeling lonely.' She looked up, her head slowly travelling around the barn of a lounge. 'This house is so big, so empty. Neither Karen nor Max needs me anymore. Dave used to come in the afternoon when he was on the middle shift. He was good-looking and a lot of fun. Kinky though. He liked taking these photographs. He promised to burn them. I wouldn't have let him take them if he hadn't promised that.'

'When did he take this photograph?' Frost asked.

'That afternoon. Just before Karen came bursting in on us. We had the shock of our lives when that happened.' She shuddered at the recollection. 'Dave said he wouldn't be coming again after that, but I would have talked him round. And when I read in the paper that he had been killed . . .' She finished her drink and poured another.

'When did your husband find out?' asked Frost casually.

She stared at him, eyes wide open in horror, shaking her head from side to side. 'My husband? God, surely he doesn't know. He'd kill me, Inspector. You can't imagine how violent he is.'

'I think we can,' said Frost. 'We think he is so violent that when Karen told him what she saw, he took one of his expensive shotguns, went out to find Shelby, and blasted his

face off. Would you like me to show you a photograph of
how your lover looked after that, Mrs Dawson?'

The glass rattled on the bar top as she set it down. She
backed away from him. 'Max doesn't know about me and
Dave. If he did he would have killed me first and Dave
second.'

Frost pulled the scarf from his pocket and buttoned up his
mac. 'Well, let's hope he's got an alibi for yesterday.'

She clutched his sleeve. 'You're not going to tell him? For
God's sake, you're not going to tell him about me and Dave?'
She paused. 'Wait a minute. What time yesterday?'

'From five o'clock onward.'

She thought, then she smiled. 'That's easy. He was shooting for his club — The Denton Small Arms Shooting Associ-
ation. There was some challenge match with another club.
Max was there until long gone nine.'

'What guns did he take with him?' asked Webster.

'An automatic pistol and a shotgun.'

'We'll check with his club,' Frost told her. 'If his alibi
holds, we won't bother you or him further. We'll see ourselves out.'

As they opened the front door a young, very good-looking
man was standing on the step. He carried what appeared to
be an overnight case in his hand.

'Oh, I do beg your pardon,' he said. 'I appear to have
come to the wrong house.'

'I don't think so,' replied Frost. 'She's waiting for you
inside. Have you brought your camera?'

For reasons he didn't explain, Frost wanted to check the alibi
on his own, leaving Webster to wait impatiently outside the
exclusive Denton Small Arms Club. After fifteen minutes, the
inspector emerged, shoulders slumped as he slouched down
the stone steps to the car.

'Well?' asked Webster, when Frost had slid into the passenger seat.

'Dawson arrived there before five and didn't leave until

well after ten,' said Frost gloomily, 'so there's no way he could have done it . . . more's the bloody pity.'

Webster raised his eyebrows. 'Why do you say that?'

'Because if it's not him, then it's got to be someone else, hasn't it?' muttered Frost, slouching lower into his seat.

They drove in silence until they reached the station, where Frost was dropped off. He had suddenly realized that he hadn't obtained the Divisional Commander's authority for the night's decoy operation.

He trotted into Mullett's secretary's office to find the grey-haired Miss Smith crouched over her electronic daisy-wheel typewriter, bashing out a report at high speed.

'Yes, Inspector?' she asked, her eyes not moving from her notebook.

'I'd like to see Hornrim Harry.'

'If you mean the Divisional Commander,' she sniffed, 'he's had to go over to County Headquarters. Perhaps I can do something for you?'

'That's damn generous of you, Ida,' grinned Frost. 'Your place or mine?' Still guffawing at his cheap wit, he wandered away, leaving Miss Smith hot-cheeked and fuming.

He ambled over to Sergeant Johnny Johnson at the front desk. 'How many men can you spare me for tonight, Johnny?' he asked.

'None,' replied the sergeant, ruling a line to finish an entry. 'What did you want them for?'

'Operation Mousetrap. A decoy operation to nab our rapist.'

Johnson nodded. Vaguely he recalled the details, but as far as he knew it hadn't been officially approved. 'Have you spoken to Mr Mullett about it?'

Frost offered his cigarettes. 'I've just come from his office,' he said truthfully.

Johnson accepted a light, then consulted the shift rota. 'How long would you want them for?'

'As long as it takes, Johnny. Two or three hours, perhaps. If he hasn't taken the bait by one o'clock, say, I'll call it off for the night.'

'Tell you what,' said Johnson. 'Providing I can call them back if there's an emergency, I can let you have four men and a patrol car.'

Frost grimaced. This was totally inadequate. Allen's plan called for a minimum of fifteen men. 'Bloody hell, Johnny. It's Denton Woods I'm trying to cover, not a flaming window box.'

The station sergeant shrugged and returned to the Incident Book. 'You can't have what I haven't got. Take it or leave it.'

There could be no question about Frost's answer. No way could the plan possibly succeed with such a pathetically inadequate force. It would be disastrous.

'I'll take it,' he said.

Webster had just sat himself down in the armchair in his room and closed his eyes for a couple of minutes before shooting off in the Cortina to Sue's place to spend almost an hour with her before they would have to leave for Operation Mousetrap. But he must have drifted into a deep sleep.

He and Susan, together with Dave Shelby and Mrs Dawson, were all enjoying a naked, sweaty, lusty foursome in that bed with the padded leather headboard when the door burst open. In the doorway, twitching with fury, was Max Dawson with the shotgun. As Dawson pulled the trigger, Webster suddenly jerked awake and the blast changed into the jangle of the phone.

It was Sue. Angry. Demanding to know where the hell he was. He looked at his watch. Damn and bloody blast! Ten minutes to ten and the briefing meeting at 10.15 sharp.

He splashed cold water over his face and leaped down the stairs to the car. By anticipating a couple of traffic light changes he was outside her flat, honking the horn, at three minutes to ten. She scurried across to the car, not looking at him. She looked marvellous. She had scrubbed her face clean of make-up and her skin glowed. Her hair was pulled back in a simple style, and she wore faded jeans and a white nylon zip-up windbreaker over a red-and-white-striped T-shirt.

Look virginal and innocent, Frost had told her. She looked so virginal and innocent, Webster was all ready to drag her straight back to the flat, into the bed, and to hell with Denton, Frost and Operation-bloody-Mousetrap.

She sat tight-lipped beside him in the car, her face set, her eyes smouldering.

'Sorry, Sue,' he said meekly. 'I fell asleep in the chair. I was so damn tired.' He clouted the horn with the palm of his hand as some idiot on a pedal bike swerved directly into their path.

Sue fidgeted with the shoulder strap of her handbag. 'It doesn't matter,' she said sniffily, staring straight ahead.

'Look, I said I'm bloody sorry . . .'

'It doesn't matter,' she repeated.

He spun the wheel, turning the car into a dimly lit side road, and jammed on the brakes. He grabbed her by the shoulders and kissed her, forcing her mouth open, finding her tongue. When they parted, they were both gasping for air like stranded fish. He offered her the radio handset. 'Call Frost and tell him you're not coming. You've changed your mind. If he's running the show the whole thing's going to be a bloody farce anyway.'

She pushed the handset away. 'I always keep my promises.'

He started up the car, then rejoined the traffic flow in the main road. 'When Operation Mousetrap finishes, can I spend the rest of the night at your place?'

Her lips curved into a well-scrubbed, virginal, simple, roaringly erotic smile. 'That's a promise,' she said.

Webster put his full weight on the accelerator and left the rest of the traffic standing. He wouldn't be sleeping alone tonight.

Unless, of course, there was another of Frost's monumental sod-ups.

They were only five minutes late reaching the briefing room. A burst of raucous laughter billowed out as they opened the door. Frost, sitting on the table up on the dais, had just reached the punchline of some crude joke and was chortling

away louder than any of his audience. It was a very small
audience. Five men, four of them in casual clothes. At first
Webster had difficulty recognizing them, they looked so different out of uniform. The one with the drooping moustache
and that moon-faced one, both wearing polar neck sweaters,
weren't they Jordan and Simms, the crew of Charlie Alpha?
The young kid in the zip-up leather jacket was, of course,
Collier, happy to be away from Police Sergeant Bill Wells for
a night. Next to Collier, also in a leather jacket was PC
Burton, twenty-five, a tough-looking thug with closely
cropped hair, and a very good man to have on your side in a
fight. The fifth man, PC Kenny, was the only member of the
team wearing uniform.

As Susan entered in her rapist-bait outfit, there were yells
of delight and a salvo of wolf whistles. Webster glowered his
disapproval. This was a serious business, not a pub outing. He
snatched a glance at his watch. Twenty-one minutes past ten.
So where were all the others? He was expecting between
fifteen and twenty at least.

'This is all there is,' Frost told him.

All? Four hundred acres of woods, miles of paths and a
total of seven men. It was ludicrous, farcical, irresponsible,
dangerous. 'Sue's not going ahead with it,' he told Frost.

Frost's face fell. 'Aren't you, Sue?'

She slashed a look at Webster. 'Of course I am, sir.'

'That's all right then,' said Frost, looking relieved. He
stuck two fingers in his mouth and ripped out an ear-piercing
whistle as an appeal for silence. 'Round the map,' he called.
They crowded around the wall map.

'This mass of green,' began Frost, 'is Denton Woods.
There's no way we can cover it properly, so we concentrate on
the area where he made his two previous assaults and we bank
on Sue's sex appeal being strong enough to make him come
to us, hot and panting, with more than just his tongue hanging out. Now, we know he's a cautious bastard. He sniffs out
the area in advance. If he sees cops, he stays away, which is
probably why Mr Allen's previous decoy operations failed. So
we are going to try a double decoy. We've got PC Kenny here

in uniform. Kenny will be driving his patrol car with his blue light flashing, doing the rounds of the woods, covering the entire outer perimeter. I'm hoping that our rapist will be deceived into thinking that what he sees is all there is and that as long as he keeps out of Kenny's way, he's going to be safe. In the meantime, long before Sue begins her little nocturnal walk, the rest of us will insinuate ourselves into our positions in this tight little area here.' He tapped the map. 'All right up to now?'

Webster's hand shot up. 'Supposing he follows Sue but decides to attack her long before she leads him anywhere near to where we are?'

'Good question, son, but as long as Sue sticks to the main paths she'll be all right. He never attacks anyone on the main path.'

Webster snorted in derision. 'What do you mean "never"? Just because the two previous assaults were off the main track, that in no way establishes a pattern.'

'You don't rape women on the main path,' insisted Frost. 'It's too public. Besides, his usual ploy is to wait in the bushes and grab at his victims as they walk past. The main paths are too wide. If Sue sticks to the middle, I reckon she'll be safe.'

'You reckon?' sneered Webster. 'And supposing your reckoning is wrong? It's not you who'd get raped . . . it's Sue.'

Frost shook the ash from his cigarette. 'I know that, son,' he said mildly. 'But there's a risk to everything. All we can do is minimize that risk. But if Sue wants to back out?' He raised an eyebrow at the woman detective, who shook her head. 'In any case, Sue will be in radio contact with us all the time. If she's attacked on any of the main paths, we will still be able to get to her, although it will take that little bit longer.'

But Webster would not back down. 'The extra distance could make all the difference. She could be unconscious and raped by the time we finally get to her.'

'Sue isn't helpless,' replied Frost. 'She's been trained in unarmed combat and karate. She could have broken his John Thomas in six places by the time we got there. Everyone happy up to now?'

All heads turned to Webster, daring him to complain further. He folded his arms and stared straight ahead, his face a solid scowl of displeasure.

'One last point. I've got a theory that our rapist will be in the disguise of a jogger, so look out for men in track suits or running shorts.' He indicated a pile of walkie-talkie sets on the side table. 'Now everyone grab a radio, and make sure it works.'

While the team surged around the table, sorting out the communications equipment, Frost drew Susan to one side. 'I know it's a ramshackle operation, love, but I think it might work. The important thing is you must take no chances. Anything the slightest bit suspicious, let us know — even if it means warning our rapist off. I'd rather abort the whole operation than have anything happen to you.'

She smiled. 'I think I can trust you, sir.'

'You're mad if you do,' said Frost. 'I wouldn't trust me a bloody inch. Let's fit you up with your radio.'

Susan's transmitter-receiver was concealed in her shoulder bag, the aerial wire running under the strap. A small hearing-aid-type earpiece enabled her to receive messages, and a tiny microphone disguised as a CND badge and pinned to her wind-breaker would transmit information.

She was sent outside into the corridor to test the equipment, the men all holding their receivers close to their ears with the volume turned down low. They didn't want the sound of police messages to scare their man off. A long pause with nothing coming through. They all checked their receivers and adjusted the fine tuning. Still nothing. Frost opened the door and yelled to ask if Susan had started transmitting yet.

'Can't you hear me?' she called from the far end of the corridor. She fiddled with the CND badge, and suddenly there was a loud click and a rustling sound from all the receivers as Susan's voice rang out loud and clear, 'Testing, testing, testing . . .'

Frost radioed back and she confirmed that the receiver was working.

'Hadn't we better change her radio?' asked Webster, worried that the initial failure might be repeated at a less convenient moment.

'That's the only one I could find,' said Frost. He sent Sue out again for another test, and this time it worked perfectly. Webster still wasn't happy. This entire operation was a botch-up, cobbled together at the last moment. It was too risky. Too much depended on luck, which usually stayed away when it was wanted most.

Frost looked up at the wall clock. Eighteen minutes to eleven. 'Time to leave,' he called.

Collier and Burton travelled in the Cortina, Webster driving and boiling over because he always ended up the chauffeur. Why couldn't one of the others drive for a change?

Kenny went on ahead in the patrol car, its lights flashing, the siren warbling. Sue would be travelling with Jordan and Simms in the station's unmarked van, which would follow on later to give Frost's team a chance to get established in their concealed positions. Everyone felt excited, laughing and cracking jokes. No-one, apart from Webster, seemed to be taking it seriously.

As the Cortina pulled out of the car park, Burton turned his head and looked out of the rear window at Susan in her tight jeans and T-shirt, waiting by the van. He gave her a wave, then nudged Collier and leered. 'Cor, if the rapist doesn't oblige, I think I'll have a go raping her myself. Rumour has it she's very tasty.'

Webster's face turned crimson. He slammed on the brakes, jerked his head around, and yelled, 'Why don't you shut your face, you coarse bastard!'

Burton rose from his seat, fists clenched, his lip curling back like a snarling mongrel. 'Why don't you try and make me, you hairy sod.'

Frost stuck his arm between the two men and pushed them apart. 'Pack it in, you two. You're like a pair of bloody kids.'

They drove on in uneasy silence. From time to time Burton would whisper something to Collier and the two of them would snigger; Webster's knuckles, as he gripped the steering wheel, would get whiter and whiter.

Frost smoked, ignoring it all. His mind was going over his plan again and again, searching for weaknesses and finding plenty. The car slowed down. He looked through the window to see the orange sodium lights of the ring road. He nodded for Webster to stop and let off Burton and Collier, who would approach the stakeout area from this direction, while he and Webster would drive on and approach it by another route. They didn't want the rapist to see a gang of men all walking up the same side path.

'Control your bloody temper, son,' said Frost when they were alone in the car. 'You'll end up hitting someone.'

Yes, you for a start, thought Webster, coasting the Cortina into a lay-by and tucking it tight against a hedge. He made one last appeal to the inspector. 'Call this damn thing off before it's too late. It's never going to work.'

'I think it will, son,' said Frost, unclicking his safety belt.

'Then you're a bigger bloody fool than I took you for,' said Webster, throwing caution to the winds. 'You haven't got the start of a decent plan, and you haven't got anything like enough men, and there's no backup in case things go wrong. Susan could be beaten up, attacked, raped, and we wouldn't be anywhere near her. It's the height of criminal stupidity.'

It was Frost's turn to lose his cool. He thrust his face very close to Webster's. 'Listen to me, you mouthy sod. Susan Harvey isn't just your bit of crumpet on the side. She also happens to be a bloody good police officer. She knows the score. We all do. And of course there are risks. The public expects us to take risks — that's why they chuck petrol bombs at us and kick us in the face at football matches. If by taking risks Susan can help us catch the bastard who's been raping seventeen-year-old kids, then I reckon it's all worthwhile, even if it puts in jeopardy your chances of knocking her off in bed tonight. So shut your bleeding mouth, son, because your constant whining is getting on my bloody nerves.'

Frost flung open the car door and stamped out, leaving the

constable fuming. Webster fought to regain control, then locked the passenger door and climbed out after the inspector. Perhaps Frost was right. Perhaps he was being overly protective about Susan. But that didn't make this threadbare decoy operation any the safer.

A gentle wind was ruffling the tops of the trees, which seemed to twitch and shrug off its advances. But it was a cold wind. Frost looked up at the sky. Black, the moon obscured by clouds. And the woods were dark and heavy with menace.

Frost shivered, but not from the cold. He suddenly had a feeling that things were going to go wrong. Webster was right. He hadn't enough men, the planning was half-baked, and it was dangerous. If Webster hadn't been so smart-arsed about it, Frost might have listened to him, but that scowling, sneering face and waggling beard just increased his stubbornness.

It was darker than Frost had expected. Not too bad when they stuck to the main path, where some of the glow from the sodium lamps filtered through, but as soon as they branched off and plunged deeper into the woods, where trees and shrubs pressed in on each side of them, they had to slow down and almost feel their way through. They needed a torch but daren't risk drawing attention to themselves at this stage.

A torch! Frost clicked his radio on. 'Frost to van. Is sexy Sue there?'

'Sexy Sue here,' came the reply, her voice sounding childlike and breathless through the loudspeaker, almost like the young Marilyn Monroe's.

'Take a torch with you, Sue. You'll be able to find your way about better, and if our chum is lurking it will help draw him to you.'

Pleased with himself for having thought of this, he now felt better disposed toward Webster, who was sulkily stamping alongside him. 'We're going to get him tonight, son. I know it.'

'I hope so,' grunted Webster without conviction. He didn't share Frost's enthusiasm for the torch ploy. With Su-

san flashing the torch, the rapist could keep his distance. He
would be able to see her without being seen by her.

'I think this is where we turn off,' whispered Frost, his eyes
screwed up as he tried to penetrate the darkness. 'This is
where the seventeen-year-old was attacked last night.' Frost,
then Webster, squeezed through the gap in the bushes to
reach their pre-selected stakeout stations between two subsid-
iary paths. First Frost settled down in his position, leaning up
against the rough bark of some sort of tree, leaving Webster to
flounder on to his own allotted station. He was crashing
through the undergrowth like a wounded rhino, and Frost
gritted his teeth until the sounds finally stopped as Webster
found his position and settled down. 'Let's hope the bastard's
deaf,' Frost muttered to himself. He then checked that everyone was in his assigned position.

'Collier to Base. In position. Over.'

'Burton to Base. In position. Over.'

'Webster. In position. Over.'

Then, suddenly. 'Burton to base. Someone's coming along
the path. Too dark to see yet.'

A pause. Burton's breathing over the speaker. Then, 'I can
see him. A man — middle-aged, receding hair. He's got a dog
with him.'

Jordan's voice. 'There was a bloke with a dog lurking
about last night.'

Frost couldn't imagine a rapist bringing a dog along with
him but wasn't going to take chances. 'Which direction is he
heading?'

'He's gone on to the north path,' reported Burton. 'I think
he's heading for the main road.'

'Let's give him a chance to go, then,' said Frost. He struck
a match against the bark of the tree and cupped the flare with
his hands as he lit up and settled himself down to wait.

The smell of cigarette smoke wafted across to Webster,
who was crouching in wet grass, peering through bramble
bushes to the narrow, overgrown path. 'I don't think it's safe
to smoke,' he whispered into his radio.

'You're a bastard, Webster, but you're absolutely right,'

replied Frost, pinching out the Rothman's King Size and returning it to the packet. He changed position from one foot to the other. It was boring and tiring just standing still in the dark, keeping dead quiet and waiting. The forest creaked, groaned, and murmured. The wind scuffled leaves, making them sound like stealthy, shuffling footsteps. Twigs snapped for no reason.

Frost found he was lusting for a cigarette. He would have sold his soul for just one puff. He took the packet from his pocket and sniffed the heady tobacco smell, which only made his longing worse. Waiting was hell. He looked at his watch. 11.12. The hands didn't seem to be moving. Then Jordan called from the van, 'Van to Base.'

'Frost. Over.'

'Bait ready to enter woods. Over.'

'Has the bloke with the dog emerged yet?'

'Two minutes ago, sir.'

'Then bloody tell me,' snapped Frost. 'I'm not a mind reader. Give us a sound check, Sue.'

'Mary had a little lamb,' whispered Susan into her lapel badge.

'Loud and clear,' confirmed Frost. He did a final check on all the radios, then gave the signal for the girl.

Time: 11.15; very dark, the moon hidden by clouds. Ideal conditions for a rape.

From the van, Simms was able to watch Susan through night glasses right to the point where the main path veered around to the right. Then she was completely out of sight to the two men in the van.

She walked slowly, trying to appear unconcerned. From time to time she flashed the torch on the path as Frost had suggested. Once, she was positive there was someone right behind her, almost touching her. She could hear his footsteps, feel his breath ruffling the hair on the back of her neck. She swung around. The path was empty.

The earpiece emitted occasional bursts of static. 'Walking down the main north-south path,' she said very quietly into her lapel badge. 'So far, so good.'

'Say again?' queried the earpiece. 'We lost you then.'

'So far, so good,' she repeated.

'Roger,' acknowledged the earpiece.

It should have been reassuring to hear a friendly voice, but she was beginning to realize how astronauts must feel, thousands of miles up in space. They could talk to Houston. Houston could talk to them. But if anything went wrong, no matter how many voices were in contact, you were up there on your own. And she felt very much on her own. There was no-one else on the main path. Her feet scuffed through fallen leaves as she walked. At least the crackle of dry leaves should give her warning if anyone tried to sneak up behind her. She flashed her torch down on the path as she walked, beginning to feel more confident. But this was the easy bit. The rapist wouldn't make his move until she left the comparative security of this main pathway. And she would have to leave it very soon.

'Frost to bait. All OK?'

'Yes,' she answered.

'We keep losing you. To stop us peeing ourselves with worry, Sue, report in a position check every five minutes — unless you're raped beforehand, of course.'

'Acknowledged.' She clicked off the transmit switch. She was now at the safest point of her route, the section where the path hugged the ring road and was warmly splashed with yellow from the sodium lamps. Then the path veered toward the centre of the woods, where the black mass of trees and bushes squeezed out the light and muffled the reassuring sounds of traffic and people.

She was now off the main path, following a smaller side route. Bushes on each side clutched and pulled. Halfway down, she stopped. This wasn't the route Frost had mapped out for her. She had turned off too soon. She was walking away from the stakeout, not toward it.

She turned. And there was a man, crouching.

She backed away, one hand on the transmit button, the other bringing up the torch. Under the beam of the torch the crouching man changed into a small straggling bush. She started to breathe again and slowly made her way to the main path.

From a long way off, a diesel train bleated as it dragged itself away from Denton Station, a lonely, mournful sound that made her feel more isolated than ever. She quickened her pace. Then stopped.

Footsteps. Slow. Shuffling.

Someone was coming up the path toward her!

Her thumb hit the transmit button. 'Bait to Base. I can hear someone.'

Frost's voice, urgent, worried. 'Where are you?'

She didn't know where she was. That damn wrong turning. Frantically she looked all around, trying to locate some landmark that would pinpoint her position. 'Not sure,' she whispered. 'About a mile away from you — one of the turnings off the main path. I'm not sure which.'

The footsteps, slower now, came closer.

Webster's voice cut across the transmission. 'Let me go and find her.'

'You stay bloody put,' snapped Frost, 'and keep off the air.' His mind raced. It would be quicker if Jordan and Simms in the van sped round by road to her approximate position and got to her that way. The others could follow. He barked out orders to that effect.

Sue gripped the torch for use as a weapon and waited. It would be a couple of minutes at least before Simms and Jordan could get anywhere near. The bushes ahead shook and rustled, and the shuffling, slow and deliberate now, because he knew he had her, was coming closer . . . closer . . .

An old man, small and frail, pushing a pedal bike, gave her a nod as he squeezed past and continued on his way.

She spoke into the mike, hoping they wouldn't notice how much her voice was shaking. 'False alarm. An old man with a bike. Panic over.' Sighs of relief all round. The van was instructed to return to its previous position.

She felt ashamed of herself for panicking. What she had to do now was return to where she had turned off and find the correct path, the one that Frost had marked out for her on the map, report her position, and continue from there.

A small, fairly well-defined, side path veered off to her left. She wondered whether to take it. It should bring her back to the correct route. She moved toward it, then hesitated. Frost had stressed that she must keep to the allotted route or they might not be able to find her.

It was while she was hesitating that the man struck.

A noise. From far off. Webster's head jerked up. Was it a scream? He radioed to Frost.

'Did anyone else hear it?' the inspector asked. All replies were negative. 'You're out-voted, son,' said Frost, wishing he had never included Webster in the operation. The man was too involved with the decoy. He shifted his position from foot to foot and stretched. Every limb was aching from standing still. He was almost ready to defy Webster and have a surreptitious smoke when the radio clicked, and there was the bearded wonder bleating again.

'Shouldn't Sue have radioed in by now?'

Frost brought his wrist up to his eyes and squinted at his watch. 'How long since she last called in?'

'Five minutes,' replied Webster. 'Shall I give her a call to see if she's all right?'

'Give her another half minute. She's not staring at her digital, counting the seconds.'

'She knows she's supposed to call in every five minutes,' hissed Webster. 'What's the point of having check calls if we ignore it when they're not made.'

Frost snorted with exasperation. Webster was really getting on his nerves. He flicked the transmit switch. 'Base to Bait, come in please.' He released the transmit, returning the set to receive. A rush of empty static. 'Hello, Sue. Frost here. Come in please.' He violently thumbed the switch over to receive as if the set could be bullied into answering. No answer. Back to transmit. 'Frost to all units. She should be near the main path, somewhere. Let's go and find her.'

Webster charged ahead, not caring how much noise he

made. Frost, hard on his heels, getting the backlash of branches forced aside by Webster. On each side of them, Burton and Collier smashed their way through the under-growth. A stitch in Frost's side almost made him cry out, but he gritted his teeth and forced his legs to keep going.

They reached the main path. Webster looked to right and left. 'Which way?'

'Right!' panted Frost.

They hammered along, sobbing for air. The first turnoff. Burton was sent to investigate. On to the second. Webster's torch slashed the dark. On the pathway, a CND badge. 'Here!' he screamed.

Ahead something white. Then a crashing as someone broke from cover. A man. Zigzagging. A naked man. And there was Sue, on the ground, her clothing torn, her face bleeding.

In the dark distance bushes shook, marking the path of someone running.

'After him, son. I'll see to Sue.'

Webster charged on. Frost radioed for the van to try and head the man off, then homed in Burton and Collier to join the pursuit. That done, he knelt beside the girl. 'Sue?'

She eased herself up into a sitting position, wincing as she did so. 'I'm all right, sir.' She gingerly touched her face.

'You're not all right. It looks as if he gave your face a real right bashing. Take it easy, I'm going to send for an ambu-lance.' He raised the radio to his mouth, but she tugged his arm down.

'I don't want an ambulance, sir, honest. I'm fine. I just want to get home.'

'We'll take you to Casualty. If they say you can go home . . .'

'No . . . please. I'm all right.' There was blood on her face from a split lip. She found a tissue in her bag and cleaned it up.

Frost was relieved but couldn't help feeling that her wish not to go to hospital was for his benefit. An injured officer needing hospital treatment meant a special inquiry to ascertain blame. And how Mullett would love that, especially as this failed, botched-up operation was put into effect without his authority.

She made an attempt to get up, but he restrained her. 'I can stand,' she insisted.

'So can I,' said Frost, flopping down on the path beside her, 'but I'm so bloody nackered I'm going to have a rest. So what happened?'

'I wasn't expecting him. Suddenly there was something black over my face. It felt like plastic.' She paused. 'It had buttons — I felt buttons.'

'You mean, like a plastic mac?' asked Frost.

'Yes,' she said. 'That's what it was. A plastic mac. He threw it over my head, then started hitting me, punching my face. His hands moved down to my neck and he started to squeeze.' She touched her neck and flinched. 'I managed to pull his hands off, but he started punching again. I couldn't see. I'm sorry.'

Frost poked a cigarette between her bruised lips, stuck one in his own mouth, then lit them both. 'No, love, I'm the one who should be saying sorry. I sodded it up. We were too far away from you, and I should have called it off when your radio packed in.'

She drew on the cigarette. 'I couldn't see. I couldn't breathe. He kept hitting . . .'

He took her hand and patted it. 'I know, love. I know.'

Webster staggered back and leaned against a tree, his legs sagging, his mouth open as he tried to satisfy the demand of his lungs for air.

'Any luck, son?'

Between gasps, Webster shook his head. 'I thought I'd got him, but he must have doubled back and suddenly shot away behind me. Chased after him, but he was too far ahead. Heard a car drive off.'

'Are you sure it was our man?'

'Positive. The bugger was stark naked. How's Sue?'

'Beaten up, but not too bad. Take her to Casualty, then drive her home.'

She pushed herself up to her feet and began brushing leaves and pieces of dead grass from her clothes. 'I don't want to go to Casualty, I just want to go home.' She picked up her shoulder bag, then looked around for her torch.

'Well, drive her home anyway,' Frost told Webster. He then radioed all units requesting they stop and search all cars driving away from the vicinity of Denton Woods. They were helping Susan back to the car when the radio blurted out.

'Kenny to Mr Frost. Come in, please.'

'Frost here.'

Kenny's voice was triumphant. 'I've got him, sir. I've got him!'

THURSDAY NIGHT SHIFT

An almost liquid surge of warm relief flooded over Frost. He could hardly take in what Kenny was saying. Kenny had spotted the man charging out of the woods, stark naked. The man had jumped into a car and roared off, but the police constable had managed to swing the patrol car across his path and bring him to a halt.

'Where are you?' asked Frost.

'In the slip road, about four hundred yards southwest of you.'

They cut across until they could see the sodium lamps and the flashing blue of Kenny's patrol car, which was sprawled across the road, hemming in a metallic silver D-registered Mercedes. The windows of the Mercedes were misted with streaming condensation.

Kenny had a man in an arm-lock, bent across the bonnet. The man was not quite naked. He wore red socks and black shoes.

'You dirty bastard!' snarled Webster.

Frost moved to block Webster, who seemed ready to lunge at the man. 'Put the cuffs on him,' he said. Kenny spun the man round, then snapped handcuffs on his wrists.

'Well, well, well,' commented Frost, running his eye over their captive, who was about thirty-five, short, plumpish, and looking absolutely terrified. 'Is this him, Sue?'

'I don't know, sir. I didn't see him at all.'

'Would you mind telling me what this is all about,' squeaked the man, bringing down his handcuffed wrists to cover himself.

'Don't you know, sir?' asked Frost, mockingly. Then his eye caught a movement inside the Mercedes. 'Who've you got in there?' The misted windows blocked his view. He yanked open the rear door. 'Flaming heck!'

In the back seat, frantically trying to get into a dress, was a young woman, naked except for a pair of briefs. The heater had been going full pelt and the interior was overpoweringly hot and thick with the lingering cloy of cheap perfume and sweat. The woman snatched up the dress and bundled it to cover her breasts. 'Shut that bloody door,' she hissed.

Frost slammed shut the door. The first doubts crept in. 'Who is your passenger, sir?'

'None of your business, officer. Would you please allow me to get dressed. I'll end up with pneumonia.'

Frost risked the passenger's wrath and opened the rear door again. 'You're not being raped by any chance, are you, madam?'

'No, I bloody well am not,' she snapped. 'Now piss off, all of you!'

The inspector closed the door yet again. 'Your friend has a charming way with words, sir. Would you care to explain what you are doing here?'

The man raised his eyes to the dark, moonless sky. 'Are you sure you're a detective? We're in the car. I'm stripped. She's stripped. What do you think we were doing, playing bingo? What I'd like to know is what the hell you are doing here?'

'Attempted rape, sir. About five minutes ago.'

'Well it certainly wasn't attempted by me, Inspector. It's taking me all my time trying to keep up with that nymphomaniac in the back seat. Now, can I please get dressed?'

Frost shook his head. 'You weren't in the car when my officer first saw you, sir. You were running, stark naked, from the area where the attempted rape took place.'

The man snorted with exasperation. 'All right. If we have to go into detail then I'll go into detail. I left the car because I felt the need to relieve myself. I also felt the need for a bit of a break. It's like working a treadmill trying to satisfy her in there. I'm having a nice, quiet restful pee under the stars when suddenly there's someone charging up on me. I think it's her husband so I race back to the car to get the hell out of there. Next thing I know I'm in a scene from "Starsky and Hutch" — sirens . . . skids . . . police. I pull over and I'm yanked out of the motor and spread-eagled all over the bonnet. I've committed no offence and I don't see why I should be treated like this.'

Frost signalled for Kenny to unlock the handcuffs. The man rubbed his wrists, then snatched up his clothes from the front seat and started dressing as quickly as he could.

'Who is the lady, sir?'

The man looked to left and to right, then lowered his voice. 'She's my secretary. We're both married so, for God's sake, be discreet.'

'Of course, sir.' Frost stepped back so Kenny could take down names and addresses and details of the man's driving licence.

'Can I go now?' asked the man, zipping up his trousers. Frost turned inquiringly to Kenny, who was on the radio to Control, checking the driving licence details with the central computer. Kenny nodded. The details all tallied.

The man stuffed the driving licence back into his pocket and peeked inside the car where the misted windows were now clearing. 'Look at that,' he hissed. 'She's not even bothered to get dressed. Well, if she expects me to carry on where we left off after this fiasco, then she's got another think coming.'

He hurled himself inside the Mercedes and slammed the door. A querulous babble of conversation, followed by a snarl from the man, and the car jerked into gear and shuddered off.

'We'll hang on to her address,' murmured Frost, watching the dwindling taillights. 'It might come in handy if time drags one night.' He pushed his hands deep into his mac pockets and stared up at the night sky. Operation Mousetrap was back to being a disastrous balls-up — the rapist clean away, a policewoman knocked about, the farce with the couple in the car, and to cap it all, he had no bloody fags left.

A searching wind found where they were and punched away at them. Susan shivered. It was cold and everyone was feeling dejected. Frost told Kenny to take Sue and Webster back to her flat. He would go home in his own car.

He was trying to find the Cortina when Collier called him on the radio. In the excitement he had forgotten all about the rest of his team.

'We're still searching, Inspector. Haven't spotted anyone yet.'

At first he considered telling them to pack it in. But, what the hell, there was nothing to be lost by letting them rummage around for a while longer. He radioed Jordan and Simms, asking them to join the other two and do a sweep of the section. If they found nothing in an hour, they should report back to the station. As senior officer he supposed he should really show willing and join them, but he wasn't in the mood.

The patrol car drew up outside the flat. Webster helped Sue out and slipped his arm around her. She was shivering. 'Are you sure you're all right?' he asked.

'I'm fine.' She smiled. 'I'll take a couple of painkillers when I get in and I'll be as right as rain.'

He took the flat key from her shoulder bag and opened the door for her, turning to wave to Kenny who had been summonsed to a reported break-in at Beech Crescent. His wave was acknowledged by a toot on the horn.

The flat was warm and cozy. She had left the gas fire on and the bed had been made, the covers invitingly pulled back. No sign of a nightdress. Susan slumped into an armchair and held her hands out to the fire. She looked all in.

'I'll do you some hot milk,' said Webster, opening the fridge. There, on the rack, chilled to perfection, was a bottle of white wine, and on the shelf, a cold roast chicken. Everything laid on for a marvellous night that now wasn't to be.

She shook a couple of aspirins onto her palm and swallowed them down with the hot milk. She was hunched in front of the fire, still trembling, unable to get warm. 'Run me a hot bath, please.'

He turned on the taps and swished in the bath crystals. She was in the bathroom with him, peering at the steam-misted mirror, which she wiped clean with her hand. 'Don't I look a fright?'

He wished he could say she didn't. But she did. Her face was swollen, all greeny-black around the eyes.

'You can stay if you like,' she said, testing the water and pulling off her T-shirt. 'But I just want to sleep.'

'Yes, of course,' said Webster.

He let himself out.

Rot in hell, Frost. Rot in bloody hell.

Jack Frost sat in the car. His hands explored the door pockets, but there were no cigarettes. Damn. He scavenged the ashtray for a decent-sized butt and lit it, almost burning his nose with the match. The smoke from the resurrected cigarette tasted hot and bitter, but it suited his mood.

Then he noticed the bulge in the door pocket on the passenger side. He hadn't thought of looking there. His hand dived down to meet something cold and hard. He pulled it out. A bottle. Lots of bottles, the spoils from the party of two nights ago . . . the night they had found Ben Cornish's dead body. The retirement party! Mullett kept dropping unsubtle little hints about Frost's own retirement. Well, he'd be dropping even bigger ones when he learned about tonight's monumental foul-up.

He tore the metal cap from the vodka bottle and took a swig. The spirit tiptoed over his tongue with the velvet delicacy of a cat's paw, but as it reached his stomach the scratching claws came out. He shuddered. Neat vodka wasn't his favourite drink. He found a miniature whisky. With his head thrown right back, he poured it down to flush away the vodka taste. A little furnace roared in his stomach. He felt good. The next bottle made him feel better. In fact he felt like taking a drive round to Mullett's house, heaving a brick through his window, and yelling, 'Come on, you bastard, sack me!' The more he thought about this, the more the idea appealed to him.

'Control to Mr Frost. Come in please.'

What the hell was that? His eyes focused on the radio. He decided to answer the call first, then drive round to Mullett's house. He fumbled for the handset and pressed the transmit button. 'Frost here. Over.'

Bill Wells sounded excited. 'Jack, can you get over to the station right away? Burton and Collier are bringing in the rapist.'

Frost's heart skipped a beat. He was now stone-cold sober. 'Are you sure it's the right man? I've already had one disappointment.'

'Positive, Jack. They nabbed him in the woods about ten minutes ago. He was carrying a black plastic mac. It was stained with blood.'

Burton was waiting for him in the lobby, grinning all over his face. Over his arm was a cheap black plastic mac.

The desk phone rang. Wells answered it, his face changing as he listened. 'It's for you, Jack,' he called, holding the receiver at arm's length as if it might explode. 'Mr Mullett.'

Mullett had heard about the decoy fiasco. His message was icily terse. 'My office, nine o'clock tomorrow morning.' A click and then the dial tone. Pretending the Commander was still on the line, Frost said loudly into the phone, 'Why don't you get stuffed, you miserable old bastard?' He hung up. 'That's put the po-faced bleeder in his place,' he told the others, who were looking horrified. He beckoned to Burton. 'Let's go and see what Superdick looks like.'

The man in the interview room was hunched at the table, his back to the door, watched over by PC Collier. As Frost and Burton entered, the man turned around. Frost's euphoria burst and his heart took a sickening nose-dive down to his bowels. The alleged rapist, spluttering with indignation, was Desmond Thorley from the converted railway carriage. 'I demand an explanation, Mr Frost. This is an outrage.'

'I'm as outraged as you are, Desmond,' said Frost, sinking wearily into a chair. 'We've both been dragged here on false pretences.' He searched his pockets for a cigarette, then remembered he was out. Behind him, Burton and Collier were exchanging puzzled glances, wondering where they had gone wrong. 'You pillocks,' he told them, feeling dead tired. 'The Denton rapist rapes women. Desmond wouldn't know what to do with a bloody woman if she came into his bedroom stark naked.'

Desmond shuddered. 'What a repulsive thought.'

'But he was carrying the mac,' insisted Burton. 'There's blood on it.' He opened it out to display the stains.

Jack Frost took the garment and examined it. 'It's blood all right,' he agreed. He folded it carefully and placed it on the table. 'So what's the answer, Desmond? Are you our rapist? Are you AC/DC? Does your plug fit all sockets?'

Thorley's face flushed at the insult. 'The very idea!'

Again Frost searched his pockets for a cigarette. Infuriatingly, Desmond had none and neither Burton nor Collier smoked. A mental picture of the silver box in Mullett's office swam before him like the mirage of an oasis to a thirst-crazed man in the desert. He excused himself, sneaked into the Commander's office, found a key on his bunch that would unlock the desk drawer, and liberally helped himself from the Divisional Commander's special stock.

He returned to the interview room, puffing happily. 'Right,' he said, diffusing expensive Three Castles smoke, 'let's get down to business.' He pointed to the mac. 'Where did you get this, Desmond?'

'The man dropped it. If that thug of a policeman had asked, I'd have told him. But no, he hurls himself at me, frog-marches me to a dirty old van, and when I try to protest, he yells at me to shut up.'

'He's a courtesy cop,' explained Frost, letting the smoke trickle slowly from his lungs. 'Who dropped it?'

'I don't know. He bashed into me — nearly knocked me over.'

'Start from the beginning,' said Frost.

'Might I have a cigarette?'

Frost puffed across a steam of smoke so Desmond could savour its quality second-hand. 'These are really too good for you, Desmond, but tell me about tonight, and if you don't leave anything out, you might get one.'

'Well,' said Desmond, clasping his hands together, 'I was out on my little nocturnal expedition, looking for courting couples, when I noticed this great big car parked very suspiciously. It was bouncing up and down on its springs and the most peculiar noises were coming from inside. I tiptoed over and peeped through the back window, and what do you think I saw?'

'A disgustingly naked lady underneath a plump little man in red socks?' offered Frost.

Desmond's eyebrows soared in admiration. 'Who's a clever boy then? Anyway, while I was peeping, the man looks up from his endeavours and shakes his fist at me.'

'You sure it was his fist he shook?' murmured Frost.

'Anyway, I beat a hasty retreat. Good job I did, because a short while later there's crashing and yelling and police whistles. I thought they might be after me, so I took one of my little shortcuts. Then this man suddenly looms up out of nowhere, carrying something bundled under his arm. He barges into me and sends me flying. When I pick myself up, there's no sign of him, but the mac is lying on the ground. I picked it up, intending to hand it in at the police station . . .'

'I bet you were,' scoffed Frost.

'When,' continued Desmond, 'this oaf of a policeman hurls himself at me. That is every word the gospel truth.'

Frost chucked him a Three Castles and lit it for him, then prodded the mac. 'Nothing in the pockets, I suppose?' he asked Burton.

Burton looked embarrassed. 'I don't know, sir. I didn't look.'

'Well, look now,' said Frost.

Picking up the mac, Burton went through the pockets. The left-hand pocket was empty, but in the other, something he first thought was the bottom of a pocket turned out to be a crumpled plastic bag. He pulled it out and, as he did so, he felt something else. Something the bag had wedged tight in the depths. A key. An old, worn Yale-type key. Not an original, but a copy, with no identification number.

Collier was sent for some fingerprint powder just in case the rapist had forgotten to wipe it clean. He hadn't!

The screwed-up plastic bag was straightened out. Two holes had been cut from it. The inspector pulled it over Collier's head. The holes matched his eyes. They had found the 'Hooded Terror's' famous mask. Originally a waste-bin liner, it didn't look at all impressive.

Frost turned his attention to the key. He placed it in the centre of the table and stared at it.

'It could be the key to the rapist's house,' suggested Collier.

'Yes,' agreed Frost. 'All we've got to do is try it in every front door in the county. If it fits, we've got him.'

'Rather like Cinderella's slipper,' said Desmond.

'Trust you to think of fairy stories,' said Frost, dropping the key into his pocket. 'I'll try it in Mullett's front door tomorrow. You never know your luck.' He rose from the chair, all the tiredness and depression coming back.

'Can I go now?' asked Thorley.

'Take his statement, then chuck him out,' said Frost. 'And get that mac over to Forensic.'

He left the interview room and drooped across the lobby, shoulders down, his scarf dragging behind him.

'You all right, Jack?' asked Wells. 'You don't look too good.'

'Just tired,' Frost told him. 'I need some kip.'

'Don't forget you've got to see Mr Mullett at nine o'clock sharp.'

'I won't,' said Frost, stepping out into the cold, dark, friendless night.

FRIDAY DAY SHIFT

He took the key from the black plastic mac and tried it in the lock. It slid in easily. He turned it. The lock clicked and the door swung open on to a long, narrow passage. At the end of the passage was a woman, young, stark naked, her arms wide open, warm, welcoming. He ran to her, but there was Mullett barring his path. An angry, snarling Mullett.

Frost woke with a jolt and opened his eyes to blazing sunlight. Sunlight? He sat up in bed and snatched up the alarm clock, staring in disbelief at what it was telling him. 11.30 a.m. It couldn't be! The alarm was supposed to have woken him at seven. He had an interview with Mullett at nine. He tested the winding key. It was fully extended. Either he had forgotten to wind it last night or it had rung itself to exhaustion and he had slept right through it. Damn.

Swinging his bare feet to the floor, he screwed shut his eyes against the harsh probing jab of the morning sunshine. Who wanted sunshine on a day like this? If he was going to get a bollocking, let it pee with rain.

He broke all speed records dragging on his clothes, which were in a heap on the floor. Then he stopped, sat on the bed, and lit up one of Mullett's cigarettes. What the hell? There was no point hurrying. If he skipped a shave, skipped breakfast, and roared nonstop to the station he would still be nearly three hours late.

So why not be four hours late? A leisurely wash and shave, followed by a fry-up and plenty of time to try and think up some novel excuse, some heart-rending sob story that would stop Hornrim Harry stone cold in his tracks.

Whistling happily, he bounced down the stairs, scooping up two letters from the mat, and taking them into the kitchen. The first was a statement of account from Bennington's Bank. He wasn't ready yet for more bad news, so he tossed it, unopened, into the kitchen bin. The second envelope was a mystery with handwriting he didn't recognize. Propping it against the bread bin, he filled the electric kettle and switched it on. Two dubious-looking rashers of bacon sweated and cowered in the corner of the fridge. He took them out, sniffed them, and decided to chance it.

The rashers were laid into the frying pan with a generous chunk of recycled dripping, then two eggs were cracked and dropped in, and everything started sizzling and spitting and filling the kitchen with greasy smoke. He turned his attention to making the tea. No tea bags left. Damn and flaming blast!

He ferreted around in the rubbish bin and found a swollen, soggy used bag looking like a drowned mouse. Beggars can't be choosers, he thought as he dumped it in his cup and drowned it again in hot water. Then he buttered some bread, tipped the contents of the frying pan onto a plate, fished a knife and fork out of the washing-up bowl, and settled down to eat.

Something white caught his eye. The letter. Sliding a greasy knife under the flap, he slit it open. A birthday card. He frowned and took another look at the envelope, which immediately explained itself. It was addressed to Mrs J. Frost. Of course. Today was his wife's birthday and the card was from someone who didn't know she was dead. The handwritten message inside read 'Happy Birthday from Gloria . . . still at the same address . . . would love a letter.' He closed his eyes and tried to remember. Gloria? Who the hell was Gloria? He thought he had let everyone know. Giving up, he replaced the card in its envelope.

He had forgotten today was her birthday. But then, he always did forget. Time after time that awful realization as he descended the stairs and saw the pile of cards on the mat.

He recalled her last birthday, when she was in hospital and looked nearly twice her age. And the birthdays when they were first married, when she was different, when everything was different, when his jokes made her laugh, when they were happy together. How had it all changed? He was no different.

He never changed. And that was the trouble. She wanted him to change, to be a big success. But he couldn't.

He jerked himself back to the present and to the cold food congealing on the chipped plate. 'Happy birthday, love,' he muttered, dropping the card on top of the bank statement in the rubbish bin. He supposed he ought to put some flowers on her grave, pretending that this time he had remembered. Pushing the plate away, he lit up the last of Mullett's Three Castles and decided no flowers. It would be hypocritical.

Mullett buzzed through on the internal phone yet again. 'Is Inspector Frost in yet?' A routine that was fast becoming a regular feature of his day.

'I don't think so, sir,' said Sergeant Johnny Johnson. As if there was any doubt! He knew darn well Frost wasn't in. Hadn't he been ringing his house continually since five to nine getting only the engaged signal? The inspector must have left his phone off the hook again, but Mullett couldn't be told that.

'I want to see him the second he gets in . . . the very second,' said Mullett grimly.

'The very second,' echoed Johnson, who seemed to know this script by heart. He banged the phone down and yelled for Webster.

'You went to Mr Frost's house, Constable?'

'Yes, Sergeant,' replied Webster. 'As I told you, his car wasn't outside.'

'Did you knock on his door?'

'No point, Sergeant. If his car wasn't outside, then he wouldn't be in.'

'You go straight back to that house, Constable, and you knock, kick, and bang at that bloody front door. If you get no answer, then go and find him. And next time I tell you to do something, do it properly!'

'Hear, hear,' said a familiar voice. 'Morning all.'

'Where the hell have you been?' Johnson yelled at the inspector. 'Mr Mullett's been having kittens!'

'Kittens?' frowned Frost. 'I thought we'd had him doctored.'

The sergeant could only bury his head in his hands. 'It isn't funny, Jack. Look at the time! It's gone twelve. You were supposed to see him at nine.'

Frost made a great show of consulting his watch. 'I can spare him a few minutes now if he likes.'

Johnson snatched up the internal phone and punched out Mullett's number. 'Mr Frost is here now, sir. Yes, sir. Right away, sir.' He turned to the inspector. 'The Divisional Commander's office, Jack. Now!' He replaced the phone, then clicked on a smile to greet a woman who wished to report strange goings-on at the house across the street.

Frost spun on his heels to answer the summons when Collier called him back. 'A call for you on your office phone, Mr Frost. A woman. She wouldn't give her name.'

'Right,' said Frost, making a sharp right-hand turn toward his office.

Johnson looked up from the complaining woman. 'Where's Mr Frost gone?'

'His office, I think,' answered Collier.

'His office?' screamed the sergeant. 'Mr Mullett's waiting for him. Attend to this lady, would you.' He pushed Collier toward the woman.

The internal phone rang. Mullett was getting impatient.

'Leave it!' yelled Johnson, too late. Collier answered it and held the phone out to the sergeant. 'The Divisional Commander for you.'

'Run and fetch Mr Frost,' shrilled Johnson, pushing Collier in that direction.

'What about me?' snapped the woman.

'Be with you in a moment, madam,' replied Johnson, his head spinning. 'Yes, sir,' he told the phone. 'Yes, sir, I did tell him. I think he had another urgent call, sir. Yes, sir. Right away, sir.' He replaced the receiver and wiped a hand wearily across his face.

'They're always at it, morning, noon, and night,' said

the woman. 'Here . . . where do you think you're going . . . ?'

Frost pressed the phone tighter to his ear. 'No, we haven't got
your sovereigns back yet, Lil. I know we're a load of lazy
good-for-nothing bastards. Have I ever denied it? When I
have some news, I'll tell you . . . and the same to you, Lil.'

He hung up, looked at his desk and shuddered. It was
awash with papers. Where did they all come from? He
scooped up an armful and transferred it to Webster's desk so
he could have a frown at it when he came in. He poked a
cigarette in his mouth and pressed the top of the gas lighter
he had found in the kitchen drawer. A six-inch column of
flame seared past his nose and reminded him why he had
stopped using it.

The door crashed open. A panting Sergeant Johnson. 'For
Pete's sake, Jack!'

'Oh blimey,' said Frost. 'Hornrim Harry!' He sprang to his
feet for the sprint to the Commander's office and then saw
the other shape behind Johnson. Mullett, his face tight with
rage.

'My office, Frost . . . now!' He spun on his heel and
stamped out. The ambient temperature seemed to have fallen
by thirty degrees.

'I tried to warn you, Jack,' hissed Johnny Johnson. 'I'll
start a collection for you.'

'You worry too much,' said Frost, marching to the Star
Chamber with his chin held high.

Miss Smith, Mullett's mirror, was at her typewriter, her face
simmering with displeasure. His anger was her anger. With a
passable impression of the Commander's glare, she stared
icily at Frost as he passed her.

'The Commander said you were to go straight in,' she
snapped.

Frost had been caught out like that before. He knocked.

A snarl from the inner sanctum. 'Come in!'

Mullett sat stiff and straight behind the satin mahogany

desk, Frost's personal file open in front of him. It was his intention to bring up again all of the inspector's past misdeeds and to suggest without equivocation that Frost should look elsewhere for employment as he clearly lacked the attitude and discipline necessary to be a police officer. He kept his eyes down, ignoring Frost's ambling entrance. But before he could pull the pin out of his first grenade, Frost got in first.

'Sorry about this morning, Super, only I suddenly remembered it was my wife's birthday. I thought I should put some flowers on her grave.'

A brilliant preemptive strike which put Mullett completely off his stroke. 'My dear chap,' he said, 'do sit down.' He made a mental note to ask Miss Smith to check the files to ensure the date was correct, then he paused and bowed his head for a few seconds to show respect for the dead. That down, he steeled himself for the unpleasant task in hand.

'Operation Mousetrap, that unauthorised fiasco of last night. You knew my permission was essential and would only be given if I was assured the plan was viable. Why didn't you ask me?'

'Sorry about that, Super,' said Frost, his legs crossed, his unpolished shoe waggling. 'I tried to see you, but you'd sneaked off somewhere.'

Mullett's lips tightened. 'I was at County HQ. You only had to pick up the phone, but instead you flagrantly disobeyed standing instructions and went ahead regardless, and if that wasn't bad enough, you gave Sergeant Johnson the impression that I had agreed to it.'

'He must have misunderstood me,' said Frost brazenly. 'Still, no harm done.'

Mullett leaned back in his chair, wide-eyed with incredulity. 'No harm done? A police woman was injured.'

Frost shrugged. 'A few bruises and a black eye. I've seen brides come back from their honeymoons with worse than that.'

'She could have been killed, Inspector.'

'She could have won fifty thousand pounds on the pools, sir, but she didn't.'

Burying his face in his hands, Mullett felt like crying. How could you reason with a man like this? He picked up a newly sharpened pencil from his pen tray and twiddled it between his fingers. 'I'm taking you off the case, Inspector.'

Frost's jaw dropped. He looked disbelievingly at Mullett as if the man had taken leave of his senses. 'You're bloody what?'

The pencil snapped in two between Mullett's fingers as he stiffened with fury. 'Don't you ever speak to me like that again, Frost,' he croaked, anger making his voice barely audible.

'Sorry, Super,' said Frost in the tone of a man pulled up on some minor and obscure breach of etiquette, 'but I want to stay with this one. I think I'm close to cracking it.'

'Yes . . . the plastic mac and the door key,' said Mullett, referring to his notes. 'Pass them all over to Mr Allen. It's his case from now on. By the way, how are you getting on with your murder inquiry — that drug addict?'

'Not too well,' said Frost, mentally adding 'as well you know, you four-eyed git.'

'Then you'll have more time to concentrate on it now you're off the rape case, won't you?' smiled Mullett, showing the interview was at an end by pulling his in-tray toward him and taking out the letters for signature. 'One last thing. The Chief Constable is very concerned at our mounting number of house-breakings. Let that be your number-one priority. That will be all, Frost.' He unscrewed the cap of his fountain pen and began signing his letters only to see his pen jump and splutter ink all over Miss Smith's pristine typing as Frost left, slamming the door behind him with unnecessary force.

He put the letter to one side for retyping, then buzzed Miss Smith for some aspirins. There had to be some way he could get rid of the man.

The door slamming was repeated as Frost fumed back into his own pigsty of an office, where he further vented his rage by giving his in-tray a right-hander, sending the contents flying all over the floor. He spun around on Webster, who was regarding his tantrum with amused tolerance. 'Don't just sit there plaiting your beard, Constable. Help me pick this lot up.'

Without a word, Webster began gathering up the papers, smirking with inward satisfaction at Frost's rage. Obviously he had been given a roasting by the Divisional Commander for last night's debacle. And it served the stupid fool right.

Frost was down on his knees after a couple of burglary reports that had found their way under his desk just out of reach. He poked at them with a ruler and managed to fish one out. 'By the way, son. As of today I'm off the rape case.'

Webster grunted noncommittally.

'How's your girl friend this morning?' said Frost, reading through the form.

'She's come to work,' the constable told him, 'wearing dark glasses to hide the black eye, but otherwise OK.' And no thanks to you, he added under his breath.

Frost flung himself into his chair and read the burglary report again. 'Do you know anything about this attempted break-in at Beech Crescent?'

'Just the bare details,' said Webster. 'PC Kenny was called to it last night as he was dropping Sue and me off at her flat.'

According to the report, a Mrs Shadbolt at number 32 saw a man climbing over the fence into her back garden, so she dialed 999. Kenny did a search of the area and found that the back door of a house a couple of gardens away had been forced open. Kenny woke up the householder and they went over the premises from top to bottom, but nothing had been taken.

'Hmm,' muttered Frost, scratching his chin thoughtfully. He swivelled around to the wall map to locate Beech Crescent. Most of the streets adjoining the woods were named after trees, and he found Beech Crescent not too far from the spot where Sue was attacked. He had a feeling that this might be worth following up. 'Get the car, son. We're going out.'

They had just started out when Control radioed. Sammy Glickman, the pawnbroker, had phoned. The man with the sovereigns for sale was back in his shop with another batch.

'We can be there in five minutes,' said Webster, looking out for a turnoff.

'No,' said Frost firmly. 'We're following up the burglary.' He told Control to send an area car to the pawnbroker's immediately to pick the man up. He would interview him on their return. Webster couldn't see why this attempted break-in was so important all of a sudden, but Frost was the boss.

Mrs Shadbolt, her grey hair dyed lavender, wore bright orange beads over a fluffy mauve cardigan. Under her arm she carried a tiny overweight Pekinese, which she called 'Mummy's darling.' It was a sour-faced animal with a protruding tongue, continually snuffling and panting as if its oxygen supply was running out. The woman had another dog, a French poodle, its hysterical bark hitting the eardrums at a frequency bordering on the threshold of pain. To its Gallic fury, it hadn't been allowed to bite the two detectives, but had been dragged by the collar to the kitchen and shut in. Its incessant high-pitched yap threatened to shatter all the glasses in Mrs Shadbolt's display cabinet.

'The poor dear gets so excited when we have company,' explained Mrs Shadbolt.

'Tell us about last night,' shouted Frost over the noise.

'Well, I was upstairs in bed . . .'

Frost heaved himself out of the chintz-covered sofa. 'Let's re-enact the crime,' he suggested. Anything to get away from that bloody castrato barking.

Up the stairs, past pictures of kittens romping with balls of wool on the walls, and into the little bedroom overlooking the garden. A nightdress holder in the shape of a fox terrier sprawled across the twin pillows of the double bed.

'My bed,' Mrs Shadbolt explained.

'Make a note of that, Constable,' Frost muttered to Webster.

'I retire every night at ten on the dot, Inspector. I'm a creature of habit, regular as clockwork. Bed at ten, up at six forty-five.'

'Is there a Mr Shadbolt?' asked Frost, eying the twin pillows.

She dabbed an eye with a tiny handkerchief. The Pekinese snuffled in sympathy. 'He passed over six years ago.'

'Sorry to hear that, madam. So you were in bed . . . ?'

'Fast asleep. I go off the instant my head touches the pillow. Then Fifi started to bark. I woke up instantly.'

'Yes, I imagine you would,' said Frost. 'Where was Fifi?'

'Up here with me. Fifi sleeps on the floor; Mummy's darling sleeps on the bed with Diddums.'

'Diddums?' queried Frost.

She simpered and patted the fox terrier nightdress case. 'We call him Diddums. Fifi was leaping up at the window, barking incessantly. I got out of bed and opened the window.'

They all moved over to the window in question. Frost opened it and looked out on to the garden below. A tiny garden, a wooden fence on each side, a brick wall at the rear. Beyond the brick wall were the back gardens of the houses in the street running parallel to Beech Crescent. Mrs Shadbolt's lawn was infested with green and red plaster gnomes, some peeking through bushes, some sitting cross-legged on plaster toadstools, others fishing down a plastic magic wishing well.

'Very tasteful,' murmured Frost, thinking he had never seen anything so ghastly in his life.

'I looked out,' continued the woman, 'and there he was climbing over the fence into my garden, right down at the end, near the gnome on the toadstool. I just screamed and screamed and he immediately leapt over the fence.'

'What, back the way he was coming?' asked Frost, pulling his head back in.

'Oh no,' Mrs Shadbolt told him. 'He carried on across my garden and over the fence into next door.' She indicated the wooden fence to the right.

Frost spun around, frowning. 'Are you sure?'

'Of course I am. It was dark, but I could still see him. And the fence shook as he clambered over it.'

Frost looked out of the window again. 'Where's the house of the bloke whose back door was forced?'

'To the right. The way the intruder was going. Next door but one, number 36.'

Frost sat down on the bed and wriggled because he was sitting on something uncomfortable. He pulled Diddums out from under him and dropped it on the floor. 'This isn't making sense.'

'It's making sense to me,' said Webster, who couldn't understand why the inspector was wasting time on this piddling little abortive break-in. 'The man climbs over the fence into Mrs. Shadbolt's garden. She screams, so he climbs over the next fence. Where's the problem?'

'Probably nothing,' said Frost, seeming to lose interest. 'What are the people like at number 36, Mrs Shadbolt?'

'I can't really say, Inspector. They only moved in recently but they seem a nice couple.'

'Right,' said Frost, standing up. 'We'll have a chat with them. Thank you so much for your help.'

Out in the street, as they turned toward number 36, Frost said, 'Do you ever get the feeling that things are suddenly going to start going right, son?'

'I often get the feeling,' said Webster, 'but never the follow-up.'

'Me too,' muttered Frost, 'but I'm hoping today might prove the exception. Now, what's this geezer's name?'

'Price,' said Webster, 'Charles Price.'

Charles Price was a shy-looking man in his late thirties with dark hair and an apologetic smile. He was painting the front door of his house and was so engrossed in his work, he didn't hear the two policemen walking up his front path.

'Mr Price?' asked Frost. 'We're police officers.'

He spun around, startled, the paintbrush shaking in his hand. 'You did give me a turn,' he said. 'I never heard you. Is it about last night?'

Frost nodded. 'Just a few questions.'

'Nothing was stolen,' said Price. 'He must have been scared off. Your police constable was on the scene in minutes.'

'All part of the service,' said Frost with a smile. 'Do you think we might come in?'

Methodically, Price replaced the lid on his tin of yellow paint, wiped the brush with a rag, and immersed it in a jam jar half filled with white spirit. 'Trying to get it all finished before the wife comes back,' he explained, wiping his hands on another piece of rag. 'We only moved in three weeks ago and there's so much to do to get the place shipshape.'

Warning them to be careful of the wet paint, he guided them through the passage and into a small lounge, which was spotlessly clean and had double sheets of newspaper laid over the floor to protect the carpet. 'If I spill so much as a single drop of paint, my wife will never let me hear the end of it.' Noticing the inspector's dirty mac, he spread another sheet of newspaper across the settee before inviting them to sit down. 'She's very fussy about the furniture.' He brought a kitchen chair over and perched himself on the edge.

'Just a couple of questions, then we'll let you get back to your decorating,' said Frost, the newspaper crackling beneath him as he tried to get comfortable. 'You've been here only three weeks, you say?'

'That's right. We used to live in Appian Way, over by Meads Park, but we had to move. My wife couldn't get on with the neighbours.'

'And where is your good lady, sir?' Frost was wondering if it would be possible to light a cigarette without causing a towering inferno with the sheets of newspaper.

'She went to Darlington on Tuesday to look after her sick mother. The poor old dear is eighty-seven and can't do a thing for herself — can't even get to the toilet. My sister-in-law usually looks after her, but she had to go into hospital with her varicose veins.'

Frost cut in quickly before they got the entire family medical history. 'I see, sir. Thank you.'

'She's not due back until tomorrow,' said Price, 'but she was away when the man broke in, so she wouldn't be able to help you. Is it all right if I patch up the back door where he broke in? She'll be furious when she sees the damage.'

'Perhaps my hairy colleague and I could take a look at it first, sir.'

They tramped over more newspaper, past skirting boards glistening with newly applied white paint, as he took them into a small utility room. The room housed a large chest freezer and the gas and electricity meters. On the far wall was the back door, which opened on to the garden. This was the door the intruder had forced. As the lock was now useless, the door was bolted top and bottom to keep it shut. Price unbolted and opened up. The back garden was similar to Mrs Shadbolt's, but overgrown and minus the gnomes.

Frost stepped outside and filled his lungs with fresh air to get the taste of paint out of his mouth. He and Webster examined the door. The jamb was crushed and splintered where it had been jemmied open.

'He was determined to get in, wasn't he, sir?' muttered the inspector, straightening up. 'Was anything taken? Are all your tins of paint accounted for?'

'The constable kindly went through the house with me. Everything was intact. We haven't really got anything worth stealing, but he might have thought the previous occupants were still here. They had lots of expensive silver, I believe.'

'That's probably the answer!' Frost exclaimed delightedly. 'You should have been in the force, Mr Price.'

Price blinked and beamed his pleasure, then a shrill whistle screamed from the kitchen. 'The kettle! Would you like some tea?'

'Love some,' said Frost. 'Be with you in a second.'

As soon as Price had retired to kitchen, Frost scratched his chin thoughtfully and advanced on the chest freezer. 'Had a case once, son. This bloke strangled his wife and buried her under the floorboards, telling the neighbours she had gone to visit her sick mother. When the body started to niff a bit, and the Airwick was fighting a losing battle, he dumped her in the freezer and started painting the house so the smell of paint would mask everything else . . .'

Webster groaned. 'Surely you're not suggesting . . . ?'

'I bet you tuppence she's in the freezer.' He flung up the

lid, looked inside, then let it thump down again. 'Tuppence I owe you.' Something tucked down between the back of the freezer and the wall caught his eye. He leaned across to peer into the dark space. 'Something down there, son. Give us a hand to shift this thing.'

What on earth is the prat up to now? Webster struggled to ease the fully loaded freezer away from the wall. At last there was room for Frost to poke his arm down. It emerged clutching a pair of rusted garden shears, the wooden handles missing.

'Hooray!' exclaimed Webster sarcastically.

'I'm doing my Sherlock Holmes stuff and you're taking the piss,' reproved Frost. He held the shears to the light. 'See these small splinters of wood stuck on the blades? They're off that door. This is what our burglar used as a jemmy, my son.'

Webster took the shears and offered them to the door jamb. 'You could be right,' he admitted grudgingly.

'Don't strain yourself,' muttered Frost. He carried the shears out to the garden, his head bent, searching. With a cry of triumph he pointed to a shear-shaped indentation in the earth of a flower bed that ran along the fence. 'And this is where our burglar got it from.'

'So?' said Webster.

'So,' Frost continued patiently, 'he didn't bring it with him. Not a very well-equipped burglar, was he? Didn't have anything on him to open a door, so he had to use an old, rusty pair of shears that just happened to be in the garden. And wasn't he lucky finding them in the dark?'

'Tea's ready,' called Price.

Frost put the shears on top of the freezer, bolted the back door, then called, 'Coming!'

They took tea in the lounge. It was served in dainty china cups on a tray containing milk, sugar, and a selection of biscuits. Price's wife had him well house-trained. Frost praised his tea.

The man smiled modestly. 'I can turn my hand to most things. Take a biscuit.'

Frost took a custard cream. 'I forgot to ask you, sir. What's your job? You're not a house painter, are you, like Hitler?'

'I'm a night maintenance engineer with Broughtons Engineering Works on the Industrial Estate, but I'm on holiday this week.'

The custard cream was delicious. Frost took another one. 'Night work? What hours do you do?'

'We start at eight at night and finish at six the following morning. The machines are going nonstop all day, so repairs and maintenance have to be carried out when the factory is closed.'

Frost parked his cup on the arm of the settee. Price snatched it up and put it on the tray. 'Are you there all alone, sir?' He brought out his cigarettes.

Price jumped up to fetch an enormous ashtray which he placed in front of the inspector. Then he opened wide the window. 'My wife can't stand the smell of tobacco smoke.' He returned to his chair. 'No, I don't work on my own. There's two of us, the senior engineer and the deputy. I'm the deputy. You will be careful with your ash, won't you?'

'I'll swallow it if you like,' said Frost, starting to get irritated. He thought for a moment. 'The Industrial Estate. That's not far from the golf links where those two girls were raped?'

'That's right,' agreed Price, fanning Frost's smoke out the window, 'The nurse on April 4th, the office worker on the 5th.'

Frost stiffened. Price had the dates exactly. 'You've a good memory for dates, sir?'

'Not really. The police questioned me about it. I was able to help them.'

Webster and Frost exchanged glances. 'In what way, sir?'

'It'll be on your files,' said Price.

I haven't read the bloody files, thought Frost. 'I'm sure it is, sir, but tell us anyway.'

'Your lot suspected our senior engineer, a man called Len Bateman. He'd been in trouble with the police years ago for messing about with young girls. I was questioned by a Detective Inspector Allen. Do you know him, Mr Frost?'

'One of our junior officers,' said Frost.

'Anyway, I was able to tell Mr Allen that Len Bateman had been working right alongside me at the time of all the rapes, so there was no way he could have done them.'

Frost took another custard cream. 'Does Bateman still work for your firm?'

'Oh no. A few weeks later the works manager caught him stealing engine components. He was sacked on the spot and a new man took his job.'

'When was he sacked, sir?'

'About mid-April.'

'Which was about the time the rapings stopped,' said Frost thoughtfully. There were no more custard creams left, so he helped himself to a chocolate digestive. Price moved the tray out of his reach.

'I don't know if you've noticed the coincidence, sir,' continued Frost, munching away. 'Three of the rapes took place near where you work, and two at Meads Park near where you used to live. No sooner do you move down this way than the rapes start up again in Denton Woods, almost on your doorstep.'

'I hope you're not suggesting it is anything other than a coincidence?' said Price, rubbing a rag on a speck of white paint he had noticed on his chair leg. 'I couldn't have done it, I was at work. Ask Len Bateman, he was working alongside me.'

'You're quite right,' said Frost. 'You've got a cast-iron alibi.' He thought for a moment. 'I used to know a bloke who worked nights just like you. He worked with one other bloke — just like you and Len Bateman. They used to get up a fiddle between them. If one wanted a night off, the other one used to clock in for him. No-one ever found out.'

'I wouldn't dream of doing a thing like that,' said Price.

Frost beamed at him. 'Of course you wouldn't, sir — it's dishonest. But just supposing you and Bateman did work the same fiddle. There would be nights when you'd be all on your own in the factory, perfectly free to nip out for the odd rape when the mood struck you. And if Len Bateman was asked, he'd have to swear blind he was with you all the time because your alibi was his alibi.'

Webster shifted uneasily in his chair. He hoped Frost wasn't going to make some wild accusation without a shred of evidence.

Completely unabashed, Frost carried on. 'A new man took over when Bateman got the sack, so you couldn't work your fiddle any more. Which is probably why there were no more rapings for nearly four months.'

No-one could have looked more stunned than Price. 'This is some kind of nightmare! My house is broken into and the investigating officer is almost accusing me of multiple rape.'

'Almost?' cried Frost. 'I didn't mean to be as vague as that.'

Price stood up and, as forcefully as he could, said, 'I must ask you to leave. This is most upsetting.'

Frost didn't budge. 'Does your wife visit her mother very often?'

'Two or three times a year.'

'Leaving you all alone in the house. I wouldn't be at all surprised that if we started comparing dates, we'd find you were either at work on your own or all alone in the house when the rapes took place.'

'I really can't believe what I'm hearing,' exclaimed Price, his eyes blinking rapidly.

'Let's take last night,' said Frost, lighting up a second cigarette. 'There was an attempted rape in the woods, just across the road there — a police woman, a very tasty bit of stuff, young, big boobs — the sort you like. You had a go at her, but she fought back. The cops came running, so you had to scoot off.'

Price just shook his head at every word as if unable to believe anyone could be so stupid or so cruel.

Webster kept his face impassive and stared out the window in case the inspector wanted to involve him in this flight of fancy.

Frost carried on doggedly. 'You wore a track suit, jogging

trousers with no pocket, and a sweatshirt with no pocket. Under your arm you carried a plastic mac — the mac you used to chuck over their heads before you half strangled them. You ran off like mad, but in the dark you bumped into someone, which made you drop the mac.'

Price's Adam's apple was travelling up and down like an express lift. 'This is nonsense!'

'Trouble was,' continued the inspector, 'when you lost your mac, you also lost this.' From his pocket he produced a tagged Yale key which he held out for Price to see. 'Your front-door key. Which presented you with a problem. How do you get back inside your house? You can't knock up your wife; she's away in Darlington.'

Price turned in appeal to Webster. 'I didn't leave the house all night. You've got to believe me.'

'Can you prove that?' Webster asked.

'How can I prove it?' Price said hopelessly. 'I was here on my own. It's like a nightmare.'

'It was a nightmare for those poor girls, sir,' said Frost. 'Anyway, back to our poor old rapist, who you say isn't you. It's not his night. His dick's been disappointed, he's lost a perfectly good mac, and he hasn't got his front-door key. So how is he going to get back inside his house? Too noisy to smash windows, and the front door is too exposed and too solid. Which leaves the back door. This means climbing over garden fences. Unluckily for him, old Mother Shadbolt's yapping dog wakes her up and she screams blue murder and rings for the law.'

'Whoever Mrs Shadbolt saw,' insisted Price, 'it wasn't me. It was the burglar.'

'A bloody weird burglar, sir. He's spotted by a screaming woman. Instead of doing what any self-respecting house-breaker would do — get the hell out of there as fast as he could — he calmly hops over another couple of fences and starts to jemmy open your back door with a pair of rusty shears he finds in the pitch dark in your back garden. He enters your house, hides the shears behind your freezer, then nips off unseen without taking anything. That was no burglar, Mr Price. That was you, breaking back into your own house because you'd lost your key in Denton Woods.'

Price stared first at Frost, then at Webster. He put a sheet of newspaper over a dining chair and sat on it. 'What can I say?' he mumbled, almost on the verge of tears. 'I'm innocent. It wasn't me. What can I say?'

Frost shook his head in unstinted admiration. 'You're a bloody good actor, sir, I'll give you that. But let's put it to the test, shall we?' He tossed the tagged key over to Webster. 'Go and see if this fits the gentleman's front door, would you, son?'

Webster left the room. Frost sat on his sheet of newspaper, watching Price through narrowed eyes. Price, on his sheet of newspaper, fidgeted uncomfortably.

They could hear Webster's footsteps as he walked toward the open front door. Then came the click of the key being inserted into the lock. A pause. Webster came back into the room and handed the key to the inspector.

An uneasy, cold, prickly sensation crept up Frost's spine. 'Well, son?'

'It doesn't fit,' said Webster. 'It's not the right key.'

Frost seemed to crumble visibly. Webster almost felt sorry for him. The big buildup, all the pieces apparently fitting until the last, vital ingredient. It was the wrong key.

'Are you sure?' asked Frost flatly.

'Positive,' said Webster. 'The key doesn't fit the lock.'

'Well, Mr Price,' said Frost. 'It looks as if I've made a bit of a balls-up. I can only say I'm sorry.'

'Not your fault,' said Price generously. 'You were only doing your job. I must feel thankful that I've been eliminated. Now, if you'd excuse me, I've so much to do before my wife returns. I presume it's now all right for me to repair the back door?'

Frost nodded. Webster stood up, ready to go, but Frost remained seated, his mind racing, re-examining the facts. He was so bloody sure he was right. He felt it. He knew it. So where had he gone wrong? But at last he was forced to admit defeat. Slowly he heaved himself up. 'Thank you for your co-operation and for your understanding, Mr Price.'

The door bell rang, loudly and insistently.

Price jumped to his feet. 'I'll get it. You wait here.' He sped from the lounge, closing the door firmly behind him. Frost darted for the door and opened it a crack so he could see right down the passage.

Price opened the front door. A hard-faced woman, a key in her hand, stood in the porch alongside a suitcase. She wore sensible tweed clothes, flat shoes, and her greying hair was pulled back into a bun. She must have been some twenty years older than Price.

'Maud!' exclaimed her husband. 'I didn't expect you back until tomorrow.'

'Mother's dead,' said the woman, lifting the suitcase into the hall. 'Now what on earth has been going on? Why doesn't my key open the front door? Have you changed the lock or something?'

From the lounge, Frost charged down the passage. In his haste he sent a tin of yellow paint flying all over the floor.

While Mrs Price was insisting on knowing what on earth was going on, Frost snatched the key from her hand and compared it with the one from the plastic mac. There could be no mistake this time. The two keys were identical.

The colour drained from the man's face as he edged toward the door and escape. But Frost darted forward to block his way.

'Who is this man?' demanded the woman of her husband. But he could only open and shut his mouth and shake his head.

'I'm a police officer,' Frost told her. 'Terribly sorry to hear about the death of your mother, Mrs Price. But I'm afraid I've got even more bad news for you.'

'She wasn't like a wife,' said Price tonelessly while they waited in the interview room for Webster to come back with the typed statement for signature. 'She was always strict with me, always laying down the law about what I should and what I shouldn't do. She treated me like a child, even when we had sex. It was horrible — like making love to my own mother. It made me feel unclean. I wanted someone young and innocent. I was driven to those young girls, I couldn't help myself.'

'You could have left her,' said Frost, 'gone off with someone younger.'

He shook his head, horrified at the enormity of the suggestion. 'She wouldn't have let me do that. She'd have got so angry.'

Frost felt irritated. Here was the swine who had smashed and kicked and violated those poor girls. He should be elated that he had caught the bastard. He should be revelling in the thought of what other prisoners, who loved to wreak vengeance on sexual offenders, would do to Price once he was put away. But the man was so ineffectual, so pathetic, that Frost had to fight hard to stop feeling sorry for him.

Webster came in with the typed statement. He slid it across the table to Frost, who checked through it, then passed it over to Price.

'This is a typed copy of the statement you have just given us, Mr Price. Please read it through carefully. Unless there's anything you wish to change, I'd like you to initial every page, then sign it at the end.' But Price, anxious to get the unpleasantness over, initialled the pages automatically with barely a glance at the contents, endorsing the final page with a signature in almost childlike handwriting. Frost and Webster witnessed it.

'No chance of bail, I suppose?' Price asked hopefully.

'No chance,' confirmed Frost.

'I've got some books hidden under the bed,' Price confessed shamefaced. 'Dirty books. It would be awful if my wife found them. Any chance you could get to them before she does?'

'Happy to oblige, Mr Price,' smiled Frost. 'We don't want you to get into any trouble.'

·   ·   ·

He took a copy of the signed statement and marched with it, in triumph, to Mullett's office, pausing first to chat up Miss Smith. 'You can take your rusty chastity belt off, Ida,' he smirked. 'We've caught the rapist.' She stared right through him and continued sealing the flaps of envelopes marked Confidential. Not in the least put out, Frost asked, 'Is Dracula in his coffin?'

'The Superintendent is off,' she snapped, encouraging a flap to stick with a thump of her fist and wishing it was Frost's nose. 'He won't be back until tomorrow.'

Damn, thought Frost. He's never here for my rare moments of triumph and never absent when I foul things up.

When he got back to the office, Detective Sergeant Hanlon was chatting up Webster. Hanlon, beaming from ear to ear was bursting with news.

Sod your news, thought Frost, you listen to mine. 'We've caught the rapist, Arthur. The flower of Denton womanhood can safely walk knickerless in Denton Woods tonight, as long as you stay at home.'

Hanlon giggled. 'Well done, Jack.'

Frost slumped into his chair. On his desk was a subscription list for the widow of PC Shelby. He saw Mullett was down for fifty pounds so, out of spite, he put himself down for sixty, which he could ill afford, and tossed it into the out-tray. He looked up to see Hanlon grinning down.

'Why are you still hanging about, Arthur? Do you fancy me or something?'

Hanlon pulled up a chair. He had a lot to tell. Charlie Bravo had sped off to the pawnbroker's shop in time to arrest the man who was trying to sell Glickman a further quantity of stolen sovereigns.

'Marvellous!' exclaimed Frost. The earlier message from Control had completely slipped his mind. 'I'm solving so many cases these days, I can't keep track of them all.'

'You haven't solved this one,' retorted Hanlon. 'I have. They've coughed the lot and I've charged them.' He handed Frost the carbon copies of two statements.

'Why are there two statements?'

'Because there are two prisoners,' explained Hanlon. 'They're brothers.'

Responding to Glickman's phone call, Charlie Bravo had roared round to the pawnbroker's and apprehended Terry Fowler, twenty-four. Fowler had thirty-three Queen Victoria sovereigns in his possession. He was brought back to the station and searched. Six packets of a substance believed to be heroin were found in his jacket. The drug squad was informed, and a team went to Fowler's digs, where they arrested his brother, Kevin, twenty-five. The room was systematically searched. Taped to the back of the wardrobe was a plastic bag packed tight with white powder, which tests confirmed to be heroin of the type being pushed around Denton for the past couple of weeks. The drug squad was overjoyed. They had found the two new pushers.

'The Drug boys will take all the credit for this, Arthur,' said Frost, skimming through the statements, 'just as you're trying to take all the credit from me.'

The brothers, Trevor and Kevin Fowler, came from Poplar, east London, but were now of no fixed address and were continually moving around the country. Two weeks ago they arrived in Denton, taking a room in a bed and breakfast boarding house near the railway station. The metropolitan police knew them and had teleprinted details of their past form, which included petty theft, robbery with violence, and possession of drugs.

'If they've only been in Denton a couple of weeks,' observed Frost, 'then we can't push all those petty house-breakings on them.' This was a big disappointment. He had been hoping to clear up his backlog of unsolved burglaries in one fell swoop.

'They only admit to the sovereigns, Jack, not to anything else,' said Hanlon. He showed Frost the recovered coins. Thirty-three of them.

Tipping them onto his desk, Frost counted them. He only made it thirty-two. Webster counted them for him and made it thirty-three, which, added to the five already sold to Glickman, made a grand total of thirty-eight. Mrs Carey had reported seventy-nine stolen, so where were the other forty-one? 'Turn out your pockets, Arthur,' he said.

Hanlon grinned. 'The drug squad tore their place apart, Jack. There were no more sovereigns. Both the brothers say that's all there was. Mrs Carey must have been mistaken.'

The inspector shook his head. 'She never makes mistakes about money.' He scooped up the coins and returned them to the bag. 'Still, I've got more important things to worry about. Now take all this junk off my desk, Arthur, and get the paperwork tied up. This is your case now.'

'You're letting him have it?' asked Webster when Hanlon had left. 'He only came in on it at the death.'

'I've got more than I can cope with, son,' said Frost. He rubbed his chin thoughtfully. Something was worrying him. 'Those two blokes were only in Denton a couple of weeks. Ma Carey lives in a shitty little house down a back street. How come they picked on that house to rob? How did they find out she had all that money?'

'They could have overheard someone talking about her,' suggested Webster.

'I suppose so,' said Frost, but he still looked doubtful.

'You're not suggesting they've confessed to a crime they haven't committed, are you?' asked Webster.

'Of course not, son.'

Webster fed a sheet of paper into the typewriter. 'Do you want me to do the report on the rape arrest?' He knew that if he didn't do it, it wouldn't get done.

'Yes, please.' He gathered up the subscription list for Mrs Shelby and took it out to Johnny Johnson in the lobby, where he received the sergeant's congratulations on nabbing the 'Hooded Terror'.

'You'll be in all the papers tomorrow, Jack.'

'Unless something bigger breaks,' said Frost, 'like Allen finding Shelby's murderer.'

'Shouldn't be long now,' said Johnson. 'Stan Eustace can't hide much longer.' The phone rang. He answered it. 'And who is it speaking, please?' He offered the phone to Frost. 'Lady for you, Jack. Won't give her name.'

Even before he took the phone he knew it was Sadie Eustace, but he hoped against hope he was wrong.

'Jack?' she whispered.

He picked up the complete phone and moved as far away from Johnson as the cord would allow. 'I can't talk to you, Sadie,' he hissed into the mouthpiece. 'I got in too much trouble last time.'

'You've got to help, Jack. Stan's been in touch . . .'

He cut her short before she gave anything away. 'Sadie, whatever you tell me, I am going to report it.'

'He's frightened, Jack. The police have framed him for this killing and he's terrified at what they might do when they catch him. He'll give himself up to you if you meet him — just you, no-one else.'

'Where is he?'

'He's . . .' She broke off as a series of soft clicks cut into the conversation. 'What was that?'

'No idea,' lied Frost, realizing that Allen had her line tapped.

But she knew what it was. 'The bastards! They've bugged the phone!' The line went dead.

He replaced the receiver and returned the phone to its original position. 'Sadie Eustace,' he told Johnson. No point in keeping it a secret now. He thought for a second, then made his way to the murder incident room.

The room was empty except for Detective Sergeant Ingram crouched over a large Revox reel-to-reel tape recorder, looking tired and drawn as he listened through earphones to the replay of the conversation between Sadie and Jack Frost. Seeing Frost, he pulled the earphones off and rubbed his ears. Quickly, he scribbled a note on a pad and dropped it into an in-tray marked 'Mr Allen — Immediate'. 'Pity she twigged,' he said. 'She was going to tell us where Eustace was hiding.'

'A great pity,' agreed Frost, looking around the room. Empty desks, silent phones, and the wall map marked with red pins indicating the numerous Stan Eustace sightings. 'Where is everybody?'

'Tea break. They should be back in a minute.' He shook

his head at Frost's offer of a cigarette. 'We could do with a lead,' he went on, knuckling tired eyes. 'He seems to have gone to ground.'

'Mr Allen's only looking for Stan, then?' asked Frost. 'He isn't keeping his options open?'

'Why should we look for anyone else?' asked Ingram in a puzzled voice.

Frost didn't answer. He shuffled over to the other side of the room to look at the various notices fastened to the cork bulletin board: duty rosters; search areas; phone numbers of off-duty men, a list headed Police Marksmen with names and phone numbers. Frost saw that Ingram's name was on this list. 'Why police marksmen?' he inquired.

'Eustace is armed,' replied Ingram wearily. He wished the inspector would go. He was tired. He didn't feel like talking or answering questions. He just wanted to go somewhere quiet. For the past three nights he had hardly had any sleep.

'I don't want him killed,' said Frost.

Ingram nodded. 'I'll let Mr Allen know.' A green light flashed and the spools of the Revox began to revolve. Another call coming through on Sadie's phone. Ingram turned up the volume control. The ringing tone. A click as the receiver was lifted.

Sadie's voice. 'Denton 2234.'

A man's voice, tired, despondent. 'Sadie. It's Stan. Did you talk to him?'

Sadie's voice, shouting. 'Hang up, Stan. They've tapped the line.'

Click. The dial tone. Silence. The tape recorder switched itself off.

Behind them the door opened and closed. They turned to see Detective Inspector Allen. 'We've found Stan Eustace's old car,' he told Ingram. 'It was abandoned under the railway arches, so he's obviously nicked something else. Advise all units.'

As Ingram was phoning through to Control, Allen gave Frost an unfriendly nod, then moved to his Immediate Action in-tray. 'Phone call 16.37. Sadie Eustace to Inspector Frost.

Tape Index 033.' He grinned mockingly at Frost. 'What was that about, Inspector? Were you and Sadie arranging another clandestine assignation?'

'I wish you wouldn't use such long words,' said Frost. 'You know what an ignorant sod I am.'

FRIDAY NIGHT SHIFT

Ken Jordan gently coasted Charlie Alpha down the side street, past the public toilets and into the empty parking space alongside four other parked cars. Seven o'clock in the evening and time for an unofficial coffee break. He leaned back in the driving seat and stretched his arms as his observer, Ron Simms, unscrewed the top of a thermos flask and the smell of strong, hot coffee filled the area car.

Taking their plastic cups with them, they climbed out of Charlie Alpha to stretch their legs. The night was chilly and there was a fresh wind blowing. 'Isn't that where they found that tramp's body?' asked Simms, nodding his head toward the red-bricked building with its creaking enamelled sign.

'Yes,' muttered Jordan, but he wasn't looking in that direction. His eyes, ever alert, had detected a movement inside one of the parked cars, a grey Honda. It was as if someone had quickly ducked down because he didn't want to be seen. Jordan drained his coffee, took a torch from the door pocket, and strolled across for a closer look. The beam of his torch flared on the wind-screen. A face jerked up. The engine coughed, then roared, and the Honda leaped forward, forcing Jordan to jump to one side. He spun around, catching sight of the driver's face as the car sped past.

'After him!' he yelled to Simms, clambering inside Charlie Alpha.

'What's all the panic?' asked Simms as the police car, its siren wailing, bulleted after the Honda in hot pursuit.

'It's Stanley Eustace!' shouted Jordan. 'Radio Control and tell them we need all the assistance they've got.'

The red dots of the Honda's rear lights were increasing in size. They were gaining on him. Closer and closer. Soon they would be able to pass him, to swing in front and force him to stop.

The road took a sharp curve. The rear lights of the Honda suddenly disappeared. Around the bend at full speed, tyres screaming in agony.

No sign of the Honda. The road shot straight ahead. You could see for miles, but the Honda had vanished.

Simms twisted his head to look through the rear window. 'Back there!' he yelled. Far behind them, getting smaller and smaller as they roared on, was the Honda. It crouched on the grass verge, lights off, driver's door open. Jordan slammed on the brakes and the Sierra shuddered to a stop.

'Three units on their way to assist you, Charlie Alpha,' radioed Control. 'You are reminded that the suspect is armed and dangerous.'

'What shall we do?' asked Simms, warily eyeing the grey car, which appeared to be abandoned.

'We don't just sit here like bloody Charlies,' snapped Jordan, reversing back to the other car. They got out and cautiously approached. There was a rustling in the grass to one side of them, and before they could turn, a shotgun barrel was rammed into Jordan's face.

'Don't force me to do anything stupid,' said Stan Eustace, the gun shaking in his hand, his trigger finger twitching. He looked tired, frightened, and desperately dangerous. 'Facedown on the grass.'

They flung themselves, facedown, on to the wet grass.

'Move and I'll blast your heads off,' croaked Eustace.

They stared at wet grass. A rustling sound. Simms jerked up his head. A shot blasted out. He banged his face down, hugging the ground as tightly as he could.

The slam of a car door. A car driving off at speed. Silence. Simms carefully lifted his head to see Charlie Alpha disappearing into the distance. They leaped up and raced to the Honda, then stopped dead. The front tyre was flat and peppered with shotgun pellets.

'Shit!' said Jordan.

Faintly at first, from a long way off, came the sirens of approaching police cars. Jordan moved out to the centre of the road to flag them down.

Jack Frost ambled into the station about eight o'clock, hoping he might catch Mullett. The news of the arrest of the Denton rapist should have put the Divisional Commander in a sufficiently good mood to allow the inspector more men to help with the Ben Cornish investigation. No-one seemed able to whip up much enthusiasm over the death of a junkie dropout who was living on borrowed time anyway.

'He's been in and gone out again,' Johnny Johnson told him. 'He's with Mr Allen at the house.'

'What house?' asked Frost. 'The house at Pooh Corner? The house that Jack built? The house of ill repute?'

'I thought you knew,' said the sergeant, delighted he had someone to break the news to. 'It's Stanley Eustace. They've got him cornered in a house on Farley Street. Allen's in his element — police marksmen, the press, television cameras. Stanley's broken into this house and is holding a family at gunpoint. It's a hostage situation.'

Detective Inspector Allen was leaving nothing to chance. He opened up a detailed street map of the area and went over the various points one more time with Detective Sergeant Ingram. 'Are all the adjoining houses empty? Has everyone been evacuated?'

'Most of them,' said Ingram.

'Most of them? I told you to shift all of them, Sergeant.'

'The family in number 25 refuse to leave, sir.'

Allen's voice rose. 'Refuse? Who said they had a choice? Get them out. I don't care how, but get them out.'

Ingram delegated this task to a uniformed constable, then looked up as a police car, flanked by two police motorbikes, screeched up with the rifles and handguns from County HQ armoury.

'Right, Sergeant. Issue the guns,' ordered Allen. 'And

make sure our marksmen are positioned exactly where I indicated. And emphasize that they are not, repeat *not*, to fire a single round unless they have my explicit authorisation. Is that clear?'

'Yes, Inspector,' said Ingram. He handed out the Smith & Wesson specials to the five police marksmen, keeping a Ruger .222 rifle for himself. Ammunition was carefully counted out, allocated, and signed for. He made sure they all knew their locations, repeated Allen's instructions, then sent them out to take up position.

Ingram's own position was in the top room of a house across the street. From this vantage point his telescopic sight could shrink the distance across the road and the garden and let him look directly into the top back room of number 57, where Eustace was holding his hostages.

Allen had arranged for the street lamps to be turned off and for batteries of spot lamps to be directed to the back of the hostage house. If Eustace looked out he would only be able to see the blinding glare and the darkness beyond. He checked with his radio that the marksmen were all in position and again reminded them they were only to fire on his express command.

He turned his head impatiently as a black van edged its way along the cleared side street. The uniformed man whose job it was to turn back traffic had waved the van on. Didn't the fool have the sense to check with him first? The van pulled in to the kerb and an officious looking swine strode out. 'Who's in charge here?'

'I am,' snapped Allen. 'Who are you?'

'Detective Inspector Emms, Communications. What's the situation?'

'The situation,' said Allen, 'is that we have a police killer armed with a shotgun holding a woman and two children hostage in the top back room of that house over there. He's threatening to kill them all if we don't meet his demands — a Concorde to take him to Rio or some such rubbish.'

'Have you made contact with him?'

'Only through the loud hailer. He won't let us get near.'

'You've got to make voice contact,' said Emms. 'You've got to establish rapport.'

'You're not teaching a bunch of bloody rookies,' snarled Allen. 'I know what we *ought* to do. At the moment we can't do it.'

Emms looked up to trace the direction of the overhead phone lines. 'There's a phone in the house. I can wire you into it. If he picks up the receiver, he'll be directly through to you.'

'The phone is downstairs. Our man is upstairs. I can't see him trotting down just to see who's ringing him, but wire it in anyway.'

'Right,' said Emms, pleased to have the chance to show off his expertise. He disappeared into the back of his van.

Allen's walkie-talkie paged him. 'Reporter from the Denton *Echo* would like to talk to you, Inspector.' Allen's first thought was to tell the man to go to hell, but, on reflection, it wouldn't do him any harm to get his name in the papers. 'Send him over,' he said.

The communications expert emerged from the van. In his hand he held a telephone on a long length of cable which trailed behind him. 'It's ringing,' he announced proudly, offering the handset to Allen.

'When I want you to ring him, I'll bloody well tell you,' said Allen, snatching the phone. He listened. The ringing tone, on and on and on. He looked for someone to take the phone over. 'You . . . Constable!'

PC Collier came forward. Allen pushed the phone at him. 'Listen to this. It's ringing in the house. I don't suppose he'll answer, but if he does, keep him talking and let me know immediately.'

A man in a duffle coat ran down the street toward him. 'Mr Allen? My name's Lane — chief reporter Denton *Echo*. What's the story?'

'The man with the gun is Eustace, Stanley Eustace, but I don't want his name published. There are other, more serious, charges pending.'

The reporter lifted his pencil from the page. 'What charges?'

'Strictly off the record, Mr Lane, the charge will be the murder of Police Constable David Shelby, but that is not for publication at this stage.'

Lane nodded. Nothing linking the armed man with any other offences could be printed as it could prejudice the chances of a fair trial. 'Who are the hostages?'

'Mrs Mary Bright, thirty-four, separated from her husband, and her two children, Bobby, seven, and Scott, eight.' Allen looked over Lane's shoulder to Collier, still holding the phone tightly to his ear. 'We've got a direct line through to the house. It's ringing, but he won't answer. I'll try the loud hailer again in a minute.'

Allen squinted as car headlights hit his face and another car pulled up. Farley Street was starting to look like a public car park. He was about to yell for it to be moved on when he saw Mullett climbing out.

Mullett marched briskly over. He nodded to Allen, then raised an inquiring eyebrow at the reporter.

'Mr Lane, chief reporter, Denton *Echo*,' Allen told him.

Mullett clicked on his professional smile. 'Mullett — two 'l's and two 't's — Superintendent Mullett, Commander of Denton Division.' While the reporter was writing that down he asked, 'How do you intend to play this, Inspector?'

'As long as the hostages are in no danger, sir, we're prepared to sit tight and hang it out. We hope to commence a dialogue with Eustace soon, when I'll try and get him to release the children. Our aim is for a peaceful conclusion.' Allen said this loudly for the reporter's benefit and was pleased to see his words being taken down verbatim.

'It might be better,' Mullett told the reporter, 'if you put that down as if I had said it. It's my directive, and Mr Allen is acting in accordance with it.' Allen fumed inwardly.

'He's still not answering the phone, Inspector,' said Collier, whose ear was starting to ache.

'Quiet everyone,' called Allen. 'I'm going to try and make contact.' He thumbed the switch and raised the loud hailer to his mouth. His amplified, metallic voice reverberated over the back gardens. 'Eustace. This is Detective Inspector Allen. I'd like to talk to you.'

From his vantage point in the opposite house, Ingram, squinting through the telescopic sight, saw movement inside the room. He clicked on his radio and reported to Allen. 'He's coming to the window, sir.'

A terrified woman was pushed to the window. She turned her head away from the blinding glare of the lights. Eustace was well behind her, his arm crooking her neck, the shotgun in his free hand. Ingram shifted the sight slightly to the left and the crosspiece was dead centre of Eustace's forehead. 'There's enough showing, sir. I think I can get him.'

'No, Sergeant,' snapped Allen. 'There will be no shooting. Confirm.'

'Confirmed, sir. No shooting.' Ingram sounded disappointed.

'Listen to me,' shouted Eustace in the darkness, his voice shaking. 'I'm only going to say this once. You've got thirty minutes. I want a car with a full tank, I want it left outside, then you all piss off.'

'Release the woman and the kids, Stan, then we can talk about it.'

'No. They come with me. You've got thirty minutes.'

Allen took a chance. He raised the loud hailer to his mouth and, as he talked, started to walk toward the house. He wanted to be able to talk without shouting. The loud hailer was forming a barrier between them. 'Do you want any food, Stan? We can have it sent in. In fact . . .' A shot blasted out and pellets splattered high on the far wall. The woman screamed. The children inside the room started crying.

'No farther, Mr Allen. I'm cornered and I'm desperate and I've got nothing to lose. Just get me the car and stop ringing that bloody phone.'

Allen retreated back to his old position. 'Cut the phone,' he ordered.

The woman was dragged away from the window.

'What do you think?' Mullett asked.

Allen scratched his head. 'I don't know, sir. My every instinct tells me to rush him. I'm sure he won't harm the woman or the kids.'

'He'd use the gun,' said Mullett. 'If not on the hostages, then on our men, and I'm not having anyone hurt. We'll sweat it out. Time is on our side. Hello, who is this?'

A patrol car skidded up. PC Kenny and a woman got out.

'It's Sadie Eustace, Stan's wife. I'm hoping she can talk some sense into her old man.'

Sadie, an old coat flung hastily over a blue dress, almost ran over to Allen, her eyes crackling with anger at the sight of the armed men and the press and the spotlights. 'What are you bastards doing to him?'

'Now take it easy, Sadie,' soothed Allen. 'He's got a gun and he's taken hostages.'

Sadie turned her back on Allen and appealed directly to Mullett. 'I'll get him out. Let me go in there and talk to him.'

Mullett looked over her shoulder to Allen, who firmly shook his head. 'I'm sorry,' said Mullett. 'I can't let you go in there.'

'Why not? He won't harm me. I'm his wife.'

'The point is, Sadie,' said Allen, 'you might try to help him.'

She spun around to face him. 'For Pete's-bloody-sake! I want to help him. That's the whole point of the exercise.'

Allen smiled his thin smile. 'You might try and help him get away, Sadie. If you were with him, he'd have an extra hostage, extra bargaining . . . and you'd be a hostage we could never be sure was on our side.'

'You've got to trust someone, Inspector.'

'Forgive me, Sadie, if I can't trust you. You can talk to him on the phone if you like. We've got a direct line through. Try and persuade him to release the hostages and then come out with his hands up.'

She nodded her agreement. Allen clicked on the loud hailer. 'Stan. Go down to the phone. Sadie's here. She wants to talk to you.' Stan's voice shouted out into the darkness. 'Are you really there, Sadie?'

'Yes, Stan,' she shouted back. 'I want to talk.'

She took the phone and waited for her husband to go down the stairs with the hostages. Allen stepped back, and when he was well out of earshot he raised the radio to his mouth and very quietly called Special Units 3 and 4. Once Eustace was distracted by the phone call, he wanted to try and sneak some men inside the house. When he had issued his instructions he moved back. Sadie was speaking to Stan.

'Stan, it's me, Sadie. You've got to give yourself up.'

'And spend the rest of my life in the nick for something I didn't do?'

'But Stan . . .' A movement caught her eye. Allen appeared to be signalling to someone in the back garden. She turned her head. Three men, one with a revolver, were inching forward toward the back door.

'There's one thing I should mention, Stan,' she said, keeping her voice steady. 'There's a cop with a shooter creeping up to the back door.'

Allen spun around, furious, his eyes blazing. He made a chopping motion for Emms to cut the connection. At that instant there was a splintering of glass as a gun barrel smashed through the downstairs window. The blast of the shotgun split the darkness, and a small shrub to the right of the approaching armed policeman disintegrated.

'Get back!' bellowed Stanley. 'The next shot goes into the hostages.'

The three policemen scuttled back.

Allen, white with anger, turned to Sadie, 'You stupid cow.'

'You stinking bastard,' returned Sadie, equally furious. 'You used me, you bugger.'

Mullett charged over. 'What happened?'

'He fired at one of our men.' The walkie-talkie buzzed. Allen raised it to his ear. 'But he's OK, sir, not a scratch.'

'Right,' said Mullett. 'We sit tight. We play it cool. We make no more moves.'

Ingram called Allen over the radio. 'Eustace is back in the

top room with the hostages. The kids are crying, the woman looks as if she's passed out.'

'And what is Eustace doing?' asked Allen.

'Keeping well back, sir, pacing up and down. I think I could get a shot at him, sir. He's away from the others.'

Allen could see Sadie, ears straining, listening to every word. He lowered his voice. 'We're playing it cool for a while. But be prepared.'

Sadie moved off into the darkness.

Frost had been talking to the drug pushers. A right pair of sullen charmers who were determined to say as little as possible. They wouldn't enlarge about the sovereigns. They stole them and that's all there was to it. They were vague about the details, both apparently unable to remember where in the house they had found the coins. And as far as the quantity was concerned, if the old girl said there was more, then the cow was lying.

Webster had been dispatched to check with Lil Carey. She had no doubts at all about the number of sovereigns. Why, thought Webster, was Frost making such a meal of it? They'd caught the thieves and they'd got a confession. There was no reason for the men to lie about how much they had stolen; the sentence for the theft would be trivial compared with their sentence for pushing drugs, and it would run concurrently anyway.

But Frost kept niggling away at it, chewing it over and over. It was a welcome diversion when Wells stuck his head around the door.

'Lady to see you, Mr Frost,' said the sergeant in his official voice.

'I'm not undressed yet,' said Frost. 'Who is it?'

It was Sadie Eustace. She looked a mess. She'd been crying and her hair was in disarray. She declined the offer of tea but accepted one of Frost's cigarettes. 'They've got Stan holed up in a house in Farley Street.'

'So I hear, Sadie. Nothing I can do about it, I'm afraid.'

'The bastards are out to kill him, Jack. They've no intention of letting him come out alive. You've got to help.'

Frost folded his arms and leaned forward on his desk. 'It's not my case, Sadie. It's Mr Allen's. He may be a bastard, but he's straight. He won't let anything happen to Stan.'

'Look at me, Jack. I'm bloody desperate.' She held up her face, which was drawn and tear-stained. 'Get him out of there, please!'

Frost opened his door and yelled to Sergeant Wells. 'What's the latest on the siege?'

'Stanley's now threatening to kill the hostages one by one if his demands aren't met by midnight.'

'He doesn't mean it, Jack — it's just a bluff,' Sadie blurted. Frost waved her to silence.

'And what are his demands?' he asked Wells.

'A fast car, fully tanked up, no pursuit, and one of the hostages to go with him. There's no way we're giving him that.'

Frost closed the door. It was half past eleven. He retrieved an opened packet of salted peanuts from his in-tray and shook a few into his hand. There was nothing he could do for Stan, nothing at all. But he wished Sadie wouldn't look at him like that. He sighed and shot the salted peanuts into his mouth.

'All right, Sadie, what exactly do you want me to do?'

'Get Stan out of there alive, Jack, and name your price.'

'My price is twenty pounds for a short time, fifty pounds for all night, but I'm willing to do it for free if you treat me gently.' He stood up.

'You'll do it?' gasped Sadie.

'If I can, love, but a lot depends on Stan. If he blasts my brains out as I come up the stairs, then I might have to let you down.'

'No chance of that, Jack. He trusts you.'

'Then he's a bigger fool than I take him for.'

He unhooked his mac from the coat peg, then slowly wound the scarf around his neck, hoping that Wells would come crashing in at the last minute, like the United States Cavalry, to announce that Eustace had given himself up.

'I'm going to get myself into trouble, son,' he told Webster as he fastened the final button. 'If you want a laugh, come with me. If you want to keep your nose clean . . . stay here with Sadie.'

'I'm not bloody staying here,' said Sadie defiantly. 'I'm going with you.'

'What's your plan?' asked Webster.

'Plan?' said Frost. 'Since when did I ever make plans? I shall just barge in and hope for the best.'

Webster reached for his coat. 'I'll come with you.'

'You're a bloody fool, too!' said Frost.

The situation at Farley Street had suddenly worsened. Eustace was showing signs of cracking up. Allen's last attempt to talk to him had ended with the gunman screaming abuse, waving the gun wildly, and showing all the signs of losing control. There was now serious concern for the safety of the hostages. Indeed, Eustace had reiterated his threat to kill them one by one if the car wasn't ready and waiting at the stroke of midnight.

Allen was now pinning his hopes on a plan to get some men inside the house by hacking a way through to the roof space from the premises next door. This was proceeding very slowly, as the task needed to be performed silently, and the midnight deadline was fast approaching.

And as if there wasn't enough to worry about, he now had that half-wit Frost to contend with. The man had barged in with some harebrained scheme involving his getting inside and talking Eustace out.

'No way, Frost. I don't want any bloody heroes, thank you. The man's trigger-happy and cracking up. He's itching for an excuse to kill someone.'

He moved away and radioed the men working on the roof space for a situation report. 'We're getting there slowly,' he was told, 'but we keep hitting snags. There's pipes and steel joists all over the place.' When he turned around again, Frost had gone.

'Where's Mr Frost?' he demanded of the constable guarding the entrance to the back of the garden.

The constable pointed. 'In the garden, sir. Trying to get to the house.'

'Why the hell didn't you stop him?'

'Stop him, sir? He said you had given permission.'

'Mr Allen!' Ingram was calling over the radio. 'I can see someone in the garden, sir.'

'I know. It's that bloody fool Frost!'

Frost was flat on his face, inching toward the back door. Stan wasn't a killer. He knew he wouldn't fire, just as he had known that doped-up kid at the bank wouldn't fire, the one who had put the bullet hole through his cheek.

He was crawling through wet grass and wished he had never started this. Something tugged at his neck. He froze, then, very slowly, looked around. A rose bush had snagged his scarf. He unwound it from his neck and left it behind.

Inspector Allen was aware of someone hovering at his side, trying to attract his attention. 'I'm busy,' he snapped. Then he saw the gleaming silver. 'Sorry, Superintendent . . . didn't know it was you.'

'What's the position? . . . Is that Frost? You surely haven't allowed Frost . . . ?'

Allen cut him off. 'I told him not to, sir . . . specifically told him not to. He disobeyed my order and now I'm wasting my time trying to prevent him, and the hostages, being killed through his own stupidity.'

Mullett's jaw set. This was intolerable. This was the last straw. He could feel the nerve in his forehead starting to pulsate. 'Get him out of there,' he snapped.

'We can't, sir,' replied Allen. 'He hasn't got a radio. If we yelled out to him, it would attract Eustace's attention.'

'I don't give a damn about that,' said Mullett. 'If he wants to risk his stupid neck, that's his lookout, but I'm not having him risk the lives of the hostages. Call him back.'

Allen sighed but reached for the loud hailer and raised it to his lips. A car door slammed in the background. His radio paged him. He clicked it on and listened, then turned to the Superintendent. 'The Chief Constable is here, sir . . . on his way over to us.'

Mullett pushed down the hand holding the loud hailer. 'Hold it, Inspector. I don't want the Chief to know we have dissension in the ranks.'

Allen put the loud hailer on the ground. Mullett began flicking invisible specks from his uniform and smoothing down his moustache. Allen ruffled his hair and loosened his tie. He thought the Chief Constable would be more impressed with a police officer who looked as if he had been working than with an immaculate tailor's dummy.

The Chief Constable marched briskly over, slapping his gloves against his leg. 'A quick update please, Mr Mullett.' Mullett had just started to explain when the Chief caught sight of Frost. 'Good Lord! Is that Inspector Frost?'

Frost, his body wet with sweat and all his limbs aching, had reached the back door. He stretched up until his hand touched the door handle. Tentatively he turned it. The handle turned, but the door was double-bolted from the inside. Stan wasn't stupid! He wished he'd worked out the problem of how to get inside before he took this mad plunge. A fine bloody fool he'd look if, without even getting over the first hurdle, he now had to worm his way back and face Allen's wrath.

The next thing to try was the kitchen window. Pressing tight against the wall, he eased himself up and edged toward it. It was an old-fashioned sash type, and by pressing his face against the pane he could see the catch was fastened inside. To unfasten it he would have to break the glass, but could he break it without attracting the attention of Stan and his shotgun? He looked around him for something to use. In the flower bed at his feet was half a brick. He pulled it out and slipped off his mac, which he wrapped around it.

Allen, squinting through night-glasses, couldn't make out

what Frost was up to. It was Ingram, radioing through, who gave him the answer. 'He's going to break the window, sir.'

The bloody idiot! As soon as Eustace heard the glass break, he could take it out on the hostages. He might even lean from the window and shoot Frost . . . The temptation to let this happen was quickly dismissed, and Allen felt ashamed for even considering it. They would have to provide a distraction — and quickly. He radioed through to all surrounding units. When he gave the signal they were to sound their horns and their sirens and keep them going until ordered to stop. This, he hoped, would drown the sound of breaking glass, or at least divert Eustace long enough for Frost to get inside.

The field glasses to his eyes, Allen watched. Frost had the wrapped brick balanced in his hand. 'Allen to all units . . . Stand by.'

Frost shut his eyes, turned his head, and swung back the brick . . .

'Now!' screamed Allen. The cacophony shredded the night air into a thousand pieces.

'Stop that bloody noise!' screamed Eustace, dragging the woman again to the window.

'Off,' said Allen. Abruptly the noise stopped.

The contrasting silence was so tangible it could almost be touched. Gritting his teeth, Frost slipped his hand through the broken windowpane and reached for the catch. A needle of broken glass slashed his wrist. Damn. He felt warm blood trickling down. He flicked the catch back, then scrabbled for the bottom of the window, which creaked peevishly as he raised it. Up with his knee to the sill, the jab of more broken glass, then he was over and inside the dark kitchen.

'He's inside,' cried Allen. They now had no contact with him. All they could do was wait and see.

'Well done, Mr Allen,' said the Chief Constable.

'Yes . . . well done,' added Mullett hastily.

From his vantage point across the road, Ingram again called Allen on the radio. 'Sir. I have a clear, uninterrupted view of Eustace by the window. Permission to fire?'

'No, damn you,' snapped Allen. 'Only at my specific command.' He turned to the Chief Constable. 'I'm trying to bring this to a successful conclusion without a single shot being fired — by the police, sir.'

'I quite agree,' said the Chief Constable, nodding.

'All the way,' echoed Mullett, feeling rather left out of things.

Frost crouched in the darkened room and wished the gash on his wrist would stop its sticky trickle. It felt as if gallons of blood were pumping out and it reminded him of the way ancient Romans committed suicide. His knee felt wet, sticky, and gritty from embedded chunks of glass. All in all he had made rather a mess of his spectacular entrance.

A door faced him. He limped over to it and cautiously pushed it open. He could make out carpeted stairs leading to the upper rooms. Good. The carpet should deaden the sound of his approach. His impromptu plan was to creep into the room, get behind Stan, and throw him to the ground so he couldn't use the shotgun. He fought several different versions of this encounter in his mind, but somehow they all seemed to end up with Stan on top of him and the shotgun barrel rammed halfway up his nose. But this was no time for pessimism.

He padded to the foot of the stairs and listened. All seemed quiet above. He tried the first stair, carefully placing his foot well to one side to avoid any creaking. Then the other foot. A splash of blood plopped to the stair carpet, marking his progress. He paused and listened. Nothing!

The next stair, then the next. His approach was absolutely soundless. The SAS couldn't have done it any better.

He raised his head for the final stair and his heart suddenly stopped. The terrified face of a woman was staring at him. An arm encircled her neck. Jammed under her chin, the barrel of a shotgun. Behind her, a twitching Stanley Eustace, his finger quivering on the trigger.

'Shit!' said Frost. 'I didn't think you could hear me.'

'One move out of turn, Mr Frost,' said Stan, 'and I'm pulling this trigger.' And he pushed the barrel even more tightly under the woman's chin. 'Now, come up!' Frost had never seen the man as uptight as this before. He was a hair-breadth from breaking point.

'All right, I'm coming,' said Frost. 'Don't do anything daft.'

Pulling the woman back, Stanley led Frost into the bedroom. On chairs against the wall were two terrified young boys.

Eustace took the gun from the woman's throat and pushed her away from him. 'Go and sit down with your kids — and not a move, do you hear? Not a move and not a word.' He swung the gun around to cover Frost.

'Sadie sent me,' said Frost. 'She said you'd be pleased to see me. I wouldn't have come had I known it would be like this.'

'I want a car,' said Eustace. 'A getaway car. And they've got to promise not to come after me.'

'Sadie said if I came up here, you'd let the hostages go,' said Frost.

'No. I need them!' His finger kept touching the trigger then moving off.

'You don't need them, Stanley. If you want a hostage, you've got me. Besides, you haven't the slightest intention of harming them, and those kids ought to be in bed.'

Allen put down the phone. 'Eustace says he's letting the woman and the kids go, but Frost remains.'

'That's excellent news,' said Mullett.

'Is it?' muttered Allen. 'All we've done is swap one set of hostages for another. We're back to where we started.'

'Jack Frost will get Stanley to come out, don't you worry,' chimed Sadie. 'He won't let you bastards kill him.'

PC Collier, watching the garden, called out excitedly to Allen. 'The hostages are coming out now, sir.'

Frost was reaching for his cigarettes. 'Stan, if I take out a fag, will you promise not to blow my head off.'

The gun moved with Frost's hand as it dived into his

pocket. The gunman shook his head when the packet was offered to him. 'Given it up.'

Frost clicked his lighter. 'Wish I could, Stanley.' He sucked on the cigarette and let the smoke fill his lungs, then slowly exhaled. 'You've got to give yourself up some time, Stan. Why not now?'

'I want a car, petrol . . .'

Frost waved his hand impatiently. 'You know bloody well they're not going to give it to you. They've got the press and the TV cameras out there, all waiting for the happy ending — with the crook losing and the police coming out on top. Mr Mullett's hoping for a different happy ending — you blowing my brains out. But there's no way they're going to let you get into a motor and drive away.'

The man's entire body started to shake. 'If the bastards want a fight, I'll give them one. They framed me. I never touched that copper.'

The waiting and the hanging about was making Mullett impatient. 'What's going on, Allen?'

Allen wished Mullett would get back to the office and stop being a pain. All this standing behind him and fidgeting and expecting things to happen just because the great Chief Constable was there was getting on his nerves. He radioed Ingram. 'What's happening, Sergeant?'

'Mr Frost is by the window, sir, Eustace well back, the gun trained on the inspector. No chance of a shot at the moment, sir, I might hit Mr Frost. Hold on, sir — something's happening . . .'

'As God is my witness,' said Eustace, the finger on the trigger shaking dangerously, 'I never touched that copper. I never even saw him that day. You've got to believe me.'

'Stanley,' said Frost uneasily, 'with a gun rammed in my gut I'm prepared to believe anything.'

Stanley laughed. An overwrought laugh. 'It's not even bloody loaded, Mr Frost.'

'What?'

'I fired my last cartridge half an hour ago. It's empty — look.' His finger tightened on the trigger to demonstrate.

Frost's arm swung out to knock the gun away, just in case Stan was mistaken, but even as he moved the explosive blast hammered at his ears. Stanley stared, open-mouthed, in horror, pointed an accusing finger at Frost and pitched forward, vomiting blood, the red stain on his chest spreading, spreading . . .

'Get an ambulance!' shouted Frost as armed police charged into the room. He cradled Stanley's head in his arms. Outside a woman was screaming uncontrollably — Sadie Eustace.

'You silly sods!' yelled Frost. 'The gun wasn't loaded. You silly sods . . .'

Ingram had fired the shot.

They carried Stanley's body out on a stretcher, the red blanket pulled up to cover his face. As Frost emerged Sadie lunged at him. 'You bastard — you let them kill him.' Webster and a woman police officer held her back. Frost walked on. There was nothing he could say to her.

Back in the room, the post-mortem.

'It wasn't even loaded,' said Frost.

'I didn't know,' said Ingram. 'I saw him pulling the trigger. I didn't know.'

'You're not expected to know, Sergeant,' snapped Allen. 'If a killer points a gun at a police officer and then pulls the trigger, you are entitled to assume the gun is loaded.'

'I quite agree,' said Mullett. 'The person reproaching himself should be you, Frost. You placed this entire operation in jeopardy because of your cheap tactics. We'll talk about this further in my office, first thing tomorrow morning.'

'Yes, sir,' said Frost. Stan dead. Sadie widowed. That was all that mattered. He sat in a chair and lit a cigarette.

'We'd better see the press now,' said Mullett to Allen. He sighed. 'Pity that damn shotgun wasn't loaded. It would have made a splendid story.' They went out together.

Frost dribbled smoke and peered at Ingram through the haze. The sergeant looked shattered.

'I thought he was going to kill you. I saw him pulling the trigger. I didn't know the gun was empty.'

'Sit down,' said Frost. 'I think we ought to have a talk.'

Ingram sat.

'It's a mess, isn't it son?' said Frost.

'Yes,' muttered Ingram.

'I was hoping a bloke called Dawson had done it,' said Frost. 'Dave Shelby had been knocking off his wife. But Dawson had an alibi. He was in some shooting contest until late evening.'

'Oh,' said Ingram.

Frost lit a second cigarette from the first. 'He belongs to the same shooting club as you do. In fact you were both down for the clay pigeon shooting contest that afternoon, but you left early — didn't even go in for your heat. The club secretary told me. He said you left just before five with your shotgun tucked under your arm.'

'I wasn't feeling well enough to shoot,' said Ingram.

'So the secretary said,' agreed Frost. He reached in his pocket for the packet of photographs and put them on the small table in front of him. 'Shelby was knocking your wife off as well, wasn't he?'

The sergeant sprung up. 'How dare you, you swine . . . !'

'You don't have to put on an act for me, son' said Frost wearily, 'I'm an unworthy audience.' He sorted through the photographs and pulled one out. 'This is Shelby with Dawson's wife. It was taken on Tuesday afternoon. If you turn it over you'll see that these instant pictures all carry a printed number. This is number seven.' He sorted through to find another which he turned facedown. 'This is number eight, which means it was taken after the other one.' He flipped it over. 'The lady with Shelby — it's your wife, isn't it?'

Ingram stared at the photograph. Two nude figures interlocked. He didn't say anything.

'That must have been taken Tuesday night,' Frost went on. 'It couldn't have been much later because the next day he was dead.'

The detective sergeant seemed unable to tear his eyes away from the photograph.

Frost went on. 'You were at the party Tuesday night so Shelby had the coast all clear. He'd parked his patrol car out of sight near the toilets and was on his way up to your place when he noticed the grille was broken. He was just about enough of a policeman to investigate, and he found Ben Cornish's body. He was all fidgety that night. I thought he'd been up to something, but he was just anxious to be on his way for a spot of fun with your Stella and his camera.'

Ingram picked up the photograph, then turned it facedown. 'I never knew this was going on,' he said.

With tired sadness, Frost shook his head. 'You did, son. That's why you killed him.'

'Eustace killed him,' said Ingram. 'Shelby's notebook was found near his car.' He waved away Frost's offered cigarette.

'The grass in that field was wet with dew,' said Frost. 'The notebook was supposed to have been lying there all night, but it was bone-dry. I never twigged at the time, but I'm a slow old sod. It was dumped there a few minutes before it was found — and by you, my son.'

'No,' said Ingram.

Frost dabbed at the gash on his wrist. 'It's difficult to get rid of every trace of blood. You've probably scrubbed and scrubbed the inside of your motor, but I bet it wouldn't take Forensic long to find what you've missed. Shelby must have been bleeding like a pig.'

Jagged blue flashes from outside as the press took photographs of Allen and Mullett.

'Shelby and your wife expected you to be away at your shooting match Wednesday afternoon. But you suspected something was going on so you left early. You crept into the house and found them together beating the hell out of the bedsprings. Is that what happened, son?'

Ingram stared down at the floor and then had to turn his head away as he found his eyes focused on the section of bloodstained carpet where Eustace had been lying.

'No. I didn't catch them in the act, Mr Frost. I didn't want to. I suspected what was going on, but I didn't want to believe it. I got back early and there was Shelby's patrol car down the side street. I parked alongside and walked toward the house. The blinds were drawn in our bedroom. I didn't want to go in. I didn't want to believe it. But after a while, the door opened and out he came, smirking all over his damn face. When he saw me, he charged off to his car and roared away. I followed and eventually managed to force him to stop in Green Lane.'

'Where we found his abandoned police car?' Frost prompted.

'Yes. I was beside myself with rage. I wanted to hurt him. He was laughing, taunting me. He said if I wasn't able to satisfy Stella, it was no wonder she had to turn to a real man.' He hesitated, unwilling to go on. 'I will have a cigarette if you've got one, Inspector.'

Frost handed him the packet, then lit the cigarette for him.

'Go on, son. I'm a good listener.'

'The shotgun was on the back seat. I only meant to scare the hell out of him. I think that's all I meant. I don't even remember pulling the trigger. God, his face! In my dreams I see his face!' He shuddered.

'Why did you drag him to your car?' asked Frost. 'Why didn't you leave him?'

'I was going to take him to the hospital, but I soon saw it was far too late. I found a secluded spot to dump him, cleaned up the car, then drove home. I said to Stella, "Did you have a good day?" and she said, "Yes — did a bit of shopping and baked a cake." And she asked if I'd had a good day, and I said, "Marvellous." Both of us lying our heads off.'

Frost shrugged his shoulders. 'I'd have done the same, son.'

'I don't know how long I thought I could keep quiet. I wanted to tell someone. I felt sure it would all come out.'

'And then you heard about Stan Eustace and the armed robbery.'

'Yes. Everyone but you assumed Eustace had killed Shelby.

I wanted to keep the suspicion on him. I had to get rid of the notebook anyway — I'd found it in my car.'

'So you planted false evidence?'

A pause. 'Yes.'

'So it must be a godsend for you now that Stan Eustace is dead and can't tell his side.'

'You've got to believe me, Mr Frost. I really thought he was going to kill you. That's why I fired — for no other reason — you've got to believe me.'

'Supposing I'd got Eustace out of this alive and he was charged with Shelby's murder. What then? Would you have come forward, owned up?'

Ingram bowed his head dejectedly. 'I don't know. I really don't know. All I know is I didn't mean to kill Shelby, but he's dead. Now Eustace is dead and everyone believes he did it. Can't we leave it like that?'

Frost pinched his scarred cheek to try and bring some life back into it. 'It would be a nice easy way out, wouldn't it, son? The trouble is, I'm a cop. Not a very good one, perhaps, but still a cop. I don't really know why I became one, but one thing I'm sure of, I didn't become a cop to turn a blind eye to planted evidence — or to let a dead man, even if he was a crook, be wrongly accused of murder. Your way would be easy. It would keep everyone happy. But it would be wrong son. I just couldn't do it.'

Ingram took the cigarette from his mouth and hurled it through the open window. 'It had to be you, Mr Frost, didn't it?'

'I'm afraid so, son,' murmured Frost apologetically. 'I'm always around when I'm not wanted.'

'So what are you going to do . . . arrest me?'

Frost shook his head. 'Best if I don't son. Much better if I'm kept right out of it. As it was you who shot poor old Useless Eustace, a voluntary confession might make nasty-minded people less inclined to query your motives. What do you reckon?'

Ingram nodded.

'And I'd be a lot happier if we didn't have to bring these

into it.' Frost held up the photographs. 'Shelby's widow has suffered enough.'

Again Ingram nodded.

'So keep my name out of it. Make it a voluntary confession, all off your own bat. It'll make things a lot easier for you.'

Ingram heaved himself out of the chair and moved slowly to the door. He paused as if to say something, but shook his head and went out, closing the door firmly behind him.

Frost sighed and looked at his watch. A shuffling of feet made him turn his head. Webster was leaning against the wall in the corner of the room.

'Hello, son. Didn't know you were there. Been there long?'

'Not very long, sir.'

Sir? This was the first time Webster had ever called Frost 'sir'.

'You didn't hear any of that, I suppose?'

Webster paused, then lied. 'No sir, not a word.'

'That's what I thought,' lied Frost. He stood up. 'Let's have an early night, son. I've got to report to Mullett for a bollocking first thing in the morning and I don't want to keep yawning in his face.'

SATURDAY DAY SHIFT

Frost sat in his office and smoked, waiting to be summoned to the Divisional Commander's office. Seven minutes past nine. Mullett was prolonging the agony, making him sweat.

The news of Ingram's arrest had shocked everyone. Apparently he had walked up to Detective Inspector Allen in the middle of the press conference and confessed to the accidental killing of Dave Shelby. This further blow to the prestige of Denton District, following so hard on the heels of the fiasco of the shooting of the now-cleared Stan Eustace, had fanned the flames of Mullett's fury. Frost wasn't looking forward to the coming interview.

A tap on the door. The summons to the torture chamber, he thought. But that treat was still to come.

'Lady to see you,' announced Johnny Johnson.

He hoped and prayed it wasn't Sadie. Not this morning. He couldn't face her.

The lady was Mrs Cornish, straight-backed, dressed in mourning black, and clutching an ugly brown handbag. Frost sprung to his feet to shake the rubbish off a chair so she could sit down.

'What brings you here then, Ma?'

In answer, she undid the clasp of the handbag and took out a small paper bag. She tipped its contents on to his desk.

Sovereigns, all minted in the reign of Queen Victoria. Frost counted them. There were forty-one.

He looked at her incredulously. 'Where did you get these?'

'I stole them from a tin box in Lil Carey's piano,' she said. 'There were seventy-nine in all.'

'And what happened to the rest of them?' Frost asked.

'Ben took them.'

'Ben?'

She nodded. 'Tuesday evening he pushed his way into the house begging me for money for drugs. He was in a terrible state. He couldn't stop himself shaking and looked as if he hadn't eaten for days. I said I'd give him food but not money. I left him alone while I went down to the corner shop for some eggs. When I came back the house had been turned upside down and Ben had gone. He'd taken one of the bags of sovereigns. The other bag was too well hidden, otherwise he'd have taken that as well.'

'What time was this?'

She snapped her handbag shut. 'A little after nine.'

A little after nine! The pieces were all slotting together. He could visualize it. Ben hurrying from the house, desperately anxious he shouldn't be late for his meet with the two drug pushers, the sovereigns heavy in the pockets of that ragged filthy overcoat, enough to buy many little packets. But he didn't buy any. By nine thirty he was dead.

And yesterday two drug pushers were arrested with the sovereigns in their possession.

It now made sense. Better for them to confess falsely to a burglary than risk being linked by the coins to the murder.

'Those bastards killed my son,' said Mrs Cornish.

Frost scooped the coins back into the bag. 'Let's get our basic facts straight. You never stole these coins from old Mother Carey. Danny, perhaps, or even your daughter-in-law — I spotted her family allowance book in Lil's piano — but not you, Ma.'

She met his gaze and stuck out her chin defiantly. 'It was me. I'll swear to it in court.'

The internal phone buzzed. Miss Smith informing him that the Divisional Commander would see him now.

'Tell him to wait,' said Frost.

ABOUT THE AUTHOR

R. D. WINGFIELD was born in London within screaming distance of the scenes of the Jack the Ripper murders.

Until 1970 he worked in the sales office of an international oil company, writing crime plays for radio in his spare time. The success of his radio work meant the day job had to go, and he became a full-time writer. His plays have been broadcast all over the world and translated into many languages.

R. D. Wingfield is married, has one son, and lives in Essex. He is the author of four mysteries: *A Touch of Frost, Night Frost, Frost at Christmas,* and *Hard Frost,* all available from Bantam Books.

BANTAM MYSTERY COLLECTION